ALTERED
BODIES

ALTERED BODIES

RESONANT EARTH
VOLUME 3

CODY SISCO

RESONANT EARTH PUBLISHING
LOS ANGELES, CA

Resonant Earth Publishing
PO Box 50785, Los Angeles, CA 90050
resonantearthpublishing.com

First edition: October 2025

Library of Congress Control Number: 2025917502
ISBN: 978-1-953954-25-1 (paperback)
ISBN: 978-1-953954-26-8 (ebook)

Author photo by Nate Jensen

www.codysisco.com

The American Union of Nations

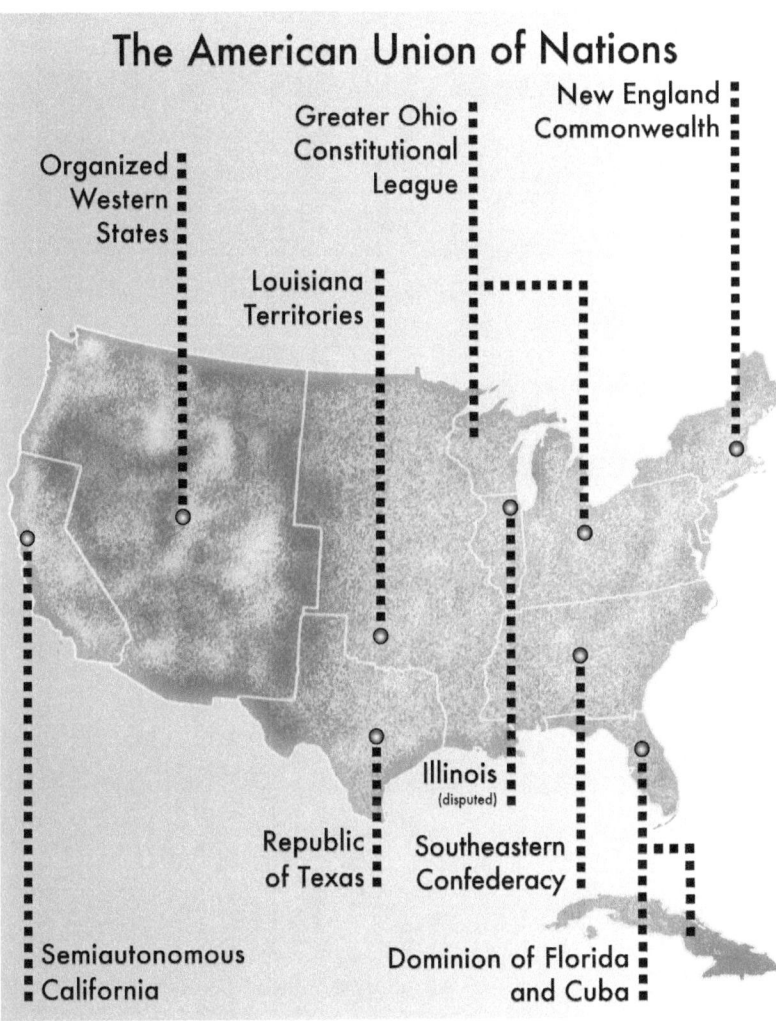

Organized Western States

Greater Ohio Constitutional League

New England Commonwealth

Louisiana Territories

Illinois
(disputed)

Republic of Texas

Southeastern Confederacy

Semiautonomous California

Dominion of Florida and Cuba

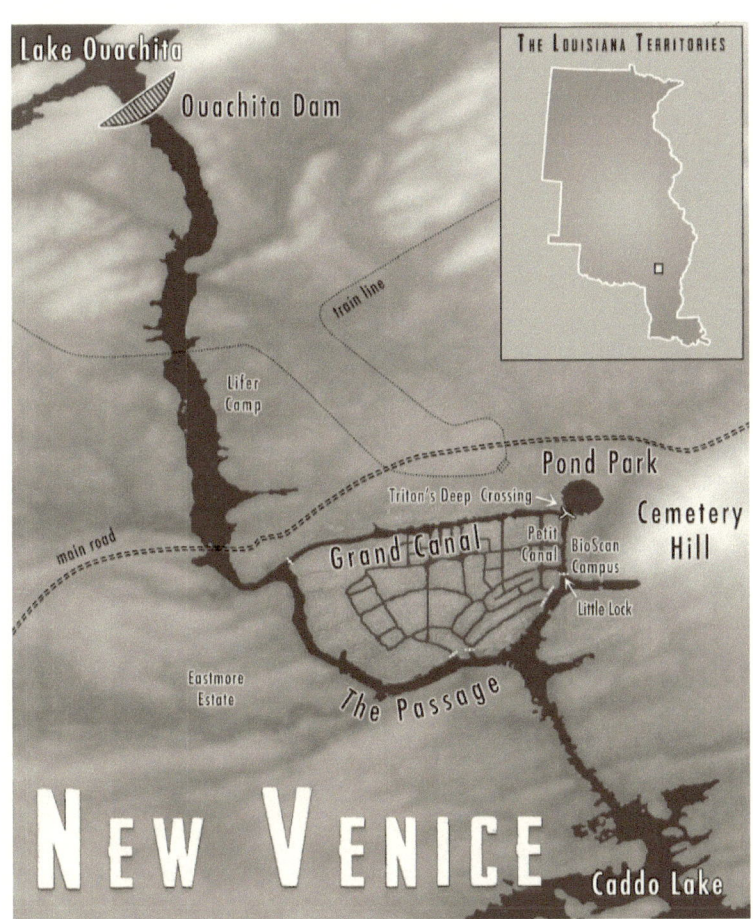

THE LOUISIANA TERRITORIES

Lake Ouachita

Ouachita Dam

train line

Lifer Camp

main road

Pond Park

Triton's Deep Crossing

Grand Canal

Petit Canal

Cemetery Hill

BioScan Campus

Little Lock

Eastmore Estate

The Passage

NEW VENICE

Caddo Lake

1

The Cold Nile Miracle was not simply the result of creative financing, poached labor, and astounding feats of engineering. The founders dared dream up a new civilization, write a new history in the sands of the desert, and emerge from the corruption and hopelessness of Manifest Destiny into a brighter future. It worked too well. See: Las Vegas and the End of Humanity.

—Robbie Eastmore, *Another World* (transmission date unknown)

12 December 1991
Las Vegas, Organized Western States

Below the glinting mirror-finish façades of Las Vegas towers, buried under markets shaded by photovoltaic fabric and cooled by fragrant and mood-enhancing mists, entombed within parched earth, a maze of machinery hummed quietly. In the subterranean darkness, though she felt cloistered, Ming Pearl knew she was never truly alone. Hearing only her own footfall and whispering breath and the gurgling of the lightstrips, any flat surface could become a holoscreen; any networked, free-ranging drone trundling down a hallway or buzzing close to the ceiling could be an instrument of surveillance. That was the price of working for the Diamond King.

Chilled air brushed against Pearl's face as she entered the door to the vault—cold and feathery, like the freezer blasts that had cooled her parents' restaurant kitchen. She paused and smiled to herself. Memories were time-traveling prayers, and there was nothing more important, more precious, than reverence. She remembered the smell of seasoned meat-filled pastries and dumplings and playing with the remains of cut vegetables—onions, zucchini, and eggplant were her favorites; they had such different personalities—while daring to hover her fingers close to the fiery pepper oil, not letting her hand fly away when the spitting oil burned her. She saw the hanging slabs of beef and poultry swinging from hooks like they were trying to fly free through the foggy air above Long Valley once again. A tingle traveled up her spine at the ghostly memory of shivering in the freezer until she couldn't feel her fingers. She let these memories take hold and savored them. In a world that had become unrecognizable, she was determined to never let them go.

Lining two sides of the vault, embalmed bodies had been placed inside individual chambers, canted down toward their heads, where wires and tubes protruded and facilitated the circulation of data and fluids. She had lowered the temperature when she first arrived as a sign of respect. A tomb should be cold, inviting reverence, especially tombs for the missing and forgotten.

"All of you are treasures," she said to the dead.

What melodrama. Here I am, performing my grief when no one is listening.

Her words echoed back from the white mycoceramic tile walls. She couldn't hear the fans and pumps—despite their presence in the vault. As with so much of the Organized Western States, especially in Las Vegas, the imperceptible was what really mattered. Someone was always listening, harvesting secrets. She pushed away political concerns with a wave of the hand. This was a cold and quiet space for her misery, a place of emergence, where her rage might recede in time or grow to consume her.

I wish you were here, Brother. I wish I could see you again. But it is better that you are safe in faraway ground.

Quietly, shuffling in soft-bellied shoes, she walked to the small, stunted body of Rigoberto Watts: nineteen, born in Dos Rios, Semiautonomous California, diagnosed with mirror resonance syndrome at age nine. He'd deteriorated, deemed Class One by his thirteenth birthday, warehoused for years in a coma, and become physically atrophied, wasted. Never to be the man he could have been.

Yet, in death, he became someone's treasure.

Rehabilitation had been an impossibility for Rigoberto as it had been for Pearl's brother, who was part of the first wave of mirror resonance syndrome patients. The recommended dose of Personil had been higher back then, deadly in the long run. Reform came too late. Not even the great Jefferson Eastmore had been able to save her brother. Grief destroyed her family, one of the many tragic echoes that rippled out from the Carmichael Massacre and that beast Samuel Miller. *Curse his name, foul his flesh, let his soul be tortured for eternity.*

Her brother could have been one of the best pilots of his generation. A captain of the sky, surveying the vastness of the earth below.

It was cold comfort that she was not alone in her suffering.

Pearl placed a hand against Rigoberto's face. His skin was hard, waxy, and as cool as the vault's air. He left behind two fathers, a mother, two sisters, and a brother. Memories of his family traveled the supple neural fibers in his brain, memories that might now be finding a new home in diamond filaments in the darkness around her.

One day soon, implants would reignite living but broken minds, drawing their consciousnesses from the dark holes where they wallowed—but not soon enough for these cherished bodies. The Diamond King could not resurrect the dead.

She traced the outline of a skullplug, from where nanowire unspooled throughout Rigoberto's right prefrontal lobe. A tiny blue light pulsed there once every sixty seconds, marking time, signaling to dumb meatbags like herself that this glorious technology was working, that it could be relied on, that they should trust it. Streams of data coursed through tendrils, firing electrical pulses throughout Rigoberto's brain tissue. The data would—if she could keep the belief alive—help the Diamond King help humanity.

Time would tell whether she was betraying Jefferson Eastmore or loyally following his plans to their intended conclusion.

Neural activity consumed oxygen, which had to be replenished. A black cylinder on the floor fed oxygenated fluid into a port at the back of the young man's skull. Waste materials were filtered. All this so Rigoberto's neural paths could be stimulated, mapped, and cataloged. Although the accumulated data was far more than experts could ever parse, it was no problem; the analysis was automated. When findings intersected with her work on the soft, human side of the research, she would be informed and consulted, and for that, she was thankful. But she knew she was ancillary. The real advances were taking place somewhere else deep within the bright, sparkling connective tissues that made the Organized Western States into a nexus of processing capacity with emerging significance.

Pearl retrieved a pebble from her pocket and positioned it on the floor, alongside others. From one vantage point, a curious scattering of rocks. From another, it was an evolving spiral pattern she had initiated as an act of reverence; each pebble symbolizing one day of her observance.

She looked again at the bodies, servile in death, at the limits of scientific advancement. All these treasures were precious and wouldn't be forgotten if she could help it. She had been in the room, present at the moment when life support was discontinued for each of them—when they crossed over from living to this new kind of undeath. She would continue to witness. One day, she would speak. The world should know what emerged from this place and what it cost.

What are they dreaming now?

She repeated her mantra, "All of you are treasures." It was a reminder that at least one person would remember them after they were gone. She couldn't help wondering, however, what dreams emerged from the dead when they were not allowed to rest.

Cody Sisco

2

American Union citizens should have been warned. The European authorities had known for months that trouble was on the horizon. The repositioning of MeshSats was not the first indication that they had a powerful cyber adversary.

Perhaps the authorities did try to educate the masses via the Mesh. Perhaps their warnings were intercepted or changed en route. Perhaps their adversary had been scheming for far longer than anyone suspected.

The bottom line is that everyone was unprepared for an onslaught they didn't see coming.

—Robbie Eastmore, *Another World* (transmission date unknown)

14 March 1992
New Venice, The Louisiana Territories

What does it take to send someone over the edge? A suggestion? A push? A weapon in hand?

Victor was deep in thought as he arrived at the BioScan meeting. All day, he'd been walking a tightrope between agitated and out of his mind. And his balance was slipping.

He passed a group of stim addicts on the bridge over the Petite Canal who pawed at him, vibing on him sexually, extricating himself by batting aside their hands, shrugging out of unwelcome embraces, and fleeing clumsily. The undignified aftereffects of their resonance—his erection and fractured attention—were undoing him. Fumewort tinctures, which he gulped down several times throughout the day, proved insufficient defense. At work, he refilled his on-the-go container from the jugs stashed under his desk, then headed to the strategy meeting.

A wave of déjà vu crested as he entered the conference room high up in the BioScan tower, where glum executives sat around a newly installed conference table. They looked up briefly, acknowledged him, and resumed their conversations. A missing memory lurked at the edge of consciousness but darted away when he tried to clutch it. It wasn't a fun combo: the feeling that everything happening had happened before alongside the feeling that parts of his brain were missing. The present was overflowing, while the past was a patchwork of cloying voids and mushy blobs. Brimming with annoyance of his extreme forgetfulness, he took a seat, gulped fumewort tincture, and stewed in self-pity. His colleagues seemed unaware of his predicament, thankfully. It was strange to share the room, pretending as if a gargantuan gulf of experience didn't separate him. But maybe the gulf wasn't that big anymore. While he couldn't fake being normal, he'd claimed his space among them. If he spoke, he would be heard. But he usually kept his mouth shut, for better or worse.

Glass walls provided a panorama of brown water, green hills, red mudflats, and the gray stone buildings of New Venice. Aunt Circe insisted on holding meetings in the new building, even though most floors remained unfurnished, and she spent most of her time in Europe.

Karine LaTour, wearing a frock that looked like white cotton balls stuck together with putty, kicked off the meeting with a bleak recitation of the company's predicament: finances trending toward insolvency, a growing and baffling patient population, and unexpected regulatory headwinds. The executives seemed resigned to the decline. Karine steered them toward "the main problem," which was all the Broken Mirrors being transferred from Semiautonomous California and what to do about their treatment. This spurred the executives to talk as excitedly as gallows witnesses waiting for the trap door to drop.

Out of phase with their rapid-fire remarks and sharp twists of conversation, Victor's mind was stuck reliving the feeling of the stim addicts' hands, their intense, hungry gazes. Animalistic grunts and moans echoed in his ears so loudly he didn't notice when the room went quiet.

"Victor, what do you think?" Aunt Circe asked. In her tone, Victor smelled rotten fruit, like disappointed expectations.

As he looked at her heart-shaped face, blankspace feathered his vision in gray, blurry streaks. *What do I think, what do I think, what do I think?* The phrase repeated itself like a virus spawning copies. Outside, a vista that was kaleidoscopically confusing. Inside, lightstrips pulsed with neon colors, swirling and changing with every flash of emotion on the executives' faces, each one beaming limbic signals directly to his brain.

Circe waited. Her curls contained shadows. Her brow was a black line of skepticism. He had no response, no answers. He was trying to focus on Circe's question amid a confusing swirl of half-memory; he would never be a leader if he couldn't speak when an opportunity arose. One of the executives harrumphed audibly at his silence—which one, Victor didn't care.

"Victor?" Circe repeated.

The budding resonant episode he'd been fighting threatened to blossom.

Focus. The wise owl listens before asking who. And sometimes, the owl speaks.

It was no use. He had no speech. He couldn't even clear his throat.

"I'll give you a moment," Circe continued, pretending she hadn't let a long, uncomfortable pause grow monstrously embarrassing. "No one is leaving this room until we have a workable plan for our new patients. I've heard a lot of hemming and hawing. We need good ideas."

Anger flared red on more than a few faces before stilted conversation returned, each executive offering self-interested, doubtlessly ineffective propositions. Victor had gathered enough focus to begin tracking the discussion better and didn't like what he heard. The deadlock was potentially fatal for the Broken Mirrors coming under BioScan's care, yet Circe let the executives drone on and on, seemingly determined to avoid taking a position herself. She paid more attention to her silver-and-black-painted fingernails than the people around the table. She was aloof, distracted, and indecisive, which wasn't like her at all. And yet, no one called her on it. They were all too deferential. Even Karine, who was usually vocal and insistent. Thus far, she had only raised her voice to correct figures, clarify mistaken assumptions, or cut off digressions—a minimalistic, fact-focused approach that was insufficient, given the uncertainty and urgency. Circe's forbearance was, it seemed to Victor, contagious.

The executives mercilessly cut down each other's suggestions and seemed more interested in jockeying for attention and influence than solving problems. If the proposed course of action didn't give their group more staff, more resources, or more sway, then it wasn't workable, wasn't appropriate, wasn't something they could get behind. More time was needed. Or more study. Or more of something else that wasn't available.

What do I think?

There are no good options.

I should say that—it's what they are all thinking, after all.

Broken Mirrors, transferred from the Semiautonomous California Classification Commission, arrived at the clinic daily, some conscious, others not. All awaited salvation that might never come.

Marilyn, the finance expert, who always wore large round rimless glasses that made her eyes resemble oversized holo-projections, spoke up. "Without offering treatment advice, I can say that maintenance care is eating a hole in our budget. Keeping comatose bodies alive is expensive."

"Are you suggesting we dump them in the canals?" Karine answered with her acid tongue. Marilyn opened her mouth, but Karine cut her off. "We know it's costly. Circe said she wants solutions, not reiterations of the problem."

Marilyn bristled, sat back, and folded her arms but didn't offer a rebuttal.

Diego Olivera, a recent hire in charge of patient oversight, despite not being a mirror resonance syndrome specialist, cleared his throat. Victor watched as Diego, who had a baby face with plump lips and ruddy cheeks, sat up straight and said, "I hesitate to say this, given recent events ..."

That got everyone's attention. "Recent events" included a hostage crisis that ended with two dead patients, one of whom was Samuel Miller, who had killed hundreds at the Carmichael Massacre. Victor still had nightmares and doubts about their final confrontation.

Diego was saying, "We currently administer Personil doses intravenously or orally, depending on the patient's status. We could stop."

Eyes widened around the table as his suggestion hit home.

"Stop treating our patients?" someone asked. Victor didn't see who it was. He fixated on Diego, who was either creatively unorthodox or a dangerous villain.

No more Personil?

When Victor had stopped taking the drug, the dullness in his mind sharpened, a gray world turned colorful, and he felt like a new person, not totally in control but at least cognizant. The cost, however, seemed to be more active symptoms and more frequent trips to blankspace—true blankspace: that euphoric, featureless expanse of near-orgasmic gray gauziness, not the counterfeit living-in-molasses feeling caused by medication. He unscrewed the cap on his thermos of fumewort infusion. Bitter, smoky, herbaceous fumes rose. He took two big gulps. *It may not be working, but I'll take two for luck.*

They'd tried stopping Personil with Samuel Miller, and the consequences had been dire. There had been a shockstick, but he didn't remember the entire encounter—another gap. A scattering of inkblot trauma obscured multiple memories.

"I don't think that's a good idea," he said.

"This time, I agree with Victor," Karine said. Her tone was light, but her taut mouth and intense gaze belied her determination, which Victor shared, to not create any more murderers.

Diego shook his head. People with mirror resonance syndrome were not inherently dangerous. It would take time to eliminate the self-hating bias SeCa had instilled in him.

"Now wait, you two," Circe said. She stood and took a few steps toward Diego, watching him. "I think it's worth considering. Go on."

Diego flashed a smile that, to his credit, appeared genuine and leaned forward. "MRS isn't degenerative under the right conditions. When the research from SeCa's Classification Commission arrived, I reviewed everything, what little there is. Personil is used to make patients easier to control. There's very little evidence it helps their condition, but there are heaps more significant, sometimes severe, negative effects. They might recover on their own."

"We've had this debate before," Karine said. "The consequences of coming off Personil—"

"Have not been fully explored. We have two case histories. Both patients are, I would say, extraordinary."

In Diego's eyes, Victor saw a pulsing blue wave of compassion.

Diego went on, saying, "The Classification Commission was not in the business of helping MRS patients recover. The law prevented them, and also the culture. Frankly, I believe it's inhumane to continue a treatment that should long ago have been repudiated. Patients from SeCa can finally receive the care they should have been given all along."

"Victor?" Circe asked with curiosity riding on the exquisite modulation of her intonation. He should be pleased that she was asking him his opinion. So why did anger clot in his chest every time he looked at her?

He lowered his head and repeated the owl mantra, whispering to himself softly, not caring if he made anyone uncomfortable. Back in Oakland, he'd taken a chance by stopping his medication and suddenly seen the world much more clearly. That included the fact that Granfa Jeff hadn't died of natural causes, and after that ... after that, a great black pit of absence opened in his memory, and he felt himself tumbling in mid-air. His throat was dry, a punishing desiccation. The subtle hiss of the air chillers sounded like a roar of planets converging in fiery collision.

He slapped his cheeks. *Okay,* he told himself, *forget memory lane. Too many potholes and dangerous obliterating chasms. Think of the future instead.*

Shouldn't the other Broken Mirrors be given the same chance he was?

But what if, by doing so, they created a horde of patients susceptible to delusions and capable of harm? Samuel Miller had been the first and only *murderous* Broken Mirror. Victor didn't want to create more.

That's fear talking. Things can't get worse than this. We have to try something.

Victor breathed several times, then said with difficulty, "Yes." It came out in a whisper. He cleared his throat and tried again. "Personil isn't helping them. We should start with a single cohort, or several small ones, lower the dosage at different rates, try different interventions."

Marilyn, who had been pecking at a MeshBit, looked up. "We would only see significant savings if we ceased production of Personil. We could sell the equipment and reassign personnel for an added bonus. If we commit to this, we're in all the way."

Circe nodded slightly. "Karine?"

She whistled quietly. "To paraphrase Diego, science is not on the side of Personil."

"But what's *your* opinion?" Circe asked.

There was a pause, and when Karine spoke, she articulated each word slowly, "We should not feel locked into a path that is merely a historical accident. Personil sales are not expanding as we would have liked, thanks to the stalled passage of MRS legislation in the other AU nations and Europe. The story of what happened here may be influencing that."

The research director, Dr. Eitel, let out an angry cough, which Victor perceived as sparks swirling from a disturbed fire. "Thanks to Lisabella," Dr. Eitel grumbled.

Circe cut him off. "Thank you, Dr. Eitel, but I'll handle our Mesh interests." Circe looked at Victor with raised eyebrows. "Will you take responsibility?" Her tone told him that *she* would not. How hard would he have to shove her to break the glass wall and push her off the tower? His hands lifted from the table.

"The wise owl listens," he whispered desperately, more breath than sound. He urged his mind to the boundary of blankspace and then beyond, dipping in for a hit of euphoric calm. Free of his body, weightless, he mentally exhaled and negative vibes evaporated.

The illusion of freedom didn't last. A familiar sensation was intensifying: blankspace wasn't empty. This time, the fullness had a shape and feeling: something was there, an object, something he was forgetting, something he'd been missing but couldn't name. There was a mystery there, one he didn't have time to solve. He had to return.

Coming back, he noticed his heartbeat had slowed. He swallowed. Circe was watching him closely. Colors still illuminated the executives' expressions, but the worst of the episode's effects had ebbed. Roar receded to a hiss.

"Victor, I need you on board," Circe said.

Diego said, "If I may? Even with drugs out of their systems, I doubt we'll see spontaneous recovery. We need to develop alternative treatment plans that might have an impact."

The research director slammed his hand on the table. "'Might!' You keep saying 'might,' but we don't know anything!"

"More true than you know," Circe said under her breath so that only Victor, Karine, and perhaps a few others heard her.

The research director wasn't done complaining, for which Victor was thankful, because it took the spotlight off him. "We're overloaded as it is," the man said huffily. "How am I supposed to get answers when a quarter of my budget has been cut?"

Rolling her eyes—a gesture Victor couldn't remember Circe making before—she responded, "I'm all ears if you have an alternative suggestion."

Circe refused to demonstrate leadership. She allowed the conversation to meander. She said she wanted a plan, but she let subordinates offer excuses and toss blame like a hot potato. *This is no way to run a company*, Victor thought. If she wouldn't take responsibility, who would?

Victor stood up. Heads swiveled toward him, gazes locked, some curious, some disdainful. His face flushed. Through a throat clogged with fear and embarrassment of saying the wrong thing, he forced out the words: "No more Personil. We can wind down the manufacturing facility and buy some time with the proceeds. I'm taking personal responsibility for the care of MRS patients. A treatment protocol will be in your inboxes within a week. Alternative therapies included." He breathed hard. *What else?* "I expect your cooperation."

He looked squarely at Circe, daring her to challenge him but seeing only a swirling, glittering orange effusion of a smile. She said, "I think we all see the wisdom in it."

Two minutes later, the executives were gone, taking their agitation with them and leaving Victor, Circe, and Karine alone. None of them spoke for a long moment.

"I'll handle the disposition of Personil-related assets," Karine finally said. "I'll get you the numbers on how many doses are left as soon as possible. I have to say, Victor, it's good to see you so assertive."

"That means a lot coming from you," he said. Perhaps their work relationship was taking a welcome turn toward the better. As far back as he could remember—admittedly, not very far lately—Karine had been his chief skeptic.

"We should also coordinate around patient intake," she said.

They made plans, shooting options back and forth over the next ten minutes. Circe ignored them, tapping on a type-pad. When Karine asked her at several points for her approval, she demurred, saying a different version each time of "whatever you two think is best." Victor caught the initial surprised look on Karine's face and watched it change during subsequent interactions into disbelief and then a heavy, grim dread. She locked eyes with him at one point and raised her eyebrows questioningly. All he could do was shrug. He knew something was wrong with Circe, but since nausea threatened to return whenever he looked at her, it was better not to think about it.

Cody Sisco

When they started repeating conversations, he excused himself. "Today was a tough day," he said before parting.

That was true, yes, but it wasn't the complete story. He'd avoided a resonant episode. He'd taken charge and cast the deciding vote against Personil. Feeling flush with accomplishment was a new experience. He *could* be part of the team. One day, he *could* lead one. Now that he had a taste of belonging, he wanted more. But he didn't belong; he knew that. He had uncommon talents. Ranging through blankspace at will was among them. Exquisite emotional sensitivity was another. People might say these aspects of MRS were imaginary; they were wrong.

There was a gaping emptiness in his mind that needed exploring. A sustained visit to blankspace in a controlled environment could map its edges and perhaps beyond. As a side benefit, if it provided a little euphoria, a reprieve from his problems, and a celebratory escape, then why not?

He left the building. Warm, humid air greeted him, and scents of sage and rosemary hinted at his satiety. The sun glittered on the surface of Qaddo Lake, where pleasurecraft were passing, some headed toward the Petite Canale locks and others southward. An anticipatory smile curled on Victor's lips, and a plan began to take shape.

It wouldn't be at all like crossing over.

3

Ozie was tinkering with his cyberarm when a feed from the Diamond King activated. *Oh, great. Lucky me.* The pathologically bizarre, stupidly wealthy, and likely murderous tech maverick of Las Vegas wanted to chat with Ozie. He ignored the feed. But then a tiny face of black, red, and gold pixels in the style of a diamond-fringed playing card appeared on his wrist. Ozie wiped his brow with his live hand and turned up the chiller to keep from roasting him alive in the van, which he'd parked in the desert sun beyond the circumference of Las Vegas.

The Diamond King's playing card visage was a simple, unmoving representation superimposed over the artificial skin, ligaments, and "blood" vessels of Ozie's wrist. *Oh, good, it's not the animated version.* Ozie *hated* the animated version; hiding his real face was only one of many annoying quirks. The Diamond King was a paranoid and eccentric supersmart coder who wouldn't let anyone see him in person, so all real-pics of his face were embargoed. Another annoying quirk: initiating feeds without warning, without asking permission. He was the man behind the curtain, pulling the strings of the mayor and city council and possibly the national legislature if rumors were to be believed. As the creator of the automated social rating and communistic economic system in the OWS, the Diamond King's digital avatar, or those of his agents, the totems, were a daily interruption into the lives of citizens. They appeared at will, haunting the nation's infrastructure and reminding everyone of the freedoms they'd traded away for peace and prosperity.

Despite the Diamond King's monstrous habit of intrusion, the voice that emerged from the sonobulb embedded in Ozie's cyberthumb was as human as could be.

"Ozie, friend, check your feed. I can't see your face."

Hypocrite! "My arm is in diagnostic mode." That was euphemistic. Most of the synthskin between his wrist and his shoulder was peeled back so he could access fuel cells and wetworks tucked within the artificial musculature. The vidcaps embedded in his hand were offline, too. "Go ahead. I can hear you."

"Reassignment details have been transmitted. Come see me."

The Diamond King's face dimmed. It was replaced by a set of glowing coordinates that indicated the Northeast Quadrant, a few blocks from Grand Park, in the commercial belt. A twenty-minute drive once Ozie finished with his arm.

"Acknowledge receipt of the message." The Diamond King's playing-card face returned, an animated visage this time, the vile and creepy one, and his square eyes blinked, becoming two black Xs under canted eyebrows. Ozie looked down, and a tiny smirk pulled at his mouth. *Have I annoyed the Diamond King? Must be tough ruling a city state all by your lonesome.*

"Acknowledge receipt of the message," the Diamond King repeated.

Ozie snapped a power gel cylinder into his bicep. "Message acknowledged. What's the job?"

He searched casually through a crate of supplies, letting his fingers pick through rolls of synthflesh, optical cable connectors, and fingernail-sized spectrum relays. His other arm lay across the worktable, his wrist shining with the image of the Diamond King's face, which "stared" at the van's ceiling. Ozie shook his head. *Unreal.* Sometimes, Ozie's life seemed like a wild dream from his teenage years. Not for the first time, he wondered if he should find a remote mountain lake and retire from everything.

The Diamond King said, "It's too complicated to describe verbally and too sensitive to discuss remotely. We'll talk when you arrive, which shall be soon."

Ozie looked at his arm with reluctance. It was becoming clear he'd have to cut short his upgrade project or risk the ruler's ire. He muttered, "You're definitely not winning the best boss prize, Kingsly."

Where's the trust?

Despite months of working together and praising Ozie for hacking jobs well done, the King seemed no closer to giving him real access. Ozie knew the value of hard work. Ever since he fled

Semiautonomous California for the backroads of the Organized Western States, he'd been hustling to get hacking gigs, building up his supplies of hardware, and learning new techniques for cracking virtual safes, hijacking Mesh traffic, and staying under the radar of law enforcement.

When Jefferson Eastmore paid him a million AUD to program a data egg with his last testament and a brainhacking program customized for Victor, Ozie had been able to level up his operation considerably—it was his big break, truth be told. He started adding code to the dark grid network that shadowed the Mesh. He created machine-brain interface programs for his braincaps. He built Springboard Café into an international hacking destination.

Then Victor showed up months before he should have, wild-eyed and confused, disrupting carefully laid plans and making a mess of things. Worse still, they hadn't exactly clicked, which hurt the most. The five years they'd spent apart could have been a century. Ozie didn't count many friends and had hoped for a better reunion. Instead of reconciliation after what went down with Samuel Miller—Ozie didn't regret supplying the shockstick and helping rid the world of that mass murderer—Victor had been hazy, in and out of blankspace, unable to track what Ozie was saying about Jefferson Eastmore's posthumous entanglements with the Diamond King and Ozie's biggest fear: that by working for the Diamond King and pursuing an uneasy, treasonous, and surreptitious rebellion with Tosh, he was putting himself in jeopardy.

Some people somewhere probably could have lived their lives never knowing a killer. And here Ozie was surrounded by them.

Perhaps his isolation was for the best, he often thought. In high-risk environments, emotional entanglements created vulnerabilities, making detachment a challenging yet necessary strategy that enabled a broader range of tactics. Or maybe he was fucking himself over. Still, the upshot was that Ozie managed to trick Victor into stealing from the Human Genome Initiative, and got him to pay for it, too. One hustle begat another, and that money enabled his biggest hack yet, one he might never surpass: realigning MeshSats in orbit, allowing him to plant his digital flags in every Mesh Tower in the southern OWS. Using the computing power to decode the gene responsible for mirror resonance syndrome was only a bonus.

For the sweet icing on his cyber cake, Ozie retrofitted his van into a totally secure digital fortress. It was the only place he felt truly safe. He didn't look forward to any excursion, let alone another work assignment from a paranoid crime lord.

Drive to a mountain lake. Set up camp. Never leave. Do it now.

"Why aren't you on your way already?" the Diamond King asked. His voice was pitched high and soft like a child's. Ozie sometimes wondered if he'd been a thespian before his ascension to his secret throne.

His cyberarm lay open like a filleted fish. He'd hoped to jam in more quantum processors, spectrum relays, and solid-state storage packs. Plenty of room to bulk up with more computing power. At some point, he'd need to refit the musculature, too, but that was a long, dreary task that would require at least one assistant, and he couldn't bring someone in to help, not while he and the Diamond King were playing cat and mouse.

An alarm blared in the van behind him.

"You won't keep me waiting," said the Diamond King.

Ozie's wrist went ominously dark. He glanced at the arm, dread gathering in his stomach like the gurgling consequences of contaminated seafood. Then he felt the van begin to roll forward. The acceleration was smooth and automated. The tools and gadgetry hanging from the walls rattled quietly. He checked the vidscreen. The van was headed toward the Northeast Quadrant. His security programs registered an alert.

Ozie began the procedure to exit diagnostic mode and return the cyberarm to normal functioning, rolling the flesh back down and securing it. At the same time, alarm bells clanged in his brain, and fireworks of panic ricocheted in his skull as a resonant episode gathered speed. He rose carefully on account of his arm, used a hanging synthleather strap mounted in the ceiling to pull himself forward, and snatched a braincap from its dock.

"Run Springboard Five," he said, donning the cap and anticipating the program's dependable and soothing relief. Alternating waves of hot and cold washed over him. Stinging pain and vibration in his limbs pulsed on and off. The resonance began to fade.

He looked down at the cyberarm, checking it had booted up properly. The braincap's transcranial magnetic stimulation made it feel like his arm was tingling even though it was a composite of metal, conduit, and translucent synthflesh.

The van is moving. How?

You know how.

Ozie gulped, pushing the thought from his mind, and concentrated instead on Springboard Five's distractions of fractal patterns and colors. The program was working. Calm fortified him and pushed back the panic.

He wasn't the type who could avoid looking at hard truths for long. His experience with mirror resonance syndrome taught him that only the cold, harsh light of rationality and deduction could be trusted.

Look at it logically.

Ozie turned to the vidscreen and read the security log.

Intrusion. Data packet, executable, self-modifying. Trace lost.

He breathed hard, telling himself not to speculate. *Get to the bottom of it.* He nodded to himself. This was a problem. A challenge. A game. Time to start solving.

The security logs didn't reveal much. Whatever foreign code had breached his defenses had vanished. That didn't necessarily mean it was gone. That meant his monitoring algorithms could no longer find it. A stealthy snippet of code could be doing unknown amounts of damage.

The van navigated autonomously, its movements almost imperceptible to Ozie, who was only vaguely aware of turns and subtle changes in acceleration. He was fully immersed in the digital labyrinth of his security system, meticulously setting up a sentinel program to monitor any anomalies. Until, without warning, the van came to a stop.

The rear doors unlocked and opened, revealing a crowd of black-clothed men and women looking at him with stoic expressions and, beyond them, a vast swath of concrete lit by lightstrips.

Someone snorted, a woman with spiky fuchsia hair and a zigzagging scar down her jawline. She waved a hand in front of her nose and said, "It smells like cooked farts in there!"

"Come on out," a tall, burly man gestured, his fingers casually holding a shockstick, its tip pointed toward the van's floor.

Ozie blinked, speechless. The value of the hardware in the van topped a million AUD easily, and his toys wouldn't take kindly to a Dirac pulse from the man's shockstick.

"Coming! Easy." Ozie climbed out of the van and was tightly flanked by the Corps mercenaries. They outnumbered the solar panels surrounding Las Vegas, and their numbers rose in proportion to proximity with the Diamond King. The woman slammed the van doors shut. Ozie ran the locking program and heard a click. Not all his software rebelled from his command.

Not yet.

"This way," the tall Corp gestured, leading them through the parking garage. The space was windowless, with lightstrips mounted in parallel rows that cast bands of shadows on the cold, gray floor. The air was chilled, with a faint scent of ozone, suggesting they might be underground.

The Corps hustled Ozie to an elevator and packed into it with him. They rode up thirty floors in a matter of seconds. Ozie realized he was still wearing his braincap. Oh well. He didn't care what the Corps thought of him, and when he met with the Diamond King, well, the man knew Ozie well enough to know his dependency. The Diamond King was well aware of mirror resonance syndrome; he had expert knowledge direct from the great Jefferson Eastmore. Ozie sometimes wondered if the Diamond King had once been diagnosed. Perhaps that was why he lived as a shadowy figure that only showed up via vidfeeds, text messages, and by proxy via looming war-ready, tech-enabled thugs.

And now he'd sent bizarre bits of code that might still be lodged in Ozie's van's systems. The damage they could do was almost unthinkable.

Ozie had designed his security system architecture as a set of concentric defenses. They were connected via encrypted links, some hard-wired and some quantum entangled. Each had independent kernels and backup routing. A breach in one shouldn't affect the others. And yet, the van had moved. He thought *he* was the Diamond King's top hacker. If someone else was brought in to usurp him, this could spell the end of his employment. Or worse.

The elevator ride ended with Ozie stepping out while the Corps remained behind. "We'll come back for you," the tall Corp said as the doors closed.

"Oh, I'm *so* relieved," Ozie muttered, not caring whether the Corp had heard him. The Diamond King's monolithic authority ensured Ozie's physical safety via a protection order, a clause in his contract, while a Corp who disregarded the Diamond King's missives risked pain worse than death. It was rumored that

Cody Sisco

somewhere in the city a building imprisoned thousands of dissidents who were chemically, physically, and mentally tortured according to the King's terrifying system of justice. Punishment was said to be doled out in direct proportion to contract violations.

There were also rumors about bodily experimentation.

People were released sometimes, injured and suffering, into Grand Park, unable to care for themselves. If no one dared help them, the bodies were removed after an appropriate amount of time. They were burned in the desert at a facility downwind of the city. The Corps were obedient unto death, serving death.

Ozie moved away from the elevator and stared at his surroundings. He was high in a tower. It wasn't a room but an entire floor, punctuated by support pillars clad floor to ceiling with mirrors. Through the windows, a vista of buildings and roads encircling the greenery of Grand Park.

A weight lay on his heart, and fatigue sapped his reserves. The cityscape reminded him of Oakland & Bayshore. When he was twelve, his class had toured the national archives and the courthouse. A breezy history conveyed in plaques and infographics erased the true history: how refugees and political protesters were criminalized and shunted to Long Valley, how mirror resonance syndrome became an excuse to demonize the most vulnerable people in Semiautonomous California, and how the Mesh was used to control what people knew, thought, and believed. On that trip, Ozie realized that SeCa's shiny modernity housed a cruel, xenophobic, and simple-minded people who were rotten to the core.

He never thought of Las Vegas that way. He believed in its self-mythologizing hype. A technocratic paradise. A communal utopia. The future arrived here first. People immigrated to be somewhere optimistic, push the boundaries of scientific and technological possibilities, and pursue unconventional personal growth. He didn't want to think it was all a distraction from a more disturbing, hidden truth. He didn't want this seemingly sustainable oasis to be nothing but a mirage.

Vidlenses were conspicuously mounted in the ceiling, but Ozie guessed they were mostly for show. A few eye-level vidlenses could capture everything via reflection off the mirrored pillars. He wandered to a window and looked down until a pinging sound intruded on his consciousness. He followed the sound around the elevator bank and found the Diamond King. His image was displayed on a darkened window—the dynamic playing-card visage with a golden, bejeweled crown and a glitter-belted waist.

The Diamond King's voice descended from a ceiling-mounted sonobulb. "This location will be furnished and equipped to your specifications. The whole building is at your disposal."

If brains could roll, Ozie's would be tumbling in a rock polisher. "You want me to *live* here?"

"It would be most efficient."

Was the Diamond King teasing him? The whole point of the van was to be able to pick up and move, to flee, at a moment's notice; he didn't like being stuck in one place.

The Diamond King would have deduced that, of course.

"Have I done something to anger you?" Ozie asked, disgusted by the plaintive whine in his voice. Trying a more assertive tone, he said, "I'll come and go as I please." It was no good. He sounded like a terrified peasant. He bit back the urge to say "m'lord" and bow. He wasn't confident it would come across as sarcastic. He would probably just sound like a brown-noser.

It galled Ozie to take orders this way. Every interaction seemed intended to reinforce the Diamond King's virtual authority, his ability to show up wherever he wanted, while everyone else was a meatspace prisoner. The Diamond King's physical personage was likely less than impressive—otherwise, why bother with the whole charade?—but it was effective. The psychological challenge of interacting with a virtual avatar successfully put Ozie off his game. That was the point, of course, and he wasn't the only one afflicted by it. Centuries after monarchies had been consigned to historical footnotes, the ruler of Las Vegas, although not real royalty, seemed focused on flaunting his status of Last King Standing, and it pushed the world's buttons hard.

It also sparked in Ozie a desire to rebel, perilous as that would be. In that moment, he grasped the immense power, hope, and defiance that had been distilled into the nineteenth-century, Europe-wide slogan "Topple All Kings."

But, Ozie wondered, *what do you do when a king wants to work with you?*

The pixel mouth moved in time to the words: "You're going to help me rebuild our world. The terms of your employment contract have been updated. Review them."

Ozie didn't bother looking at his arm when it pinged. Excitement fluttered in his chest. "What does that mean?"

"The Corps require an upgrade to go global. We've reached the limit of cooperation using current technologies. You will help us improve the efficiency and effectiveness of centralized command and coordinated field tactics."

When Ozie opened his mouth, only a quiet squawk emerged. The Diamond King's influence, centered on Las Vegas, was said to extend somewhat into the Organized Western States but barely a whisper beyond that. The King and Ozie's interests intersected at the nexus of mirror resonance syndrome, stims, and brain augmentation research, and with their combined intellects, perhaps they could transform the world.

However, this global ambition was new and troubling. From what Ozie could glean from the dark grid, the Diamond King engaged in low-level mafioso shenanigans and shadowy political maneuvering, not serious geopolitics, as demonstrated by the Corps' cartoonishly aggressive activities in the Republic of Texas. They were considered thugs, not operatives.

Ozie had pursued this gig to honor a promise he'd made to Jefferson Eastmore, but more importantly, he was here to satisfy his curiosity and gain access to tech that seemed decades ahead of anywhere else in the American Union. What did he know about his boss's ambitions? Probably next to nothing. And ignorance could be dangerous.

"What? Like, an army?" Ozie said.

The Diamond King chuckled. The avatar's eyes shifted from black to red, and the diamonds haloing him spun like whirring saw blades. "Think of it as a defensive force."

"An army by another name."

"Army. Battalion. Brigade. Each term is more archaic than the next. I don't care how the Mesh reports it. I need willing bodies to expand my reach and deflect any counter-maneuvers. If the Mesh wants to call it a war, so be it. We've got a lot of work to do. Read your job description and then let's talk."

It was at this moment Ozie realized spying was a shit job and that ambition was never a reliable guide.

I didn't sign up for a war!

If the Organized Western States, despite its utopian ideals, planned to go to war, its American Union neighbors were obvious targets. Perhaps the Republic of Texas was already at war by another name with the OWS. The Louisiana Territories could be next, unless the Diamond King turned his gaze westward; SeCa couldn't put up much of a fight. They had a meager defense force and always ran a deficit that Europe grudgingly financed. Europe, as a target by proxy, was ludicrous. Calling the conflict asymmetrical would be a charitable way to put it. "*Ass-symmetrical*" *is more like it.* And the OWS would have few allies against Europe. Fatalist pacifism was entrenched throughout the other nations of the AU, thanks to the not-yet-faded memory of European troops on the American continent. During the War of the Atlantic, the United States armed forces, which had been depleted by the need for colonial defenses in Asia and deprived of electricity by European-sympathizing saboteurs, had been incapable of coordinating an effective resistance. No one could want a repeat of that disaster: technological superiority had carried the day, and the imbalance had only worsened since then. How could the American Union ever mount a defense when Europe could take down the Mesh with the push of a button? The Union's citizens were living through the inevitable consequences of their defeat and were unlikely to pull together to resist the Diamond King.

Ozie scratched the stubble on his cheek. It was frustrating to work with someone who only showed themselves on a screen, hiding away somewhere out of reach. The emptiness of the office was creepy.

"Stay focused. There's a printed contract in your office," the Diamond King said.

My office?

A light came on, visible through glass partitions, illuminating the only furnished section of this floor. Ozie walked over and sat in a chair that he suspected was real leather and skimmed the contract.

He should tuck his tail, run, and get far away from whatever big plans were being hatched. Still, there was no doubt more profit and power to be gleaned from the Diamond King than he ever could have hoped. Not just that—they could make a brilliant team.

As he flipped through the pages, noting what was mostly a boilerplate employment contract, Ozie considered what he'd heard via the dark grid over the last few months. A cyber battle for Mesh assets was heating up, emerging from the repositioning of

MeshSats, something he'd done without considering the potential consequences. And he was likely wanted by European operatives for it. Furthermore, the satellites he'd commandeered to enable the processing of the genetic data that Victor stole from the Institute of Advanced Biological Sciences was a smoking gun, and the Diamond King was blamed for the shenanigans. So now Ozie was on *his* radar.

Good to see a blank check for legal protections included. That alone could be worth millions, Ozie noted.

As a result of the MeshSat Crisis, as it was being called, sanctions were placed on Las Vegas and the other cities of the OWS. The American Union was staying true to its appeasement roots and had not issued any statements, referring all inquiries to the OWS. In the absence of consensus by the member nations, the AU foreign office chose to say nothing. And consensus was lacking, big time. The Republic of Texas praised the sanctions, as did, somewhat surprisingly, Semiautonomous California. The Louisiana Territories called for talks, eager to insert themselves as a neutral arbiter—they loved that shit. The other nations issued lukewarm statements reflecting their generally prostrate stance toward Europe; they couldn't care less about the OWS. Wealthy as it was, there just weren't enough people to justify any kerfuffle.

And yet, Ozie thought, as he looked out at the towers and further at the mountains surrounding the desert plain, there was something *special* here. The Cold Nile Miracle was real. They were rocketing into the future. Multiple scientific and technological revolutions were spinning a tale of progress faster and louder than anything that had come before.

This could be Ozie's destiny.

Curing Broken Mirrors and ...

Creating mind-machine interfaces and ...

Eliminating the global resource and biodiversity crisis and ...

Resolving political differences peacefully and ...

The Diamond King's pixelated image was roving back and forth across the screens in the room in a digital facsimile of pacing.

Ozie looked out the window and spotted cranes in the distance where another segment of the quadrant was under construction. Las Vegas was on track to double its population in less than ten years. Its economy was more than booming; it was exploding, not the flash-bang-smoke of a chemical bomb, more like the fusion explosions that powered the sun: sustained, powerful, almost too bright to behold. Among the many genius economic policies enacted by the OWS, there was another force working in its favor: rapid and effective immigration, assimilation, and indoctrination from all the beleaguered populations fleeing climate chaos, economic stagnation, and political suffocation. They were doing it right there. And the economic system ensured that everyone shared in the growth.

Why risk all that? If the Diamond King started a war, Europe could shut off Mesh access to the continent. They would withdraw their satellites. They would try to sabotage MeshTowers or take remote control of communications and anything linked to the Mesh—automated factories, drones, and autonomous vehicles. The economy would unravel. Ozie couldn't see how war would result in anything but disaster. Unless the Diamond King had an ace up his sleeve. Which was pretty likely. Very likely. Almost certain.

Ozie could be part of this future. He could control it. He could harness it to finally turn mirror resonance syndrome into a superpower. If he played his own cards right and kept them close to his chest.

"Okay, focus. You've read the contract. What do you think?" the Diamond King asked from a vidscreen on the desk.

"This says all my potential legal costs would be covered."

"Of course. But both you and I know that's not what's motivating you. It's the science, unraveling the mystery, isn't it? Mirror resonance syndrome will unfold its secrets. You'll finally get your answers."

The Diamond King was right. This job would allow Ozie to work on sophisticated, cutting-edge tech brainhacking, with the wealth of Las Vegas backing him. He hated the idea of getting more deeply involved with the Diamond King, but part of him wanted desperately to stop going it alone. It was too late for regrets. He'd become isolated, with few connections to draw on and partners in crime who were unreliable. Being a loner had been a point of pride, insulation from society's ills, and a kind of freedom. Now he saw it was a trap, a vulnerability easily exploited, a grave mistake. The Diamond King was giving him hope that things could change.

He couldn't refuse. The offer was too good to pass up, and he had no alternatives. Besides, the Diamond King would kill him if

Cody Sisco

he refused. Or worse.

"There's one more thing," the Diamond King said.

A fearful chasm opened in Ozie's chest; The Diamond King was crazy enough to do anything. "Let me guess. We're going to launch a rocket that'll destroy Moonbase One," Ozie shot back.

"Not at all. The rockets come later. I want you to tell me everything you know about Victor Eastmore and crossing over."

A cold chill ran down Ozie's spine. *Crossing over* was Samuel Miller's euphemism for murder, believing that a quantum-triggered shockstick would deliver his victims into another world. "What? Why?"

The Diamond King's eyes flashed red.

Ozie rocked back in his seat, an innate fear response, and a foolish one, since the King's image couldn't hurt him. Still, this personal interest in Victor was disturbing, given that the Diamond King's history with the Eastmore family also included procuring the polonium used to poison Jefferson Eastmore. Now, he was targeting Victor?

"Begin speaking," the Diamond King said. "I'll tell you when I've learned all I need to know about Victor."

Ozie's cheeks heated up. Was his value to the Diamond King based on his association with Victor? Had he gravely overestimated his own importance?

He cleared his throat. "Victor and I met ..."

4

It was my own fault I got hooked. After my injury, I couldn't do the things I loved: playing catch-and-carry, rowing up and down the Passage, or being with my kids. Just a little hit, I thought, when I need to feel better. There's no harm. Boy, was I wrong! I felt like a shooting star. But when I came down, I had burned everything I loved.

—BioScan journal entry titled, "Patient notes from New Venice"

20 March 1992
New Venice, The Louisiana Territories

Alia Effendi had emerged from the hostage crisis with the Human Lifers battered and shaken. Changed, too, not for the better. She looked for things that *hadn't* changed while waiting for the MeshNews interviewer to arrive. From her perch on the balcony overhanging the BioScan lobby, she checked on her town. Colorful boats still moved languidly through the canals. Shops alongside sold crafts of every kind: carved totems, woven cloth, and beaded jewelry. The restaurants and bars fronting the Passage were connected by a charming rickety wooden boardwalk that promised romance and discovery or, at the very least, an enjoyable evening.

A thriving center of the Permanent Enlightenment, New Venice was a special place where the harms of slavery were amended. After New Orleans had been abandoned, due to rising waters, New Venice became a unique cultural hub and refuge. Change was plentiful, but unrest was an unfamiliar state of affairs in the tiny tourist town. When politics moved in, as it did every election season, the debates were always respectful, the tone elevated, and the ceremonies dignified.

But everything had changed with the hostage crisis. Afterward, disgraced Human Lifers had been run out of town, which set a bad precedent. New Venice was famously welcoming, but was that still true? After the recent ruckus, people returned to prosocial, foundational patterns. Nevertheless, every resident's heart was home to a troubling doubt, a suspicion that things couldn't go back to how they'd been, not completely, and the new arrangement of affairs was strange, confusing, and unpredictable—a change for the worse, undoubtedly. Over the past few weeks, Alia noticed a pervasive sense of glum resignation wherever she went. People seemed more hesitant and closed off.

She wouldn't mention any of this during the interview. Her goal was to set the frame positively for the future and give BioScan, New Venice, and Torsten most of all a boost of good publicity. This was an opportunity to put the past in the ground and stand ready to face the future. Alia would meet the moment with a determined, if not fully genuine, smile.

Lisabella Binglioto arrived and greeted Alia with the bubbling excitement of the hot springs east of New Venice. Alia feared, however, that the woman was just as poisonous as the toxic waters. This new celebrity Mesh reporter in their midst was using the crisis with the Human Lifers as a career springboard and seemed determined to spread false-faced cheer wherever she went. A bright smile, an eager tumble of words, expressions that strobed across her face in dizzying succession, and a penchant for wearing skin-tight clothing that covered every patch of skin yet left nothing to the imagination.

Her reporting during the crisis had made her a household name throughout the Louisiana Territories. Mesh officials had bumped her stories to the tops of people's feeds to shine a light on the Human Lifers and the stim addict crisis. Lisabella was the face of a changing political climate, one that demanded an end to the American Union's practiced equanimity and non-interference that purported to be principled but was, in fact, the resignation of the defeated. Alia feared New Venice was simply a territory on her map of geopolitical influence and ambition.

"Right this way, Lisabella," Alia said. She smiled, determined to evince enough positivity to not seem a dour sloth compared to Lisabella's frantic glamour. However, when Alia caught a glimpse of their reflections in the glass wall of a conference room, she noticed they made an attractive duo, and she loosened up a little.

They went first to the tower under construction up the hill. The tour of the BioScan facilities had been Lisabella's idea, proposed directly to Circe, agreed to, and then it became Alia's responsibility. She knew it was likely for twin reasons: her prominence was elevated by her fiancé Torsten, and she'd been through the hostage crisis herself. Never pass up an opportunity to tell your story, Torsten would say. But that's why he was the politician, not Alia. She wanted to be checking off her tasks, making sure all the patients were comfortable, that their needs were met, and that they were being cared for. If she could show Lisabella how important this work was, maybe that would make a difference.

They hiked up the stairs slowly, making chit-chat, not wanting to break a sweat. Alia led Lisabella through an unfinished floor of the new tower, which was a capstone of the Eastmores' investment in New Venice and truly something to behold, as monumental in its way as the canals it loomed over. Caution tape warned them away from where the windows would soon be installed. The open-air drop to the ground ten stories below made Alia queasy. Her breathing began to quicken. When Lisabella asked if she was okay, Alia blamed it on the stairs, a partial truth. Thankfully, the momentary panic passed.

Lisabella seemed intent on fulfilling her promise of portraying BioScan positively and of fairly reporting the dilemma of treating mirror resonance syndrome patients when a cure was still out of reach and the challenge of helping a fast-growing population of stim addicts.

The only tough question Lisabella posed provoked a moment of mute fear in Alia.

Lisabella asked, "The crisis was a tragedy. You mentioned the patient who regrettably passed away after missing their medication. However, that wasn't the only casualty, and there are conflicting accounts of what happened. So, I wanted to ask you, do you regret the death of Samuel Miller?"

Alia took a breath. The world whited out, then came back fuzzy. She shook her head to clear it and hoped Lisabella would read that gesture as her answer. What bothered Alia wasn't the man himself or his death in suspicious circumstances. It was how he'd inspired the Human Lifers to follow his madness. It was so infuriating, so puzzling, so irrational. How could they all lose their minds at the same time? They might have remained a curious, extreme offshoot of the Puros, forgotten and overlooked. Instead, they'd made Samuel Miller their spiritual leader, besieged BioScan, and drawn the wrong kind of attention to her small town. The inquiry would sort out exactly what happened during the hostage-taking and how Victor and Samuel came to be in a drug hut with a lethal shockstick. Alia didn't want to step into the limelight by saying that the murderer got what he deserved.

It took a moment for her to respond in a calm, neutral voice, "In the healthcare profession, every death is regrettable."

Lisabella's lips quirked, and she moved on.

After the tour, Alia rushed out, declining Lisabella's invitation to lunch. It was undoubtedly a ploy to pick Alia's brain about Torsten's campaign. She really couldn't stay, she said, a wedding. "You know how it is, I'm sure."

A quick autocab ride took her to the highway north of town, stayed on it until the next exit, and then ascended Cemetery Hill Road to Torsten's cabin overlooking Pond Park. She changed clothes, brushed her hair, put on a necklace and gloves, and then rode in the same autocab back down to the Botanical Garden, which was set on a bluff overlooking all New Venice's buildings and the Grand Canal below. She was thankful it was such a small town that she could dash home to change, rather than changing at work.

She walked through the Rose Garden and took in the view. Chairs had been set in two groups on the lawn with the townscape behind them. Further in the distance, rolling hills and the gray waters of the Passage. A dais festooned with flowers completed the scene, and she paused to inhale their sweet scent. A wave of dizziness nearly tipped her over. Had she forgotten to eat lunch? She steadied herself.

Guests mingled on a broad patio, where tents would protect them if it rained. However, looming thunderclouds had retreated, and the sky was now striped by thin cirrus formations that looked like frothy white Gulf waves on a breezy day.

Alia found Torsten sitting with the mother and father of one of the brides and joined them, apologizing for her lateness. Torsten kissed her, squeezed her hand, and continued an earnest though somewhat rehearsed-sounding recitation of priorities for economic development in the LTs. No one would want to talk about the stim crisis or security concerns during a wedding, and he was seizing the opportunity to put forward his broader vision for prosperity. The bride's parents were listening with serious expressions, nodding, moving in small degrees toward the optimism

Cody Sisco

and confidence that Torsten inspired. Few could resist his potent combination of charm, logic, sincerity, and passion. His words gently lapped at the shores of her preoccupation; she wished it would bowl her over.

Inhaling, she could still smell the lush and pungent flowers from across the lawn. Then, something clicked into place, and she recognized with disbelief all the components of a nineteenth-century throwback wedding. The placement of the flowers. The arrangement of the audience. The pastor presiding over them in his tidy tweed suit like something out of a posed, sepia photograph. The cross—Laws, how had she not noticed it when she walked in? A six-foot-high wooden crucifix propped up where everyone could see it, too big to be anything but a joke. Or maybe it was a genuine testament of faith but in horribly poor taste. Who could say?

Alia nudged Torsten. He turned, and she raised her eyebrows at the cross. A smile quirked the edge of his mouth, and he shook his head slyly. They'd talk about it later.

He was holding up well, considering the rigors of the campaign and the fact that his brother Anders had gone missing. Not that it was entirely out of character for Anders. He was his brother's opposite: emotionally unstable, volatile, and as prone to outbursts of hysterical sadness as to quiet, seething anger. Going missing during the campaign was, in a way, convenient, but Alia knew Torsten was worried. Anders was his only blood kin left.

This wedding assembled so many close family members, all their history and memories intertwined in complicated vibrancy. Her wedding would be nothing like this. Her parents' memory would be crowding the shadows. Her friends … Who was she kidding? She had her work, she had her work friends, and she had Torsten. There couldn't be a bride's and groom's sides in the seating arrangement because the imbalance would tilt the world on its axis. There would be hundreds of people who were there for him, surely. Who didn't want to join the bandwagon and hop on the Torsten train? The wedding would be planned as precisely as a campaign event: there would be spectacle and optimism and good cheer. But intimacy? Knowing someone better than you knew yourself? That was for the two of them only, later, when the campaign was over. Alia often wondered if it would ever end, though.

She tried pushing away such thoughts and looked at the boats on the Grand Canal. Few passed under Triton's Deep Crossing into the Pond, surrounded by a growing number of tents belonging to stim addicts and refugees from the Republic of Texas that popped up with the fecundity of springtime buds. Windows installed on the BioScan tower's lower half reflected the gray chaos of buildings and canals across the way. Below the tower on the slope and adjacent to the Petite Canal was the administration building, where a patient had died, neglected by the medical staff who were themselves prisoners of Wonda and her Human Lifers. Alia had begged and bargained to be allowed to treat the patient. Wonda had been callous, empowered, unrelenting, and very pleased with herself. A pure ideolog. Did Wonda regret that patient's death? Lisabella should ask *her*.

Throughout the conversation with the bride's parents, Alia smiled, nodded as if she followed their words, and chimed in when she could edge in, but her gaze strayed.

What bothered Alia wasn't any of the wedding details—flowers, crosses, decorations—but the ritual of it, the enforced process, the echoes of all that was bad about the previous century. The racism and slavery, economic imperialism, religious fanaticism, nationalism and manifest destiny—the list could go on and on. Everything that was counter to what the Permanent Enlightenment had achieved: reparations, progress, equality, secularity. Why, then, did the brides choose *this* ceremony?

Far out in the Passage, the Qaddo Lands were where the Human Lifers had retreated, protected by the tribe's sovereignty and reluctant, unofficial sanctuary. Having spent so much time there in her youth, she knew both how much of a violation and disruption their presence would be and how honor-bound the tribe would feel to help outcasts and refugees, especially those that had a similarly complicated relationship with modernity.

There were limits to Alia's empathy, however. Wonda had been cruel and ruthless, using terror and power as means that couldn't be justified by any end. She deserved to lose everything.

But a question that had been vexing Alia for months arose again before she could quash it: *How much of the patient's death had been Wonda's fault, and how much had been her own?* If her guilt could be accounted for in discrete pieces, like bits in a computer, or decimalized to hundredths or thousandths, maybe Alia could calculate her portion and live with it. Likewise, despite what a monster Samuel Miller was, she should have stopped Victor before his final visit to

Cody Sisco

the drug hut. And when he came to her with the shockstick after, she should have done anything other than throw it in the canal. She remembered, again, the feeling of the shockstick in her hands after Victor urged her to take it. His instructions. How she hadn't questioned him. She'd gone to Bozart's Bridge with the shockstick and dropped it in the water. Only during its seconds-long fall had she stopped to wonder what she was doing. She felt the weight in her hands so intensely that she looked down. She was holding her clutch, not a shockstick, gripping it tightly. She rolled her shoulders, releasing the tension in her neck.

Her crimes, she was sure, would never become a legal question, despite the official inquiry. No sane judge would side with the Human Lifers over the staff of the most important employer in the LTs. No lawyer would dare raise the question. Rather, it was a matter of ethics. But for the first time in her life, Alia couldn't be sure if she was on the side of right or wrong.

The law protects saints and sinners alike, her mother had used to say, back when Alia still listened to her mother, more than half a life ago. Samuel Miller was the worst of the worst, responsible for the slaughter of hundreds in Carmichael. *But that didn't give Victor the right to*—Alia stopped herself. This was too dark a hole to fall into during a wedding.

With a silent gasp of dismay, she noticed that everyone— Torsten and herself included—had moved to the seats and were waiting for the ceremony to begin. Gooseflesh crawled up her arms. She had no recollection of the past five minutes.

Is that what going blank was like? It couldn't be. *This is nothing like blankness,* she told herself. *Too busy thinking about my own problems and not paying attention, that's all. Nothing like blankness.* She clasped her hands in her lap to keep them from shaking.

She put a smile on her face and watched a bride lead her favored guests to the front of the gathering. The bride was a handsome woman, one of Torsten's political connections. She wore a black suit with a white collar and cuffs in the masculine tradition, indicating the politicization of a sacred event. Later, Alia would remark to Torsten that it was ill-suited to the modern day.

The other bride, Alia's friend from school, walked down the aisle, accompanied by organ music that elicited a few giggles from the crowd, like a questionable word shouted in church. She was beaming, beautiful. Alia had always known her to be kind and thoughtful, with a booming and infectious laugh. She deserved to have her wedding how she wanted it. But that didn't stop Alia from wondering: why like this?

Alia's unease deepened as they proceeded to recite verses and vows. This throwback ceremony somehow pressed all her buttons at once, she realized. Marriage had been redefined over the past hundred years for good reasons. It was no longer a transfer of property from a woman to a man; spouses were defined as equal partners, regardless of their gender. The bond of marriage no longer signified an indelible right to a woman's fertility or exclusivity for either party. Childbearing and fidelity were decided by discussion, not paternal-colonial systems of progeny and puritanism.

Unease pounded in her temples. What was worse, she couldn't sublimate and redirect her feelings, try as she might, which wasn't like her. Torsten noticed her squirming because he placed a reassuring hand on her knee and squeezed gently. But had he wrapped an arm around her, she might have leaped up, screaming, "I'm my own woman!" Marriage was an agreement between two individuals, crafted on their terms to fit their relationship, wants, and passions. Each bond was unique. How could it be anything else? The only hope for lasting marriage was resonance, connection, and attraction.

Leave it behind, she told herself. And yet she couldn't. This ceremony was an abomination, a relic, a backsliding.

As the pastor declared permission for the husband to kiss the bride, a symbol for the taking of her virginity, everyone clapped.

"Not on my wedding day," Alia muttered, her words masked by the cheers and claps around her. Everyone stood, and she rose as well. She worked up a smile as the brides passed by. Their echoed smiles were exuberant. Their gazes noted that both Alia and Torsten were there, a quick mark of thanks as they rushed onward to their joint destiny.

Alia heard a quiet snort from Torsten. With every bit of will remaining, she shoved her thoughts away and turned to him. "A lovely ceremony, don't you think?" she asked, her arm circling his waist.

"Total boner killer," he whispered. "It's like we went back in time."

"Here's a glimpse of the future." She brought him close and kissed him deeply. They saw the world for what it was together. That was going to be enough.

But as they walked back through the rose garden, she worried that perhaps she was starting to understand a bit too well the feeling of being caught in a resonant episode—it was isolating, unbalancing, and with no clear path back to belonging.

5

After the BioScan meeting, Victor crossed Bozart's Bridge into town. Today was the day. No backing out. He would cross into blankspace and go as far as he could.

At the boating supply store, he picked out an entire spool of synthsilk because it was easier than specifying the exact length he needed, and he honestly didn't know how much each loop and knot would require. At the register, the clerk moved slowly. She was a grim and wiry woman whose hands and bare arms were so wrinkled they looked like the fabric of a loose-knit sweater. One finger pecked at a type-pad, while her other hand held the spool. The obnoxious label faced him, a red and gold cartoon spider with multiple eyes and a filament of web hanging from its mouth like thick white drool. "Spider strong!" the label read. "No one makes better synthsilk!"

The clerk handed him the spool, saying, "Thanks, and you have a great day now, you hear," ending with a tight-lipped smile. She moved to the window pretending to scan the narrow street and the esplanade fronting the Grand Canal, while actually monitoring him with side-eyed suspicion.

Victor took his purchase and left, muttering "good day," already thinking about where he would cut the rope and how to twist and loop it. He'd earned a basic boating credit from the Craft Corps when he was seven, and this was the first time he would be putting his knot-tying skills to good use.

At the center of town, the streets were closely packed and buildings towered three, four, or five stories in some places. They never experienced direct sunlight. The streets' cobblestones smelled dank and moldy thanks to shopkeepers who insisted on spraying the day's litter into the canal. As Victor passed by a dark alcove, someone's stoop, he smelled an appalling, potent cocktail of bodily excretions and glimpsed a figure, covered in ragged blankets, slumped on the step. He crossed to the other side of the street, preoccupied—the trick would be to use knots that tightened the more they were pulled—and then he stopped. He'd already made so many mistakes and was only twenty-five years old. It was past time to try harder to do the right thing.

He returned to the alcove and leaned in, holding his breath. It was a woman. Dirty face, eyes closed, maybe forty, with a fading bruise on her cheek and what looked like dried blood on her hairline. The waft of stim metabolism, like rotting fruit, was unmistakable. He couldn't tell if she was breathing.

"Hello?" he asked.

No response.

He reached out and gently nudged her shoulder. If she was alive, it was his business: BioScan's, to be precise.

She stirred, but her eyes didn't open as she sighed the kind of sigh—a languid erotic moan—that would make anyone blush. It hooked into his brain's pleasure center before he knew to be on guard.

He turned away, embarrassed by a burgeoning erection, wishing he weren't so easily imposed upon. Having mirror resonance syndrome shouldn't be a liability in matters of sexuality; it should be a spectacular, mind-rending-in-a-good-way bonus, with arousal charging a feedback loop of erotic energy spiraling upward toward earth-shattering orgasms.

But it never worked out like that. Instead, he was perving on a stim-addled wretch.

Victor recrossed the street and retrieved a MeshBit from his pocket. He activated the cigar-shaped device by pressing his thumb on one end and then called the hotline.

"BioScan StimAlert, how can I help you?"

The voice, although it sounded like that of a young and competent individual, was actually a rudimentary form of algorithmic intelligence, capable of conversing within predetermined parameters but rapidly becoming repetitive and annoyingly obtuse if the caller deviated from its anticipated script.

"There's a body—I mean, a person—on Albion Way, half a block from the Grand Canal. She needs help."

Victor hung up without waiting for a response. Someone would fetch her. She was no longer Victor's problem. Like all the others, she would be taken and admitted to an intensive intervention facility for a few days while the worst withdrawal effects ravaged them. Then she would be placed into co-housing, most of which was located at the former campsite of the Human Lifers near Ouachita Dam, though some of the drug huts arrayed on Cemetery Hill still served that purpose for patients deemed a risk to themselves or others.

The drug huts were Victor's destination, even though he should be back at the clinic, helping however he could. It was a crisis; he didn't have time to indulge in blankspace.

Victor crossed the Petite Canal and began hiking up the hill, staying clear of the administration building and the half-finished tower.

I just need a break.

Earlier in the week, Karine caught up with him and began asking odd, elliptical questions about his aunt, probably trying to drag him into another of their disagreements. This morning, Alia spotted him from down the hall, looking at him like she wanted a confrontation. That was just the in-person hassling. The pings and queries via his MeshBit were also distracting. Ozie sent him several messages per day. Those went unread. Same with his parents. He paid for updates on Chico's status every four hours from a med tech in need of some extra cash, although the updates were always only ever "comatose, no change." Elena would have to appreciate that he was doing everything he could to help Chico and fulfill his promise to her. They had let each other down repeatedly. He didn't want to strain their friendship further.

The world wanted to intrude. Victor wanted to hold it at bay.

He needed a place where he could get to the bottom of mirror resonance syndrome, what it *really* was, without interruptions. He'd wasted so much time searching for a cure when the answer he truly needed was inside his own skull.

Summer was ebbing in New Venice. Bees picked over pollen-scarce flowers. Limp leaves hung on tree branches, desiccating, loosening their grip, and twisting in the breeze. Drug huts perched on the hillside, precariously balanced on tall stilts above the precipitous drop as the sun slipped behind the hills to the West.

Victor looked at the drug hut where Samuel Miller died. It was fitting yet macabre to use it today, but there was nothing left to try. After considering his room, in his office, everywhere he could think of where privacy and quiet might be available to make his attempt, he'd decided this was the place. Today, he would enter blankspace, and he wouldn't leave until he had answers.

Jefferson Eastmore always called blankspace a fantasy, a byproduct of mirror resonance syndrome with no more substance than a hallucination. Samuel Miller believed blankspace was how one could cross over to other worlds and attain a kind of immortality through quantum suicide: using the randomness of subatomic particles to trigger a lethal weapon. Samuel had believed that dying in one world of the multiverse resulted in living on in another. Compared to quantum murder, which Samuel used in excess in Carmichael, Victor supposed that quantum suicide was the better option.

Victor knew from experience that blankspace was no mere illusion. He'd approached its far border, glimpsed nebulous and distorted visions of the other side, and felt the boundary to be thick but permeable. He would have to cross over fully to discover the truth and was determined to do it without going to Samuel's extremes.

He entered the drug hut. The living room looked like the set of a stage play depicting normal life. There was a cozy, stuffed rocker by the fireplace and a table and chairs in a dining nook. And yet, didn't the strangest things often happen in ordinary places?

Victor locked the front door behind him and went into the room where the shockstick had misfired when he confronted Samuel. The door of the room didn't have a lock, for the safety of patients and staff—not that that had helped. Victor sat, took a pair of scissors from his pocket, unspooled a length of synthsilk rope taller than he was, cut it, and got to work.

He'd imagined this moment for days. He started with his feet, binding them together at odd angles so he couldn't do the blank-minded equivalent of sleepwalking. Then came the hard part: tying his wrists to his feet while still having enough flexibility to finish the last knot. He tested the knots and was satisfied they weren't going to give. To free himself would require undoing a series of them, which he was certain he wouldn't be able to manage while blank. He slid the scissors far away under the couch. This was the safest way to do it. He wouldn't go wandering off a cliff or wake up naked with strangers—again.

Satisfied, he began to take stock of his mind, a prerequisite for clearing it. Images of Samuel Miller swirled around him: the black-clad man in Carmichael, the drooling Personil-suffused vegetable-person, the earnest-though-crazed patient begging Victor to help him cross over. Victor didn't know what blankspace was, or what might wait beyond its far, fuzzy borders, but Samuel's claims were surely madness. Pure corruption. Corruption worked in small doses over long periods to poison everything it touched. He noticed his chest tightening and tried to suppress this train of thought. There was no time for an errant brain today. He envisioned a wise little owl who knew better, flapping its wings at the corner of his vision. His focus returned.

The blankspace mystery needed solving. His previous attempts had been tentative, only dipping a toe in the blankness while trying to hold on to the reality around him. He had been less than fully committed. He also hadn't bothered tying himself up before. Now, the preparations were made, and he would do whatever it took to cross over, and his body, once his mind left, would be trapped here, unable to harm himself or anyone else.

He breathed. He was ready.

Euphoric excitement buzzed in his groin as he began to slip into blankspace, falling inside his skin—

Loud knocking interrupted. Someone was outside. Someone mad.

"Victor!" Elena yelled.

He opened his eyes. "Laws, not now," he breathed.

"Victor!" There was a storm in her voice. "I'm going to rip your face off! Get out here!"

He wanted to ignore her, but she wouldn't stop until he came out. There was no way he could cross over now.

"Victor!"

"I'm coming! Give me a minute."

"Get out here now!" Her voice was closer to the window now, and he could see a dark shape silhouetted against the translucent pane.

"I am," he called out. "It's just—it's going to take a moment."

She harangued him while he picked at the knots ineffectively, crawled to where the scissors had gone, pressed himself against the couch, reached under to retrieve them, and started cutting. She'd sought him out several times over the past week. He thought he would be able to avoid her today. She must be spying again.

As he cut his knots, he saw that they hadn't been half-bad, but there were a few twists he'd do differently next time. There had to be a next time. The mystery of blankspace was like a splinter in his finger that swelled and festered. It kept him from achieving anything approximating sanity.

If he didn't *know*, he couldn't *live*. *The wise owl listens until the answer comes.*

"You've done nothing for Chico," Elena said from the other side of the window. "He came in needing help, and you've done nothing. At least he was shambling before. Now, I can't get him out of bed. I don't think he's been awake for a week. They say his vitals are trending down, and what are you doing for him? Nothing! What are you doing now? Masturbating with echoes of Samuel Miller?"

He swallowed bile. She'd brought Chico to New Venice because she didn't trust Texan doctors to help a Puro, and Chico's behavior as he fell ill was bizarre and unsettlingly familiar, like an MRS patient's decline, only faster. He understood her reasons. But he was at the end of his patience with her snooping. He unpicked the last knot that tied his feet and stood. He folded the rope, picked up the spool and scissors, and reached the front door, ready to curse her out.

As soon as he opened it, Elena pushed in, fear and concern all over her face, threatening to infect him with her anxiety. "What took you so long?" she asked.

He dipped into blankspace to get a little dose of bliss. Then, returning, avoiding her gaze and glancing down at the rope, he couldn't resist saying, "I was tied up."

She followed his gaze. Her eyes, usually greenish brown like new plant growth, flashed red. *Warning! Danger! Danger!* his mind screamed in hyperbolic synesthetic code—and then the colors on her face flickered pink and teal as she suppressed a retort.

She grabbed his arm and hauled him out the door. "Come on."

He let himself be dragged along by her strong and determined grip. Just before they passed over one of the cute garden bridges that arced over a hot spring, perhaps to prove a point, he slipped out of her grasp, and they crossed single file, him in the lead.

He said, "You know I'm not the best person on staff to help Chico."

"I don't care. You're going to go in there and raise a stink. *You* can at least do *that*, Mr. Eastmore."

The least he could do was also the most. He didn't know how to help Chico. Elena was headed for bitter disappointment.

They turned uphill toward the tower. Maybe she was right. The stim crisis made everyone at BioScan more flexible and creative in getting the job done with limited resources. Perhaps all that was required was a strong push.

At the foot of the tower, a worker blocked the automatic doors, so Victor opened the side door for Elena. "We're in the middle of a crisis," he said, trying to keep his voice level and not incite her further. "We're doing all we can, but Chico's just one piece of the puzz—"

Elena grabbed him again and spun him around so they were face-to-face. "You never loved the family business. Don't pretend now. I'm asking you to put someone else first for once."

That stung. He wouldn't be working so hard for purely his own sake. The mirror resonance syndrome patients needed his help. He'd accepted responsibility. But she didn't care about them. Chico was her new cause, and Elena was most herself when she was righteous and frustrated. He said, "So, if I can't help him that proves I'm an awful person? Your premise is flawed. I'm trying. But I'm not a miracle worker."

Her hands, clenched in his shirt fabric, released. She muttered quietly, "It's not a fucking premise. It's his life."

Victor was moved by her sadness, though gratified to no longer be burned by her anger. More softly, he replied, "We'll go see him. I promise. But since I'm here, I need to check on a few things first."

She frowned, looking lost and desperate. For a moment, he thought she might take his hand. He couldn't remember the last time she'd been tender with him. Several months, at least. Perhaps during that brief period, living in Amarillo while she was on stims and manically happy.

He moved down the hallway reluctantly. He didn't want to see Chico again. They'd tried everything, and nothing had helped. Chico was going to die.

6

We survived. We tallied the body count. We pushed back when we could.

We knew the Corps were backed by the OWS. Of what would come later, we had no idea. I never believed I'd live to see the Republic fall.

—Elena Morales, "Requiem for the Republic of Texas"

20 March 1992
New Venice, The Louisiana Territories

Elena watched as Victor supervised a macabre assembly line of bodies. They lined the wall of the room holding MAMA, the functional magnetic resonance imaging machine, and stretched into the hallway. Alive but unresponsive. Locked in some private hell and dependent on a world they couldn't perceive to keep them alive. Her skin crawled, but he didn't seem bothered. With delicate care, he waved a small device across each body to check for any metal implants that could cause problems with the strong magnetic fields generated by the truck-sized machine.

"What then?" she asked. "Once you've got them all scanned, so what? There's no cure."

"I know that," he snapped. His brow knotted, and his lips pressed together in a grim, taut line. "We're going to try everything, every intervention we can think of, and we'll be sequencing the hell out of their genomes and running them through this brain scanner as often as necessary. It's taking too long, though. Circe says we already have the best and there's no budget for more. This will have to be enough. But it's not."

The machine, which filled half the room, was worth more than most people would make in their lifetime. Compared to MAMA's magnificence, Elena and he were specks, who would one day pass into dust while this hulk survived decades longer, maybe centuries. Like the great human creations of eons ago—the cliff caverns of

Mesa Verde, the rock formations of Atacama, reef spirals off the coast of Crete—MAMA was monumental.

In terms of curing Chico, though, the machine was irrelevant. Elena's patience was dwindling fast. If she were a mere speck in the universe, that was more reason to do something useful—unlike Victor, who wasted time and energy trying to fix something no one understood.

"I'm sure they'll be grateful for the effort," she said, trying not to sneer at him.

Her snipes were becoming offensive, and she was pushing him away, the way her abuela pushed everyone away with her needling, caustic, bloody attitude. She didn't want to become that kind of person, but the transformation felt both easy and beyond her control. "Can we go see Chico now?"

"Yes, let's go." He didn't move, though. "Maybe they will someday," he said after a moment in a gentler voice than she'd heard in a while. He was looking at a young woman, clothed in a hospital gown, her head shaved and face sunken with waxy skin taut over the curvature of her skull.

"I feel like I'm forgetting something," he said.

"A way to treat them?"

"Maybe. I don't know."

She looked down at the comatose woman. "How do you make sure their muscles don't atrophy?"

"Some of them have been like this for years. Samuel Miller's the only one who ever recovered."

"And you don't know why?"

"No. Something Jefferson did to him, maybe. Some ..."

He trailed off, staring at a corner of the room. Elena followed his gaze and saw nothing unusual—lightstrips, ceiling tiles, a poster on the wall about safety precautions showing metal objects whizzing toward the fMRI machine—nothing to hold a normal person's attention. She looked at Victor and saw a lax puppet-human, the thing that remained when his mind went to blankspace.

The quiet became stifling. She couldn't hear the bodies breathing or see their chests rise and fall. They were so close to death in practical terms, death-like, and yet they remained half alive. What was going on inside their heads? Did they go to blankspace too?

She heard her breathing, ragged and jumpy. She wanted to run and felt foolish for it.

Whenever she'd done stims, she hadn't experienced blankness. It was rather the opposite. She'd been filled with euphoria, a sense of interconnectedness, and a wellbeing that nothing—not sex, not food, not laughter—could emulate. It was like biting a power line. But then the comedown arrived, which actually did resemble a kind of blankness, an emotional void that was accompanied by long periods of thinking about nothing at all, not fullness, not "crossing over."

Was he crossing over now?

"Victor!"

She called his name a few more times with no effect.

Then he blinked.

"Sorry. I'm back. I'm here. I thought I remembered something, but ..."

It looked like he would go blank again, so she grabbed his arm and shook him. He looked down at her hand and smiled an exultant, satisfied smile that was as powerful and contagious as it was rare. "Still here. Thank the Laws you still have the magic touch."

Her mouth turned up in response for a split second before she locked it down. *The fool. The stupid, broken fool.* She was thinking of something to say that didn't make her sound awful when her MeshBit chimed. It was her father.

"Fa?"

"Elena?" Her father sounded tense and out of breath. An engine droned in the background.

"I'm here. What's wrong?"

"We're leaving. Your mother's packing up now. I'm on my way home and then we go south. Julia, too." His voice was shakier than she'd ever heard.

"Go south?" she asked. "Why?"

"It's not safe. Los diablos azules—los Cuerpos—son locos! They started asking questions about the dogs. I got out quickly. Will you meet us, hija?"

"Papá, I—"

Elena glanced at Victor and saw the blankness in his stare. He'd gone away again. If he was Chico's best chance, there was no hope, and though she cared for both of them, admittedly with mixed feelings, there was nothing she wouldn't risk for her parents. "I'm coming, yes. Don't tell me where. If the Corps are after you, they might be listening. Leave a clue with you-know-who. Keep Mamá safe, okay? I'm coming."

"I'll call again when we're safe. I love you, Elena. Te amo."

"Te amo, Papá. Cuidado. I'll see you soon."

The connection ended.

Tears slipped down her cheeks while she stared at Victor, who was vacant-mouthed, eyes unseeing. She grabbed a pen on a nearby desk, took hold of his hand, and wrote on the back of it a single word in block letters she knew he'd recognize as her handwriting. *Adios*.

7

People assume that the truth will set them free. That's not the case at all. Lies are strands in the web that keeps truth aloft.

—Anonymous Biographer of the Diamond King

6 April 1992
Las Vegas, Organized Western States

Ozie scratched his head and ran his palm over a day's growth of stubble. He'd taken to shaving using a laser that vaporized hair while leaving skin intact, yet he'd forgotten to use it this morning, maybe also yesterday. Things were starting to get blurry timewise. Another unasked-for perk of having access to nearly unlimited resources and new tech was that he could opt out of the diurnal cycle, keep odd hours, snack whenever he wanted, and sleep in brief sojourns away from his screens while relying on braincaps to keep his MRS symptoms in check. *Heavy is the head that wears the crown.*

He ran his brainhacking programs continuously. Without them, his condition, exacerbated by stress and inconsistent routines, would rapidly deteriorate. "Vegetableizing" is how he thought of it—not inevitable, but definitely possible the way he was sprinting toward the project's end.

Finding evidence of the Diamond King's role in Jefferson Eastmore's death was a tiny part of Ozie's motivation. More important was access. Money. New technology. The levers of power to transform the world. *Who could say no to all that?* Although he now wondered, *What if I'm just another tool in the Diamond King's toolbox?*

Ozie looked at the assemblage of computing cores arranged around him like honeycomb bricks, the hollows dedicated to liquid cooling circuits, each column topped by a narrow-beam spectrum relay to provide speed-of-light linkages to other computing stacks in the room. The construction, which was replicated a thousandfold and filled several additional building floors, amounted to more processing and storage capacity than had previously existed throughout Las Vegas, including the resources contained in the Institute for Biological Sciences. And this was only a test of the architecture that would be replicated a thousandfold if all worked as planned. The machines ran their final checks and put out a green signal. After tweaking the settings for days and days, installing new equipment to stabilize and monitor things, he'd finally coaxed the system into a state that met his ambitious—no—bat-shit ludicrous pie-in-the-sky aims.

The diagnostic on the vidscreen should have been a single line: System Nominal. Instead, the program had spit out a hundred or so lines of code. As he read the logs more closely, the back of his neck tingled. The logs didn't make sense. It reported that the spectrum relays routed external traffic to the processors amounting to 80 percent of their capacity. The problem was they weren't connected to anything. He'd built the whole thing in an isolated virtual workspace, wanting to work out the kinks and protect it from any foreign code. Of course he'd had to install base software, but he had done so from pre-checked and pristine source code. Systems, once operational, always gathered complexity, but this system should have been a fully controlled, predictable entity. It shouldn't—it couldn't—be doing anything new or unexpected.

And yet, it was doing *something*.

A wave of nausea overtook Ozie. He stumbled to an overstuffed synthleather chair printed with galactic whorls and stars. When he'd ordered it, he joked to himself that the chair would make him feel like the king of the universe. But kings don't panic about errant code, and he recognized he wasn't, in fact, King in these parts.

Ozie snapped his fingers a few times, and Raoul, a roving bot similar to the one he'd programmed back at the Springboard Café, brought him sparkling water spiked with anti-anxiety meds and fumewort. *If it works for Victor, maybe it'll work for me.* He sipped the beverage and turned his attention beyond the office windows to the circle of Grand Park and the curved wall of buildings that comprised the inner core of Las Vegas. From thirty stories up, the view rivaled any vantage in Oakland & Bayshore. Artificial lakes and lush greenery gave the impression of abundance and fecundity.

Cody Sisco

Beyond the city limits, however, all was dusty sand-etched rock and sediment. He could see it from here, an escape that promised only hardship and privation, and still he yearned for it. His office offered every comfort except freedom.

It offered mystery as well, and that's what kept him going thirty-plus hours at a time without sleep and who knows how many hours since his last meal—the robot was always good about cleaning up after him and whisking away dirty plates and silverware. Could he indulge now in creature comforts and take a desperately needed sip of sleep? No, he had to stay on top of his project.

He returned wearily to the control bay, faced the array of six large vidscreens, and began querying the system to uncover exactly what it was working on.

As minutes and hours flowed by, he began to get a hunch that grew in certainty: none of this was an accident. He'd developed the system to eventually serve as the nerve center and command station for a new initiative by the Diamond King to exert control over the Corps via an undisclosed communications protocol developed by some other team. The idea was that an initial group of mercs would test the system, and it would be progressively rolled out to more units, generally teams of six to ten operatives trained in communications, combat, search and rescue, crowd control, and other authoritarian power plays. The Diamond King had shared his plans in other terms, of course, forcing Ozie to decode his true motives.

As he investigated further, Ozie learned that what he had initially thought was a problem was not. The system functioned as designed. Somehow, it was linked with the outside world and functioning autonomously, again, as designed. And yet Ozie had never "pressed play."

Fearing the confrontation but no longer able to suppress his curiosity, Ozie pinged the Diamond King. Within a minute, the playing-card face and torso appeared on a vidscreen, blinking at him in a mechanical yet oddly organic way that led Ozie to think a vidcap and processor setup must be recording the man's physical movements and expressions, rendering them digitally, and relaying them to this avatar.

"The system is up and running," Ozie said.

"Yes, I know. Its performance meets my expectations."

"But I don't understand how. I never linked it to anything outside this room. Unless you've got spectrum relays built into the walls and a program capable of squeezing into my code ..."

Ozie trailed off. He looked around at the mirrored pillars throughout this building's floor. Of course. He should have seen it sooner. He also should have kept his mouth shut—better that than reveal how his stupid, dumb, bogged-down brain malfunctioned by missing what was in plain sight. He'd assumed the pillars were purely structural, but how much computing infrastructure was hidden from view behind the glass?

He sprayed typepad cleaner into the air. Seconds later, a green glittering mist flared where it intersected a spiderweb of lasers above his head. The network, running on optical connections, was there all along, waiting to hook into the nerve center that Ozie built. That explained the hardware puzzle, but how did the Diamond King break into his software?

The avatar smiled, revealing a mouth with white cogs for teeth. "You've exceeded expectations," he said. There was no warmth in his voice. Still, Ozie felt relieved. One served at the Diamond King's pleasure, or one served as worm food.

"Can you tell me how you made the integration work? I thought my system would remain isolated," Ozie said.

"I will send you a summary. Sleep now. We'll begin again when you're rested."

The jagged scarlet, white, and yellow face disappeared. Ozie was staring at his own dim reflection. Exhaustion washed over him as if on command.

Don't forget to ask about the next phase. To outsmart a fox, you must lay a good trap.

I've got to find out what he's hunting.

Ozie stumbled and then crawled across the floor to reach his bed in the other room. His last thought as sleep began to take him was that his cyberarm was tapping a beat he didn't recognize.

Sometime later, Ozie opened his eyes and looked around. He was sprawled on his galaxy-patterned bean bag, not having made it to his bed before he passed out. Thick, fragrant sludge-spit coated his teeth and gums. His shoulder ached where the cyberarm weighed on it. He was blinking, trying to wake fully, when he heard the elevator chime.

A woman in a lilac pantsuit turned the corner and didn't miss a step as she strode toward him. He sat up slightly but didn't rise. Exhaustion still lay on him like a heavy blanket.

"Hello." Her voice was sharp and accent-inflected in a way that reminded him of a European-born professor he'd once had for a civics course. Her head was shaved except for a top-shock of dark blue hair that flopped to one side. A broad smile showed laser-straight teeth, and her eyes sparkled behind the bright lime frames of her glasses. "My name is Grette Sinapoulous. I am happy to be working with you, Mr. Smythe."

"Are we? Working together? The Diamond King mentioned something … I was supposed to read a summary, I think." Ozie looked around guiltily, expecting to see the royal image on one of the pillars scowling at him, but he was alone with Grette.

"May I?" She gestured to a neighboring bean bag, also galaxy patterned, which he thought of as Andromeda, and sat down, leaning forward with her hands clasped between her legs. "We have much to discuss."

"I didn't read it. The summary. I'm not sure—"

"I watched you sleeping."

"I'm sorry?"

"*He* tells me to wait until you have awoken. Now we can talk. This project is my life's work. We will be starting surgery—"

"Hang on a minute. Please. I'm going to need some caffeine or something." He stood and massaged his temple with his human hand. "Raoul, coffee," he said.

"We can walk?" Grette asked, gesturing in a loop.

"Yeah." He sighed. "Slowly, we can walk." If she caught his imitation of her slightly off-kilter syntax, she didn't remark on it.

"I am a seven," she volunteered out of nowhere.

Ozie hesitated. The ritual of status exchanges was one he had witnessed many times during his few and brief sojourns to what he called "civilian life" in Las Vegas, and he'd participated in a few. It still took him off guard. When would it cease to give him gooseflesh?

"I'm a nine," he responded after a moment.

She nodded, smiling, glancing his way briefly in an expression so honest and endearing that he almost felt bad she was caught up in all this. But he understood "life's work." There wasn't really any choice. The path led to where he must go.

He picked up a protein bar from one of his stashes and offered one to her, which she declined. They continued walking slowly around the office perimeter.

"I am eager to work with you to obtain his approval." Grette gestured back to the elevator, where Ozie assumed she had last exchanged words with the Diamond King. Her statement poured cold water on his sympathy. She was a believer and a sycophant, and if she ever learned of Ozie's ambivalence and his inclination to disloyalty, she would denounce him gladly.

"He told me this project was the top priority," he told her, unsure whether he was boasting, testing her knowledge, or hoping his fears would be allayed. "Budgetless."

"It's a dangerous thing," she answered, "to try to meet expectations from one so ..."

During her silence, Ozie pictured bodies laid out in Grand Park, exposed, scoured by the wind and dried in the sun and heat. They turned a corner and saw fields of solar towers and mountains in the distance.

"Genius," she finished.

A minute later in their perambulation, Raoul rolled alongside, extending a platter upward. Ozie stopped, took a cup filled to the brim with real coffee, and sipped carefully from it. As Grette explained "her life's work," Ozie grew increasingly impressed. She had long been working on the implantation of electronics in the brains of primates, including humans. As computing power escalated and brain hacker scripts were inducted into neuroscience, Dr. Sinapoulous had laser-focused her research on "skullplugs."

"You've put these in humans?" he asked.

"Oh, yes, many humans. For the treatment of epilepsy and prevention of dementia, depression, and other mental illnesses. The trick is filaments, which grow through neural tissue like climbing ivy. That was my breakthrough, keeping them in place. The filaments transmit and receive electromagnetic impulses. Over time, they map the brain's structure, improving our ability to alter its state. The plugs need a long period to exchange data and commence reprogramming. This is where I seek your help."

A network of plugs. Autonomous processing. Feedback cycles. The challenge was already starting to crystallize in his mind. To link the plugs, characterize layered data, and pass abstracted information between spectrum relay nodes—the project he'd just

Cody Sisco

completed was already the cornerstone of what would be needed as a solution.

She offered a partnership and access to resources to explore a fascinating new field of science, ensuring he wouldn't be alone in the endeavor. The discoveries would unfold at an astonishing rate.

She interrupted his thought process. "Not only a network of plugs. A network of minds. To be able to convey this rich information from one mind to another. To share among the network. It would be a form of communication beyond words. We do this together."

A network of minds?

He said, "Oh, yes, yes indeed; we do this."

8

I told myself that I'd been through worse, that I'd survived far more terrifying circumstances. But that feeling of helplessness, of having nowhere to turn. It's the same pain every time.

—Mía Barrias, Mesh interview with Lisabella Binglioto

10 April 1992
New Venice, The Louisiana Territories

The bodies arrived in New Venice on refrigerated train cars after a long journey east. *Patients: they're patients, not bodies,* Karine reminded herself. The wrong terminology could make or break an interview. Standing under the shade of the depot's cantilevered roof, she consulted with Gustav, the square-faced logistician she was grooming for a promotion. She was relieved to find their patients' vital signs stable. This latest shipment would tally zero fatalities during the voyage, continuing their record. Quite a feat, considering. The whole affair required more risk than was prudent, and the logistics taxed even her abilities, yet everything seemed to be going to plan.

"*Everything is going to plan, Lisabella, and that's all we can ask for.*"

No, much too confident. It's begging for something to go wrong.

"*The effort is not without certain challenges.*"

Better ...

Or how about, "*It's hard work saving all these lives.*"

Ding-ding. We have a winner.

Gathering Class One Broken Mirrors from facilities across Semiautonomous California had been a wretched task. Thankfully, Mía Barrias, SeCa's favorite crusader, had assumed the heaviest burden, sending dispatches of what she found in those sad, decrepit places: neglect, illness, dull-eyed staff, and comatose bodies. Karine was genuinely surprised: the reports she'd reviewed during her brief stint as a commissioner must have always been sanitized and the data criminally misleading. Of course, she'd gone to several facilities when she'd first joined the Classification Commission. Perhaps she hadn't been paying enough attention. Anyway, she suspected those had been handpicked showrooms, ship-shape with their gleaming surfaces, attentive nurses, and clockwork administration, which served to hide a darker truth: the Class One facilities were warehouses for people forced into insentience by SeCa but whom, due to its tortured morality, it couldn't deliberately destroy. Mía reported patients wasting away, riddled with tumors unchecked and raging. To allow someone to die of cancer, let alone fail to provide treatment immediately following a routine early diagnosis—it spoke to the binary, good-versus-evil absolutist logic of the Cathar mindset that lay behind every failed policy in SeCa.

No. No. No. Don't criticize SeCa. Its Classification Commission is not your problem anymore. Focus on the Louisiana Territories.

Try, "I love the heartland. The care we're providing these patients is unparalleled around the world."

The train station was abuzz, everyone busying themselves according to plan—thank the Laws for small mercies. This wasn't where she expected to end up. But really, what could she have done differently? The chaos of the last two years at Gene-Us, then BioScan, the unflinching, unceasing effort to bring some order, to apply all she learned from the trial-by-fire assignments that were the strength and terror of the European education and internship system—organizational development, structure, and process—those skills had been up to the task. She'd done as much as she could. Yet it wasn't enough, and the company was failing.

Nothing is ever enough if we don't give ourselves some grace. Show yourself some kindness.

She marked off a few completed tasks on her typepad. At least now there was some predictability to the shipments of bod-ies—*Patients! They're called patients, even if they're as sentient as cucumbers. Don't say "cucumbers."*

Maybe she could even allow herself to believe that this time she could make a difference.

The train engine's humming ebbed to silence. It was a short, three-car assemblage with an engine and two cars of "sleepers."

A fleet of vans waited nearby with BioScan staff running through their checklists. She gave Gustav the go-ahead, thinking of the money this operation drained from company coffers. Careful as she was being, it would run out soon.

Karine mentally returned to the pitch she would make to Lisabella. A positive Mesh story would be a nice upside and strong leverage with Circe during the inevitable squabble.

Begin with the obvious challenge … context.

Say, "After gathering up the MRS patients from facilities in SeCa, they were shipped to the OWS border. A harrowing transfer was effectuated. Tensions between the two nations have never been so high."

No, too cold. Too abstract. You need to define your role. Doer. Chief-in-all-but-name. And lose the acronyms. People hate alphabet soup.

The cooperation between Semiautonomous California and the Organized Western States would have failed without Karine's persistence. She shuddered, remembering long days under harsh sunlight with only scrub and cactus, except the thin, improbable line of verdant landholdings that subsisted on the Cold Nile Miracle's bounty. How such a herculean engineering feat arose in that backwater was legendary.

"What do I think of Las Vegas? Lisabella, I'm so glad you asked."

To see it with her own eyes had diminished it. Up close, the fabled city became a child's set of Tinkertoys. Why not carve a thousand-kilometer-long canal between the Columbia and the Colorado rivers? The audacity! Yet today it was taken for granted. And then, for the sake of redundancy and efficiency, wouldn't a railroad running the same route be advisable? And since no infrastructure was sustainable without maintenance and security, shouldn't communities be seeded in the back of beyond to look after the investment? A long, thin line of civilization strung out in the desert like holiday lights, leading to its terminus of bright, shiny, orderly towers that comprised Las Vegas.

The city was a mirage, one with a promise so attractive that since it burst into existence less than 100 years ago, it came to rival the long-standing research and manufacturing centers of the New England Commonwealth. A mirage ruled by another mirage, if rumors of the Diamond King's insubstantiality were to be believed. Bookies in Oklahoma City had good odds on him being a front for the Corps criminal syndicate.

"Why, Lisabella, yes, I do have some theories about him."

Of course, she'd long suspected that Jefferson Eastmore and the Diamond King had some business entanglements. She was even willing to entertain the idea that those entanglements may have resulted in Jefferson's death. After Victor's accusations about her own culpability, her curiosity intensified, and she started digging into the Diamond King's history. Each new fact she uncovered brought a fascinating glimpse of a mystery far more intriguing than even the best crime novel. Who was the man behind the digital avatars? No one could say for sure. What was the extent of his influence on government policy and society? Inestimable. Why had he hidden himself from view for so many years? That was the trillion-dollar question.

Karine blew air from her lips. Foolishness. Secrets that needed to stay hidden. This was no time for silly fantasies of disclosure and scandal. BioScan took every minute of her waking hours and gnawed at her sleep. She needed to focus on the task in front of her.

Bodies taken from the train were loaded onto stretchers, looking small and vulnerable. The sight was dispiriting. How this could bode well for BioScan's fortunes escaped her. The search for a cure to mirror resonance syndrome, which remained elusive as ever, was wasting her talents. She doubted Victor could do much to reverse their condition. He would fail, and she wouldn't mourn the fact. She'd celebrate. He'd been coddled and privileged too long. And if Victor didn't fail on his own, Karine might just give him a push. No, she thought, she'd give him one last chance. That was the high moral ground. Anyway, she needed him as an ally to defend against whatever was going wrong with Circe.

Karine signed the paperwork. Fourteen bodies transferred to the vans in this group, bringing the total of live, comatose Broken Mirrors in their care to sixty-seven, with three times as many ambulatory Class Three MRS patients and stim addicts currently enrolled. She had to remember to harass the accounts receivable department to follow up with SeCa officials—the payment delays were becoming a cash flow problem. She wouldn't hesitate to stop the patient transfers in retaliation. There was no excuse for tardiness when it came to money.

Her MeshBit chimed and she cleared a notification; it was time to meet Circe back at the office.

She eschewed traveling with the comatose patients and walked along the trail down to Pond Park. Her hiking boots, though cinched tight, still wobbled around her feet every time she took a step. It was an uncanny incongruity that she had such a large frame and slender feet. If her young self could see her now, tromping around the American Union heartland, dodging stim addicts and refugees as she made a wide arc around the pond befouled by duck shit, and shrugging off raindrops falling listlessly from a gray sky—that ambitious, motivated girl might have made different choices. Maybe she'd have joined a citizen's choir in Mallorca and spent days fishing or serving tourists on the beach, making eyes with pretty men and women from all over Europe, taking them in their hotel rooms, crisp sheets, and sea breezes. Laws, she ached for home and simple comforts.

Karine had just enough time to update the patient intake manifest. Then, it was time for her meeting with Circe, who occupied a modest temporary office within the administration building.

"Shut the door, please," Circe said primly. She stacked a pile of paper on the corner of the desk, returned a pen to its holder, ran fingers through her hair exactly three times, then crossed her arms and waited.

Karine shut the door and observed her boss's preening with faint amusement. There had been a time when Circe seemed more carefree, her movements more fluid, her smiles quick and infectious, but that time had passed. Their friendship had fractured bit by bit, unnoticed, until only dust remained.

"Remind me," Circe commanded.

Karine did not doubt that Circe remembered why she'd asked for this meeting, but they were no strangers to such gambits.

"The cash flow situation," Karine said delicately.

"Ah."

"I don't want you to panic."

Circe smiled. It was a tight, efficient expression that disappeared moments later. "Hardly a chance of that. Please sit."

"We have been through a lot," Karine said, lowering herself onto an uncomfortable half-moon seat. "The current problem is that New Venice is making a blood-red loss and the rest are trending in that direction. I don't see any of it turning around before we have a liquidity crunch. We need a transfer from our Europe accounts within sixty days—our other AU accounts likely wouldn't cover it. Your Mesh friends may need a heads up; we wouldn't want unexpected delays."

Circe contemplated her fingernails. "You're ringing the fire alarm over burnt toast."

Karine fussed with one of her hiking boots, letting her hair fall across her face. She hadn't expected this line of defense: an attack on her judgment. She would have to proceed more carefully.

"I'll go over the figures with you," Karine said, brushing the hair from her brow. "Some of the trends are clear, others not so much. The problem, as I see it, is the Louisiana Territories' payment formulas. We expected more per patient when we cut the deal."

Circe nodded. Yet she still seemed reticent. "They've been a bit opaque about internal disagreements."

"We can't wait out the next set of budget negotiations."

"See what you can do about our vendors."

Karine tensed. She couldn't have been more unnerved than if a bird smacked into the window. BioScan was known for its rigorous vendor management and in a good way: fair terms, timely payments, and proactive communications. To try to squeeze money from vendors would be a marked shift.

Circe ran her fingers again through her hair, again exactly three times. "We are the biggest game in town. To some, we're the only game. What's the point of strategic purchasing if we're not getting as much benefit as possible? Find some trees to shake and use the cash to plug the holes."

"I'm not sure how prudent—"

"I don't want to talk about nickels and dimes. Am I clear? This region is set to blow up, and you're playing with spare change."

Karine bit back a response. Circe wanted to have it both ways. Going after vendors *was* a nickel-and-dime prospect. What was her game? Why was she so twitchy and curt?

She saw it immediately. Circe was *scared*. About what, Karine didn't know, but that explained her uncharacteristic snappiness and her wanting to pass the buck. Something had her spooked. The summit was coming to town, and Circe was due to host the dignitaries. Had some bad geopolitical news reached her ear?

Karine said gently, "I'll look again at how we can solve this problem. I may need to work with our AU affiliates."

"Fine, but try not to overburden them," Circe said, rising from her chair. "Come back with a workable solution."

Karine hesitated, moving toward the door slowly. What she'd missed before was now plain as day. Thinking back, she couldn't remember when she'd seen Circe so rattled, not even during the hostage situation. "If there's anything—"

"No, thank you."

Karine left the room and shut the door behind her. Her mind reeled. That had been a disaster. If she'd known Circe would be so obstinate, she'd have managed it differently. Lost in thought, Karine exited the building on the downhill side and then had to hike up a set of stairs and double back toward town.

Leaning on vendors would be a mistake. Karine had no doubts about that. Maybe they could tighten up operations and squeeze out a few weeks of cash. But a truly balanced budget, absent additional revenue from the government, would require deep cuts. There was no way to do it without affecting patient care. What was Circe really asking her to do? And what was she so concerned about?

A few years ago, a youthful, more optimistic version of Karine would have confronted Circe. They would have hashed it out over a bottle of wine. Uncountable possibilities for how to solve a problem would have been their playthings. When had she let go of friendship and chosen ambition instead? What did she have to show for it?

Karine straightened her shoulders. This was no time for mopey immaturity. She had a lot of numbers to crunch, but first, Alia would have to spill a few beans about the summit. She stopped when her MeshBit beeped and displayed "Inpatient Intake."

"What is it?" Karine asked, thinking perhaps one of the patients might be causing trouble.

"Karine? This is Diego. I'm reviewing the records of the Class One patients who were supposed to arrive today on the train. We're missing a few. Four, to be exact."

Karine felt a flash of heat around her eyes. "There must be some mistake. Everything checked out. I was there personally."

"I have the manifest here that you signed off on. It matches the computer record. But that's the problem: the computer record is wrong too."

"What do you mean?"

"It's been changed. I have a printout from last week. I keep paper records because ... I've run into problems in the past. I used to work in the ROT. We had problems like you wouldn't believe. So, I'm looking at the paper record, and I can say that we're missing four patients. They've been deleted from the digital records, and there's no trace of them. No audit trail. Nothing."

"Then we do have a problem. I'll be right there." Karine's mind whirled as she hurried back to the administration building. A confrontation with Alia would have to wait. Investigating Circe's budget buffoonery would have to wait. Regrets about a fading friendship could be conveniently brushed aside. There was a mystery in her hospital, and that wasn't something she would tolerate.

9

In effect, the Qaddo subsumed other tribes to create a renewed hybrid people. There is no such thing as a pure heritage or a culture in isolation. They made the wise decision to find a new path to build on the strength of their mutual support and appreciation. The West has a lot to learn about the importance of living in accordance with what works.

—Shoshanna Crowcaw, *Qaddo on the Front Lines of History*

14 April 1992
New Venice, The Louisiana Territories

Feeling outright dictatorial, Victor assembled the medics and doctors who played a role in Chico's care, forcing them to endure their colleagues' curious, amused, and quietly disdainful looks as they passed. With Elena gone, he could have breathed easily and let them off the hook. He didn't dare. He had no hope of keeping her friendship, or deserve to, if he didn't save Chico.

Victor asked what more could be done. The medics rolled their eyes at the waste of one patient taking up so much of their time. The doctors were perplexed by Chico's condition, full of excuses and empty of advice. All were fearful that they wouldn't be able to meet an Eastmore's demands and humiliated to be unable to help a patient "circling the drain," as one of them put it. A few spoke aloud Victor's private assessment: that Chico was a lost cause—a sentiment he wouldn't dare let cross his lips, whether in Elena's presence or not. He'd made sure they were out of earshot of the comatose young man to assuage a particular wariness about treating unresponsive people like inanimate objects.

The problem was that Chico had been cured of the infection he came in with, a rare and puzzling bacterial infection that had ravaged his organs, and yet he hadn't recovered. *Spirocetacae* didn't typically reside in humans; it preferred to make its home within the circulatory system of ticks and occasionally in wild mammals. Tick bites enabled the bacteria to emigrate to a mammalian host, and humans *could* be infected. Still, cases of this particular bacterial infection reported over the past few decades numbered only a couple dozen. Although there had been no rash on his skin, a telltale but rare side effect, doctors concluded a tick had probably bitten Chico. A course of antibiotics would usually knock out the infection, which did happen. By then, however, Chico had already been debilitated and put on life support. Lab tests of his blood showed nothing remaining in his system to cause concern, save for the admittedly toxic byproducts of organ damage, which was to be expected. However, he showed no signs of wakefulness or responsiveness and was as close to death as someone could get. Recovery wasn't out of the question; it was simply not likely with standard treatment. In a way, he fit in among the unresponsive mirror resonance patients.

Victor's circular conversation with Dr. Midge Lansdotter, a cheerless yet competent professional who recently moved from Akron, continued while the others returned to their responsibilities.

"There's nothing to be done," she told him.

"We've got to find something," he said. He could be strong and resolute for Elena. And every vulnerable person deserved someone standing up for them.

While the doctor gazed at Victor with a baffled expression, behind her, he spotted Alia stalking down the hallway. Her headscarf blazed green, red, and yellow, hues reminiscent of jungle flowers. The look on her face was one of determination and seething anger. Victor took a few steps back and looked at her hands to see if they held a weapon.

"There is one option we haven't considered," Dr. Lansdotter said.

When Alia came abreast of the doctor, her manner shifted, and she politely smiled, waiting for the doctor to finish her thought.

"Oh, hello, Alia. I'm glad to see you. As I was saying, Victor, the problem might be neurological. The inflammation caused by the infection may have damaged parts of his brain. We could run him through MAMA and see what there is to see." She looked pleadingly at Alia as if to abdicate her responsibility.

Cody Sisco

Victor nodded at the mention of MAMA, relieved to have some way forward. He'd spent countless hours with the machine, both inside it to check on his condition and running patients through its maw to track their progress. Running Chico through would be easy.

Alia said, "If you'll excuse us, I'd like a word with Victor."

"I'm running behind as well," Dr. Lansdotter said, squeezing Alia's arm and giving Victor a solemn nod before she turned and strode down the hall.

The gooseflesh on Victor's arms rose, and he became aware of Alia staring at him, a storm of colors fleeting across her face. His emotion-color-coding system was no help when confronted with such a tempest.

She grabbed his hand and pulled him through a door into the nearest stairwell. After she'd checked that no one was lurking on the landings above or below, she turned to him and hissed, "You've been avoiding me."

Victor blinked. This was a different side of Alia. She was usually so smooth and diplomatic, putting her feelings aside for whatever the needs of the moment, the group, the company.

His heart thudded in his chest. "I don't—"

"I got dragged into the inquiry last week. They wanted my opinion on your behavior during the hostage crisis."

"You did the best you could. We all did." He recalled the transformation of the clinic from a place of healing to a source of conflict. The protests outside. Masked figures with shocksticks giving orders. The days spent sleeping inside BioScan's rooms. It had been an impossible situation, created by Wonda, enflamed by Samuel, and fueled by the blind faith of the Human Lifers. It was naivete compounded by insanity, and it had sucked them all into its vortex.

Alia said, "I bit my tongue until it was sore." She paced in front of him, crossed arms squirming, looking like they might burst free. Each intermittent, accusatory glance darting his way stung like a wasp.

Victor focused on the tips of his shoes. "Circe said it's only a formality."

"'Circe said'!" Alia hissed mockingly. "You're not above the law, Victor."

"That's not what I'm saying. Look, this is a big gray area."

She stopped pacing. Her icy stare made him look for an escape route. He ran through the owl mantra in his mind, afraid she'd mock him if he said the words aloud.

The wise owl listens before asking who.

The wise owl flaps away when there's trouble. I should grow wings.

Her furious whisper gutted him. "You brought him a weapon."

He gulped. There was no denying it.

"And then you asked me to ..." Alia looked around.

No vid caps were visible, but the security features on campus were state-of-the-art. Audio and visual footage could be captured almost anywhere—not that the security staff would have any reason to review it. Even less reason to hand it to authorities. Still, better to choose their words wisely.

"He wanted to cross over," Victor whispered. "He would have found a way eventually. Wonda wanted it for him, too."

"She's not a reliable judge of right and wrong, Victor, as you know."

He blushed; a red flame ignited within his chest and scoured his throat. He swallowed and choked out, "I know. I'm sorry about what happened. I am. I think about how it could have gone differently all the time. I'm sure it's difficult for you, Alia. But it just happens to be one more horrible event in a long string of them since—I was going to say since—I ..." He couldn't remember. There was a gap in his memories. A black hole from which nothing could escape. What could have fallen in? He shook his head to clear it. "My bad luck ruins whatever it touches."

Her stance softened. "You're not—"

"Please. You didn't come here to give me a pep talk."

"No. I want to know what happened. In the room with him. Did you mean to?"

Victor took a breath. He knew what she was asking. "I'm not sure."

"You're not taking responsibility."

"I'm not the only one with an unexplained death." Wonda had forced Alia to withhold treatment from the man who died. Alia would be imagining his face: waxy, pebbled with sweat, smelling of food gone sour during his last moments, dying in disgusting conditions.

When he met her eyes, he saw that she had gone rigid, her hands clenched into fists, arms stiffly at her sides. A vein throbbed

Cody Sisco

in her temple, pulsing underneath her headscarf, making the whole thing seem to wriggle like a coil of serpents. Victor closed his eyes and breathed. She didn't have snakes in there; his brain was acting up. He said quietly, "I didn't mean that."

"I don't want this to cause a rift between us."

"You'd be better off if it did," he said.

"Lisabella's doing a profile about me on the Mesh, calling me a hero. It feels so dirty—dishonest! I feel like I'm losing my mind!"

"I'm sorry," he muttered and turned.

"Wait!" she said. "You're not alone in this, you know."

"Thank you," he said. He meant it. But he had to go. Her despair threatened to consume him. He rushed down the stairs and out of the building. Trees passed in a fuzzy gray blur. He didn't regain his full senses until he stood on a rise, looking out at the muddy waters of Qaddo Lake and the Passage. Shadows clustered around New Venice as the sun lowered.

Alia wanted a reckoning he couldn't give her. He tried to remember what happened, but there was no image of the moment of Samuel's death in his memory—though that wasn't the black hole, was it? No. His memory was a sieve.

Regardless, he'd been terrorized by the echoes of Samuel's massacre in Carmichael all his life. He shouldn't be hauled to task for the Man from Nightmareland's demise. Samuel had wanted to cross over via quantum suicide. Victor had brought a modified shockstick capable of doing the job. He'd entered the room … after that, who could say what really happened? He was the least reliable witness imaginable.

Worst of all, he knew, was the fact that he wasn't seeking answers to these questions. He was focused on solving the MRS mystery. Alia's reckoning with the past, Elena's demands to save Chico, and his stewardship of the MRS patients. All of these were secondary to the question that had haunted his entire life. He wouldn't stop, wouldn't hesitate, wouldn't let himself be derailed. That was his intention. But he feared whatever dark bird fluttered in his lapsed memory would show itself soon enough.

10

The Mesh was never intended to foster a national culture. The European authorities used it to cement control, to expand surveillance, and to keep a tight rein on a rival power. However, its cultural orientation was always local, grassroots, and nominally apolitical. Artists were a non-critical voice of support, otherwise they regularly found their accounts neutered and censored with little recourse.

—A Brief History of the Mesh

14 April 1992
Checkpoint Domino, The Louisiana Territories

The passenger van bucked and shimmied on the road, which decades of disrepair had left in a sorry state. Elena didn't mind. Each kilometer of jostle and lurch brought her closer to her family. That felt good, but there was more to it, more than a return home. She hadn't felt this good since her gender transition. The steadiness she'd had before stims had come back, along with something more: she was full of purpose.

Maybe I'm finally emerging.

She smiled to herself, wryly thankful for this moment of self-solidarity.

Hours earlier, a message from an anonymous number arrived and said only, "santuario," so she knew her parents were safe somewhere deep in the ROT. With that anxiety quenched, not even the rough journey could bring her down. This was the worst crossing she'd experienced. But when the main border checkpoint closes, what were you supposed to do?

She'd never seen so many LT gendarmerie trucks and personnel gathered in one place. Their efforts were divided into two: prevent refugees from streaming across from the ROT, which made up the lion's share of the difficulty, as far as she could tell, and prevent people like Elena from crossing in the opposite direction. She exited the vehicle, leaving it idling empty and awaiting instructions, and squeezed through a crowd of people who were angry and inconvenienced by the closure. At the edge of the barricades surrounding the checkpoint, a family were huddled, speaking hushed words while a farmworker with a black beard and bushy mustache spoke to a tall, handsome gendarme with skin that shone with sweat where it wasn't covered by armor. Elena sidled up to eavesdrop on their conversation.

"I heard this here'll be closed for two weeks," the man drawled. Something about his accent sounded fake to Elena's ears, but then again, she'd spent much of her childhood in SeCa and didn't know what strange, homespun accents flourished in the AU wilderness. He didn't quite sound Texan, that she was sure about.

The gendarme stopped scanning the crowd for one quick glance at the farmer and then at Elena before resuming. "No idea." When he looked her way again, she smiled wider. She very much wanted to get home.

"It's never been this difficult to get across before. What's new?" she asked.

The farmer looked at her, squinting against the sun over her shoulder, then he tipped his hat and said, "Word came down from Oklahoma City. New rules. Used to be all you had to do was pay. Not anymore."

Elena grimaced, realizing how much she'd taken for granted free movement between the AU nations. True, it had cost her tens of thousands of AUD over the past few years to move around, and most people couldn't afford to do it once, let alone regularly, but much of that had been on the Eastmores' dime or the Puros'. Now, when she was paying, it didn't seem there was enough money in the world to get her across a stupid patch of dirt that showed no sign of being a border except for this crowd of people in the desert and the invisible line they could not cross.

Of course, money was not all her nomadic life cost her. She couldn't name a single friend. Her relationship with Victor was far more complicated and painful than friendship should be. The few acquaintances she'd had in Texas had soured when she'd turned to stims.

But she was back, reforged, sober, stronger, and ready for action. She had allies and family. And she had a purpose. Those were more than enough.

"I'm just trying to get home. They're not letting *anyone* through?"

"Said Corps might be pretending to be refugees. Or moving weapons south. No one's getting through. Not here anyway," the farmer said, voice softer, with a glance at the family nearby, still huddled, sharing scraps of food, oblivious to the conversations around them.

The gendarme gave the farmer a sharp look but didn't say anything.

"Somewhere else?" Elena asked.

"The main crossings are all closed. But the top dogs in Oklahoma don't want it, said they closed all of them. I heard people can get through in a few places."

"You heard," Elena repeated skeptically.

"You got a good reason to cross?" he asked.

"Family," she said, wondering how much she could trust him. *Shock it*, she thought. "They were in Amarillo, but the Corps moved in, so now they're headed south."

"Corps are there too."

"Bastards are everywhere."

The gendarme appeared not to be listening, mostly, but she'd noticed him frown whenever they mentioned the Corps. They didn't have any friends in the LTs either, it seemed. Certainly not in the armed forces called up to police a border to keep them out. And all these people were suffering collateral damage. What a waste.

"You look thirsty," the farmer said. "I have iced tea in the back of my truck."

It was hot, and he seemed genuinely kind. Something about him, though—maybe the lines across his forehead or his taut jawline—suggested to her a hard edge. Maybe he was more than he appeared. "Lead the way," she said.

They skirted the crowd, walking along the road's edge through the crunching gravel and brittle, dry underbrush that poked and snagged at their clothes until they reached a makeshift parking lot, a flat, dusty expanse cleared of vegetation with vehicles parked at haphazard angles.

"You have a thing against the Corps?" the farmer asked while filling a plastic cup from a thermos. He handed it to her, filled another for himself, then sipped. She followed suit, her idle suspicion of being poisoned coming and going quickly. Something seemed peculiar about this guy, but not in a way that meant her harm.

"I want to put them in a cave and blast the entrance."

He laughed, loudly, explosively. "I guess you do. But aren't you safer here in the LTs?"

"Who says I'm looking for safety? My family is in trouble, and I need to help them. Do you know where this crossing is?"

"I do."

She stiffened. His drawl had evaporated.

"You're going to need more than money to get through, though," he said in a neutral tone that sounded educated, Continental. *Laws, is this guy European?*

"Like what?"

"Credentials. I can get you smooth, quick access to a border agent who won't look twice at your MeshBit as he waves you through."

"You would do that? Why? I know I don't look rich, and I'm not so—"

"See this?"

He took a device from his pocket and held it up. She took it from him and looked at it in her palm. A normal, typical Mesh device that lacked any distinctive features. Cheap. "Yeah. And?" she asked.

"Take that with a couple hundred just like it and pass them out to whomever you meet who might want a fresh perspective. They don't connect to the Mesh now that it's been compromised. Only each other. We call it the Alt Grid. They're unhackable. And they've got more news about the OWS than the Diamond King wants to get out."

"Who do you work for?" she asked.

"That's a mighty impertinent question, young miss," he said, with a fake accent again, smiling at her.

"Don't 'young miss' me again, or you'll miss me soon," she quipped. "Okay, you get me across the border. I hand these out to people who seem—what? Non-Corp-oriented? Why?"

"How else do you organize a civil defense when the Mesh is compromised?" He was definitely European. She saw it now in his face, in how his mouth moved as it formed sounds that were not quite as exactly American-sounding as a born-in-the-land citizen. Should she help him? He was promising to help her.

Perhaps the ROT's future wasn't as desperate as she feared. It felt like a burden being lifted.

"Show me the way," Elena said.

11

Looking back, after those few months in New Venice, I developed a false sense of confidence. Something was missing. I didn't know where I'd come from or what I'd been through. My recall was a yo-yo spinning low, about to come up and bonk me in the face.

—Victor Eastmore, *Apology to Resonant Earth* (transmission date unknown)

20 April 1992
New Venice, The Louisiana Territories

Victor told Alia that he was going to see Wonda. Big mistake.

"But I don't understand why!" Alia said.

He said, "She's dangerous." It wasn't the real reason, but it wasn't untrue. It was also easier than explaining that his memory was spotty and how desperately he wanted to patch it up. "We have to keep tabs on her. And I think it would help explain how things went down."

"*You* have to keep tabs on her, you mean. I want nothing to do with her. Why would you want to see her again after what she did?" Alia crossed her arms and looked at him with narrowed eyes.

Victor looked away and said, "I feel partly responsible for what happened."

Recognition bloomed on her face in ember-smoky swirls, and she seemed at a loss for words for a moment, then managed, "I can see how you would think that."

She reached up and wrenched the headscarf off her head, smoothed her hair into an intricate pile using jerky, shaking hands, and re-wrapped it. He noticed that she was silently mouthing all the recriminations that she wanted, but hadn't yet, pummeled him with. He deserved every word of it. Yet her agitation concerned him.

"Are you okay?" Victor asked.

Alia reared back a little, seeming surprised. "I suppose not. Among everything else, I'm worried about Torsten. The campaign is going to ramp up, and with his brother out there somewhere doing who knows what to get himself in trouble, it seems like there's no end of things to be worried about. And the situation here ... well, this isn't exactly a refuge either." She looked at him and smiled slightly. "Thank you for asking. I consider you a friend. I really do."

"Thank you." Her gratitude was a heavy lump in his throat and a sad sweetness on his tongue. "I'm sorry I ... I'm trying my best to put things right." *In my head*, he didn't add aloud. "I don't know if there are any good options. There's something ..."

He didn't know how to say that his memory was a leaky vessel, that something important was missing, and he needed to explore the contours of his missing memories to fill in the gaps, without making her more anxious than she was already. If she knew how broken he truly was, if she found out, could they remain friends?

Instead, he explained that he wanted to see how much of a lasting effect Samuel Miller had on Wonda, whether she had begun to recover, if she ever would.

"It's dangerous for you to see her," Alia warned.

He hated that everyone saw him as malleable and easily manipulated. But how else could he be when susceptibility was a consequence of his condition? Maybe she saw the resolve in his expression because she sighed and then wished him well through gritted teeth.

The kayak paddle dipped, pulled, rose, and dipped again in a soothing, steady rhythm. Victor wished he had such a simple, predictable mechanism for knocking loose the memories that clung to the deepest recesses of his brain. Something he had forgotten was exacerbating his condition, eroding his confidence, and eating at the edges of his sanity.

Pearl would say he should let the past go and live in the emerging present. But she didn't have a wayward brain and the lives of so many patients on her conscience. Her herbs helped take the edge off his anxiety, even if the fumewort and bitter grass tinctures, each taken ten times a day, failed to fully clear the fog from his mind. An insidious blankness lived inside his skull; an uncanny chill filled his bones. His dreams showed glimpses of

Cody Sisco

foreign places—a stone room; a mist-shrouded forest; an impassable desert, rose-colored by a rising sun. They were mirages, he'd decided, but that didn't explain why he could see them so clearly while his past was obscured.

A vital truth was hidden in his missing memories, and he needed to dislodge it. The best way he knew how—based on hundreds of hours of therapy with Dr. Tammet while sheltered in Oak Knoll Hospital—was exposure. This trip to see Wonda would reignite darkened neural pathways. Memories lost to blankness would be recovered, he hoped, and provide a searchlight in the dark.

With every pull of the paddle, the vessel thrust forward. Hot, aching muscles in his back and shoulders begged him to stop, but he focused on the choppy waves around him, churning the water into a chaotic cauldron. He fought on through the squall, rocking, pulling, lurching forward with maximum effort and minimum gain but pleased to know he would be tired when he encountered Wonda. Otherwise, he might hurt her.

She'd done monstrous things to him. Used him. Corrupted him. Twisted him around her finger. She pushed and manipulated; worse, unforgivably, she'd turned him into her sex puppet. Hers and Tosh's. The details were hazy, eluding his grasp. Not for long, he hoped.

The bulk of Cemetery Hill to Victor's left dropped away as he left the Passage behind and crossed an imperceptible border; he was now traversing Qaddo Lake, and what limited sovereignty was afforded the Qaddo tribe now applied.

The mudflats extended for kilometers, sometimes partitioned by the streams of red and yellow mineral-saturated water that flowed from the hot springs in the hills. A decrepit dock lay across the flats like a snake sunning itself and lolling its tail end in the water. He reached the dock, lashed his kayak, and climbed ashore.

Wonda would likely resist helping him. She blamed him for Samuel's death and hated him now as much as she'd revered him before. But, maybe, if he helped her and the Human Lifers, she might help him fill in the missing pieces of his memory. It would gall him to do anything on behalf of fanatics, but to get what he wanted, he was prepared to make sacrifices. She'd been repeatedly messaging him for weeks with a single question, "Are you ready to talk yet?"

Victor wasn't sure how much of a problem it was that his throat oozed acid whenever he thought of her. Was that a fair reaction? Half-memories of her caresses as he faded in and out of blankness were clouded with disgust. She thought she was helping him by keeping him locked in her trailer, comforted in her embrace. She'd fucked him while he lacked consciousness and then pretended they had a relationship. She'd enthralled him into a relationship while he didn't have the wits to know what she was doing. The most damning fact of all, though, was that he stayed with her after he'd awakened. He'd been robbed of his choice but then failed to exercise it when his wits returned.

The dock gave way to a gravel path wide enough for a single vehicle and pockmarked by dips filled with undrinkable water. The smell of sulfur wafted by in bursts. Dotting the landscape, mud pots bubbled and puffed palls of white steam. Somewhere in the upland clefts, according to childhood lore, in places so sacred and secret that only Qaddo elders knew their true names, erupting geysers had sculpted exotic geothermal crevasses, shelves, and terraces.

As he walked, the mudflats ceded ground to grasslands punctuated by scrubby bushes, birds flitting between them, pecking the ground for seeds. There were shacks, each trailing a trash shadow where occupants flung their bottles, cans, and other pieces of rusted metal. Finally, the single paved route through the Qaddo territory came into view. He crossed it and continued upward to the building where Wonda was staying with hardcore Human Life hangers-on.

Trudging forward under a leaden sky, he felt every gram a city boy venturing into the wilderness on a naive quest. Those tales never ended well.

And then, the shack. He knocked on the unpainted door frame and waited. With a loud creak, the door opened. Wonda's hair, dyed beet-purple, was stringy, as if she had taken a shower and never toweled it off. Dark circles under her eyes stood out from her pale skin. She acknowledged him with a wry quirk of her lips. Her face, once animated with faith, testifying that everything in the world always worked out the way it should, was now gaunt, sallow, and wasted.

The instant he saw her, a pit opened in his stomach, a longing that was physical, bestial, and made worse because it couldn't be acted on. Their history was a barrier more impenetrable than rock. He had no illusions about where the blame lay. They were both toxic and destroyed anything and anyone that got close. A good match, in that way, at least.

"I knew you'd come eventually," she said, "but I'm not giving it up easy."

Victor was stunned. His stomach twisted, and yet a thrill grew deep in his groin. It took a moment for him to collect himself. At last, he managed, "I'm not here for that. Sex is the last thing on my mind."

"Sex?" Wonda looked puzzled, and then understanding blossomed on her face as she cackled. "You think I want to fuck you? Right now?" She gave him a long look of such cold, cruel scrutiny that Victor felt his balls retreat.

"Well, what else did you mean?" he asked.

Her expression hardened, her eyes like two pieces of midnight sky during a new moon. "I'm not playing games. Go away."

Victor felt his body shudder as he resisted the urge to turn and walk away. He breathed and forced himself to relax. "You can't make me do anything anymore."

"Is that what you came to say?"

"No!"

"Well?" she asked.

He tried to start again, but his mouth froze up. Her pale, round, freckled face—a young woman's face—was visible, partly, beneath a sediment of difficulties laid down by the past few months. Her wide eyes were no longer bright, no longer eagerly consuming everything in sight; they rested heavily on Victor, weighing down his sore shoulders. "You messaged me," he reminded her.

"To make a deal. But you—" Wonda seemed to give up mid-sentence and closed her eyes.

A deal for what? She's always scamming. And she doesn't look well.

Opening her eyes again, she said, wearily, "Stop looking at me like you're staring at a vidscreen and go."

"I'm here to check on you."

"To check on me? That's so much garbage it could bury you."

"I've been thinking about what happened. It must be hard depending on people who don't exactly want you here. Do you need anything?"

She recoiled. "We are on the edge of obliteration, and you want to see what I need? How generous you must be feeling. How much like a fucking savior."

"Well ... no ... but," he said, gulping and forcing himself to do what he came there to do, "I have some questions about Samuel Miller, too."

Wonda was stony-faced, but he could tell she was moved. Tears formed, swelling then streaking down her cheeks. She'd always been quick to cry, but it was surely earned this time. He blinked back wetness in his own eyes as revulsion gurgled in his belly: how could she feel anything like sadness toward such a monster?

Maybe Wonda was sad to have lost her leverage. Samuel was the magic in her poison potion.

She cocked her head at the barren yard. "Might as well give you the tour so you can tell everyone in your stupid town how awful it is for us. They'll be happy to gloat."

She stepped out, closed the door, and trudged around the side of the house. He followed a few steps behind, breathing deeply to calm himself. Despite the occasional sulfurous whiff, the open air lifted some of the gloom and apprehension he'd felt about seeing her again. Ducks whirled in the sky and came to rest on the lake. Someone nearby clobbered a drum. Cars passed slowly with the crunch-scrape sound of tires on gravel.

He remembered that sound, and a flash of the past illuminated. He'd been driving somewhere barren like this, surrounded by mountains and dusty roads. There'd been danger, and someone beside him in the passenger seat. Was it Wonda?

Before he could lock onto the memory, it faded, called back by whatever part of his brain had briefly let it escape.

Victor glanced around and realized that he had lost track of Wonda.

Wizened faces stared from dark, screened-in porches. He hurried forward, figuring she must be ahead when his shoe crunched on broken glass. He stopped, looked down, and saw the remains of a stim cartridge, the shards barely visible against the gravel scattered over red earth. He was about to ask what stims were doing in a Human Life camp when he saw a more peculiar sight: an open box, piled next to a dozen others beside a building. Inside were dozens of plastic goggles and straps. They didn't look like the ones he'd seen on a trip to Little Asia, the leftovers from protests against Semiautonomous California's crackdown on refugees, when sedative gas had filled the streets of Oakland & Bayshore. Rather, these goggles looked expensive, fresh-made, like something from Tosh's arsenal.

The crunch of gravel behind him announced that Wonda had returned. He went over to the box and lifted a pair, dangling it by a synthleather strap so she could see. "What are these for?"

"Swimming," she said with crossed arms.

"And where did you get the money for them?"

Wonda huffed. "You're not my bookkeeper. Not that you really care about us anyway."

Victor looked toward the lake and the reddish-brown mud ringing the shore. Water that flowed down from Ouachita Dam through the Passage and New Venice's canals was no clearer than sludge. He glanced up at the hills where mineral water springs cascaded and pooled, steaming, usually at a temperature close to boiling. He shivered, remembering Great-Granma Florence's story of a little Eastmore girl who'd fallen into one of those pools and died. He was glad Wonda was banished to such a wretched place, but he didn't think she would learn any lessons from it.

Wonda said, "There's more to see," and then, after watching him drop the pair of goggles back in the box, led him onward.

"About a dozen people share that outhouse." She pointed to a shack that seemed to shimmer from an aura of flies, though Victor allowed that might just be his imagination. "Fresh water from a well," she said, "what counts as fresh. It tastes like metal. They give us their stale bread, leftovers from the communal kitchen. Bedsheets that smell of sulfur but maybe saw a washer sometime in the last month. The Qaddo are keeping us alive, so we're all very thankful for that—life being more important than purity, as we all know." Her voice oozed scorn and something else: self-pity, maybe. She seemed more broken than ever. Victor wondered if she wished she'd never come to New Venice to sink to such lows.

Victor made a peace offering: "I can try to convince BioScan to—"

"I grew up poor. It's not so hard for me. Some of the others left behind comfortable lives. They don't complain, though. The ones who stay—they like the privations. Brings them closer to purity. A blessing, in a way." She gave him a look like he was a bug she wanted to smash. "Don't say 'BioScan' to me again."

He felt his nostrils flare and realized that hers had done the same moments before. "You don't actually believe all that stuff. Blessings? Purity? You took what Deliberation built and twisted it beyond recognition. You took his people from him." If she could harbor wayward beliefs so out of tune with the natural, scientific world, what use was anything she might tell him?

"They followed me. They have faith. What I believe is not so different from what you believe. We're both searching for the truth."

She led him to a large natural rock pool about five meters in diameter with blue water fringed by precipitated rings of milk-, red wine-, and lemon-colored minerals. A wooden platform downstream bridged a trickling outflow that likely went to the lake. She leaned over a railing and stared into the pool. Bubbles rose to the surface, releasing belches of steam laden with sulfur and trace elements from deep within the earth's crust.

"Ask me and get it over with," she said, though her voice wasn't cruel, just tired.

She had faults, it was true, but she did know how to read him well. He blurted with relief, "I feel like something's missing. There are things I don't remember. I think it's got something to do with blankspace and what's on the other side."

She looked at him with a steady and level gaze, her eyes slowly widening. "You're not all here, are you? Have you seen the other side?" she whispered, looking briefly again like a young woman with the whole world to discover.

Victor shook his head. "Not clearly."

She moved to the railing and gripped it as she bowed her head, whispering faintly.

He rested a hand on hers and said gently, "This kind of worship is crazy. I don't understand how Samuel won you over. You've got to let it go."

"You believed him," she said insistently.

"I didn't!"

"Are you sure? You're still trying to cross over, aren't you?"

Revulsion whip-cracked through him, and he snatched back his hand as quickly as if he'd been stung by a bee.

Cross over? No. The term was so loaded with baggage that its meaning was lost. It could mean suicide by quantum devices. It could mean descending into catatonia. It could mean something unexperienced and unexplained, a mystical singularity akin to Emergence. What he was doing was entirely different.

"No. I'm not that delusional," he said. "For all my problems, I'm not the one who trusted a mass murderer, who worshipped him."

Wonda grimaced. "He didn't do it."

"Huh?"

"He didn't," she repeated.

"Didn't what? You don't think he crossed over?"

"No. I don't think he killed those people."

"What?"

"I don't think Samuel was responsible for what happened in Carmichael."

She looked at him calmly. In his synesthetic vision, her face was a blue matte hue superimposed over her pale skin. She wasn't mocking, wasn't trying to persuade. She was simply stating what she believed. She was officially crazier than he was.

"That's—that's delusional. It's recorded. I mean, there are records. It happened. *I was there.*"

"You were a child. I'm not surprised you misremember. What I know is that the Samuel Miller who was here in New Venice wasn't responsible."

"*The* Samuel Miller who ...? What are you saying?"

"He crossed over. Switched places. It was a different Samuel in Carmichael who planned the murders."

"You're talking nonsense."

"You're avoiding what you already believe to be true. If you believe in crossing over, and I'm sure you do, whether you want to admit it or not, then it's logical to assume that a person who crossed over once may have done so before. So, if Samuel crossed over from here—"

"He didn't cross over. I saw his body. He's dead."

"You were there when it happened, weren't you?"

In the thump of a single heartbeat, Victor realized he'd been tricked. Wonda was leading him on, trying to get him to admit he'd killed—no, that's not what happened, there'd been an accident. Victor wasn't to blame.

"You did it, didn't you? You killed him. Or did he cross over? I need to know."

"This is nonsense, a waste of time," he said, turning away from the hot spring.

"Wait, Victor," Wonda said. "I spoke with Samuel, you know. Near the end."

Victor blinked, thinking back. From the time he woke up in the Human Lifers' camp to when they'd taken hostages at BioScan, his memories were relatively clear and crisp. Still, it had been a wild couple of days at the clinic. He'd been shuffling between the prisoners and the Human Lifers, trying to keep Wonda and Tosh from hurting them, searching for a resolution. There were plenty of moments when Wonda could have gotten Samuel alone.

With growing dread, Victor remembered Samuel saying that a woman had visited him, and they'd talked. Victor had assumed it was his Aunt Circe. Why though? Blankness reared up, and he spun away, desperate to clear it. What if it had been Wonda instead? She'd been so obsessed. She still was. Maybe she couldn't ever put Samuel to rest. Why was his madness so difficult to counteract?

"Victor!" Wonda shouted.

He glanced down to find his feet had wandered to the edge of the platform past the end of the railing onto the flaky, dried mud bordering the pool, where wisps of steam drifted toward him, warming his pant legs. He retreated to safety.

She grabbed his arm. "What did your grandfather think about crossing over? He dealt with Samuel for years. He scanned his brain. What did he learn? You think about that. Run along now. You'll be back when you figure it out."

At the mention of Granfa Jeff, nausea returned, doubling him over. Why? He didn't know. There was a slippery gap in his memories, a black hole that obliterated and shamed him. He could never get close due to the plasma-hot disgust circling the event horizon.

Wonda advanced again. "And your aunt—"

He straightened and grabbed her shoulder, pushing her dangerously close to the pool's edge. "Don't talk about my family!"

Her expression turned sour, flinty. "Control yourself," she said in a low voice close to a hiss.

He loosened his grip. Why did she insist on provoking him? With deliberate slowness, he let her go.

"Good. Now leave." She emphasized each word. "Get. Off. My. Property." Her hand flew to her mouth. When she lowered it, she was smirking. "My dad always said that. Everyone was coming and going. They had eviction orders from the bank. He said, 'Get off my property,' more than, 'I love you.' I can't really say it here because none of this is mine."

"You're not okay," Victor said. "You're living in a lie."

She gave him a long, cool look. "Leave. Don't come back until you've figured yourself out."

Victor turned, and his shoes scraped on the gravel. Wonda didn't always make sense, but he'd been right to try to come here for answers. She knew something. She might know him better than he knew himself right now. And she was right; he would be back after he downed a gallon of fumewort. And there would be a reckoning. What had she said about his granfa and aunt? It was slipping away. There was some link between the holes in his memory and his family. Everything told him to turn to them for answers, but it was like grasping a river. Maybe it was time to take the plunge.

12

Why would people allow themselves to live inside a lie? In normal societies, there's give-and-take between the government and its critics, a sense of balance in the public sphere, of using tension to find a workable middle ground.

Las Vegas and the OWS didn't have a public sphere, per se. Not in the way we think of them. Each individual had their own relationship with authority: a seemingly positive, nurturing, supportive partnership.

What did we learn? That extreme individualism is a road to desolation.

—*A History of Las Vegas* (author unknown)

3 May 1992
Las Vegas, Organized Western States

Ozie surveyed the first batch of pluggers. They stood at attention, toeing a line in the dirt on the outskirts of Las Vegas. Large solar towers stood behind them, spindly and sleek photon harvesters powering everything from bioreactors to digital avatars like the Diamond King's entwining, infiltrating, maddeningly invasive presence. The pluggers wore customized braincaps, Ozie's handiwork, which interfaced via spectrum relays with the plugs implanted in their skulls. He couldn't take much credit, however. Grette had supplied the specifications, designs, equipment, and the team to implant the plugs. Ozie's task was merely to program the interface. It was an achievement that—if he could share it with researchers outside the OWS—would probably make their heads spin.

Once implanted in the skull, the plugs' spools of conductive nanowire began threading through gray matter to find neural clusters to deliver precisely timed surges of electrical current. The wires transmitted and received, sensing their environment and altering it when commanded. If the Corps weren't wearing braincaps, the only visible signs of the surgery would be thirteen slightly red patches of skin, no bigger than a thumbnail, on their bald heads. These Corps had been re-assigned to the "black diamond" team, and today was testing day. Through his cyberarm interface, he could now issue commands. Not that he wanted to.

He rolled back his shoulders. He said, loud enough to be heard over the desert breeze, "You'll each be given an objective, which will consist of finding an object." He waved toward a dusty sprawl of tumbleweed and rocks. Strewn across the terrain were household objects and gadgetry: a wicker chair tipped on its back, a faux café brewer, a cobalt-blue sock, sunglasses, a bag of oranges— nearly fifty items that Ozie had placed himself, alone, in the hours before dawn.

One of the Corps, a pale and freckled man who was a heavy steroid user, asked, "You going to tell us which one and get this started?"

Ozie avoided his gaze. These guys had no idea what they were in for. He wondered, not for the first time, why they had become Corps and what they thought their fate would be. Certainly not *this*.

He tapped a command on his arm.

The freckled Corp straightened with a grunt, looked around, and strode toward the field of objects.

The woman he'd been standing next to said, "Woah. Are we starting?"

Ozie sent her a command to find the bag of oranges and eat one.

"Oranges," she said aloud. "It's crystal clear in my mind." She broke into a broad grin. "This is amazing."

"It is," Ozie said. She turned to her task, and he continued issuing desires until the ten Corps hunted through the dirt like children playing catch-a-tiger. These grunts could become his friends if he made an effort, if he knew how to not hold himself back, if he didn't know in his core that he was always meant to be alone.

The freckled Corp had gone a hundred meters or so; far enough to become a tiny figure overshadowed by the mountains behind him. Ozie considered urging him to keep going, walk into the wilderness, and never return. The only relief, the only safety from the Diamond King's commands, would be somewhere without Mesh access, a remote valley, or maybe an ice cave way up north.

Or, and this thought intrigued him, inside a Faraday cage, the walls of which would need to be charged with electromagnetic—

A surprised moan of pleasure from the nearest Corp interrupted Ozie's imaginings. The man, a short guy packed with muscle, held a spoon to his face, looking at it. His other hand roved down his chest and settled on his groin. "Oh, Laws, that feels good."

Ozie checked the man's settings, which were in line with the others. Groans came from a few more Corps, receiving a reward for their efforts. Yet it was one Ozie hadn't issued. Someone else was in the system, making adjustments, sending sensations.

Ozie looked down at his wrist to see the Diamond King's avatar.

"I have another task for you," it said.

"You gave them a nice treat." The words were meant to be sarcastic, but they sounded rather envious. *Am I so pathetic now that I want my emotions served up via spectrum relay?*

"Now they know what happens when I'm pleased."

"And when you're not pleased?"

A scream erupted somewhere behind Ozie. The man with the spoon was upright, shaking, vibrating like he was being ripped apart.

"Stop," he implored in a whisper. "Don't hurt them on my behalf." He licked his lips and swallowed, his throat suddenly tight and dry. It wasn't good to talk back.

"What's going on?" the woman pleaded. She wiped orange juice off her lips and began to cry.

Ozie shouted, "Come here, all of you, listen up."

They were in it now. There was no going back. All that remained was survival.

"Rewards and punishments flow from your service. Please the King and be pleased in return. Upset him, and he has the power to end your life in the time it takes to blink. Keep training. We'll debrief after."

"Don't be upset," the Diamond King said as Ozie returned to the van. Waves of calm cascaded from the top of his head downward. He tore the braincap off his head. He had no plugs. The Diamond King couldn't get all the way inside his head. But he'd hacked into Ozie's braincap.

Ozie wanted to scream.

"I need you to go to New Venice," the Diamond King said from the patch on Ozie's cyber wrist.

Ozie responded grimly. "I'm happy to oblige." He didn't worry about trying to sound eager; he had no delusions that the Diamond King cared a smidge how he felt.

"You shall bring me the neurograms of Samuel Miller and Victor Eastmore."

An icy chill like a mountain stream ran down Ozie's back.

He recalled the long recitation of facts the Diamond King had coaxed from him earlier, including Jefferson Eastmore's requests for help to create an unhackable repository of data; Ozie's efforts to track down and program a data egg so that it held the neurograms of a madman and an old friend—two mirror resonance syndrome patients with uncannily intertwined lives; Jefferson's death; and Victor's subsequent quest to uncover the truth. He'd been entirely forthcoming, because withholding information seemed like a doomed strategy for surviving the Diamond King's thralldom. The stakes were too high, and he couldn't rely on flimsy excuses, such as loyalty and circumspection. Ozie still didn't understand the interest in Victor and so, while it had seemed strange and made him feel dirty to divulge what he knew, it hadn't seemed very problematic. Ozie was starting to wonder, though, if he should have been so honest. And how, during the entire recitation, had the questions been so precise, as if the Diamond King were excavating a tomb he had built himself?

"Why?" Ozie asked. He had hoped the Diamond King's curiosity about Victor would fade. "You want to try to decrypt it again?" When Tosh stole the data egg and delivered it to Ozie, he'd used all the King's tools to try to crack it open. He'd been unsuccessful. A stab of icy fear wedged between Ozie's ribs. Maybe the other hacker, his replacement, could do it.

"This is not the time to discuss it. You'll go to New Venice, get the data egg from Victor Eastmore, and bring him here."

Ozie swallowed, telling himself whatever the reason, the Diamond King wanted the data egg, Ozie was obliged to retrieve it, and there was no harm in it.

No. No fooling yourself this time. You need a clear conscience and pure motives.

This might be an opportunity to salvage his friendship with Victor, but only if he was a hundred percent truthful.

"I'm not sure I can do that without knowing more," Ozie said.

"Do you need help persuading him?" the Diamond King asked.

Ozie's gut cramped. He'd seen the Corps persuading people. It didn't end well. "I don't want him hurt."

"We won't hurt him. We'll negotiate with him."

"What can I offer?"

"We're going to help his Broken Mirrors recover."

Ozie capitulated, of course. He was in too deep to stop cooperating. He needed to start looking after his interests and find a way to permanently extract himself from the Diamond King's control. He would make his attempt soon. If that failed and he had to rely on Victor for help, he wasn't sure he could keep any hope alive.

13

There was no compelling reason to unite the lands beyond Appalachia into a cohesive union. Rather than genocide and, subsequently, an uneasy coercive cohabitation, the vast continent could have continued to evolve unhindered. The excesses of capitalistic exploitation could have been avoided. And the scourge of the twenty-first century would never have been born.

—*The American Union: A Failed Experiment* (author unknown)

7 May 1992
New Venice, The Louisiana Territories

It was a perfect day for politicking. A warm sun, intermittent cumulus clouds, and a feather twitch of a breeze took the edge off the heat. If nature's vote weren't enough, free food and drink would help convince the citizenry. Alia kept a pleasant but vacant smile on her face, hoping to deflect everyone's attention toward her fiancé as he turned up his charm to eleven.

Torsten Lund surveyed his campaign's picnic preparations while taking advantage of the shade of a large oak tree within the grounds of the Mesh House, a change of location calculated to show he was keeping up with the changing security situation. Banners and bandstands were erected along key sight lines to hide the refugees living in Pond Park. Families were arriving, most via the steps leading up from the canals, while others emerged from a long line of autocabs that inched forward almost imperceptibly. Kayaks were stacked in vast rows by campaign staffers while autocabs would go find new customers in town.

Alia watched Torsten closely. Her mood brightened to see him in his element. He was always a bit tense before a big event, but the glad-handing, quick-shuffle hellos, how-you-beens, and vibrant community vibes soon lifted him to new levels.

Today held new challenges, though. Alia had counseled him that morning to avoid making specific promises and not get sucked into shifting sands. She hoped he took her advice. He was a candidate for an old era when things made sense and the status quo was broadly appealing. The environment had shifted so quickly. No one knew what was coming next. What was needed next was unclear. Change overtook them and propelled them down a chasm, cliff-shrouded, toward unknown waters.

There were at least two hundred guests already filling the grounds. Volunteers were busy cooking and serving drinks amid rows of picnic tables fitted with printed tablecloths featuring Qaddo artists' designs. The plan was to allow guests to mix and mingle and eat and drink during the first hour, then Torsten would make a brief speech, a band would play, and games would be organized on the lawn for the children. There were sports competitions for the older kids, including sprinting and rowing, as well as activities like face painting and drawing for younger children. Sheriff deputies, including the handsome but frosty Chris Spaulding, supervised the crowds. A few children ran around the picnic tables while newcomers continued to arrive and chatter excitedly. Alia was close enough to hear them clearly, yet far enough away to be politely excluded, which was fine with her.

She stiffened as Lisabella approached Torsten. A white-and-purple sundress, in the gaudy European trend-of-the-month style, billowed around her; her shape, hidden for once, rather than accentuated. Her family had donated generously to Torsten's campaign, giving him a reasonable excuse to be seen talking to her. Still, bad feelings about the Mesh and its functionaries ran deep in the LTs.

"Will you miss all this?" Lisabella asked.

"It will still be here." Torsten smiled genuinely, easily. Was he taken in, or did he want to project friendliness? Alia would have to ask later. "As will my house, my wife, even myself as often as possible, if you'll believe it. I hope to be here more often than Oklahoma City."

"Poor Alia. He'll be gone so often. I certainly wouldn't allow it."

Alia smiled. Lisabella was lingering. Was a realignment toward Europe part of the new normal in the LTs? How exhausting that would be.

Torsten smiled his I-won't-indulge-you-much-longer smile, then changed the subject definitively. "I'm going to need something

Cody Sisco

beautiful to put in my new office. Would you be willing to part with one of your 'New Venice at Sunset' paintings? Maybe the one from the vantage of the dam?"

Lisabella smiled. "Of course," she said. She nodded toward a banner that masked the view of the park. "I have one of the park—pre-refugees, that is—and the Grand Canal, too. It's yours if you want it."

"Yes, I do."

"It's been lovely to see you. I won't keep you." She walked back into the festivities.

Alia moved closer and adjusted Torsten's tie, cuffs, and hair. They'd been talking about an art deal, but that was a pretext. Her presence here meant that Mesh authorities took an interest in his campaign. Their backing was valuable but also risky. She kissed him on the cheek and launched him into the crowd, where he could greet and smile at each person one after the other. He did it with ease and a genuine good feeling, which is why the campaign staff encouraged these events. He made and received introductions, stressed the importance of the election, repeated a few choice campaign positions, and looked serious when answering constituents' questions. Smart, warm, passionate. She was proud of him.

After twenty minutes, he broke through the crowd more purposefully, still nodding and smiling but not stopping. He motioned to Alia that he needed a moment of her time, and she saw where he was heading: Victor had arrived. Her chest tightened. If excitement and anxiety felt the same in the body, this was what a double dose felt like.

Although Torsten greeted Victor warmly, she sensed strain and tension in his smile. She watched their interaction and was ready to intervene if necessary. She wanted them to get along. Victor wore a smart suit in shades of lavender and gray. His hair was slicked back, curling in the rear. He was as put together as she'd ever seen him. He and Torsten looked handsome, standing side by side, and the MeshNews feeds would likely get a boost from the photogenic pair.

"Alia tells me you've been spending a lot of time with your great-grandmother. I met her a few years ago. Please give her my regards."

"I will tell her," Victor answered.

So, that was it: the need for Eastmore endorsement. Alia expected Torsten to pivot onto the next campaign imperative, but he lingered. "Send Circe my regards as well. I had hoped she'd be able to attend."

Victor's face darkened, and it was a moment before he spoke. "I'll do that too."

"I heard the MRS patients are under your supervision now. I'm sure you'll be able to help them. I know the LT bureaucracy can be tricky to navigate. If there's anything you need, just say so."

"That's generous, thank you. I'm sure Karine will be in touch."

A campaign staffer was signaling to Alia that Torsten was needed. Strange that he didn't notice. Alia was going to catch his attention, then hesitated. She was curious. Why this sudden interest in Victor?

"I'm sure it's a lot to keep tabs on with new patients always arriving. Make sure the numbers don't get away from you." He patted Victor on the shoulder, one of many gestures to project strength and reassure.

Victor shied away and looked down. "I'm good at numbers. Multivariate analysis. Bernhardt signal analysis. Numbers that are a bit more complex than reading a poll."

"Hahaha, I'll bet you are. All I'm saying is that when we're talking about people, about patients, those are the really important numbers to get right."

Victor looked up and cocked his head, seeming to understand something that was lost on her. Despite her misgivings, it was good to see Torsten trying hard to make friends with Victor.

Torsten reached out and almost patted Victor's arm again but seemed to think better of it. He changed tack. "You know, when I was little, my parents both died, just months apart from each other. So, I know something about grief. It was rough. Rough for me, but especially for my brother. To this day, he hasn't dealt with it, and that's probably because I pushed him to grieve. I wanted him to feel what I was feeling. But he didn't, and I just made it worse. By trying to pull him close, I was pushing him away, if you see what I mean."

Sometime during this speech, Victor had gone glazed and blank. Torsten looked to Alia, confused. She had seen enough episodes that she wasn't alarmed. What was important was getting Torsten back on track for this evening's plans. She took his elbow firmly, and he rose, letting her lead him back toward the stage.

She glanced back, and Victor seemed to have come back to himself. His attention was now locked on Lisabella, who had been circling and was now moving in.

On a day full of choreographed remarks, stage-managed interactions, and sincere gambits for the future, a few lost people were searching for answers. They navigated around façades to create paths where there had been none. To overcome the obstacles along the way. The details were messy, and the conflicts were real. She felt them all in her heart, a beating pressure to rise and rise and rise. This was her home; her family surrounded her, and they were working toward something bright and vibrant. There was nowhere else she'd rather be.

Torsten was ten minutes into his speech when Victor lost patience. On a low stage a few steps above the crowd, the candidate was weaving the Human Life crisis into his remarks while trying to frame the issue in terms of emergency preparedness. He also mentioned the border with the ROT, and Victor wondered again how Elena was doing. She hadn't answered his messages in a week.

Not curious enough to stay and listen to the minutia of American Union politics, Victor wandered through the families, friends, and fringe elements of New Venice gathered to enjoy the grilled meats and slaw. Gazes darted suspiciously, voices chortled loudly, and stances shifted rapidly on steady ground. Despite the pure-white lace decorations strung between tree branches and tent poles, something was rotting beneath the surface of New Venice.

Near the entrance to the Mesh House grounds, several Human Lifers lingered and mixed with some curious townspeople. He shook his head. Their views were reactionary and ill-conceived, based on hasty pronouncements spewing from Wonda's feverish, power-tripping mouth. No genetic screening of fetuses, including for debilitating and possibly lethal conditions. A long list of unteachable scientific books and papers that should be banned. Complete elimination of all sources of radioactivity and chemicals that might contribute to mutations, even when they were needed to treat illnesses. Lunacy.

Victor wandered to the nearest cooking station and received a beef burger on a paper plate from a smiling volunteer and beer in a clear plastic cup. With these, he seated himself at a table next to a pair of sullen teenagers who gave him an appraising look and then ignored him while he took bites of his burger and sipped his beer.

Alia found Victor and sat next to him after a cool glance at the teenagers. She began, "My parents were not very supportive of me or my career. They thought the best I could expect in life was to marry a rich man and give him pretty babies. They didn't care one drop for my success. My father wouldn't give me a penny to go to medical school. My mother left me messages every day saying I was getting older and fatter and needed to marry someone soon. She set me up with dates and then made me either go through with them or call up the guys myself to cancel. They forbade all other social encounters."

He looked at her, puzzling out her intent. Both Torsten's and her intimacy came out of nowhere. Victor and Alia had been thrown into difficult situations and had several disagreements, but those had been mainly about dealing with the Human Life Movement. She had helped him as a colleague and a patient, and he sensed that, maybe, he'd helped her in some way he didn't quite understand. Perhaps the troubles they'd been through had been quietly forging a bond that hadn't become clear until now.

Alia went on, "When I met Torsten and he proposed a few months later, I said no. He kept trying. I put him off for two years, but he insisted. I finally realized that even though I'd emancipated by then, my parents were still holding me back. I was saying no because of them, their influence. We're not so different, you and me. I know what it's like to have my options constrained."

"Meaning?"

"Victor, Torsten and I are your friends now."

It clicked for him—friends, of course. She'd told him several times. He simply hadn't *known it* until now. He thanked her.

"Is it okay if I hug you?" she asked.

He paused, then nodded. When she wrapped him in her arms, it felt so good that he thought he might sob. It was nice to be held.

Her hair moved and tickled his ear. He tried to pull away, but she held him tight and whispered, "I'm not sure what Torsten was trying to tell you, Victor, but I think it was more small talk. 'Patient numbers,' he said. You need to look into it."

Patient numbers. A problem with record keeping? Why would Torsten care? It had to be something more important than that.

Cody Sisco

Victor felt a tightness in his gut. He needed to start counting bodies.

Alia waited until they'd finished dinner and the candles in the dining room had begun to sputter. Torsten had a half-full glass of wine, which he was nursing slowly. She picked up the bottle and splashed more into her empty glass. Then she asked the question.

"What was that you were saying to Victor? Something about patient numbers. I'm not sure he got the message."

Torsten put his glass down and looked away. He seemed on the verge of saying something. Instead, he remained quiet, as if the energy required to open his mouth was suddenly too much.

A sick feeling twisted in her stomach. "What is it, sweetie? Torsten?" She might have let it go on a different occasion, but her curiosity and, yes, her indignation flexed. Torsten had never taken much of an interest in Victor before. If this information was so sensitive, could it be dangerous? Whatever it was had something to do with BioScan; therefore, naturally, she would be entitled to some insight. "Torsten!"

He looked up, surprised. Her tone was aggressive and uncalled for, yes, but she wasn't used to being ignored by her fiancé.

"Whatever it is, you don't have to go into great detail. It's only—"

"I can't," he said quietly.

"I beg your pardon?" She put down her wine glass, then picked it up again to drink and stop her mouth from running. It made no sense to get upset. That didn't change the fact that she was livid. She could feel her face heating up. Torsten was looking at her with concern.

"Alia, I would tell you if I could." He smiled apologetically, an expression she'd witnessed countless times in council meetings or on campaign stages. That he would use it on her—

She pushed back from the table, grabbed her wine glass, and headed to the front door.

"Alia!" he called.

She barged onto the porch, feeling the hint of a breeze mess with her hair, and gulped down some wine. An owl hooted.

I would tell you if I could. The arrogance …

Torsten knocked on the doorframe as he came onto the porch.

"It's fine," she said. She meant it. But it still came out sounding aggrieved. "Really, I'm just … Today was …"

What was today? Not much different from anything else she'd been through recently. Nothing to set her off other than a steady, growing dread that she couldn't explain.

"You would need to get security clearance," Torsten said softly as he came to her side and wrapped an arm around her. She tensed, then chided herself for withdrawing from the one person who she needed to feel loved and safe with. She relaxed into him.

She tried to backpedal from her earlier insistence. It was a momentary obsession, and now it had passed. Security clearance meant meetings and briefings and distractions from her job. It meant losing the world of the clinic that was hers and not Torsten's. She sighed. "I don't need to. It's fine. Really. It's been a long day."

He hugged her and said, his chin resting on the top of her head, "Think about it, though. You know how much I rely on you. I wouldn't have to hold anything back."

"Maybe," she said.

"It's serious," Torsten said in a whisper.

When she turned and raised her gaze, she noticed that his expression was pained, scared even. He released her from his embrace.

"The patients are a small part of it. There's trouble, and I don't think anyone is ready to admit how serious it is."

It was her turn to comfort him. With her wine glass in one hand, she gestured at the New Venice rooftops visible through the trees, while her other arm hugged him fiercely. "I'm sure everything will be all right," she said.

But she wasn't sure. Not at all. Things were off track and sliding into an unexpected, unwanted future. Like with the Human Life Movement and the hostage-taking, a crisis that caught her by surprise. Would more foresight make the next crisis easier to manage? Ignorance wasn't a shield, but she wasn't sure she wanted to face what might be coming. She wanted to get through the campaign and the wedding and have some peace first, but that might be too much to ask of an indifferent and implacable future.

14

I tried. I tried. I tried. I tried. I tried. I tried.
   I tried.
   I failed.
   I didn't listen.
   —Victor Eastmore, *Apology to Resonant Earth* (transmission date unknown)

9 May 1992
New Venice, The Louisiana Territories

For Victor's next attempt to visit blankspace, he enlisted help from the one person he knew who wouldn't bat an eye at his oddities: Great-Granma Florence.

"What exactly ya tryin' to do?" she asked, peering up at him. Her eyesight wasn't great. Her hearing was fine, though. She complained about noises the house made, ones Victor could barely hear, as though they were as loud as a train passing from a few meters away.

"It's like meditation," he said. "I'm going to zone out for a bit and try to figure out what's happening in my head."

"Zone out, huh? We called that lazing around, gathering wool, making other people work harder because you was too busy stepping away from the worktable."

They were in her "sewing room," which was really only a storage space for more rugs, carpets, and blankets than he could count. It smelled of dust and midday naps. The only sign of modern times was an electric device on the wall that lured and zapped moths and other such threats to cloth.

Was she lonely in this big house, surrounded by keepsakes and entertained by rare moments of conversation? Most Eastmores lived in Semiautonomous California and made the trek here infrequently. Victor should have been visiting more regularly and for different purposes than metaphysical research into what was probably delusional thinking. She deserved better than that.

"Thank you, Granma. Being here means a lot to me."

"Well, okay then. Good luck to ya," she said. "Time for my nap."

She grunted as she took small steps through the door, closing it behind her. He pushed furniture to the side, padding all sharp edges. He bound his feet and hands and lay on his back, staring up at the plaster ceiling that had recently been redone. It was white and featureless, a good canvas for his visions. He closed his eyes anyway.

Blankspace exuded its familiar pull, and he let himself be whisked along in its current. He no longer felt the rope binding him or the rug beneath him. He was bodiless in a gray fog, able to move by the power of thought alone through a space where directions were meaningless. Diffused light and weightlessness imbued him with calm, steady awareness.

He was conscious of sounds, muffled at first, voices in low conversation too quiet to hear clearly. He willed himself closer, navigating upstream in a current of sound. Then he understood what he was hearing, a voice whispering familiar phrases.

The wise owl listens before asking who. The dark forest hides the loudest cuckoo.

The owl mantra. Were these his own words crossing into blankspace and interfering with his intentions? The mantra repeated again and again, its monotony lulling him into listlessness. If this was what filled up blankspace, he wanted no part of it. It was definitely his own voice, he was sure of that, and then came more words layered on top of it, still in his own voice but unfamiliar phrases.

Yours is not the only universe. There is another, where I was born.

Gray mist cleared. He saw himself in a room with a ceramic-tile floor, speaking quietly, and he sensed massive energies pooling and eddying, carrying the words beyond the room across vast darkness.

An invisible force is pushing me forward. Nothing I say or do can change its course. I'm not saying it's not my fault, but I couldn't have foreseen what would happen.

There he sat, speaking things as unintelligible as he ever heard, while his spirit self—or whatever his disembodied consciousness was—hovered, watching. His vision doubled, and a familiar, comfortable ease settled over him. He looked up at himself, floating

Cody Sisco

above, mouth agape, wondering at the apparition. He was in two places at once interchangeably.

When the time comes, you have to cross over or perish.

A wellspring of frustration burst open. He couldn't wait.

Now! I want it now.

He moved forward in his spirit body as fast as his will could compel him, straining toward the border. He felt it not far ahead, thickening at the edge of blankspace. Mass, direction, substantiality, almost within reach. He strained toward it and put all his effort into crossing over.

He collided with something. He felt it absorb his momentum; he was suspended motionless for a brief moment. Then he was flung back hard.

He woke up on the floor of the knitting room, skin soaked in sweat, bound up in rope exactly as he'd been. After a few minutes of labored breathing, he finally started untying himself. Once free, he checked his MeshBit and discovered that half an hour had elapsed.

Instead of answers, he had more questions. His other self had looked ... older? *Who was other me talking to? And why couldn't I cross over?*

His gut settled like a heavy stone. Not a single memory had been recovered. He couldn't cross over, but only now did he realize he'd wanted to. Blankspace was a Möbius strip, bending back on itself from new vantage points, a path of discovery going nowhere except where it started. If there were no answers in blankspace—

Florence knocked on the door and entered without waiting for a response. "I heard ya bangin' about, so my nap is kaput. Ya free now? I could use your help makin' lunch."

15

We all look back and agree that we missed certain signs, overlooked clear evidence, failed to recognize an emergent truth. In reality, it's impossible to predict the future, especially one that diverges so significantly from both the past and our expectations. So, don't beat yourself up. No one could foresee the birth of new gods.

—Robbie Eastmore, *Another World* (transmission date unknown)

13 May 1992
Las Vegas, Organized Western States

One week before Ozie was due to travel to New Venice, he sat alone inside one of Las Vegas's restaurants for top-rated citizens. The dining area was a street-level glass carapace jutting into the wide promenade fronting Grand Park, forcing pedestrians to squeeze past. It was a see-and-be-seen type of place, not at all his style, but they served the best enhanced juices in the city, and right now he felt more desperate than ever before.

Was he close to escaping, or were his attempts futile? He flashed back to the moment on the outskirts of town with solar towers slanting shadows across the road when the van had slowed and turned around. The controls, when he tried them, were ineffectual. The manual lever had done nothing. Looking down, where there should have been a control box, he saw a clean cut and a casing that housed nothing. The thought that someone had messed with the manual control bothered him less than the fact that none of his alarms had gone off when it happened. The Diamond King was outmaneuvering him, and Ozie was playing catch-up.

Did he dare try to leave again?

He scratched his cheek, and the stubbly sensation made him nauseous. The braincap in his bag under the table was tantalizingly close, but he didn't reach for it. Instead, he clasped his hands in his lap and squeezed. The nausea didn't pass, though it didn't get worse either. He was walking a balance beam, and on either side lay consequences he didn't want to consider. One step at a time on the line between sanity and despair, that was how he'd always played it. That would have to be enough.

The waiter came to take his order: a breakfast omelet, a side of hash browns, and two large orders of a serenity elixir with a double dose of fumewort. The perks of being in the King's organization meant that he'd been able to request that the restaurant obtain enough fumewort from Pearl to keep it stocked, and it had only taken a few days for this secret menu item to be available. When the drink arrived, tasting strongly of mango and vaguely of dirt, he slurped it down greedily. He'd always made fun of Victor's homeopathic remedies and teased Pearl about them mercilessly. *Oh, the irony. Look who's dependent on folklore and herbal dreams now.*

Dependent and alone.

Pearl avoided him. Their time as double agents seemed to be at an end. Having your ally poisoned had a way of weakening one's resistance. They were both under the Diamond King's thumb now. He sent her messages, cryptic ones that went unreturned.

Maybe he should pay her a visit in person, since he no longer trusted any devices connected to any type of network. That included the Mesh and the new Tangle network that had been rolled out in only a matter of weeks. And that wariness included most of his braincaps. The one he still trusted, an older model, years outdated and much less effective at attenuating his MRS episodes, sat in his bag. Was it paranoia to think if he used it anywhere with a vidlens nearby that the Diamond King would somehow find out and confiscate the device? Probably not. Ozie had heard several whispered examples of the consequences of extreme surveillance that convinced him he was definitely not being paranoid. Actually, yes, his life was fucked.

The people of Las Vegas had a few sayings about this. *Can't lose what you don't want*, was usually used in reference to the fruits of lawless, dangerous behavior; *frame it up*, was an admonition to live a virtuous life and ignore ubiquitous vileness; and there was the phrase *The King knows*, because incredible as it sounded, he seemingly did know what went on everywhere. Who knew what army was employed to watch all the footage, filter through it, and act on what was observed? Or what clever algorithms? But despite

Cody Sisco

the improbability of the feat, the Diamond King appeared to know it all. That was precisely the problem Ozie faced: How could he escape a system that knew what he was doing in real time?

A shiver grew and buffeted him, strong enough to cause his chair to scrape and screech against the floor. He couldn't use the braincap; too risky. He would have to regain control on his own. He sucked down the second elixir, muttering a brief thanks to Pearl and her herbs as the shaking subsided. Maybe he could pass her a note. But what would it say? "I don't like the bed I chose to lie in"? He imagined her dry, gristly laugh. "The future will emerge," she would say. *Yeah, but what if it sucks?*

After the omelet and hash browns arrived, he tucked into them. The only thought running through his mind was a pop-song refrain from his childhood on repeat with all its major-chord sing-song variations: *Run away, run away, run away, little mouse.* Ozie had never been one for mantras until recently. Filling a head with nonsense was better than letting it stew in paranoia. *Run away, run away, run away, little mouse.*

But what if I can't run away?

The little mouse singer was a Class Three Broken Mirror, it was later disclosed. They burned his music in the streets of Oakland.

Ozie finished his food, got up, and started walking back to his office, a full quarter-turn around Via Orbis. *Run away, run away, run away.*

He walked back through the lobby without a word or nod to the security. They knew him and his rating. In the elevator, he began making a plan. He would need devices with no spectrum relays that could only talk to each other via hard wire. He needed code he trusted. He needed time unobserved. Together, those challenges would be enormous, but he could start with baby steps and go from there. One step at a time toward freedom.

Ozie got to work, looking at the relay traffic among the pluggers over the last several nights. They'd been complaining about trouble staying asleep, and the Diamond King wanted answers. Without warning, the Diamond King materialized on the vidscreen, growing larger, while the frames Ozie had been looking at swam into the background.

"Go check on floor six."

Ozie's eyebrows rose, but he remained seated. There were many floors in this building that he'd never been to before. He tried them all over the past few weeks, riding the elevator to heights unimaginable in Oakland, picturing the shell surrounding his body and what it would look like, what it would feel like if the steel and glass surrounding him vanished to leave him floating in the wind before an inevitable fall. Some buttons hadn't done a damn thing when he pressed them, including the number six.

"What's there?"

"New patients." The Diamond King's image blinked out.

Ozie opened a small chiller below his desk, reached into it, and took out a bottle that held iced tea brewed with fumewort powder, a disgusting concoction, but these were desperate times. The drink wet his throat and almost made him gag as he walked to the elevator and descended.

When the door opened, he stepped out, immediately noticing that this floor was laid out like a hospital, with corridors branching off, doors concealing whatever they concealed, and stations for nurses positioned centrally. A small robot rolled up to him and immediately reversed, then did it again. *Cute.* Ozie followed it, and as they passed an open door, he couldn't resist and peeked inside, surprised to find an operating room with beeping machines and an unoccupied surgical table at the center.

Then he looked up, and a slow-dawning horror glued him in place.

The ceiling for each floor in the building was a standard five meters, which in most cases meant an airy feeling with lots of unused space. Here, though, in this room, looming over the bed, machines, and accoutrements of surgery, was a creature-like thing of nightmares. Made of shiny metal and plastic surfaces, it hung in the shadowed upper reaches of the room. Some tubes, like tentacles, were coiled above, while others unspooled from its belly, trailing down, like the underside of a jellyfish.

"Excuse me," a woman's voice hissed behind him, and he was pulled back by the shoulder out of the room. He turned and saw an entire medical team crowding the hallway and a mobile bed holding a patient, who was unconscious and so fully swaddled and covered with apparatus that nothing could be seen except the patient's nose, sticking out underneath googles, and their shaved head. Ozie moved out of the way. The woman muttered, "Thank you," and issued orders to her team as they rolled the patient into the room underneath the machine, which began to click and beep. Vidscreens leaped to life around the room, displaying the patient's vital signs: respiration, blood pressure, and indications of the amount of anesthesia circulating in the bloodstream. Ozie's view was cut off by the closing door.

The little robot he was following beeped and blinked at him, moving down the hall and back again in short bursts that Ozie would swear in a court of law meant that the thing was impatient. He followed again, this time not seeking answers and glimpses, his mind still fixed on that jellyfish machine hovering in that room. Of course, computer-assisted surgery made sense, but Ozie wouldn't be caught lingering anywhere within reach of a tentacle's grasp.

At the end of the hall, the robot neared a closed door, which swung open independently. Heartbeat pulsing in his neck, Ozie passed through the doorway and looked around the dimly lit glass-walled room. Bodies. Ten, maybe twelve, in all. They lay in beds lining one wall. Each had a complement of monitors fixed to their temples and IV lines in their wrists. Attendants moved between them. One checked a MeshBit, looked up, saw Ozie, and approached. He recognized Grette by her cropped hair and hawk nose.

"You are here to see the new patients."

"The King said I should check on them," Ozie said.

"Yes, yes. They have undergone the procedure, and it all looks good."

"I wouldn't know."

"You will not find them very interesting yet. We have normal post-surgery surveillance." She watched him carefully. After a moment, she asked, "You do not know why you are here?" Grette's voice had the cadence of a teacher who was disappointed and amused by her student's ignorance.

"I have no idea, actually. I guess maybe you can tell me, or I'll ask the King." *But I really don't want to.*

"You are here for your expertise. These patients are recovering from surgery, but that is not why they are unconscious. They are Class One Broken Mirrors, understand?"

Ozie blinked. He understood very clearly what he was witnessing. SeCa's blatant injustice: forced medication, institutional brutalization, minds deprived of the vitalities of freedom and joy until they receded from view, trapped in the body. At least the dead were free to wander. These poor souls. Why were they *here*? Oh, he understood, and he didn't like it.

"Where did they come from?" he asked. *SeCa, of course, but how did they wind up here?*

"Does that matter? They are our patients, and it is your responsibility to help them."

"They may be our patients, Doctor, but I'm not a doctor, remember?"

"Yes, I know this. But you will help them. Perhaps this is a conversation you should be having with him."

There was no need to name the Diamond King.

"I will leave you, then. If you have questions, you may reach me," she said.

Ozie looked at the people lying on the hospital beds. The way they were lined up made him think of pillars, fallen into rubble, things he'd never seen with his own eyes, only in documentaries smuggled out of the Ultimate Sultanate.

The King's voice piped up from somewhere to Ozie's left. "I chose these patients because they were the farthest gone. If we're going to claim victories, we should be reaching the highest peaks, don't you think?"

"They've all been plugged, I notice."

"All that's left is to connect them."

Ozie sighed. He'd seen plenty of strange things during his time in Las Vegas. He shouldn't be surprised at one more, but he'd reached a point of rawness, of exquisite sensitivity to changes in the balance of bad and worse that surrounded the Diamond King. Every new development chafed like a sandpaper towel. The Diamond King wanted him to connect these broken minds to the network. *Fine. And then? What's the point?* They were comatose, one step removed from death.

"For your part of this project to succeed, it is necessary that you be made aware of two things. First, the treatment protocol will focus on interrupting the feedback loops inherent in mirror resonant syndrome neurotypologies. You have experience with this within a single brain. The challenge becomes managing the signals passed through the network."

"That doesn't seem likely. Look at them. Not a lot going on."

"Why would you, of all people, expect mental activity to be apparent to an external observer? Sloppy thinking, Ozie; you should know better."

Ozie opened his mouth to object but thought better of it.

Arguing with the Diamond King could lead in dangerous directions. The Diamond King launched into a narrative of each patient's circumstances. Ozie could have just read all their files, but it was a different depth of learning to talk about a patient's medical history while looking at them, imagining them as a walking, talking, and relatively healthy person before the decline of their faculties led them to lie in front of a stranger, helpless, immobile, and without hope. At the end of the lengthy tutelage, Ozie said, "Got it. I need to hook all of them together in a way that can manage the cognitive feedback loops. What's the second thing you want to tell me?"

"There is a signal."

The room was silent. Ozie got the sense that he was supposed to know what the Diamond King was talking about, but he didn't have a clue. "Okay, what signal?"

"That is the question. What kind? From where? Manmade or natural phenomenon? Does it carry a message? What is it?" The Diamond King's voice was a whispered hint of revelations that fell flat and died on the tile floor.

This smells like paranoia. Laws, what kind of mess am I stuck in?

"You lost me," Ozie said.

"Something is affecting the neural activity of each patient. We can deduce that not only are they experiencing something like a dream state, but also that this state is coordinated. Patterns of activation are not just being shared. They are emerging simultaneously across distances that would be impossible to bridge without surpassing the speed of light. There must be an explanation."

"They're entangled?" Ozie walked down the row of patients, noticing now that they each had small, round areas on their skulls that were red and inflamed. The plugs would extrude nano filaments deep into brain tissue, map the activity, and store the data for later transmission once he'd hooked them up. However, in a sense, the Diamond King was suggesting they were already connected without needing relays, wires, or any discernible means of communication. Now he was interested.

"You're saying their brains are receiving some sort of signal?"

"Theirs and yours."

Ozie stopped. A vein throbbed in his temple. Was the Diamond King deliberately trying to freak him out?

"It's a phenomenon we don't see in people without MRS, and not every Broken Mirror. There appears to be a tipping point, a trigger, if you will, that activates the resonance. Epidemiological studies are underway. You'll be interested to learn the epicenter."

"Epicenter? You mean a place?"

"Perhaps. We can see that the trigger is somehow associated with Carmichael, Semiautonomous California."

The fumewort-infused liquid in Ozie's stomach surged up. He doubled over and breathed, praying that he wouldn't heave all over his shoes.

"Indeed," the Diamond King said. "Which is why, once you've connected these to the network, you'll need to find a way to block the signal or at least its effects. Once you've done that, you can go to New Venice, as we've discussed, to retrieve the missing puzzle piece."

Ozie's mind churned through all this information with the speed and urgency of a jetliner. A signal somehow linked to Carmichael caused Broken Mirrors to begin to—well, to experience their condition. To worsen by having stronger resonant episodes more frequently. To slip toward catatonia that was, in fact, a dream state.

Laws, what if the trigger had been Samuel?

"That's why you want the data egg," Ozie said.

"It contains what I need to unravel this mystery. Bring it back, and while you're there, convince Victor to pay us a visit."

16

The Louisiana Territories had always been a welcoming place in need of home-steaders, farmworkers, and artisans. People tended not to migrate west given the Euro-trade-fueled economic growth along the eastern seaboard, and labor shortages in both Semiautonomous California and the Organized Western States. Through incentives and careful planning, the Louisiana Territories saw a consistent though slow-growing demographic and economic expansion after the Repartition. There was land to fill and markets to grow. They couldn't afford to turn anyone away.

—Robbie Eastmore, *Another World* (transmission date unknown)

14 May 1992
New Venice, The Louisiana Territories

Alia stood at the top of Triton's Deep Crossing. People would come from all over the Louisiana Territories to stand where she stood, before touring the canals of New Venice, passing through the locks, and taking a ride out into the Passage. No tourist trip was complete without climbing to the top of Triton's and taking in the view that Alia had enjoyed countless times as a child. She remembered hands sticky with candy floss and the crunch of the last bite of ice-cream cone that had been filled with her favorite combo of strawberry swirled with chocolate. She recalled, too, the small chirping birds that always came for the seeds one of the shopkeepers flung out every half hour.

As an adult, some of the shine of these memories had worn off. The need to keep her hands clean. Ice cream flavors too sweet and artificial. Birds nothing more than filthy pests. Like so much else in life, when a grown-up learned too many things, the mystery of the world revealed itself, and the truth beneath the gloss turned out to be less wondrous, less idyllic than a child's eye view.

To her right were the squat stone buildings of New Venice and gentry who were fearful and uncooperative. On the opposite embankment, the BioScan campus, where careers came with serious baggage. Behind was Pond Park, where hundreds of stim addicts were now camping out, mixed with refugees from whatever latest calamity drove them from the Republic of Texas. She'd never seen her town like this: divided, desperate, and under siege.

Except she had, hadn't she? During the Human Life insanity. She didn't want to remember it, but the memories resurfaced slowly, begrimed, the way bicycles buried in the canals slurped as they were pulled from the muck. The feeling of being trapped with insanity running rampant. Those stupid, white-robed fools and their false-idol worshipping. And the smart people unable to extract themselves. The casualties.

And yet this could turn out to be much, much worse, here and everywhere. Torsten had told her as much as he could while her security clearance application was being processed. Expect the unexpected. Expect the Organized Western States to target the Louisiana Territories somehow. It was vague and scary enough to make her grind her teeth at night and feel lightheaded for no reason. Her mind spun dozens of scenarios, everything from invasion to pathogen to economic warfare.

They had to get ahead of the problem and improve their security, and that meant getting a tight handle on the town's social conflict. There was no other option. The future of the town was at stake, its safety during a looming, dangerous storm.

Alia descended from the bridge. Volunteers from the local Humanitarian League were surveying the denizens of the park, seeing who needed food or toiletries, making arrangements for the shared shower facilities that had been set up in a spare lot by the train station, making sure the "public use" areas of the park remained a safe place for New Venetians and tourists to take their kids on picnics without having to get too close to the addicts and refugees making the park their home.

She filled her days off volunteering for patient outreach. BioScan could help people with a substance-use disorder with simple improvements to their lives. More beds were coming online soon at the former Human Life Camp up by Ouachita Dam, places to stay that were monitored, where stims were banned and patients could avoid temptation. Where someone looked out for your wellbeing. It wasn't much, but it had been shown to help.

As she rounded the pond, she saw several clusters of people talking closely, glancing around furtively, looking shifty. How many of them were trading stims? Probably all of them. She could see others lying on the grass, staring up at the clouds, blissful smiles on their vacant faces.

Alia wished they had a better line of defense against stim addiction. There was no treatment to reduce cravings, no salve for the withdrawal symptoms. They could offer little more than a safe place to stay and a sympathetic ear. Medicine was good at some things and bad at others. The crisis tested their abilities, and they were failing.

She made her way to a woman who sat on the grass staring at the fountain in the pond. A white foamy jet sprayed erratically from the center, tens of meters high now, then subduing to a short, frothy dome, its patter-splat-smashdown growing louder then softer. The woman appeared sober, though she made no sign of acknowledgment when Alia sat down next to her.

Polite niceties came across as disingenuous when the real motive for the conversation became known. She eschewed chit-chat and got straight to the point. "I'm with BioScan. My name is Alia Effendi. If you or someone you know needs treatment for stim addiction, help is available."

The woman glanced at her and smiled weakly. Alia thought there might be hope in the expression.

"I don't mean to presume," Alia went on. "I know many people here recently arrived from the ROT to escape the troubles there."

"Troubles," the woman echoed. "Yeah, you might say that. Tell me, if you're willing to help us now, why weren't you willing to help us when Texas was being invaded?"

"Invaded?"

The woman's expression soured. "First came the stims, then the Corps. And all the while, we begged for help. And no one came. So now we're here because we're looking for someplace safe. It turns out we may be too late. There are rumors."

Alia said, "We can help you overcome the addiction. We have beds. You could get off the street."

The woman smiled wearily. "Yes, that does sound nice. Tell me, Alia, what then?"

"I don't understand."

"I suppose I'll need to apply for asylum and wait. Then maybe if my papers come through, I can find a job. If there's one available for someone like me."

"We've always welcomed people in tough times."

The woman continued as if Alia hadn't said a word. "And then maybe I can start to feel normal again. And then what?" She looked at Alia plain in the face as tears slipped down. "What's the point when nothing will ever feel as good as this?" She held a stimpipe in her hand, cupped, her wrist limp, like it was far heavier than it appeared.

Alia breathed. "The point is that the other stuff is real. Real-life stuff. It may not feel as good, but it's real."

"I guess we'll have to agree to disagree. You may as well go try to help someone else."

"You don't have to struggle alone. I'll leave my card."

"Sure. Good luck to you, Alia."

"Good luck," she responded.

With a leaden heart, Alia got to her feet. She was only several steps away when she heard the woman's sharp intake of breath. Looking back, she saw the stimpipe in her limp, outstretched hand as the woman lay on the grass, motionless, staring at the sky with a luxuriant smile. Her head lolled toward Alia. "So much better."

The next few conversations went about the same. Although most people she talked to at least acknowledged the hope of getting clean and didn't share the first woman's nihilism. She would do what she could but wouldn't expect the impossible. They must want to quit using; that was the most important thing. And it was out of her hands.

She was nearing the end of her stamina when a voice behind her made her turn. "Look at you, Ms. Goody Good. Helping the wretched with your salve."

It was a short man, barrel-chested, not yet wasted away like so many heavy users who no longer remembered that eating and taking sustenance was advisable. She thought she recognized him. A local? She couldn't place him, though. "I'm doing what I can," she said, walking away.

"Oh, and we appreciate it, surely." He spoke in a sing-song tone that mocked her. And she remembered. He was a Lifer.

"You were there. At the clinic," she said, turning to him. Poisoned vehemence dripped from her words. It surprised her. She thought she'd been holding herself together.

"That I was. Back when purity was oh-so vital. Some things don't last, I'm afraid. The death of idols has a way of changing things."

A thrill of revulsion tickled her skin. He looked unchanged, maybe a bit more hangdog around the eyes, deepened wrinkles and crow's feet. *Death of idols?* She realized he was referring to Samuel. "You worshipped him," she said, disbelieving.

"It was easier believing in miracles before I saw his body burning out on the lake."

Her stomach churned at the memory. What was this man doing here? He should be in the mud with the other Lifers.

She bit her lip. No. She wouldn't be so heartless. She wouldn't be twisted around by her personal feelings. The Qaddo had taken in the Lifers when they had nowhere else to go. It was a kindness that showed true moral fortitude. No matter that the Lifers were a bunch of lunatics under Samuel's sway. And Victor's, she reminded herself. Laws, what a mess they'd all made of her little town.

"You're better off leaving us to it," the man said, gesturing to the destitution around the park.

"We can help."

He stared at her with naked hatred. "We don't want your *help*. We know where the stims come from."

She resisted the urge to take a step back. This was her town, her workplace. She wouldn't be intimidated. "What are you talking about?"

"'Treatment' you call it. You want us dependent. You want us weak."

"Of course I don't. You're not making any sense."

"We know you're causing it. You and the Eastmores. Spreading stims so you can feed us bogus pills. Greedy plutocratic scumbags."

She almost laughed. "That's ludicrous."

"No one is getting better at your clinic. I know that."

"This stuff about the stims. It's not true. Where did you hear it?"

"Does the Mesh lie?"

Alia sucked in her breath. *Shocks, not again.* The last time infowar propaganda hit the town, the hostage crisis had blown up. If there was another set of vicious rumors about to wash over them …

Realizing this was exactly the type of thing Torsten might already know was coming, Alia turned to go.

"That's right. Go talk to your bosses and claim you had no idea they were causing this."

She turned. "It's not true. Believe me. We're trying to help."

"Psshhh," he waved her away.

Alia took out her MeshBit and was about to ping Torsten but stopped. Her clearance hadn't arrived yet, and a conversation might foul things up for him. She pinged Lisabella instead, who picked up right away.

"Alia, it's nice to hear from you. I so enjoyed the picnic."

"We have a problem. When can we meet?"

"What is it?"

"A rumor circulating on the Mesh—we should talk in person."

There was a long silence before Lisabella spoke again. "Can you come to the Mesh House?"

"Now?"

"Now, please."

"I'll be there."

The connection was severed.

Alia thought of calling Karine, Victor, or possibly Circe, but now that her heartbeat had slowed to normal, she thought better of it. Spreading rumors, even to debunk them, would tarnish her as amateurish and untrustworthy. And her security clearance application was still being processed.

She walked hurriedly along the Grand Canal embankment, waving when she passed someone she knew, though not stopping to chat. Last year, that would have been impossible. The character of New Venice was changing. People drew inward, eschewed connections, and fortified their psyches; Alia was a prime example. She had excuses, of course. Busy with BioScan, busy planning her wedding, and helping Torsten's legislative campaign. What they didn't know was that she was mostly busy wrestling with the aftermath of the hostage crisis, and she feared talking about it. And now, this pressure of impending catastrophe pinned her tongue into silence. She passed on by busily.

The MeshHouse path was a switchback cobblestone stairway up a grassy slope. Thunderheads piled skyward in the south, bulbous and weighty. Across the Passage, tidy green hills studded with patches of trees blended into the forest. She was heading into enemy territory for help, and the irony was not lost on her. The MeshHouse represented occupied lands: first wrenched away from natives by American imperialists and now usurped by European technologists. The daily, uncontested nature of the occupation did nothing to diminish the transgression; that was perhaps its most galling aspect. Europe controlled countless pockets of land across the continent, a pincushion pierced a thousand times by Mesh Towers and Houses. It always sought more, usually achieving its aims without a murmur of protest. More land, more control, more power. The exigencies of empire always demanded more.

Was she really asking for help from Lisabella and her Mesh employers? It had seemed a natural, easy, productive action—and that was precisely the problem.

She shook her head to clear it. Too late to have these concerns. They shouldn't have had Torsten's picnic here. The grand realignment was already underway. Yet another nation of the American Union brought further under Europe's sway.

When will we rise up and resist?

She knew better than to hope for revolution. How about a little pushback? One woman's grudging hesitancy wasn't enough. Maybe the fault lay in feeling individually responsible rather than collectively. If Torsten could rally people in New Venice ...

"Face facts," he would say.

The New Venice MeshHouse was just one more hole in the moth-eaten tapestry of the American Union. In the years following the Repartition, it had been a lookout post for the Louisiana Territories gendarmerie. Then, it was relinquished by an administration disinterested in maintaining the facilities. On the slope's plateau, she could see a former barracks, a lookout tower, and several Reconstruction Era buildings with wrap-around glassed-in porches that served as offices. Skillful negotiating on the part of the European Foreign Service resulted in a transfer of title to the local Mesh administrator. Decades later, that arrangement seemed more of a steal than a deal.

The guard checked her identity and let her pass the gate. Lisabella met her at the MeshHouse front door, but they didn't go inside. Instead, Alia was led to a low-slung concrete building.

Lisabella unlocked the front door and led Alia into a small storage room with racks filled with plastic bins.

"What are we doing here?" Alia asked.

"You need to see the source of the rumors," Lisabella said. She took down one of the bins and popped open the top. Inside were hundreds of devices, small models, the size of a finger, with displays that could only show a few words at a time that moved in synch with the eyes.

Alia looked around the room at the bins. "Are these all MeshBits?"

"In a way. They're unregistered. More show up every day. I am—we are not responsible for their content."

"What does that mean?"

"They carry messages, unsanctioned lies, that somehow piggyback on the Mesh network."

Alia swallowed. "It's the drone drops all over again," she said.

Lisabella nodded. "To the user, the experience is identical. They think they're on the Mesh. The sources appear to be the same. But the content is different. This is the most sophisticated propaganda tactic we've seen. And it's getting worse by the day."

"The OWS?"

Lisabella nodded.

Alia shivered, thinking that the last thing she could handle was another problem she didn't know how to solve.

"There's one other thing," Lisabella said. "I managed to track down Anders—well, sort of. He was spotted in Las Vegas a week ago. We think he's still there."

17

Be prepared to nurture an understanding of your relationship's idiosyncrasies. No two monogamies are identical; take that complexity and multiply it exponentially. Polyamory pushes the limits of what's possible. You don't need a degree in psychology, but it might help.

—*A Socialite's Guide to Polyamory*

15 May 1992
New Venice, The Louisiana Territories

The clean-up crew pulled a dead body from the canal as crowds of tourists and residents gathered to watch. A BioScan patient ID implant provided the deceased's name: Alessandra Fieri. She was a former SeCa citizen transferred from one of the Class Two "ranches" only a week ago. She'd been heard to say that it wasn't that life in the Louisiana Territories wasn't for her; it was that another world was waiting. She only needed to cross over. Apparently, her version of quantum suicide involved a lethal dose of morphine administered via a trigger in unstable superposition rigged to a Skinjector while she stood on the lip of Bozart's Bridge. Alessandra had been both resourceful and dramatic.

Victor stood on the opposite side of the canal embankment from where the corpse was laid out on the cobblestones. Across the way, a group of New Venetian citizens and refugees commingled and lollygagged. It was the second death in as many days, though this one wasn't as messy. A stim addict, having found a stash and lost his bearings, jumped from a sixth-floor rooftop and splattered on the street along the Petite Canal, horrifying tourists and locals alike. New Venice had changed, and not for the better; there was rarely a day without an unnatural death.

Within the confines of BioScan, things were looking a bit better. The installation of brain-mapping bays proceeded a pace.

Already patients rotated through for hours at a time, starting with the healthiest patients, the idea being the more self-sufficient the patients became, the more resources would be freed up for expanding the program to the less healthy. Alessandra, a Class Two, had not yet been rotated through. She'd been scheduled to start in two weeks.

Victor's call for more resources was brushed aside. Karine commiserated, saying, "C'est de la merde! But what can we do? You know our financial situation as well as I do."

A flicker of shame crossed her face. The company's fate was on the line, and she took that as a hit to her pride. Circe was absent again, having traveled to Europe, and was due back in a few weeks for the family reunion.

The crowd on the opposite embankment swelled. People were four or five deep in places, jockeying to glimpse the tragedy below. Big crowds meant trouble. After the Human Life protests, Victor knew anything could happen.

New Venice had never been a town of wide-open spaces. Real estate was scarce because the islands had been literally scratched out of the earth. Locals tended to stay put; longevity in the community was directly correlated with wealth and status. Newcomers put up with tedious long-term apprenticeships to earn their shares. A tight-knit community, certainly. But it had never felt this claustrophobic.

People grumpily elbowed past Victor's perch at the railing, glanced to see what caught his attention, then stopped and gawked, pressing against him. He elbowed them back. A figure loomed behind him, and a second later, someone grabbed his shoulder. Although the touch was gentle, he shrugged away hard. He despised being touched. The hand returned.

He turned, exclaiming, "Hands off!" and saw that he was facing his parents.

Linus and Linda stood with their arms linked with an additional man and woman at their sides. His mother's hair hung in two salt-and-pepper braids. A houndstooth beret capped his father's head. The two of them, along with the other man and woman, wore simple tunics in various autumnal colors belted at the waist. They all wore black tights and pairs of real leather moccasins sold by tourist shops that claimed to sell Qaddo goods but, in fact, did not. They were imported from the Christian make-work prison factories of Florida. His parents ought to know better.

Victor blinked. He hadn't expected them to arrive for at least another week.

"We're here," his fa said, not exactly smiling. It was more of an anxious grimace.

His ma unlinked arms and approached Victor, hugging him tentatively, which he accepted if not appreciated. She knew him well and expected him to at least suffer this from her. He could do her that much of a favor, she'd said hundreds of times. His father nodded, a gesture of acknowledgment if not affection. Having lived through the trauma of Carmichael and then doubly cursed with an imperfect son, his parents had always been somewhat distant and awkward figures in his life.

He knew not to expect too much from them. They had their interests and priorities, and he was fine with that. He had his own issues, including a big black spot in his memories, and no reason to hope it would go away now that the blankspace mystery had deepened into absurdity and transformed into a house of mirrors.

"We want you to meet our found family," his fa said.

So that's who those two were. Victor looked again. The man was somewhat attractive in a round-headed and doughy way—like the simplest, smiliest, down-to-earthiest pushover one could find. Perfect for his opinionated parents. The woman wore a serene expression, not quite a smile, but Victor appreciated how unreactive she was—though plain-faced, he could see what his parents saw in her. She didn't arouse any negative emotions, a rare quality to people as sensitive as the Eastmores.

"Sally and Carson-Ray, meet Victor, our son."

He shook their hands obligingly, trying to think of something to say that would be polite, neutral, and forgettable. "Welcome to New Venice." The business of the dead body and the crowds didn't seem to faze them.

"We decided to come early," his ma said. "We have some business with your aunt."

"Oh?" Victor said. He wondered what it could be.

"Just paperwork. Nothing for you to panic about," his fa said.

Maybe the reunion was an occasion for more legal wrangling than he'd thought. "What a relief," Victor said, deadpan. In the long list of possible panic points, paperwork was not one of them.

"It's great to finally meet you and in such spirits," said Sally. "We've heard so much. Your parents are proud of you."

Victor lifted his eyebrows. "That's good to hear." *Haven't heard a thing about you*, he added silently to himself. Then again, he hadn't done more than skim the messages they'd sent him.

Carson-Ray said, "We're found family. It's so important we get along with heritage family."

Victor eyed the man skeptically. He wasn't unaware of all the terms used to describe polyamorous relationships, and he knew they varied somewhat across the AU. In Semiautonomous California, the righteous could get away with just about anything, while those deemed fallen were constantly harassed and put down. Polyamory was a righteous privilege, officially, and Eastmores tended to avail themselves of as many of those as they could.

Victor wasn't habituated, however, to being called "heritage." Family was family to him; at least it had been up to this point. He wondered how exactly his relationship had been redefined now that these two had entered the mix. He didn't want to wonder what blend of physical and emotional comfort they provided each other—it wasn't a direction he would let his mind stray.

He said, "It's nice of you to come with my parents and stand by their side while they do … paperwork. Money is crucial to a family's future." Victor deliberately echoed Granfa Jefferson's tone, knowing the mantra would be familiar, especially to his fa.

Linus reacted exactly as Victor suspected: defensively, with an exasperated gasp. But when he spoke, his words were a complete surprise. "That's why we're so concerned. Circe's going about this all wrong. We came to avert a disaster."

Victor had a sinking feeling in his gut. "What do you mean? What kind of paperwork are you here for?"

"We don't want to complicate things for you," his ma said. "It's not important."

"It is important, Linda," Sally cut in. "You've said so many times."

The sound of a bullhorn and someone saying, "Please clear the embankment," interrupted their conversation.

A flush of anger hit Victor suddenly. Whatever paperwork and haggling about money his parents might be relishing, he couldn't ignore the fact that people were dying. Alessandra's body was on a stretcher being carried up the steps to a dark coroner's van. Officials had managed to push the crowd back. *What would Pearl say?*

"Goodbye, Alessandra. May your crossing bring you peace," Victor muttered.

"We want to have dinner with you tonight," Carson-Ray said, moving close and leaning over the railing.

"I have plans," Victor lied with only a slight twinge of guilt. His relationship with his parents had been irreparably ruptured by the way they dismissed his concerns about Granfa Jefferson's death. They probably still believed he was deluded. And he no longer had a piece of the man's irradiated tongue to prove it and change their minds.

"There's a crisis here, and dealing with it keeps me busy. I hope I get to see you again soon," he said, and before any of them could respond, he slipped under the railing, dropped a meter to the canal bank, scraping his back on the rough stone but not regretting it, and headed toward the nearest bridge. He needed to try to understand how they'd failed Alessandra.

18

When I first heard about Personil, I dropped to my knees and sobbed. We'd hoped for a solution, but those first few years were hard, and there were many reasons to doubt we would find one. I worried that Carmichael would be the first in a string of calamities. The history of the West, we knew, was full of failed promises and miserable ends. Personil was an answer to my prayers.

—Mía Barrias, *Five Years After Carmichael* (1976)

7 April 1992
North Bayshore, Semiautonomous California

Mía Barrias rode in the train car reserved for "friends of the government," which included anyone who'd served in the legislature, as an aide in the executive branch, or who had scored a publicity contract in support of public morals. She had been raised in Semiautonomous California and had been through fire there—fire and smoke and reeking death. After many years of mind-fuckery to obliterate Samuel Miller's legacy, she now had a new mission, one that would force a reckoning with her legacy and forge a new one.

After only a few months in the Louisiana Territories, her view of the world had enlarged, fractured, and shifted. She'd been myopic before, consumed. She was changed now and knew she was changed because the world looked different. Little details piled up, their dots connecting in unfamiliar ways, creating meanings that hadn't been apparent.

This train car, for instance, was reserved for the privileged who toed the party line. The dining tables had handcrafted ceramic plates on them and woven place settings. Stained glass windows cast rainbows across the chairs and aisles. Real leather seats everywhere—*Laws, the expense!* To the Cathar mindset, these luxuries justly rewarded the good and faithful. The relative impoverishment of the "disregarded" train cars at the rear was deliberate. They were served faux café, sat on synthleather, and the furnishings were stark and economical.

Bad begets bad, as the saying goes.

Why did no one question who decided? Why did they accept without resentment that those in power deserved to be there?

She sighed at the irony and half-smiled to herself despite a hangover headache. After all these years of fighting to achieve her goals for the Classification Commission, she was trying to dismantle it. As an insider, she urged SeCa toward a revolution that the masses weren't ready for. Yet again, she was one woman seeking to transform the world around her. Why did it fall to her to fix? Could the hole in her heart heal without a crusade?

Yet, thinking back to what she'd seen in Carmichael on this trip, she was more motivated than ever. The disarray at the Classification Commission's ranches and facilities concerned her. The quicker they could be closed, the better.

The map on the vidscreen of her MeshBit showed they were nearing the outskirts of Bayshore, leaving behind the marshes and estuary where the rivers of the Long Valley spread into the delta.

She was about to put it away when her MeshBit pinged a high-pitched signal for an urgent top-priority communiqué. It was Ishelem, the Governor-General's assistant.

"Yes, this is Mía. What is it?"

"Where are you?" Ish asked. She sounded concerned.

"On the train. I should arrive at Central Station in half an hour. Why?"

"Oh, Laws! I thought so. Okay, everything is going to be fine. Let me just ... there. We're sending a team of drones, and the National Guard should be on site soon. Fifteen minutes max."

"What's going on?" Mía felt a lurch in her stomach as the train decelerated rapidly. Out the window, the shantytown of Crockett's Landing sprawled down the hillside and stretched to the water.

"I don't know how the rumor got started. They think there are Broken Mirrors on the train with you."

They think ...

Her gut lurched again. Regardless of the truth, rumors like that were dangerous. There would be protests. The opposition party would use this to discredit the administration, circulate their conspiracy theories, and manufacture exactly the hot-button political situation they'd been trying so hard to avoid. The transfer of MRS patients was a win-win for the SeCa government and BioScan only so long as it happened quickly and quietly.

Mía looked out the window, caught sight of crowds assembled in the slums below, and gulped. She no longer needed to ask who *they* were. People streamed through narrow alleyways, bright flares held aloft and moving purposefully up the slope. "Can't we just zip past?" her words sounded whiny and fearful, not at all the commanding voice honed through years of speeches.

"They've blocked the tracks somehow."

Ish's tone did more to startle Mía than the entirety of the conversation thus far. She got to her feet and moved toward the exit. "There are no MRS patients on this train."

"I know that. The troubles on the border leaked though, and everyone is assuming—"

"What trouble?" The train had stopped, and Mía opened the door with the emergency handle, stepping down onto the gravel. She was on the uphill side of the tracks and couldn't see who might be approaching from downslope. Tall iron rods with mesh strung between the poles fenced both sides at a remove of twenty meters or so. "Never mind that for now. I need you to find a security gate"—Mía checked her MeshBit—"somewhere between klick marker 12 and 13, and open it."

"How do I—"

"Get rail security on the line. They can open the gates."

"Are you going to wait there?"

"Wait a minute. I'm about to get a view." She climbed over a short retaining wall and up a chaparral-pocked slope to the fence line to get a view beyond the train cars. Gusts of wind blew her dress against her calves as she surveilled the scene. Several fires burned below. Only one or two structures gathered flames, but those would spread rapidly. "Call the fire authority as well—scratch that—make sure the Governor-General speaks directly to the fire chief. We don't want any misunderstanding."

Mía returned to the train and started banging on the door to the "disregarded" caboose. A man spied her through the glass and looked at her in confusion for a second. Then his eyebrows rose, and he opened the door.

"You're Mía Barrias."

"I am. And I'm ordering you and everyone else off this train. Follow me quickly. We don't have much time. There's a mob gathering in the shanties. We're going to be gone when they get here. Find someone to spread that message forward. I'll handle the privileged car." The message had to come from her, or someone like her, for anyone in those cars to believe it. "Got it?" she asked.

He opened and closed his mouth, unsure, and then he nodded.

"Good. Go. Now!"

She headed to the first passenger car and bluntly told them to leave the train and why with none of her usual sophistry and emotional appeals. They began to follow, and soon she was walking north, away from Oakland, with a long line of people behind her. She had to turn and scold some for trying to pull their bags from the storage compartments, almost wishing she could leave them behind for their stupidity.

The mob was now attempting to break through the fence. They were using spark cutters. She wouldn't want to get close to any of those. The group's pace increased to a trot. All the while, she could hear Ishelem on the sonobulb liaising with the emergency team.

Mía said, "Ish, when you have a minute—"

"What is it?"

"How far are we to the gate? You have my coordinates?"

"A quarter klick."

Mía couldn't see the gate. There was a bend toward the east. It must be beyond, but not by much.

"I think we'll make it. Tell me what happened at the border."

"The official story is that the Broken Mirrors were turned back, and they're at a holding facility somewhere north of Lake Tahoe."

Mía spotted the gate and breathed with gratitude. To Ishelem, she said, "There's nothing up there."

"Yep, that's why we ran with the official story."

"Then what really happened?" Mía asked with a sour taste in her mouth. Truth had always been malleable in the mouths of good SeCan spokespersons.

"They were taken," Ishelem said.

"Taken? Taken where? By whom?"

"We don't know for sure. It was a hasty thing. Patients moved by trucks, not trains, without supervision or medical staff. The trucks vanished. We think it crossed into the OWS on an old logging road. Someone went out to check. The road... it was freshly paved."

"Laws. How many did we lose?"

"Twenty-six. It was two caravans, technically."

"So, from a leak about Broken Mirrors missing at the border—"

Ish finished for her, "A rumor started that they were headed back to Oakland, and that didn't go over well. Not much violence in the city center yet. Some protests. But Richmond and Little Asia are burning. Like the riots."

In the 1960s, laws had been enacted to control the movement of asylum seekers arriving in SeCa as the Great Asian War reached its devastating apex. The descendants of previous immigrants had protested and then rioted when the crackdown turned violent. In the end, the SeCa government enlisted the help of European social engineers to manage the situation. Citizens were afforded the privileges of Mesh IDs and free movement, which led to the gray markets and slums on the outskirts beyond the border walls.

"You weren't born then," Mía reminded her.

"I've seen the vidfeeds," Ishelem said.

Mía reached the gate beyond, which was a hill covered by the dry and brittle grass that gave SeCa its nickname of Brown Hill Nation. There was no latch. She tried to push it open, unsuccessfully. "We're at the gate."

"It should be unlocked."

"It won't open."

"Try again?"

She did. "Could it be stuck mechanically?"

There was some muffled conversation on the other end of the line.

"Our boards are green. It shows open." They read each other the numbers: Mía's on a small copper plate beneath the gate, Ishelem on a vidscreen somewhere safe in an Oakland office. They matched.

Mía enlisted a few people at the front line to try shoving the door. It didn't budge. The mob was a half-kilometer behind them, approaching with torches and arc welders in their angry, clenching hands.

"Everyone, keep moving!" Mía yelled at the train passengers. "Go. Keep distance between you and them. The police will be here soon. We need to give them time to arrive. Go now!" The crowd took off at a jog, some carrying children in their arms or hustling the ones too big to carry. A few hung back with her. "You don't have to stay," she said.

"We're not leaving you," a worker said, appearing to speak for a small assemblage of passengers. "Better if we all run, isn't it?"

"I might be able to calm them down."

"They might take you apart before you get a word in."

Would the crowd see her as the woman who'd protected them from Broken Mirrors, or the traitor who had lately changed her tune?

"Okay, let's catch up with the others then." She was beginning to turn when she heard the whirr of drones.

Ishelem's voice crackled over the sonobulb, "Are you still there? If you're within sight of the mob, you're too close. Get out now!

"Why? What are they ..."

Mía could see the drones now. They weren't surveillance. They were attack drones. The three at the head of the pack were aiming a sound cannon at the mob.

A piercing voice rang out, "Halt! Lower your weapons! Kneel on the ground, or we will use force."

The mob hesitated for a moment, then pulsed forward again, even faster, as the people in the lead sprinted toward Mía.

The drones shuddered. The air between them and the mob shimmered.

Bodies dropped, dust whirled up, and Mía saw nothing as skin tugged against her bones and she was flung on her ass. *So much for the targeted use of force.* She hauled herself to her feet, blood on her hands from the gravel. She gathered up the handful of other passengers, and they continued fleeing through dust, their ears ringing loudly, their dreams of peace scattered by the winds of justice.

All this because someone decided to spread rumors about Broken Mirrors and derail her plans to transfer them quietly out of Semiautonomous California and begin undoing the harm she'd caused? Her fists clenched. Whoever it was, that person would find that she wasn't someone to fuck with.

Cody Sisco

19

For years, I found it helpful to tell myself that I wasn't responsible for my actions. Because MRS warped my perspective, I wasn't to blame. Because people lied to me, I couldn't have foreseen the traps I fell into. Because my intentions were good, I could be forgiven. Now I know better.

—Victor Eastmore, *Apology to Resonant Earth* (transmission date unknown)

16 May 1992
New Venice, The Louisiana Territories

Every day for weeks on end, Victor had done as much as he could to speed up the process of brain scanning the addicts and patients coming off Personil. The work was both fuel and fervor. Back in Semiautonomous California, ensconced in his family's privilege and predilections, in awe of Jefferson Eastmore's zeal and legacy, there had been no room for Victor to dream of his own accomplishments—aside from keeping his sanity and avoiding a fate like Samuel Miller's. Now, leading the charge at BioScan half a continent away, he saw clearly what he must do: help the mirror resonance syndrome patients who were stuck living under a punishing and unfair regime. He had influence and resources, and he would push himself to the limit to save them.

Along with the New Venice clinic's teams of technicians and medical assistants, he worked at shaving minutes then seconds off the time it took to move patients into the queue, to run them through the imaging machine, and to return them to their lives. The data amounted to brief slices of time showing their neural activity, warehoused in an array of data storage units filling an entire floor of the new BioScan tower, waiting for analysis. There had been no spontaneous recoveries, no obvious changes as the Personil cleared from their systems. Trials had begun: fumewort for some, transcranial magnetic stimulation for others, ultrasound, stimulants, physical therapy, and the list went on. There were some signs of increasing awareness and fleeting blips of lucidity, but the data did not show any persuasive patterns. It was still early days, but anyone hoping for a dramatic or quick result faced disappointment and the need for patience.

Now, Victor hiked up the path toward the drug huts simply to be away from people, taking a rare yet deserved break for a moment with his thoughts in the hopes that his memories would spontaneously return. Little chance of that, but he'd tried everything else. Why not a dose of silence?

The path was crowded with large, bee-friendly bushes sprouting conical bursts of purple flowers. He was listening to the buzzing hum and letting his mind loosen up when he saw a figure sitting on the front stoop ahead—it was Ozie, backdropped by a building they both knew held dark significance.

Ozie looked haggard, crazed even, as he attempted a tight-lipped smile. There was no hiding the anxiety pulsing and thrashing behind eyes that were shot through with angry red filaments. His gloved fingers twitched around the top of a synthleather travel bag in his lap. He probably made a mess of things out west and needed a refuge like Victor did when he came to New Venice. Ozie conjured trouble like a cursed magician; everything he touched spun out of control.

Not unlike me, Victor thought.

"Victor, it's been a while."

A knot of unease tightened in Victor's gut. They hadn't parted on good terms—colluding in murder, alleged murder, didn't make for friendly relations. It would take dire circumstances for Ozie to return—that, or he wanted something. As Ozie stood up, Victor noted he wore a long coat, the same one he'd worn months earlier to hide his artificial arm. *Any new body parts missing?* he wanted to ask.

Victor took an uncertain step forward, not bothering to hide his surprise and annoyance. "Welcome, I guess."

Ozie closed the distance, and Victor endured a hug that lasted too long with Ozie's artificial limb resting heavy on his shoulder and smelling faintly of biofuel algae that rode on stronger musty waves of sweat and unwashed hair.

"Can we go inside?" Ozie asked. "I'm thirsty. I'm not used to floating."

Victor paused as he opened the drug hut's front door. "Yeah. Um? Floating? Is that code—"

"Balloons." Ozie pointed to the sky, where there was nothing but a pale and listless blue. "The Diamond King's blimps are efficient with everything except time. I saw—" Ozie rubbed his throat with his gloved cyber hand. The fingers jerkily massaged his larynx. When he spoke again, his lips twitched, and the words sounded shaky. "I saw the way the horizon bends. Clouds towering high up. I saw more stars than I'd ever imagined." He was breathing heavily, and sweat had broken out on his brow. Victor wondered what kind of stimulant brew Ozie had been living on and was maybe still in the throes of. It wasn't "aura," the stim that had hooked Elena—he would recognize that.

They entered the dim interior of the drug hut, and Victor raised the blinds of the kitchen window. He filled a glass of water from the tap. "There's a train, you know. Why didn't you take that?"

"The Diamond King wanted to show off. And the trains aren't so reliable these days." Ozie glanced down at his wrist like he was checking the time and removed his coat. The synthflesh on his cyberarm looked like a gray eel. Bioluminescent blues and ambers flickered inside. It was much lighter in color than his dark skin.

Ozie had been run ragged, and for what? All the money in the world wasn't worth your health. More than that, Victor suspected Ozie was kept in the dark about the ultimate purposes he was serving. He was clearly an instrument, and a brittle one that might break.

"Did you finally meet him? You've been working for him long enough," Victor asked.

Ozie glanced down at his wrist again. "He's why I'm here."

Victor sat down, not liking how the cushions clutched him. He guessed Ozie would talk the whole time about a hacking job or some other scheme rather than what had gone on between them, what was still going on: a rupture in trust they might not be able to repair.

Ozie said something else, but it didn't register.

Did Ozie even realize how bad things had gotten between them? Victor knew his own feelings had changed. The mixture of attraction and repulsion he'd always felt had tipped decisively toward the latter. Ozie was too mercurial, too full of misdirection, always spinning stories within stories. Once, that mystery and complexity may have fascinated Victor, but now that he'd grown and got his bearings and become more able to navigate his life and mental disarray, stability was what he cherished. Above all, he wanted people around him with whom he could *stay* stable. Ozie was always mucking up the gears of Victor's mind.

"How long are you here for?" Victor asked.

The look on Ozie's face was quizzical and concerned.

"I'm not saying you shouldn't have come," Victor reassured him. He didn't want to set them on an adversarial path, and Ozie was sensitive enough to take *anything* as a slight. "It's just that with all the patients and my parents here now, it's getting to be a lot."

Ozie asked, "Your parents? But it's June. Isn't the reunion usually in August?"

"They're early. And they brought partners."

Ozie raised his eyebrows.

"They're in a quad." Victor didn't meet Ozie's gaze. It would be full of gleeful mockery. Ozie believed any romantic relationship—coupledom, throupledom, quadrupledom, all the bigger ones—was an assault on an individual's autonomy, and the strength of the assault increased with each additional participant. Victor would just as soon not think about the complicated head-spinning psychological dynamics.

"Ha! Of course, they are." Ozie held up two fingers from each hand and intertwined them, contorting them like wriggling worms.

"Gross. So why are you here?" Victor asked.

"I told you."

"Sorry, I've been ignoring messages. I've been so busy with the MRS patients." He fingered the MeshBit in his pocket. He should check it more often. And he should respond at least some of the time.

"No. I told you like a minute ago. You didn't hear me? I need ..."

White-misted vision, cotton-filled ears—

In the space of a few breaths, the room dissolved. Dim and fuzzy shapes moved in gray gauzy mist. Then, it started coming back like sea fog clearing, moving offshore.

Ozie, continuing with implacable dourness, said, "We're going to trade."

Victor looked around the room. He was in the drug hut on the couch. Birds chirped outside, and he heard a boat motor drifting up from somewhere below. Blankspace was gone. Though it was never far.

"Hey, Victor, you there?"

"I'm—I am now." Something was wrong; his thoughts were opaque and slippery; nothing stuck. He blinked and repeated the owl mantra to himself. "What were you saying about a trade?"

Ozie cocked his head and raised an eyebrow. "Okay, fess up. What's going on with you?"

"Nothing."

Ozie only stared back.

"Nothing," Victor repeated more confidently. A bit of normal cognition returned. "A life of MRS. Comatose Class Ones and a town full of stim addicts. A deathbed patient who, if he does die, will cause me no end of grief with Elena. Missing persons. Dead ones. I mean, aside from all that, I'm actually managing fine these days."

"No. I'm not interested in your spin. What's wrong in there?" Ozie tapped Victor on the side of the head with a surprisingly soft fake finger. "This is an uncommon presentation of symptoms." Ozie looked at Victor with intense curiosity.

"What symptoms?"

Ozie took a braincap from his bag. "I brought this for myself, but I think you might need it."

"I'm fine."

"Victor, listen to me. The two times I brought up why I'm here, you either ignored me or went sideways. A return trip to blankspace, gone and back again, with a singular stimulus. That's bad news. I'm going to repeat myself in a moment and test a hypothesis. First, put this on, pay attention, and tell me what goes through your head."

He held out the braincap. Urgency in his tone convinced Victor to cooperate. Though he didn't like being told what to do, he knew something was off, way off. Ozie was uniquely qualified to help if he could let him.

"Okay," Victor said. He put on the braincap, not liking how it mashed his hair down, and waited. Pressure built in his chest. His secret wanted to come out. Maybe honesty was the right path to take with Ozie.

Victor added with a sigh, "I have been missing some memories."

Ozie said something unintelligible, and blankness surrounded Victor.

20

Mesh authorities hereby advise the citizenry of an unauthorized entry into the airspace of the Louisiana Territories and Semiautonomous California. Please report sightings of any aircraft using the form below. Keep your eyes on the skies for safety and sovereignty.

—Official Mesh advisory (13 June 1991

16 May 1992
New Venice, The Louisiana Territories

Victor wobbled on his feet and grabbed the chairback as he lowered himself to sit. "I'm woozy," he said. "But I didn't hear you."

"That tracks. You stood when I suggested it. But any mention of"—Ozie's words were garbled—"and you go blank. Let's try again." Ozie took a deep breath, tapped a command on the wrist of his cyberarm, and then, emphasizing each word slowly, said, "I'm here to get the data egg."

Blankness flooded the room, obliterating color and depth, leaving only the sketchy contours of objects like tentative scribbles on tracing paper. Ozie was a gray blur, moving closer. Victor felt his hands being grasped, lifted, though only faintly, as if his hands and arms were numbed from sleeping on them. Beneath him, unseen, a vortex sucked at his consciousness, heavier than anything he'd experienced, pulling like the gravity of inevitable sleep at dawn after a night of restlessness. He resisted going, heard Ozie's voice, and focused on that. He didn't want to slip away into nothingness.

"What's going on, Victor? Tell me."

He ran his tongue against his teeth. He was sitting on a couch as Ozie held his hands. Everything else was an illusion, including the bass notes thrumming in his chest and the howling in his ears. He focused on shaping each word, fighting against the sensation of falling. "I'm here. But I'm being pulled down."

The grip on Victor's hands disappeared. He floated alone, pin-wheeling in nothingness, an insubstantial puff of air. "Don't go," he tried to shout. It sounded like a whisper.

"I'm still here," Ozie said in a voice that was muffled but close enough to provide some comfort.

A sensation settled on Victor's head, faint as a breeze, a prickling. Then, a cooling weight cascaded like water running down his back. He was solid again. The mist began to clear. Blankspace's gravity was not pulling so hard. He wanted to break away. "It's weakening."

"Don't come back completely yet," Ozie told him. "Tell me what you see." Ozie was gripping his hands again.

Victor visualized a tiny version of himself moving up and taking in the scene, a light and lithe observer. His body was poised above a dark maelstrom, where the room itself twisted and swirled, and at its center was the hole, its shape not spheroid but oblong. It had a shiny surface shot through with blood-colored cracks like lacework.

"It's an egg. Black with tiny red lines," he said.

"Do you remember the data egg?"

Blinding light shot from the darkness. The egg cracked open and exploded with the force of a supernova. Victor blinked in pain; then he was back in his body. The chasm beneath him had vanished. The room was vivid. The blankness was gone. Hands at his head, his fingers traced the curves of a device, a braincap, that rested on his head.

"Do you remember it now? The data egg?" Ozie asked.

Victor breathed and fought back rising bile. "Yes," he hissed when he could speak again. He stared daggers at Ozie. He wanted to tear off the braincap but didn't dare interrupt whatever it was doing.

Ozie, looking relieved, sat back against the cushions and rubbed his face with his human hand. "Glad I could help."

It wasn't only the fact of the data egg that had come flooding back. It was images and events piling up, smothering him. "How could I forget? Jefferson! Circe! What the Laws have I been thinking for the past few months?"

"Pretty creative avoidance tactics, actually."

"What do you mean?"

"My guess? It was ... What's the term?" Ozie huffed in frustration. "You were thinking *around* the things that hurt you. You didn't want to deal with them, so you sealed them off. You forgot anything remotely having to do with—"

"I remembered Samuel!"

"It didn't hurt you to lose him. Jefferson was different. How he went, the aftermath ... I wonder ..."

Ozie paused too long. "What?" Victor's patience was thin.

"We thought the data egg was suppressing your episodes, right? I wonder if this was a side effect, or maybe your memories didn't form properly ... no, you have them now ... maybe they were, I don't know, shunted or firewalled or something. Or maybe they had, like, a sort of common frequency, from a cognition perspective, that allowed your mind to hide them. Like a mental immune response." His expression brightened, a bright yellow manic glow. "I remember now! It's called dissociative amnesia."

Victor thought back to when the data egg opened for the last time, a memory he'd hunted for unknowingly that was now accessible, how Jefferson had cast blame on Circe for his death, the heavy weight of a legacy that Jefferson demanded Victor carry. His anger felt like a fever, radiating from his skull, crisping his skin, parching his mouth.

He looked at Ozie, remembering how they'd touched each other to short-circuit resonant episodes to channel their crazy, racing brains in the directions of arousal and orgasm. For a moment, he wanted that again. Ozie's eyes widened in recognition.

But it was too late, too pathetic. There was too little time. He'd lost months fiddling around.

"There was also my concussion," Victor said.

"That too."

"When the data egg opened," Victor said, "I ran from it. Mentally, I mean." He coughed to shake off the huskiness that had crept into his voice. "I went to bury the data egg, and then ... that's when Wonda found me. At the time, I think I remembered." He stared at Ozie, who looked relieved. "How could I forget again?"

"Look, Victor, our brains are—flexible—no, that isn't the right word. They're malleable. They change. And you and I have more experience than most trying to make that change happen, usually to stop our episodes from taking over." Ozie got up, filled a glass of water in the kitchen, and drank it while Victor watched him from the living room, feeling the distance between them as a kind of suction. "In this case, your brain responded to a trauma by trying to forget it. Buried it. A common response. It's normal."

Victor snorted. "Sure. Normal. Fuck me."

"So, was it like plugging in a memory drive?" Ozie wore a sly grin that Victor wanted to slap off him or press against with his lips.

"Yes, exactly like that," Victor said. "No, you twit. Everything was always there. The memories, the feelings. It was just … I don't know. I guess, when I got close, I didn't even know what I was close to uncovering. My brain wouldn't let me think about it. And there was so much else to keep me busy."

"Did you say you buried it?" Ozie asked.

Victor saw the urgency on Ozie's face and hesitated. He looked like he'd used to when a robot waiter at Springboard Café had set a bucket of fried pickles in front of him.

"Yes," Victor said after a moment.

"Well, let's go get it."

Victor remembered what Ozie had said earlier about the Diamond King. His short-term memory seemed to be working okay now. "You're here for him. Why does *he* want it?"

"Like I said. We're going to trade."

"For what?"

"A treatment for Broken Mirrors as miraculous as raising the dead. I'll tell you about it over lunch."

They found a corner table on a rooftop restaurant overlooking the Passage. Victor sat facing away from BioScan so he wouldn't have to be reminded of its cold hallways and rooms full of abused patients.

On the walk over, he'd removed the braincap and, thankfully, he hadn't had any sort of relapse. Hopefully, whatever change the braincap had wrought was permanent. Or maybe when truth finally manifests, there's no avoiding it.

Ozie ordered heaps of food and a pitcher of sour ale. Victor partook, eating some fried plantains and rice and slowly sipping from his glass while an erection pressed tightly against his underpants. He was glad to feel whole again. But a libido resurgence, kicking up sexy dust all around him, well, he could do without that kind of distraction.

"You said a trade. What can the King give me?"

"You know all about my braincaps already."

Victor nodded.

"Well, he's found a way to make them more effective. The research teams at his disposal, they're doing stuff I would have thought was fifty years in the future. Anyway, he's got a way to map the brain and influence cognitive states."

"Influence cognitive states? Mind control? No thanks."

"It's not like that. Not entirely. You and I know the strain of maintaining equilibrium when the slightest thing can throw us out of whack. His tech does that for you. It prevents an episode from gathering steam and going full bloom."

Victor knew that was something Personil couldn't do without damping down cognition overall. "I guess that's fine for us if it works and there are no side effects like, I don't know, loss of will, personality changes, cognitive decline. Big ifs. What about Class Ones?"

"That's where he started. It was a smart move. I won't get into all the details, but the same tech works on them, too. It stimulates their arousal centers—not erotically—don't look at me that way. I mean the other kind of arousal, basic consciousness. It fills in for deficient inhibitory circuits. The patients aren't unconscious, you know. They're dreaming."

Victor stared at Ozie, whose glasses reflected light from a window with a view of the Passage. *Dreaming?* "I can't believe that."

"Their neural activity intermittently resembles REM sleep once you've corrected for ..."

"For?"

"I'm getting ahead of myself." Ozie took a long sip, finishing his sour ale, and wiped his mouth with the back of his hand. "A few of the recovered Class Ones said it was like waking up from a dream, so that's one of the hypotheses we're looking into."

He'd always imagined MRS as a long, slow decline into catatonia, a one-way trip to blankspace, a lapse into mental nothingness. What if he was wrong? Was blankspace full of *dreams*?

Victor looked around the bar, imagining groups of recovered Class Ones hanging out, drinking, and sharing their impressions from years of dreams the rest of the world never had.

His throat constricted with emotion. He'd been puttering around at BioScan with no idea what he was dealing with, even while the problem pulsed inside his skull. Like a good friend, Ozie pointed him toward what really mattered.

Victor said, "We haven't had any Class Ones recover."

"That's why we have to help them," Ozie said. "There's some other stuff about how the tech works that needs to be explained better, even to me. But that's the gist."

"I want to see them. Talk to them if they're capable of it."

"Of course. We'll show you everything. Victor, I have to ask: what do you have here that's better?" Ozie pointed over Victor's shoulder at BioScan's buildings arrayed on the hillside, glinting in the setting sun. He knew what Ozie meant. Broken Mirrors were no better off here than they had been in SeCa. They awaited exactly the kind of cure that Ozie was promising.

Too good to be true? Probably.

Better than waiting for a miracle? Absolutely.

"All he wants in return is the data egg? Really?"

"He wants to scan you too. There's some aspect to MRS that fascinates him." Ozie glanced down at his wrist. "I wouldn't be shocked to learn that he'd been diagnosed. Half the time, I think his weird playing-card avatar is a trick to prevent excessive excitatory feedback." Ozie mimed signals bouncing between his and Victor's brows.

Victor took that in and made a mental note to ask more about that later. "And the other half the time?"

"I don't know what to think. Reclusive genius?" Ozie shrugged. "Or maybe he just decided one day to opt out of all the normal stuff because he could, and this is what's left."

"And that is?"

"Really. Weird. Shit."

While Ozie sat at the bar on the east side of the Petite Canal ordering drinks and flirting with the tall, muscular bartender, Victor walked the restaurant's perimeter while repeatedly tapping his MeshBit to request a connection to Pearl. The hole in his memory was gone, and in addition to scenes from the past few months returning, confidence filled him. There was a problem to be solved, and he was on it, not flapping around in a hurricane of indecision and confusion. It was like biting the apple, bit by bit consuming chunks of sweet, nourishing fruit. The MRS patients needed experimental treatments to recover; Class Twos and Threes could opt-in, no problem, but the Class Ones? Patients were supposed to provide consent, but they were locked in. They would want

Cody Sisco

the treatment. Of course, they would. Anything was better than being trapped in some horrific dream state while their bodies languished. But how does a comatose person indicate consent? Maybe there was a way to reach inside their minds using Ozie's tech or the Diamond King's tricks. Maybe the problem had already been solved.

His MeshBit pinged. "Pearl, you finally picked up!" The smile that came to his face was fierce with delayed gratification. "Ozie is here to—"

"Ozie? Tell him to stuff himself. Other than that, I've got nothing to say to him." She was probably in SeCa, maybe Carmichael, attending to the small details of an opted-out life, no more drama to contend with. Victor was grateful she answered his call.

"No, hear me out. He said he has some new technology that could help patients with MRS. Some kind of braincap stimulation. We tried taking them off Personil, but we don't know if it's working. It probably isn't. He agreed to share his tech in exchange for the data egg. I give him the egg; he gives us braincaps and algorithms or whatever. We start to recover the patients' minds. It's okay, right? The data egg was Jefferson's obsession. It's not my obligation. I'm not tricking myself into thinking this is a better deal than it is, am I?"

Pearl cleared her throat. "After all that he's done, you still trust Ozie?"

"Not about everything, but about this, yes. There's only one thing he cares about besides his gadgets, and that's fixing MRS." *And maybe getting naked with me.* Victor reddened. This wasn't the time to consider his sexual prospects. All that had to wait. He was on the cusp of finally breaking through to a cure. His body thrummed with anticipation, a feeling he mistrusted.

He asked Pearl, "What do you think should I do?"

"Hold your breath."

"Huh?"

"And rub your tummy. Oh, and stand on one leg. These ancient secrets were passed down by warrior monks who could fly."

He pictured her bitter, toothy smile and the creases around her flinty eyes as clearly as if she were standing in front of him. "Thanks, Pearl, you're a real help."

"You're coming to learn what life is all about. There are no good options."

"So? What? Am I supposed to do nothing?"

"That's another bad option, in my opinion. Victor, you already know what I'm going to say."

He sighed, thinking back to her lectures about not fighting the ways of the world. "Let the future emerge."

"Exactly. It's more difficult than it sounds. And Victor?"

"Yes?"

But the connection had dropped.

The sound of a chair screeching brought Victor back. Ozie lurched to standing and staggered slightly as he walked over, a half-full glass of brown liquid in his gloved hand. Too much to drink. Victor scanned the bar for some water.

Ozie asked, "How's my darling Pearl?"

"I don't think she likes what you've been getting up to."

"That's hypocritical of her for multiple reasons. Our path chooses us, she would say, or some other guru bullshit. My path is as good as any other. Are you ready? Where are we going?"

"Yes. The Estate. I buried the data egg in the garden," he said.

"Well, this won't be the first time you exhume something of Jefferson's."

Victor looked at him for a moment, shocked, then grinned at the hideous joke, remembering when Tosh had helped him crack open the family tomb and the disgusting, necessary thing he'd done to get proof that Jefferson had been murdered. "Does the King still have the tongue?"

"It's safe," Ozie said.

"Good. I'm not done with Circe yet."

Outside the bar on the street, Victor hailed an autocab with his MeshBit. A minute later, the vehicle swung into view, rolled to a stop, and they got in. They crossed the Petite Canal into the main part of town just south of Triton's Deep Crossing and headed west. The journey became a slow crawl through narrow streets and across six or seven islands until they turned right, crossed the Grand Canal, and accelerated as the autocab joined the highway. Victor was aware of Ozie's proximity, the rise and fall of his chest. He wanted to snuggle up and see if any spark remained of the fire they'd once shared. Later, perhaps; for now, it was enough that they weren't at odds.

As they crossed the highway bridge over the Passage, Ouachita Dam was visible as a leaden eyebrow to their right. Soon, they exited the highway and traveled well-maintained gravel lanes, arriving at the gate to the Eastmore Estate. Victor got out and approached one of the tall rock pillars that supported a pair of burnished steel slabs of the gate. He proved his identity via voice print, retinal scan, and breath analysis. The gate hinged open away from them.

Leafy elm trees whispered and cast shadows like dark lace across the road. The buzz of insects sustained a disorienting intensity. Dampness and rot, not unpleasant in their subtle, intermittent wafting, cast him back into the past. He recalled kicking up leaves, scampering around bushes, screaming with joy to find refuge in the forest, away from all the emotional storms conjured by Eastmore reunions: his parents moping around, Auntie Circe leading a false-charm brigade with Robbie as her main cheerleader and fiercest defender, Granfa Jeff and Granma Cynthia holding court with wave after wave of distinguished visitors, and Great-Granma Florence surveying everything with a cool eye until finding a sensitive spot to sear with a hot poker of scorn.

He lingered at the gate, taking in a view of the grounds. Memories of Victor's visit to bury the data egg were hazy. He'd been so upset, shunting in and out of blankspace, returning to realspace only to ensure the job got done and Granfa Jeff's data egg was buried and forgotten. A job too well done, really. And now the past came crashing back.

Breathing deep to regain his bearing, Victor returned to the car, letting it take them the rest of the way.

A kilometer up the drive, the mansion loomed. Its parapets and gables always gave the impression of a root vegetable that didn't know when to stop growing. Victor climbed out and rushed away from the car. Granfa Jeff's last words and intent were buried in the cool dirt, a hard lump in fertile loam. A mystery the ants and beetles and worms contentedly ignored. It hadn't been a mistake to try to let Granfa's secrets go. But it had been futile. The past always clawed its way into the present. Maybe now he could be more objective, less teetering on the edge of insanity. Or maybe that was wishful thinking. He started brushing leaves and detritus aside with his hands. He wanted to hear Granfa Jeff's voice again.

Ozie was looking at Victor with a twinge of pity. That hadn't changed. There he goes, flailing, unprepared, to the brink. There was no hope for him to have a normal life. "I know what you're thinking," Victor said. He nodded toward the cyberarm. "You too, buddy. We're both complete messes. You want to help me dig with that?"

Ozie looked down. "I'd rather not. It's not the most hygienic thing to have an arm made of synthflesh, plastic, metal, and tubes covered in dirt. There's got to be a shovel around here somewhere." He went to look.

The dirt hadn't compacted much. Victor was able to scoop it with his hands. "Got it," he said as he grabbed the half-buried box, wrested it free, and put it on his lap. He opened the lid and blinked. He recoiled, almost swooned, rocking forward and back, a trail of syllables dribbling from his lips, intensifying, repeating a string of "No, no, no, no, no."

He beat the ground with his fists.

Ozie trampled a few ragged, picked-over tomato plants, getting closer.

The box was empty.

"Is this the right—"

"Yes, it's the right fucking box! Someone took it."

"You're sure you didn't—"

"Someone took it!" Victor tossed the box into the dirt. A moment later, he picked the box up and dusted it off. "I put it here, buried it, and—and ..." He sighed. "I can't be sure I haven't been back when I was blank. Shocks!" The fact that after he'd recovered so many memories, some things were still hidden from him galled like nothing else could.

"Who else could have it?" Ozie asked.

Victor looked around at the neglected garden. "How should I know? Tosh. Wonda. Maybe Circe took it. Jefferson's message accused her of poisoning him. Maybe she tossed it in an incinerator."

He shook his head, disgusted at the paths his meandering life took. How perfectly in character to have to chase a data egg mystery yet again? He wouldn't do it. He wouldn't walk that path again. But then what would happen to all the Broken Mirrors?

"Wait." Another memory scratched at his brain, this one fairly recent. "I haven't seen Tosh in a while because he's busy helping the refugees. And Circe is somewhere in Europe. But Wonda was acting strange the last time I saw her. She said, 'You'll be back when you figure it out.'"

He looked at Ozie, who nodded. "Let's go see."

Victor took a deep breath. "Laws. Okay. Let's go. She better not make trouble."

21

Mesh Journalist: You endured three days of confinement at the hands of people who believed in falsehoods and were willing to use violence to achieve political ends. How are you holding up?

Mía Barrias: This wasn't my first rodeo. No further comment.

—Mesh interview with Mía Barrias

16 May 1992
Oroville, Semiautonomous California

Mía was a few meters away from the exit doors of the Classification Commission's Class One facility in Oroville when her MeshBit chimed to announce a new message. Not halting her steps, she raised the device and then groaned as she read the message, stopping with a final click of her shoes echoing on the tiles.

The message from Karine read, *Big problem. Another set of missing patients. The third this month. Are you still at the facility? Can you look?*

Fantastic. All Mía wanted was a hot bath and the bottle of red wine in her hotel room. A single glass wouldn't suffice, not after this waste of a day poking around a dismal facility full of comatose bodies and individuals with severe MRS who had no idea the journey they would soon embark on thanks to BioScan. And she hadn't been able to stop herself, couldn't be bothered to stay sober since the train incident. Bunch of amateur vigilantes. Good for nothing but trouble, muddying the waters of a complex situation. She was sure they'd been fed a pack of lies. It was as pathetic as it was dangerous: gullible, Mesh-dependent kids with nothing better to do were caught in the misinformation maelstrom coming from the Organized Western States. Diamond dust scoured everything in its path. At least she'd been able to set the kids straight. The fey one with the pink hair had added her to their contacts as "Mia, hostage-mom," and she had three unread messages from them.

Karine's message demanded a response first. The only thing worse than remaining in the facility now would be having to come back tomorrow. Then she would miss the train to Oakland and need to stay in the SeCa hinterlands for another night.

She looked at Karine's message and sighed. The previous set of missing patients had led to rioting. That could not happen again.

She dictated her reply, "I was on my way out. Guess I should rethink my plans?"

The MeshBit chimed almost immediately. *Sorry to extend your stay. We need you to recheck the numbers. How many patients were transferred? Sending records now. Seven are missing.*

"Let's get this over with," Mía said aloud. Looking around, she was thankful the lobby was empty. She'd already exited the secure area. Through the glass doors of the atrium, she could see pine trees with their limbs sagging from drought, fountain grass on the verge of turning brown, and granite boulders so slick they seemed to have been wrapped in plastic. Her gaze lingered. Outside, there was heat, fresh air laden with the scent of pine needles, and freedom. Inside were decrepitude, corruption, and endings. Visitors, the few that ever came, would wait in the exact spot where she stood until someone arrived to escort them inside, perhaps warning them about what they might see, perhaps not. The employees, if they had ever been outraged to play a role in the mistreatment of their fellow citizens, now seemed resigned and beaten down. And, of course, they were all indoctrinated into the worldview of Semiautonomous California's Cathar-derived morality. Good people deserved justice, and bad people deserved punishment. The state's duty was to protect good people from bad people. The Classification Commission encoded this dynamic within its mandate, and "safety first" was the motto. Good people were protected from the bad people, Broken Mirrors, who suffered the consequences of a madman's actions decades ago: The newest, starkest example of a caste system since abolition and the Permanent Enlightenment.

Mía sighed to herself and returned her attention to the present. Seven missing patients. She needed to find out what happened.

After a glance at the grim hallway leading to the secure area, she sat down. Unfurling her MeshBit's screen, she pulled up the datafeed Karine was sending. BioScan recorded the number of patients from each facility scheduled for transfer, in transit, or arrived at the New Venice campus. These matched the official Classification Records that Mía called up. That was all fine. Except it wasn't the same as what she remembered.

She and Karine went over the figures during a vidchat three nights ago after reviewing the mission status report that confirmed the rumor was true and the previous missing patients had, in fact, disappeared. The Oroville facility had already transferred twenty patients, she recalled. The Classification Commission and BioScan numbers listed only thirteen patients.

She wanted to call Karine and ask her how this could be, but Karine had already essentially posed the question to Mía. It was now her job to find out. Groaning as she lowered her tensed shoulders down from her ears, Mía headed toward the doors that would take her back into the facility. This place messed with her equilibrium. She couldn't decide what was worse: the all-too-human reeks that were barely concealed by bleach odors, the incoherent moans of patients cursed with not having yet fallen completely insensate, or the knowledge that she was if not totally responsible at least substantially responsible for all this misery. Her minor discomfort and inconveniences weren't much atonement in the grand scheme. With Samuel Miller dead, her pain and suffering had eased, leaving a gap into which a seed had wedged itself like a green spurt of growth in a cracked sidewalk, and now it had sprouted leaves of guilt. Her life was penance; she demanded it be so; she couldn't have lived with herself otherwise. She would go in, solve the problem, and later the bottle of wine by her bed would serve as the aperitif to whatever portion of a bottle of bourbon she could finish before she passed out.

At the door, she buzzed herself back in, saw the attendant's puzzled face, explained curtly, "A few more records to check," and clacked onward. A brief stop at the computer at the nurse's station confirmed the numbers she expected to find: thirteen patients transferred. It left a cold numbness in her belly. How could BioScan and the Classification Commission make the same error by accident? The answer was that they couldn't. It must have been done on purpose. By whom and for what reason, Mía was more than a little curious. Frankly, she was starting to obsess. She continued into the facility, passing through a wing of silent bodies on cots attended only by beeping headboard monitors and the warm glow of lightstrips dialed to a twilight rose color.

When she reached the records room, it was empty of people, as expected for this late in the day. She found a drawer where files were stored for patients no longer cared for. The bulk were patients who had "expired." Although soon, hopefully, they would be outnumbered by transfers. In the recent transfers section, she found what she expected. She marveled at the audacity of the crime and the perpetrator's astonishing stupidity. There were twenty records for twenty patients. Only thirteen of them had arrived in New Venice. Somewhere during the journey from the Long Valley to the transfer facility on the outskirts of Bayshore, over the Sierra Nevadas, along a good length of the iron rails and concrete aqueduct of the Cold Nile Miracle, all the way to Las Vegas and then arcing northeast on the road to New Venice, seven MRS patients had vanished. Someone had altered two sets of digital records to hide the crime, leaving these paper records untouched. The altered digital records would have gone unnoticed if Karine wasn't Karine. She paid painstaking attention to anything she put her mind to, most recently the removal of Broken Mirrors from the care of the SeCa Classification Commission and their remainder to BioScan. Who took the trouble to alter electronic records and leave these physical ones untouched?

Footsteps in the hall approached. Mía stood, holding the files to her chest protectively.

A middle-aged male technician entered the room, carrying himself in the comically awkward and dainty way of someone sneaking around. The technician squeaked when he saw Mía.

"What are you doing here?" they both said at once.

The man looked her up and down, and his eyes widened in recognition. "Mía Barrias," he whispered.

Mía smiled, suffused with the familiar feeling of having the upper hand. She knew what to do with meek men.

"I know what you were about to do here," she said. "We've been watching you. If you cooperate with our investigation, you can avoid criminal charges."

"I ... I was just seeing if you needed—"

"Spare me!" she snapped. She plonked the files onto the desk and dragged over a chair for the technician to sit in. She flicked her eyes between him and the chair. His expression crumbled,

Cody Sisco

which she took as a sign her hunch proved correct. He sat down on his hands and rocked slightly, the misery on his face evident. Whoever had pressured him into his abortive crime had accurately pegged him for being weak-willed.

She knew his type: solitary, vulnerable, unlucky because he didn't have the confidence and gumption to seize opportunities and make his own luck.

"Tell me about these files," she said. "Start at the beginning. Who contacted you?"

In a whispered stutter with the beginnings of tears watering his eyes, the technician said, "The Diamond King. It was the King of Las Vegas. I know it was him. He said he could help me if I did this one thing for him. But when he spoke to me, it didn't look like him. I didn't know at first what to think. I didn't know anything."

"What do you mean it didn't look like him? Who did it look like?"

"Jefferson Eastmore. It looked just like him."

An hour later, after bringing in facility security to watch over the technician and scrounging in the archives for documents, Mía returned and placed a stack of papers on the table with a loud thunk. The technician winced. He was a plum-lipped functionary who'd hidden his deed deep in the facility under a paper-thin layer of lies and continued to spin tall tales under pressure. It was unacceptable. She would squeeze the truth out of him.

She prompted him. "Tell me again. The truth this time. You say this started years ago."

"Yes. No, not really, not like now. Or, at least, not like before, with the border shut now … I don't see how it could continue even if we—they—wanted it to."

"Which we don't."

"No," he admitted. His gaze flicked to the blank vidscreen on the wall. "*We* don't. But does he?"

Mía took the top sheet from the pile, skimmed its recitation of doctored numbers, misreported actions, and missing patients, and placed it in front of the technician. "This says three patients were sent by train to Petaluma."

He shook his head. "There was no train. Imagine the hysteria. If there were Broken Mirrors on a train—"

He broke off suddenly, watching her with misery spreading across his face.

Flushed with heat, her cheeks felt like hot stones in the sun. He was probably also noticing the way her breath hitched and the sweat breaking out on her brow.

"I'm aware of what happens," she said sweetly. "I was recently reminded. People lose their lawless minds." *A mess I created*, she reminded herself. She was as responsible as Samuel with his killing and rampaging. Via her tireless campaigning, she publicized his crimes and terrorized people initially unaffected. He was ground zero, but she was the vector for a contagion of fear and trauma.

"There was never any train," he said in a pathetic whimper.

Mía silently cursed the bureaucracy spawned by her advocacy, her militancy. It was as if her strength and stridency had paradoxically created a cadre of weak-willed functionaries.

Leadership without connection was leadership in the wrong direction.

All along, she'd known that it was her pain that had spawned the Classification System; only now, looking back, did she regret the form it had taken.

"Go on," she said. This part of his story might be true, even if the rest was a transparent lie.

"A van arrived in the morning after breakfast. There were no Class Ones at that point. Only Class Twos. They could all walk, eat, and use the toilets independently. We told them they were being transferred. Not that it mattered. They were all so zonked on Personil that they did whatever they were told without complaint."

"Who drove the van?"

He stared at his shoes and mumbled, "It drove itself."

Mía hissed. Aside from seeing a few of them in the Louisiana Territories, her last encounter with such an abomination was the one that drove her into the Sacramento River at Samuel's behest. They were outlawed in SeCa. It was amazing he bothered with such offensive mendacity.

"There were a few other passengers," he went on, "for security presumably. Big guys. They took the patients, and we wiped our hands of it. Mr. Eastmore watched. He was here."

"That was the first time?"

"Yes. Two years ago."

"When was the second?"

"A year or so later. This time, he didn't come in person."

"Jefferson."

"Yes. He popped onto my screen and let me know what he was asking. Then the details arrived in my feed. When the head of an organization says, 'I want this done,' you don't question it."

Mía restrained a hand that wanted to smack his lips and deepen their plum coloring. Wine-stained? Or was she just projecting her thirst onto him? Either way, when this interrogation was over, she had a date with a bottle, preferably something velvety with a bouquet of ripe berries, tobacco, and leather.

"You perhaps should have questioned why he asked you to create a false set of records."

"Mr. Eastmore had good explanations. This was before I knew it wasn't him."

"What made you think it was the King?"

"I'm certain of it."

Again, the technician had decided to lie. To create confusion? To misdirect? Mía leaned over the table, her two hands fisted, knuckles pillars to support her weight. "I don't believe you."

It was ludicrous if what he was telling her was true.

Jefferson continued appearing on the technician's vidscreen even after he'd been interred in Oak Knoll Cemetery for months. The technician hadn't seen the obituary. When a colleague mentioned the man's death, the technician thought it was a bad joke. Until someone brought in a magazine.

She cross-examined him.

"It sounded like him," the technician said. "His voice, what he talked about. How important it was that Broken Mirrors got the care they deserved. That SeCa was abandoning its responsibility, and BioScan and the Louisiana Territories couldn't be trusted; they only wanted research subjects. That's why I should help move the Broken Mirrors to facilities in the OWS, where they would be cared for and rehabilitated, thanks to a new technology that could reverse years of neglect and wrong-headed treatment."

When the technician had asked why he was talking to a dead man, the image shifted to that of the Diamond King.

Mía stood and pinched the bridge of her nose. She was getting tired. His story wasn't changing. But there had to be something she could take to the Governor-General—something that would help them make sense of all this.

"Why do you think it was the King?"

"I said, 'You're not Jefferson Eastmore. He's dead.' The figure smiled and then *changed*. The eyes ... the eyes were the worst. Something moved in them. A shadow. In the red on black of his irises, I saw it."

Shadows. Images. Hallucinations probably. "Have you been tested for MRS?" she asked.

The technician scowled. "The King threatened to take me apart piece by piece, starting with my toenails. He said the Corps would castrate me and pour acid in my ears. Seconds later, he offered money, tickets for a cruise in the Gulf of the Americas, and a job and early retirement in the oasis in the desert. I refused. And then small things happened: my garden turned black, and the whole thing was ruined. The car I was driving shut down while I was driving on the mountain road. I could have gone over the edge! I knew then. This was real. So, I cooperated. I wanted to live.

"One day—the day I'd had enough—I said I wouldn't transfer any more patients—because of BioScan and the program shutting down, and I thought, now's not the time to pop my head up for it to get whacked off. Because I knew you were in charge of the transition, and I never would have done anything to screw things up for you."

Mía held his gaze, wearing a stony mask perfected over decades in politics while her stomach churned. Sycophantic hero worship. Goal displacement. All the signs that she'd created an organization more devoted to doing her will than to doing what was right.

"What happened when you said no?"

"He said Corps would come for me. They would amputate. Fingers. Toes. Everything. One at a time until there was nothing left. So I changed my mind again. And now ... I hope I dare to end it before he gets me."

Mía straightened. He sounded serious. As mentally ill as he probably was, this could be a serious threat of self-harm. Her job had just gotten a lot more difficult.

"I'm going to take you to Oakland."

He began to sob.

"Don't you want out of this?" she asked, trying to soften her voice. What he'd done was disgusting, but considering his mental state, she supposed he couldn't be held responsible. How very un-Cathar of her. "You're safe. We'll go by armored car."

"It's too late for me," he whispered. "It's time to go. Don't stop me."

She noticed his gaze had drifted again to the blank vidscreen, which remained blank, but why would he be staring at it with such evident fear? She blinked, realizing—*Oh, Laws!*—what if it was transmitting after all?

"Don't!" She rushed forward when she saw him remove a Skinjector from his pocket—an unconscionable oversight of the security team—and place it against his neck, but it was too late. The hiss of the pressurized cartridge emptying its load of medicine into his system was the room's only sound.

He said, "I knew this day would come."

Then, the vidscreen beeped as an image resolved into a pixelated, colorful horror—a king of diamonds playing card. The technician slumped over, his body suddenly limp.

The image spoke, "That saves some trouble."

Mía felt her knees weakening as she moved jerkily toward the door. She gripped the knob and pulled it open. "I need a medic," she shouted. She glanced back.

The Diamond King's eyes mimed interest, his gaze following her closely. The mouth gaped open, showing razor-sharp teeth. "Tell your government task force that I have agents among them. You've already failed. Tell them it's too late, but they should probably keep trying. For morale's sake."

Mía breathed in the silence. Don't engage, don't reveal anything he might use against us. *Don't be terrified*—she'd earned freedom from that, at least.

"Don't worry, Mía. I can help you. I can give you resolution to what started in Carmichael."

She closed her eyes too late. Samuel's face stared at her—not the blank Personil stupor she'd come to know so well—the other version, the one with wide rage-fueled eyes and a misshapen leer—the one he'd shown her in Carmichael.

She slipped into the hallway and shut the door, determined not to run, managing a brisk trot that barely hid her panic. An hour later, as she swigged from a bottle of bourbon, she realized that in this crisis, like in Carmichael, her role would be to sound the alarm and mobilize against a threat that no one understood. Only this time, she had allies.

22

As the autocab crested Cemetery Hill, Ozie opened the window, and the breeze raised gooseflesh on Victor's bare chest and arms. They descended through a canyon of pines. Victor was sweaty, overheated from digging, and had shed his pullover. Now the wind chilled him. He twisted and reached into the rear cabin, retrieved his garment, and pulled it over his head. Ozie didn't appear to notice. He stared out the window while his flesh hand made a fist and relaxed repeatedly.

Victor was glad to have a distraction from his turmoil. "It's going to be okay," he said, placing a hand on Ozie's shoulder.

Ozie shrugged away. "Comfort yourself," he said.

They sat in silence as the autocab crossed into Qaddo territory. The road twisted through little scrubby valleys and around hardgrass hillocks as it descended toward the mudflats. The houses and buildings visible on the plain looked like they would blow away in a strong wind.

Ozie said, "There's no poverty in the OWS, you know. There's a place for everyone."

"I think the Qaddo lands are beautiful," Victor said, "in a kind of forlorn way."

"You would," Ozie muttered.

The autocab stopped, and they got out. Gravel crunched under their shoes as Victor led Ozie to the shack where Wonda lived. He knocked. She came to the door, stretching like she'd just woken from a nap. She looked at them dull-eyed and crossly.

"What do you want?" Wonda asked.

"I know you have the data egg," Victor said.

Wonda snorted. "So, you finally remembered. Bravo. Now, scram. You're not getting it back. Tosh, look who's here."

A figure emerged from the shadows at the back of the room to stand behind Wonda. It was Tosh, smiling wolfishly. It wasn't clear whether he wanted to beat Victor up or strip him naked. "Hello, boys. Ozie, you look surprised to see me. You're never alone, you know, not ever. We're each other's contingency plans."

A wary look crossed Ozie's face. Victor wondered which part of Tosh's greeting he was reacting to.

Wonda hugged herself as she said to Tosh, "Contingency? What is that supposed to mean?"

"I knew you hid the data egg even if Mr. Forgetful didn't," Tosh said. An angry, aggrieved expression turned Wonda's face red as he continued, "You took your ball and went home. Congratulations. Now, though, you'd be smart to make a deal."

"Don't call me that again," Victor warned Tosh. "Wonda, please, you said to come back when I remembered. Well, I'm here. This is important."

"So important that it skipped your mind for the past few months? Ha ha ha." Her laughter was forced and harsh, childishly taunting. She turned to Ozie, flashed a false smile, and said, "So, the robot man fixed him, huh?"

Wonda was looking at Ozie's cyberarm with loathing. Of course. Her Human Life beliefs hadn't gone away, and now she could see a prime target.

Ozie stiffened, and Victor sensed restrained violence. Maybe it was a mistake to bring him along. Working with Ozie was like twirling a lightning rod while standing on a barren plain.

Wonda hadn't finished insulting him. "I recognize you. Freak. I hold you responsible for Samuel's murder. We saw your little drones everywhere that day."

"Spare me your lunacy," he said under his breath, then more loudly. "We're here to make an easy trade." His voice carried menace and heat and enough desperation to fill Lake Ouachita.

Victor said quickly, "He's got tech to help the Broken Mirrors recover."

"Why should I care?" Wonda said.

Faster than Victor could react, Ozie pulled open the screen door and raised his cybernetic arm, advancing on Wonda until Tosh stepped forward and blocked his way.

"Tell us where the data egg is." Ozie's voice sounded hoarse.

"Ozie!" Victor pulled him away. He turned to Wonda. "I'm sorry."

She shook her head and wore a bitter smile. "If you thought you could torture me for the truth like you tried to do to Karine, you're barking at the wrong cat."

"No, of course not," Victor said with heat on his cheeks. "It's not yours, though. You can't—"

"Samuel's brain scans are my last pieces of him," she said. "I'm not giving them up."

"What if we borrowed it?" Victor asked.

Wonda snorted again. "You think I'd trust any of you to return it?"

Victor opened his mouth, then shut it again. She had a point, even if she was a crazy-worshipping idolator. To see the data egg as a holy relic raised bile in his throat.

Tosh spoke slickly, "Much as it shames me not to be the first to resort to physical violence in any conversation, I'd suggest there's room to bargain. Victor and Ozie, you'd be satisfied with a copy, right? What can you give her in exchange? Sweeten the pot."

Victor looked at Ozie, who shrugged back at him, preoccupied with his arm. "The sky's the limit? I don't know. Name it. We'll let you keep the data egg. We just want a copy of what's inside."

She yawned. "I already have the data egg."

Shocks! What will it take to remove her from my life forever?

"Wait," Victor said. "You don't want to live here anymore, right? You want out. We can find a place where you and the Human Lifers can live independently." Victor looked at Ozie to confirm it.

Ozie nodded.

Wonda appeared to consider how much she could demand. "Okay. Land," she said. "And money. And guarantees that we won't be bothered. Security, and not the security that keeps you locked in, the kind that keeps people like you out."

"The Diamond King can do all that," Ozie said.

"I need unbreakable assurances, too. A declaration of good faith. A public declaration. Nothing that can be rescinded quietly."

Ozie stiffened. "He never goes back on an agreement."

Victor wondered whether that was true and whether Ozie was a fool to believe it.

"One more thing." Wonda smiled. Her zealous fervor was returning. It was like watching a butterfly emerge: fascinating and gross at the same time. "We all go together to Las Vegas," she said.

"On it," Ozie said, turning away with his head bent over his arm.

"Why all of us?" Victor asked.

"The more people are witnesses, the less likely he is to disappear me. I know who we're dealing with. I lived in the OWS for two years after my dad died. I even met him once."

"You met him?" Tosh asked. Someone who didn't know him well wouldn't have heard the deep skepticism in his voice, but Victor did.

"Yes. He arranged for me to finish school. Education is important to him. Let's go. I'll grab a few pairs of clothes and then—"

"Wait a minute," Victor interrupted. "I'm not going anywhere right now. My parents are expecting me at the Estate."

Wonda's predatory smile would have looked at home on Tosh's face. "Make it plus three. Nonnegotiable."

Her eagerness made Victor wary, but he was tired of fighting. "Fine," he said.

"Okay, here's a preliminary agreement that says we'll meet and negotiate in good faith. There's nothing irrevocable here. Your costs of travel are covered, and your time is compensated." Ozie sent each of their MeshBits a document that named a contract administrator Victor had never heard of: Zac Willowby.

"Who's that?"

"A Corps captain," Ozie explained. "The King doesn't ever get involved legally. In anything. Ever. As far as I can tell."

"What guarantee do I have that you all aren't setting me up? Besides not telling you where the data egg is?" Wonda asked.

"Read the contract."

They all took a moment to read through the details. There were safeguards and collateral specified, duties assigned, countermeasures, and fail-safes. It looked enforceable and proper.

"Approved," Victor said to his MeshBit.

"I'll need to run this by a lawyer." Wonda looked at each of them, cleared her throat, and smiled. "Meanwhile, what's being served for dinner?"

Cody Sisco

23

Semiautonomous California was an idyllic oasis for the upper caste and an alluring mirage that trapped everyone else in a cesspit of degradation.

—Robbie Eastmore, *Another World* (transmission date unknown)

16 May 1992
New Venice, The Louisiana Territories

Mía took the train up Long Valley and worried about lives wasted. "Forever cursed be Samuel Miller's name," she whispered. It was a familiar feeling: devastating loss had been part of her identity for more than two decades. What was different now was that she was to blame. Feeling sympathy for Broken Mirrors was a new challenge, a new capability that she was still getting used to.

The Diamond King had taken the MRS patients. Where were they now? And what was happening to them?

Her brief exultation at discovering the crime had quickly turned to panic as the situation unraveled. The technician's death was a loss, but he'd revealed something groundbreaking. The Diamond King was able to manipulate video imagery capable of fooling everyone. He could interrupt, intercept, and corrupt every message. They had to second-guess everything. The Governor-General needed to know about the threat to national security, which meant no more Mesh-enabled communications, and they had to put protections in place to secure their correspondence. They would have to pass messages to each other using a courier.

The farms in Long Valley created a patchwork of green grass in a sea of brown, nurtured by a web of canals that ushered water from the foothills and deep-sunk wells that drained the aquifer below and caused the land to settle and sink. The train tracks were monitored and maintained as best possible, but speeds were limited for safety reasons.

An illusion of safety, to be sure. *We're all at risk*, Mía thought. The world is changing, and we can't see the seismic shifts underway until the earth opens under our feet.

The technician's story bothered her on multiple levels, but especially the report that the Diamond King impersonated Jefferson. Gooseflesh rose on her arms and legs, and a chill clutched her heart. Would the technician have recognized the deception if he hadn't learned that Jefferson died? Had Mía ever had a vidchat with the Diamond King or one of his minions in disguise? Such a thing had never crossed her mind before. The possibilities and paranoia raised by this feat were staggering. If nothing digital could be trusted, then hope would become a scarce and precious resource.

Her briefcase sat on the table in her passenger cubicle. Inside was her MeshBit. But was it secure? She should call the Governor-General's office and ask his staff chief to set up a meeting with a cybersecurity official. Would the Diamond King be listening in? She kept her hands clasped in her lap, squeezing, spasming, clammy things that felt like she was holding eels desperate to return to the water.

The Diamond King had impersonated Jefferson briefly and then abandoned the disguise. Why? He hadn't spun a tale to trick the technician into thinking the death had been staged, that there had been a coverup, and that Jefferson was alive and well in the OWS. Mía would understand that strategy. This was something else, a bizarre, frightening, world-upending fact that didn't seem to fit anywhere. She should go directly to Oakland and start what would likely be a cumbersome, lengthy investigation and counter-operation of cyberwarfare.

Maybe that was the point: to throw her off the scent of the missing patients. If so, the King didn't know her very well. She wasn't a one-trick pony or a one-track thinker.

She opened the briefcase, took out her MeshBit, and dictated a message. "Jean-Pierre, it's Mía. I'll be in Tahoe in three hours and would love to meet for dinner or lunch tomorrow, if you're available. There's something I'd like your help with. A frog startled me."

With the MeshBit returned to the briefcase, Mía sat back and rubbed her temples. Let the Diamond King listen in and try to interpret their codewords. Pierre would get the message, she hoped, and clear his calendar to meet with her. This would be a

Cody Sisco

pen-and-paper conversation, key details shared in writing and then burned while they caught up on each other's lives. Some things couldn't be said digitally, not when someone might be listening.

The fields became sparser, replaced by hillsides planted with orchards and vineyards. Eventually, these receded and the view closed in, blocked by forests of pines, some looking tired, brittle, brown, and dry. She dozed, rocking with the train's movement and dreaming of faces that shifted and eyes shining in darkness.

Mía's hotel room looked out at streetlights along the contours of the mountains around Tahoe Lake. Floating amusement platforms and lodging and gambling boats churned the waters. The Lake Tahoe basin was SeCa's second most populous urban area after Oakland & Bayshore, and it was a distant second, too. She wished she was home, but Pierre had said this was the only opportunity to meet in the next three weeks. What Mía had to tell him couldn't wait.

They were all under threat from a new vulnerability, the true scope and scale of which was unknown, and what little she knew chilled her worse than standing naked outside during a winter storm. The Sierra Nevadas and the distance to rival population centers meant that SeCa's strategy of aligning with Europe while pursuing an isolationist agenda had worked. The nation was relatively untroubled by global events. The main challenge was resettling refugees from the Great Asian War, which, although unfortunate for the refugees themselves, was a manageable problem, in political terms, if not humanitarian ones. The party in power believed that security trumped altruism and that refugees had no place in proper SeCa society, so resettlement camps proliferated at the boundaries of civilized SeCa areas. Never mind the security threat posed by tens of thousands of desperate and impoverished freedom-seekers. SeCa knew how to handle that problem. It was shameful, but it was stable.

This new threat struck at the stability of caste-based social relations. What if you couldn't trust the images on your MeshBit? What if the image you saw was not real? What if reality and fiction were indistinguishable? The workings of government had come to rely on digital communications. If those were vulnerable, all of the government was vulnerable. What's worse, having had no clue that this would become a problem, they had no strategy for how to respond. They would end up working out a plan in real time, and that was always dangerous.

And behind it all, a potentially belligerent neighbor with access to vast financial and material resources. The populations of SeCa and OWS, if the official statistics could be trusted, were roughly evenly matched. Could those statistics be trusted? Could anything?

Laws! This is too much!

She'd signed herself up for an arduous task, and she couldn't shift the blame to anyone else. Moving the Broken Mirrors out of SeCa was never going to be easy, but she hadn't signed up for a shadow war of espionage and subterfuge. Could she walk away and let it all crumble?

Abandoning a cause wasn't in her nature. She needed to task Pierre with the national security stuff so she could get back to the MRS stuff, finish freeing Broken Mirrors from the trauma box she'd created, and finally right her wrongs.

Mía pulled on a coat, left her hotel room, and went to the hotel bar. The summer/autumn transition meant that most tourists and families were gone, and she had the place to herself. She ordered a bourbon and ginger and an apple salad with chèvre.

She was on her third drink and feeling more than a touch maudlin when Pierre found her and swept her into a warm hug.

"It's been too long," he said, meeting her eyes. "You've had a rough time lately, I can see."

"There's no hiding anything from you."

"I hope not!" he said, smiling.

He took his position as the governor's chief of state secrets very seriously, and he'd been instrumental in organizing the transfer of MRS patients. He'd debriefed her immediately following the hostage situation in Bayshore. He was extremely competent. She couldn't imagine someone more suited to help counter this new threat. Perhaps it might not come as a shock.

"Get a drink," she said. "You're going to need it."

It was a shock. Somehow, word of a destabilizing new digital technology had not reached him until now, and she could tell he was struggling to absorb the information. After a half hour of hushed discussion at the bar, including all the right questions from Pierre, they received another round of drinks and moved to a pair of chairs in front of a fireplace made of large stones. She masked the wobble in her step and decided not to finish this drink too quickly.

"We need different methods to communicate," she said as she sat down.

He looked thoughtful for a moment, then said, "It'll have to be paper-based, people-based. We'll rely on vetted couriers, at least at first, until we can determine how to safeguard our MeshBits. Maybe the Europeans have a counterstrategy. We'll come up with something."

He gazed into the fire that warmed their alcove and powdered them with scents of hickory and ash. He was lost in thought.

"What is it?" Mía asked.

"I can't fault myself for not discovering this. It's out of the blue. But my counterparts in Europe have got to be aware of this. And they didn't see fit to share the information. That's worrisome."

"Hazard a guess why?"

"They're planning a response we won't like." He shook his head, frowning grimly. "It doesn't bear speculating about. Not while we know so little."

"If I thought for a minute that you could stop thinking about these things, I never would have suggested you join the Governor-General's team."

"I'm thankful for that." He smiled, looking her over in a way that was familiar and welcome. "I'm sure I'll be lying awake at night. I could use some company."

She returned his smile in double. "You're right. It has been too long."

In the morning, feeling if not rested then at least more lubricated, she made her way to the east end of the Tahoe Tunnel at the SeCa-OWS border. A half hour later she observed an MRS patient transfer and inspected their records, taking careful notes. All patients were accounted for.

Six hours later, after she'd returned home and was contemplating her next move and the half-bottle of grenache on the coffee table, a courier from Pierre arrived with a message. The MRS patients she'd seen off at the border had gone missing, as had their escorts. The abduction occurred out in the open, in daylight. Things were escalating. She got up and poured the bottle down the kitchen sink and pounded her palm against the counter. She was ready for a fight, but damn, the odds didn't look good.

24

The border is closed. Attempts to cross will be repelled with force. You will be turned away. Semiautonomous California citizens abroad are urged to contact their consular officials to register their location and receive updates about this unfolding situation.

—Semiautonomous California Mesh advisory notice (15 May 1992)

16 May 1992
New Venice, The Louisiana Territories

The Eastmore Estate's sitting room held several notable collections from famous Louisiana Territories theatrical set designers. Someone in the family with a discerning eye, possibly Florence herself, had made vastly disparate styles blend into one harmonious-though-hodgepodge tableaux.

Victor's parents sat on a paisley-patterned couch with their various limbs intricately intertwined among their found family, though they disentangled and stood when they saw Victor. He made a vague introduction for Wonda. Tosh had met Linus and Linda years ago. Why Victor hadn't ever been introduced to Tosh while Granfa Jeff was alive, he couldn't say, but it probably had something to do with shady dealings. Ozie, of course, knew the Eastmores well from when he and Victor were roommates at university. Thankfully, Ozie's cyberarm was hidden under a long-sleeved sweater and glove. Victor worried about what would happen over dinner and hoped that Ozie would keep his gloves on and no one would ask about them. Voluntary amputation and bionic enhancements weren't entirely appropriate dinner table conversation.

Circe managed the staff, who prepared the meal and set the dining room table. Victor supposed she had nothing to gain by poisoning additional family members—she already controlled the family business thanks to her stealthy assassination of Jefferson. He only hoped she was satisfied with her ill-gotten gains and not hungry for more death.

Of course, now that Victor remembered what she'd done, a truth confirmed by Jefferson's posthumous message from the data egg, it begged the question: what would he do about it?

Circe's dark curls, pulled taut and away from her broad forehead by a headband, escaped toward the back of her head and fell across her shoulders. Taut, too, were her cheekbones. She looked thin, ailing. Her eyes pulsed blackly like they were trying to parse a night without stars.

He would do nothing, for now, maybe not ever. The time for it had most likely passed. Even if he could re-secure the proof that Circe poisoned Jefferson, would his family ever believe him? Would anyone else? And if he was believed, then what? The idea of BioScan's responsibilities falling fully on his shoulders was enough to twist his stomach into knots like a balloon animal.

Linda approached Circe, and they entered a discussion that didn't look pleasant, judging by the frowns on both their faces. Victor's ma returned to the couch, sitting bolt upright and scowling. A propensity for relaxation didn't come easily to anyone in the family.

Wonda leaned over and whispered in Victor's ear. "Your mom's a looker."

Mouth agape, he looked at Wonda and realized from her arched eyebrows that she was deliberately trying to annoy him. He breathed out and muttered, "Too bad for you she has her hands full." Linda had intertwined her fingers with his fa and their two new mates.

"I guess a polyamorous inclination runs in the family," Wonda said.

Victor pressed his lips together. Her comment crossed the line. Victor didn't have a poly inclination. He'd been taken advantage of. "Don't kid yourself. You're a predator."

Her eyes narrowed, smugly, he thought. "A wolf? Me?" she said. "Too bad I'm leading sheep." She nodded at Ozie and Tosh.

"Yeah," he scoffed, "we three sheep be."

Now that she brought it up, though, the three of them—Victor, Ozie, and Tosh—were probably some of the toughest men there were, not in terms of machismo and brutishness, but in the tempered iron sense that they had all three been through extensive trials and trauma. "Actually, Wonda," he whispered, "I'm feeling better about this trip already."

Wonda scrutinized him, evidently trying to gauge whether he was being sarcastic. Before she rendered a verdict, the front doorbell rang, and she used that distraction to stalk toward Tosh with a determined look on her face. Alia and Torsten entered the room and made the rounds, saying hello, shaking hands, and dispensing hugs. Alia wore an eye-catching yellow-and-blue sari, while Torsten, in his sleek silver suit and manicured beard, looked like a massive, sexy space Viking. They gave Victor brief shoulder squeezes, which didn't bother him at all, something he would need to puzzle over another time.

Alia tensed when she recognized Tosh and Wonda. Though she did politely say hello, Victor was sure she'd rather not be in the same room with the people who'd taken her clinic hostage. His skin began to crawl. Why couldn't he leave behind the people who caused him harm? Why was he flypaper for abusers?

After a moment of exquisitely awkward small talk, Alia took Victor aside.

He tried to forestall a discussion of the hostage crisis. "If you're thinking of discussing what happened after you-know-who—"

"No, Victor, it's not about that. I've been reviewing the scans of the new MRS patients. Ozie showed me where to look. There's something odd I don't understand."

Victor didn't like that Ozie had been talking with Alia behind his back, but petty jealousy wasn't something he could afford to indulge in. "I'm not sure I can help. You're the neuroimaging expert. I'm the one with the advanced math skills and the odd brain."

"Very odd," she said, albeit lightly. Then she frowned. "There's a peculiar pattern that showed up in the neurograms of some of the patients, a similarity that—to be frank—shouldn't be there."

"Why not?"

"It's *too* similar. I can't see it spontaneously arising. There's a coordination among their neural states that—if someone explained it to me, I would say it isn't possible. There must be some error. I thought perhaps it was a data artifact in the scanner itself. But I can't find one."

"Doesn't mean it's not there," he said, growing more curious. "You seem rattled."

"I am. Maybe. I don't know. I'm simply exhausted. Maybe I'm not thinking clearly. But I don't think so."

"Alia, you shouldn't let the patients affect you like—"

"They're not affecting me! I mean, that's not what's keeping me up at night."

He took a step back from the heat of her anger. She ran a hand down her face, seeking composure. He noticed the deep breath she took in. Something was weighing on her.

"What is it?"

"It's not just one thing," she seethed. "Laws, I'd be thankful if it was."

"We're friends, right? You can talk to me," Victor said.

She let out a long breath. "Torsten's brother went missing a while back and—"

Ozie came over and interrupted. "He's in Las Vegas. Anders is. I heard you talking."

Alia stared at him, narrowing her eyes, trying to judge whether he was friend or foe.

Good luck with that, Victor thought.

Ozie said, "I also heard you say something about coordinated states. Victor, I can clue you in *later*."

Alia smoothed her headscarf. "Anders is a risk taker. He's been addicted to stims for months. I think he's searching for a purer, more potent high. We'd be so grateful if you could help bring him back."

Victor could inform Alia that he was going to Las Vegas. He could comfort her and tell her that he would ask about Anders and try to bring him home. But he kept silent, wary of all the questions and discussions that might otherwise ensue.

Mercifully, the dinner bell rang. They moved into the dining room and were seated around a long table that fit their group of sixteen—a few local family friends had arrived in the last few minutes—with ten more seats to spare. The weight of heavy-handled silver-lead cutlery, dishes that were dense ceramic slabs, cast-iron serving trays, and massive glass vases sprouting entire gardens that could collapse the table. But toddler Victor had escaped once or twice from his seat to wander the leg-dense thicket below and noticed the table's sturdy understory. It would survive for eons.

Florence, the pale, knobbly-knuckled, and liver-spotted matriarch, stood at the head of the table as the first course was brought in and thanked them all for gracing her with their company. Victor wondered how many more of these dinners she would see. Small and frail, wrinkled as crumpled paper, he hoped it was many more. With a sudden and unexpected dismay, he realized that she was the family member he cared for the most and had to swallow and rub his eyes to keep emotion from overwhelming him. He wasn't good at dealing with loss and shouldn't allow himself to feel things about events that hadn't happened yet.

Bowls of mushroom soup arrived. As the first clinks of spoons on ceramic sounded, Circe raised her voice and said, "So, Torsten, I hear your election campaign is ramping up."

Never one to miss the subtext or be embarrassed by success, Torsten replied with a broad smile, "It is indeed. There's a certain official in Oklahoma City who may not be too happy about it."

Victor looked around, clueless as to who he was referring to.

Alia, sitting across the table, caught his glance. "The health commissioner," she said quietly to him. "She's unhappy that someone from her own party is running against her for the LTs council seat she'd hoped she could retire into."

Victor thought, what a luxury it was to coast to victory, and what an upset to have the privileges of incumbency disrupted. Torsten must have confidence to spare to be so unconcerned with upending his own party's machinations. Victor glanced Torsten's way, noticing his sad-man sexy eyes, lush brown hair, and thick lips, and the way other diners' gazes were pulled his way. No doubt that's where his confidence came from.

Alia said to the table more loudly, "It's good to see that violating ethics has consequences. She can't continue to withhold money just because she'd rather see stim addicts suffer. I don't doubt that charges will be brought against her by the end of the year. We're optimistic."

Victor admired her boldness, intelligence, and poise in speaking against corruption. She and Torsten were good people, and they deserved more happiness and ease. He resolved to look for Anders in Los Vegas. Maybe the Diamond King could help with that too.

He wondered glumly, *If I add that to my list of asks, what debt will I incur?*

"Careful. The election is still more than a month away," Karine said in response to Alia. "Things could change."

"I'm not counting my chickens yet," Torsten said, "but it certainly makes planning for a policy change advisable."

Victor could see the remark hit home. Torsten had been vocal about requiring more oversight of private clinics like BioScan's in exchange for additional funding.

"Speaking of next year," Linus said. "We're planning a vacation to the Hawaiian Kingdom." He described the cruise ship and accommodations, eliciting interested questions from the New Venice contingent. It's funny that Victor hadn't seen before how the cares and worries of the downtrodden failed to grab his father's attention. But talking about a vacation brought him to life. More than anyone else in the family, Linus seemed to have adapted to the mores of Semiautonomous California. In contrast, the rest, having traveled more and seen more, cared more about other people's lives and would rather talk about real problems and possible solutions. No doubt he was the submissive member of the polycule. His fa went on about the cruise, and Victor didn't have to work hard to tune him out. The disconnect between what occupied Victor's mind and his fa's couldn't be bridged. He looked again at his parents. He ran away once, but it wasn't really his choice. He was forced to go. Now, he wondered if he regretted that distance or whether letting them drift further away was wiser. Whenever he shared what he really thought with them, they always found a way to disapprove, second-guess, and keep him from feeling in any way capable of running his own life. The sad part was that they were probably mostly right about that.

He shook himself. *Stop the negative self-talk.* He was plenty capable of dealing with extraordinary circumstances better than they might. And, at the very least, he cared about other people. That was new. It was a sign of his personal development that, as flawed as could be, he was not wholly self-absorbed.

His spoon clattered loudly against the bottom of the bowl as frustration welled up, clouding his thoughts and momentarily eclipsing his focus.

He didn't have to go to Las Vegas; he could choose to stay in New Venice. Instead, he was choosing altruism. He would help the Broken Mirrors. He would help find Torsten's brother. He would help Karine and Circe to turn around BioScan's fortunes. And if, by going to Las Vegas, he were to discover the truth behind MRS, that would be worth everything and more.

Victor tuned into the dinner table discussion again when Torsten mentioned the Organized Western States. The main dishes had arrived and were half-consumed.

Torsten obviously and deliberately avoided looking at Tosh and Wonda, or Victor. "After the troubles at the clinic," he said, squeezing Alia's hand, "it's become more urgent that we counter the problem of propaganda. I have no doubt we could have handled the situation better had a foreign power not flooded us with false information."

Ozie looked noticeably nervous as he grabbed a bread roll and stuffed it in his mouth with one gloved hand; his other hand, also gloved, lay heavily on the table. *His* drones had delivered the propaganda. It wasn't clear to Victor how many people sitting at the table knew that, but Torsten surely did.

For her part, Wonda put on a stony face and then surprised him by speaking. "If people could trust the official story, it might be different. The Mesh is nothing more than a different flavor of propaganda."

Circe raised her voice, "Shall we not bring up that tired refrain of revolt and rebellion again? The world has changed. We must prepare for new battles, not reenact the ones we've lost."

Linus squinted at his sister and wore a pinched, familiar smirk. Victor could tell he was itching for an argument. "You want us to make friends with Europe? Is that it? Lick their boots, too?"

"Linus," Linda warned softly.

"Please continue to use my dinner table as a debate floor," Florence said in her shaky voice. "Don't mind the rules of civility. Apparently, the world *has* changed." She threw a spiteful glance in Circe's direction.

"I apologize," Torsten said. "Florence, you're absolutely right. I hate to think I've overstepped."

She scowled and waved a hand, looking more annoyed than gracious.

"Where are you traveling next, Circe?" Linus asked. His tone, tightly controlled, barely masked a seething anger. Victor wondered if they'd fought like this all through their childhood, or whether it was a new development, and, if so, how recently it might have emerged.

"Cologne," she said, dabbing at the corner of her mouth with a real silk napkin. "Health authorities there seem to have a growing appetite for our services."

Victor spotted the look that passed between her and Torsten. Karine, he saw, noticed the exchange too, but her expression was impossible to read.

Linus said, "Oakland might be in better shape if you spent some time there. The stim crisis there is as bad as it is here. Worse even. The slums outside the city are growing. They're desperate. Refugees and drug addicts are mixing into an explosive cocktail. They rioted over Broken—over MRS patients several days ago."

Victor shot his fa a vicious look. He should know better. What else did he say when Victor was out of earshot? But, for once, his fa's concerns were selfless and earned back some of Victor's respect.

"A travesty," Torsten remarked.

"Shameful, Mr. Eastmore," Alia said. "It's a shameful situation. We house patients addicted to stims here, too. We're doing our best, but we're absolutely swamped by the scale of it."

"And you have no cure," Ozie said. It was the first time he spoke at the table, which provoked an awkward, long silence. He began to raise a glass to his lips, noticed all eyes on him, and returned it to the table. "You have no real treatment for stim addiction. Nor for mirror resonance syndrome. That's the crux of all your problems. No real solutions. More resources won't help you. Same with countering the propaganda."

His remarks met a frosty silence, though Ozie seemed emboldened as he continued, "The tools of our age are turned against themselves, a stalemate. They might nibble at the edges a bit, make you feel like at least you're doing something, but the reason why this is all at risk"—he waved his cyberarm in a leaden circle that seemed to encompass far more than Florence's dining room—"is because when alternatives are developed, and they *will* be developed elsewhere, they will be inescapably attractive. They'll meet a need you desperately want met. And they'll come before you're ready to deal with the consequences. They're already here, in fact."

In the seconds that followed—Victor involuntarily counted more than two dozen blinks among all the guests—silence endured in an uncomfortable thickness before Torsten finally spoke. Victor noticed his voice was warm and open even though the words hinted at steely accusation. "As someone who I understand now makes his home in Las Vegas, coming from you, that sounds, without much of an imaginative leap, like a threat."

Ozie returned Torsten's gaze, and Victor read no malice or anger in it, only a profound sadness and deep-rooted fear. "If it is, it's

Cody Sisco

not mine. It's a caution. The world has changed, but the truth of it is not yet recognized."

"Las Vegas," Linda mused, "is that where you ran off to? Victor was bereft after you were gone."

"Yes, please," Victor said, borrowing his tone from Florence, "let's talk all about my feelings as if I'm not here. How do you think I feel about your new polycule?"

Linda sat straighter. For a moment, he thought she might be deeply offended, but her expression softened. "I hope you're happy for me, as I am for you, now that you've found new friends and a home here. We were so worried after ..."

Victor wanted to say, *After I dug up Granfa's corpse and discovered that he'd been poisoned by polonium by Aunt Circe, who sometimes feels more like a mother to me than you, and now how do you think I'm feeling?* They'd all had enough controversy for one evening.

"I'm fine," he said. He didn't add that, if anything, the thing that threatened to throw him off balance was the necessity of traveling to Las Vegas to visit an elusive genius who could probably have them all killed as easily as snapping a finger. He smiled, nearly laughing at the sheer lunacy of it. "Totally fine. Really."

"I think it's time we said our goodbyes," Alia said.

The plates were cleared. Dessert would be served in the lounge, Circe announced.

As Alia and Torsten made their rounds of polite disengagement, Victor somehow found himself in a trio of conversation with his father and aunt.

"We won't sign," Linus said.

Circe sighed. "It's not necessary that you sign. The documents are only advisory. The changes to the trust have already been made." She glanced at Victor, weariness evident in the bags under her eyes.

Linus breathed through his gritted teeth. "That's not possible. Only father could have—"

"If you had been paying attention at all last year," she interrupted, "you would have seen how quickly his mental condition was deteriorating. I acted because I had to. The trust was changed to ensure that as he declined, there wouldn't be any surprises or discontinuities. Everything is safe now that we have migrated the holdings."

"I don't like having to ask you for a payout of what's mine," Linus said.

"Perhaps if you'd ever sought gainful employment as your son has done, there would be less need. I won't stop your payments, little brother. You don't have to worry. You'll see in time the wisdom of it."

"Will it *emerge*?" Linus sneered and then walked away.

Circe looked at Victor. "In many ways, Victor, you inherited more sense than he did."

The compliment, coming from her, made his stomach twist. In a rush of insight, he saw her in a different light. If anyone could embody a counterargument to Cathar absolutism, it was Circe with her mix of good intentions and terrible actions. "You engineered all this, taking control"—his throat tightened up, but he pushed onward—"taking care of Granfa Jeff, but I still don't understand why."

"Soon," she said grimly. "We'll talk when I return from Cologne. But not before I've safeguarded the future."

Victor bit his tongue. He'd demanded the truth for months, and she thought she could dole it out on her terms. She thought she could rule the family. It was time for someone to prove her wrong.

As Alia walked alongside Torsten toward the autocab, waiting to take them home, she smiled. She was lucky to have found someone with principles who stood up for what was right but could also be gracious and kind to a nonagenarian like Florence.

Someone came striding up the path. It was Lisabella. Had she been invited to dinner only to show up late? Otherwise, the security gate wouldn't have allowed her access.

"Alia, if I could have a minute of your time," Lisabella said breathlessly. "I wanted to tell you earlier, but I got caught in the office. I've been permitted to do a profile on you." She glanced at Torsten and nodded acknowledgment. "Hello, council member. Have you told her about the summit yet?"

Alia took a step back. "What summit?"

Torsten looked down at his feet, then up at her with his most charming smile. She crossed her arms, refusing to be swayed. He sighed. "I was going to tell you tomorrow. It didn't seem decent to add to all this tonight." He waved a hand back at the Eastmore mansion. "We're bringing together delegates from each AU nation's security apparatus. To discuss the propaganda problem. Lisabella had the idea to give you a role as facilitator."

"What?" She was dumbfounded. Facilitate an AU security summit? Why her?

Lisabella smiled broadly, eyes twinkling. "I convinced the higher-ups that it has all the ingredients of a national myth-making success story. Torsten's campaign. Your engagement. Now, the summit is coming to town. I'll be covering the summit, not from a political angle but from a personal one, focused on you as a prominent local figure."

"There's no way. I have no desire to be the focus of so much attention." Alia held up a hand to cut off Lisabella's interruption. "I don't care if it's positive. There's no way I'd agree to something like that, even if I didn't question your motives. And, Torsten"—she turned to him questioningly—"I don't see why you'd be so eager to collaborate with MeshNews."

He grimaced. "It will help the campaign to be on every MeshBit in the Louisiana Territories."

"You don't need this to win, do you? Don't make me."

"Probably not. And, of course, I wouldn't pressure you. It's just an idea. Only ..."

"There's more to it," Lisabella said. "A second pair of eyes and ears could be very helpful."

Alia drew a breath. They couldn't be thinking she would cooperate. "You want me to spy? For Europe? Torsten! Explain this."

"It's a long story, love, and I can't share all the details until you've been cleared. But essentially," he glanced at Lisabella and back to Alia, "we're on the same side this time."

"We are," Lisabella agreed.

Alia could see where they were headed, and it frightened her. "You're saying Europe and the other AU nations are allying themselves against the Organized Western States."

"Concerning cybersecurity, yes. The threat is imminent."

"Say I believe this threat, whatever it is, for the moment. Why would I agree to be part of this? Why would I need to be?"

Lisabella squinted at Alia as if the question had been relayed in an exotic, dead language. After a moment, the look on her face shifted to one of compassion and indulgence, a schoolmarmish look, the kind when none of the kids in the classroom could come up with an answer that was merely beyond their experience. In clear and crisp yet soft tones, Lisabella said, "To prevent a war, of course."

25

Hear me, please, and understand. It's not too late to change course.

—Victor Eastmore, *Apology to Resonant Earth* (transmission date unknown)

17 May 1992
Oklahoma City, The Louisiana Territories

Victor packed his bags quickly, rushing to catch the train to the Oklahoma City airfield, where he met Tosh, Wonda, and Ozie as they boarded the Diamond King's jet. Beyond the runway, the city's towers sprouted like fungal growths, reaching for maximum spore dispersal. He breathed, repeated the owl mantra, and swallowed a fumewort tincture, one of thirty he was bringing with him.

Safety instructions in a soothing voice piped through the sonofeed explained how to board the escape pods in an emergency. The jet taxied, turned, and began to accelerate in a burst of force that tested the squishiness of his seat. The fuselage shuddered as they left the ground and calmly sliced through the air.

On previous flights shuttling between New Venice and Oakland for Eastmore family reunions, Victor had gaped at the scale of Earth's geometry, the play of sunlight across varied terrain, and how small humanity's footprint truly was. This time was no different, and as before, he fought with the irrational fear that he would somehow slip out of the vehicle and fall and fall and fall, burning bright, a meteor streaking toward the ground.

Just a fear. Irrational yet stubbornly persistent.

The jet dipped one wing and circled in a tight-banking turn to gain altitude. This high up, Ouachita Dam looked like a gray slug curled next to a puddle. New Venice was a veiny gray patch amid green forests and the red-mud fringe and brown-blue waters of Qaddo Lake.

Victor looked closely at the land below and imagined plants growing and withering with the season, animals crawling along, feasting, and defecating, and the toil of workers building things up and letting them fall into rubble. Humanity's contrivances always left traces. Unaccountable damage had been done to the land visible below, and a century of breakneck industrialization, mostly in Asia and Europe, had taken its toll on the climate. Now every endeavor across the globe was evaluated for how it might impact the sustainability of human civilization and the millennial cycles of elements and molecules that foster life in a space-cold, plasma-hot solar system with only a single biosphere to nourish it. Moonbase One was the exception that proved the rule, and its inhabitants couldn't exist for long without resupply missions. There were no resupply missions for Earth.

And here he was, speeding through the atmosphere in a metal tube in defiance of economy, sustainability, and ecological responsibility. Among many other economic absurdities that sapped the American Union's vitality, jet travel had always been disgustingly expensive and, therefore, the preserve of only those institutions that could afford it: governments, corporations, and a short list of plutocratic families. In this case, although he could have justified the expense because lives were on the line, the Diamond King was footing the bill.

Below, they were crossing a fuzzy threshold into the uncolonized lands between the LT heartlands and the Cold Nile Miracle, where plains and mountains looked as they must have for millennia. While a few bright splotches signaled thriving crops, many more dull patches were fallow fields and attested to another absurdity: sequestration credits paid for the land to go wild.

The brown bear can't catch fish in dried rivers.

As a mantra, it wasn't as good as the owl one.

The intercom buzzed with an announcement. In an hour, they would touch down in Las Vegas.

Is this a bad idea? Victor wondered.

Good or bad doesn't matter. It's necessary.

The Broken Mirrors coming off Personil needed more help than BioScan knew how to provide, so treatment was worth bargaining for. Undoubtedly, he would have to provide more than access to the data egg's contents and his own brain scans.

Whatever it was, he'd deal with that eventuality. But it bothered him to have no idea what the Diamond King really wanted.

Ozie had hinted but never explained. When they boarded the jet, Victor noticed puffy bags underneath his eyes, the haunted shape of his expression, and the halting way he spoke. He worried about Ozie; none of it signaled a good state of mind.

A knock at the door roused him to his feet. He thumbed the keypad, and the door slid open, revealing Wonda leaning against the bulkhead, her body fitting snugly into its curve. Victor imagined her falling into the open air, sailing downward to her doom but never losing the smirk she wore now as she looked at him.

"I've been exploring," she said. "Want to see what I found?"

"Not really."

"There's a cabin below with an extravagant bed. It fits four."

Victor blinked as he processed her meaning. He noticed her tight-fitting black pants. Slashes in her black blouse revealed a body-hugging white bodice. He remembered the feel of her breasts, the scent of her skin, and he knew that she knew he remembered.

"Come on. I've seen how you look at Ozie. There's something between you. Tosh and me would be a nice side dish."

"I'm not hungry," he grumbled. "Go away."

"Suit yourself." Wonda didn't move.

"Goodbye," he said.

"Can I ask you something?" She stepped forward to block the door from closing. "Why do you think he wants it so bad?"

It took Victor a moment to figure out who she was referring to. "You mean the King?" She tipped her head in agreement.

Victor rubbed his neck. "It's either something to do with our neurograms"—he didn't have to explain to her whose he was referring to—"or with Jefferson's research. Or both. Your guess is as good as mine. I haven't had the opportunity to examine it closely."

"I asked Ozie," Wonda said. "Tosh, too. They looked at me like I didn't have half a brain. But I could see they were scared. Maybe I'm too stupid to be scared, but some megalomaniac who doesn't have the balls to be seen in person is too much of a weirdo to be scared of."

"And you've met your share of weirdos," Victor said and paused. He could so easily fall into bantering, but he resisted. It wasn't like Wonda to act flippant and cynical. This tit for tat was more reminiscent of his relationship with Elena.

Eyes widening, he realized something that hadn't occurred to him before.

From the moment he'd met Wonda, she'd always been earnest and perhaps a bit too over-eager-to-believe naive. Not anymore. Her innocence had been spoiled, torn away. She endured trauma as well as inflicted it. People who survived found ways to keep going. They could become grimly silent, reserving every bit of strength for the fight to keep themselves safe and sane. Or they could slide toward dark humor and cynicism. That was the fuel that had powered Elena after addiction to stims had scarred her brain, and that's what he saw now in Wonda's face. She'd been through the wringer and bounced back into a shape that Elena would recognize in a mirror.

"Where'd you go this time?" Wonda asked.

He cleared his throat, cheeks heating up. He had to stop making excuses for her. She'd cared for him when he went blank, but she'd also taken advantage of him. He'd tried to dissuade her from making a prophet of Samuel. She hadn't listened. She bore the responsibility for her actions, not Victor.

He said, "Never mind. You said they're scared. I noticed that too. It seems the King is someone it's legitimate to be scared of."

"So why are we skitter-bugging into his warm embrace?" she said. "I mean, is it the dumbest thing we've ever done?"

Probably second to worshipping Samuel, Victor thought but didn't say aloud. "We're negotiating. He wants something from us, and that gives us power."

"Does it, though?" she mused. "It could be a garden path that promises Eden and ends in suffocating muck instead."

When he didn't affirm her speculation, she walked away down the corridor.

It did seem absurd how much his hopes were pinned on a successful negotiation. Acquiring a new treatment option for Broken Mirrors, finding Anders and returning him home, and retrieving his grandfather's tongue, ripped from the corpse because it proved radiation to be a factor in the man's death. The list of things he wanted to ask for might not match what the Diamond King's was willing to provide.

Granfa Jeff believed misjudging what the other party wanted was the root cause of failure—he'd said it enough times. Victor required insight into the Diamond King's state of mind—his ambitions and desires—if he wanted to emerge victorious.

Victor left his cabin and walked toward the back of the jet, feeling the thrum of the engines in a jittering of teeth and belly rumbling. He knocked on the door to Tosh's cabin. Tosh opened the door, his face wearing a tired, unsurprised expression, and turned and reclined on the pull-out bed, which was a bit too short for him, tall as he was. Victor levered open a seat tucked into the wall and sat on it. He reached out and triggered the door to close.

"You've been working for the King for a while," Victor said, keeping his tone level. "What should I know about him?"

Tosh grimaced and crossed his arms, looking increasingly like an overgrown child. He was immature, and yet he was capable of torture and worse. How much understanding could a person like that have of others?

"What do you think you want to know?" Tosh asked.

Victor had a dozen questions on his tongue, but Tosh's twisty wording threw him off track. There was wisdom hidden in its convolutions. What Victor didn't know—what he didn't know to ask for—was probably more important than what he thought he wanted to discover. He looked again at the shadows gathered under Tosh's eyes and in the dark clefts of his cheeks and forehead etched with jagged lines of dread and resignation.

Victor asked softly, "Why are you coming with us if you're so scared?"

Tosh tensed, his neck tendons twitching like ropes being tugged. A bully exposed is a dangerous beast. After a moment, his expression softened. He shifted on the bed, lying back, and spoke while looking at the ceiling.

"The King is reasonable when reason gets him what he wants. Bargain with him, and you'll get a better deal than you thought possible. But it's a trap. It always is. He'll take something that you'll regret losing later. And if he becomes unreasonable …"

Tosh looked over to meet Victor's gaze. Victor looked away, not allowing himself to get drawn in. Tosh was not his friend, not after what they'd been through. They needed to go in different directions. Victor couldn't take responsibility for anyone else, not when he was so messed up himself.

Seeing Tosh so vulnerable should have made Victor worried or, at the very least, sympathetic. Instead, he wanted to push Tosh's face into the wall. His weakness was infuriating. It was his fault

Victor was in this mess, his and Ozie's. And maybe Jefferson's, too. They'd all *chosen* to do business with the Diamond King.

A shudder ran through him. He ought to kick himself. He might choose the same thing.

"Why does he care about me?" Victor asked.

Tosh raised his eyebrows, no longer looking afraid, more curious, an expression that suited his rugged, fatherly face. "Who can say? The data egg holds the last recording of Samuel Miller's brain, right? That's unique and unreproducible. Your 'grams are on there too."

"I don't need a reminder," Victor scolded.

"You might. I said he always plays the long game. Think about it. He collects oddities, but he also collects people. Especially the useful ones. He pulled me close." Tosh gestured to himself, likely aware of how his biceps scrunched into grapefruit-sized balls and the fabric of his shirt swelled with the curves of his pecs. He noticed Victor looking and slyly smiled. "You can't blame him."

"You fuck him too?"

Tosh laughed, a loud bark while throwing his head back. "I've never met him actually."

"What? You said—"

"I mean in person. He's a recluse. And a mystery. Depending on who you ask, he's a genius tech inventor or a bloody autocrat. I am positive Wonda was lying when she said she met him. No one knows what his real face looks like. He's loony, Victor. About as bad as you or you-know-who." Tosh smiled, showing his teeth, likely pleased to think he'd found a sore point in Victor's psyche he could poke.

Victor wasn't going to be so easily manipulated. He said stonily, "Loony is a matter of consequences; otherwise, it's simple eccentricity. Samuel killed hundreds. It sounds like the King also has a body count to his credit. Good company for you to keep," Victor said.

Tosh's smile faded. "You need to be careful. I mean it. Stay lucid. Make a deal and get out of town."

Tosh looked out the window. Victor sensed their descent. The odd, pulsing weightlessness in his stomach was unmistakable. The dark lines overlaid on Tosh's face were back.

"I understand the King is dangerous. Fine. What's really bothering you?" Victor asked.

Cody Sisco

Tosh leveled him a long stare. "The King pushes everyone to their breaking point eventually. I'm trying to figure out whether I'm there yet."

"So why go back? You could have stayed in New Venice."

"No. There's no running, Victor. Besides, you might need me." Tosh reached out and placed a hand on Victor's knee. Warmth and pressure traveled up Victor's thigh, tickled his groin. An erection swelled instantaneously, body betraying mind, the past returning like an unwelcome ghost. Victor's face darkened; he felt blood gathering, excitement, anger, and a desperate need to step out of the barriers he put up to protect his mind. Tosh's look of honest and devout tenderness was too much. How could such concern coexist with the violence Tosh had shown on so many occasions?

He stood and said, "I don't need your guilt on my conscience." There wasn't enough air in this tiny room, and they were hurtling through the sky in a metal tube that would crumple when it met resistance more solid than air.

Before Tosh could answer, Victor was in the hallway, lurching away to hide in his room, the door bolted behind him. The jet was shaking and jumping. He should have strapped himself in, but instead, he lay on the floor, cheek pressed into the cool surface, breathing deep to regain equilibrium.

Ozie came by, wanting to talk. Victor yelled at him through the closed door to go away, knowing he was making a mistake, that Ozie probably had some good info, but not caring, not wanting to think anymore, picturing his body dropping into the open air, sailing on the breeze back to New Venice.

No. The wise owl is flying toward the answers it seeks.

The Diamond King could help. Victor would trade away whatever he could and damn the consequences.

26

Never overestimate people's capacity for abstract thinking, especially groups. Mob intelligence is an oxymoron.

—*A History of Las Vegas* (author unknown)

17 May 1992
New Venice, The Louisiana Territories

Alia moved to the window, taking slow, measured steps to mask her impatience. She had a long list of questions to ask the dignitaries who would join her now via virtuafeed and would later arrive in New Venice. The seconds ticked by slowly, each diminishing the time she had left to accomplish the day's necessities.

I can do this. I can be the one to steer this ship to safe harbor.

Or I can wreck it on the rocks.

She took a deep breath. With her security clearance now in hand, she could access the network that tied together every MeshHouse worldwide. Only officials and the sufficiently wealthy or socially connected could book time in them. A few years ago, she wouldn't have dreamed of this opportunity. Maybe she should have. Torsten's ambition was a fire that climbed every hillside, crackling, searching, and devouring the LT's tinder-dry political forests. To love him was to be warmed by his passions; she hadn't realized how completely his utopian visions might become her own. She never thought she would be facilitating a discussion about security relationships among the nations of the American Union. Her training as a neurological imaging specialist was of no use here. Merely a stand-in, a body to occupy the space, a mind to run the logic to its necessary end. Nothing more. A spy, yet one with very little power. If she offered any challenging opinions, the dignitaries would be outraged. More likely, they would laugh at her bungling. She wouldn't give them the opportunity. If Victor could fly into the wolves' den of Las Vegas, she could play her role here. She would keep her words neutral, acceptable, and helpful. She was here to facilitate, placate, instigate, but never demand.

Torsten was a natural leader and should have facilitated the meeting based on his skill alone. However, that would have ruined the carefully calibrated political middle ground the LTs sought to hold. The LT chief executive had appointed him as lead negotiator to show official support for Torsten's campaign. His opponent was furious; she couldn't retaliate without seeming to attack the LT leadership, and that was too costly an option.

All that aside, Alia was a skilled and experienced negotiator. She was part of the team that secured the agreement that enabled the Eastmores to build the Holistic Healing Network Campus on land leased from both the LTs and the Qaddo tribe. She also helped calm things down when the Human Life Movement disrupted the town.

This was simply a continuation of her path. She knew how to be the best version of herself, to be what the situation called for. So be it—if her steps led to expanded vistas, wide horizons, and responsibilities far beyond her comfort zone. If she felt intimidated, she was at least resolved to keep her doubts to herself.

Examining the lacquer on her nails, a delicate lilac base overlaid by an intricate white floral pattern recently painted at Rejuvinail, helped put her at ease during this interminable waiting. *Fresh nails, fresh looks, fresh perspectives.*

The dignitaries' staff had accepted her appointment without any objection. Perhaps they simply liked the life of travel and the ease of crossing borders that so few of their constituents enjoyed, and, hence, the details didn't matter. Perhaps they knew that nothing would be accomplished at the summit, so didn't care. Or perhaps the situation had escalated to the point where they couldn't afford to be petty and bicker about the details. Perhaps they were scared.

Mía had sent a message saying there were riots throughout the Bayshore region. Oakland was in lockdown. SeCa had closed its border, which meant the main transit point at the eastern end of the Sierra Nevada Tunnel was under guard, and no traffic was getting through. But the rough terrain of the thousand-kilometer border couldn't be surveilled effectively, let alone sealed. And OWS mercenaries were known for their all-terrain maneuverability.

MeshNews reported that Europe was concerned about the prospect of conflict spreading. Reporting had commenced on the ROT, too—something they'd never bothered to do since Europe had comparatively few interests there. People were finally starting to pay attention to long-ignored complaints. Given the troubles in SeCa and the ROT, it was becoming clear that two of OWS's neighbors had serious security situations on their hands and that neighborliness couldn't be expected for long. The LT government feared, with good cause, that they, too, would soon be the target of similar unneighborliness.

Alia sat in front of the main vidscreen, straightened her spine, and waited. She was resolved to do a good job. Not only for Torsten. This was her hill to climb now, her achievement if she succeeded.

But what if the pressure became too much?

Torsten had cautioned her about keeping balanced while they were chopping veggies for dinner earlier in the week. "It's going to be a challenge, but you're ready for it. You wouldn't be content with a complete transformation of the BioScan campus, having boatloads of new patients admitted every day, not to mention the drafting of your wedding wishes."

He paused when he noticed she was glaring at him. Then he resumed, with a smirk, saying, "Don't be cross just because I completed my wishes this far ahead of schedule. I shouldn't put pressure on you before the deadline, I know."

"It's two months away," she said.

"Which means your plate is not completely full, so I found you another project, this one having to do with international relations and the security of the American Union, but I'm not sure it will be enough. You're insatiable. Truly, Alia, when will you ever be satisfied?" He waved a half-peeled potato at her and winked, softening the truth of his words. She gently removed the potato from his hands and pressed him against the counter.

"Councilor," she said, feeling movement beneath his pants. "I know how hard these matters are for you to understand, not just the heart of your beloved, but the real and pressing"—she bucked against him, maintaining a deadly serious face; his composure, by contrast, was cracking, the desired effect of her teasing—"issues of the day, which require the involvement of level-headed, dispassionate, and competent citizens to rise to the occasion." She disentangled herself from his embrace, looked at his tented pants, smirked, and returned to chopping zucchini. "You've warned me more than once about rigid positioning during negotiations."

He chuckled, returning to his potato peeling. "I'll strive for a softer stance. Eventually, we'll find our way to a more balanced routine. When our ambitions and circumstances align."

"Who was the first choice?" she asked.

"Hmm?"

"Come on. Who was supposed to facilitate the summit?"

"Oh. Circe."

"Hmm. That makes sense."

"Does it?"

She glanced over and saw him grimacing. "What?"

"I'll just say that the Eastmore prestige factor has waned quite a bit recently, and any whiff of scandal had to be avoided. It's almost like she's trying to ruffle feathers."

The heat in his voice was unmistakable, and she found herself thinking back to the awful dinner with the Eastmores bickering and two terrorists sitting at their table. The gall! Not only that, the power to decide who was part of society and who was shunned was exercised so bluntly, ineptly, and at odds with the values she held—She stopped herself and tried to change the subject. "What if I hadn't said yes? Was there a third option?"

"Not really. I thought I'd coast by on charm and bluster."

Alia stopped chopping. "With the security of the LTs hanging in the balance?" Her vision clouded, and her stomach churned. She looked down at the knife in her hand, too incensed to continue, sickened by how quickly her mood had shifted.

He approached her, stood behind her, and wrapped his arms around her. She relaxed her grip on the knife and carefully laid it on the cutting board.

"You will tell me if you think it's taking on too much." His voice was soft, his breath tickled her ear, and she heard his concern— and loved him for it. The hard heat of her anger transformed into a yielding warmth.

"It's settled," she said. She added the last of the zucchini to the bowl that already held eggplant, onions, and peppers, poured the marinade, tossed them, and set the bowl aside. She turned and glanced at his crotch. "Before or after we put these on the grill?"

Now, sitting in the MeshHouse room with blank vidscreens waiting for the emissaries from the AU nations to materialize, her

Cody Sisco

mind couldn't help but turn to the real reason she was here: an unassuaged, wrenching guilt over the Human Life disaster. This guilt could not be vanquished, only deferred.

Moments like these were intolerable. She needed to be busy. She needed to juggle too many to-dos. She needed to be preoccupied. Otherwise, memories rose like angry phantoms, and she relived the moments when her life was turned upside down.

It occurred to her that her desire to fill every waking moment with tasks would not be considered healthy. If examined, it might be considered very unhealthy mentally. But the misfires between her ears, however they might be diagnosed, wouldn't derail her from her goals. And she wasn't going to speak a word about it. Her troubles were nothing compared to the MRS patients and what Victor went through every day to stay sane.

Alia tugged at a seam on her jacket that had wrinkled. The hostage crisis was over, she told herself. She shouldn't dwell on it. She shouldn't cast blame. She shouldn't feel sorry for herself.

I can do this. For the LTs. For Torsten. For me.

The summit was a chance to prove herself and to grow beyond her limits. What could be more rewarding? She would pack her days with to-dos and take more than the daily recommended dose of responsibilities. Travel arrangements. Accommodation. Itineraries. Excursions. How to keep the stim addicts who were overrunning New Venice from ruining the summit. She wouldn't have time for second-guessing and wool-gathering and paranoid delusions of mirror resonance syndrome changing her brain.

There was a knock at the door. Lisabella came into the small room and took a seat.

"Don't mind me," Lisabella said. "Are you ready?"

Alia bit back a retort that she had been ready and waiting for twenty minutes. However, Lisabella couldn't help who she worked for, so Alia simply nodded.

"The virtuafeed should start soon. We had some technical problems."

"Of course," Alia said, ignoring the common lie. "Technical problems" probably meant that Lisabella's superiors decided to assign live, hidden monitors during the session. Everything was recorded, of course, and no doubt painstakingly picked over. Still, nothing beat a real-time monitor who could disrupt the feed at any moment if the discussion grew too sensitive and warranted more technical problems. Torsten had shared these insights casually, in a matter-of-fact voice; he was a politician, resigned to the condition of the world, while she listened and fumed, outraged at the systematic censorship in the service of oppression that was part and parcel of Europe's control of the Mesh and, therefore, the AU.

The vidscreen glowed and synchronized the feeds. Suddenly, Alia was sitting around a conference table extending beyond the tiny room's bounds to encompass representatives sitting in their own tiny rooms across the continent. The borders between them were indistinguishable. Crisp pixelated script labeled each participant's name, title, and national allegiance. Alia looked down and saw her signifiers glowing in reverse on the table's surface: Alia Effendi, unofficial summit organizer on behalf of the Louisiana Territories.

Alia began, fighting against a nervous tickle in her throat, "Greetings from the Louisiana Territories to this notable assemblage of dignitaries. My name is Alia Effendi, and I will be coordinating the summit logistics. If I may suggest we proceed first with an update on travel and lodging arrangements, then I will open the discussion of meeting objectives to you all. Let's begin, shall we?"

27

A 10 p.m. curfew is hereby enacted within Semiautonomous California. Violators who cannot provide proof of authorization will be arrested.

—Official Mesh advisory (17 May 1992)

17 May 1992
Oklahoma City, The Louisiana Territories

The jet landed with a smooth touchdown, eased by shock absorbers on the landing gear that reminded Victor of fallen socks bunched around ankles. A memory surfaced of wearing multicolored Qaddo-patterned socks around his thin brown legs, dry-cracked and dirty from long days running through fog-kissed grass and bushes in his grandparents' extensive bay-facing hillside garden—so unlike the dusty plains outside the window as to seem from another planet. Whenever he'd come inside, Granma Cynthia would yell and point, demanding that he stay off the nice furniture. Qui Hong would give him a bath followed by creams that smoothed his ashen skin. It was a pleasant memory or, more likely, an amalgam of several. Strange. He rarely thought of his childhood anymore; there was little to look back on that wasn't painful, and this particular memory seemed incongruous with the anxiety and foreignness of the present moment.

Exiting the jet, Victor and his three fellow travelers walked in tight formation through boarding tubes that were clad in solar skins, cooled by waves of chilled air, and lit by amber-green glow-strips. They reached the skyport and unclutched, looking upward at a chrome-and-glass latticework canopy arcing overhead. A few calm assemblages of families, businesspeople, and government representatives enjoyed drinks and petit fours in lounge areas that oozed wealth and privilege.

Wonda gaped, made a few timid motions to smooth her hair, and tugged at the cuffs of her long-sleeved bodice—hints of it visible beneath slashes in her dark jacket. Its white was not as pristine-white as some of the gleaming clothing worn by the sky-port's denizens.

With quick and sudden steps, Tosh veered off-course and grabbed a drink from a tray atop a whirring bot. He sniffed, then took a long gulp, a slight smile forming when he noticed Victor watching. Tosh held out the glass to him. "Scotch, or a fantastic imitation." Almost without thought, Victor reached out and tipped the remainder of the liquid into his mouth. Burning peat and smoky sugar combined smoothly on his tongue. He swallowed, relishing the warm track it made and the pooled heat in his stomach.

"Could have saved some for me," Wonda grumbled.

"I assure you, the facilities where you're staying will have an extensive selection of excellent drinks and much better views," a voice said from behind. They all turned to a tall, lanky figure. "I'm Silk. I'll be your escort during your stay."

Silk wore layers of gauzy material in delicate pastel shades, and their eyes were thickly lined with charcoal.

"Let's get moving," Ozie said, although Victor noted he didn't sound eager.

"Agreed," Tosh said.

"If you'll follow me ..." Silk turned, began walking slowly, and was soon flanked by Victor on the right and Wonda on the left.

"This is nothing like I remember," Wonda said, pitching her voice low.

"I thought you were going to be the skeptical one. Ready to immigrate already?" Victor asked. If she wasn't careful, she'd be ensnared as thoroughly and tragically as she'd been by Samuel. Not that she deserved Victor's concern, yet when she went all wide-eyed and childlike, something inside him wanted to wrap her up and keep her safe.

"Would you miss me?" she asked bitterly.

Silk proceeded as if nothing untoward had been said. "We've so much been looking forward to welcoming you to Las Vegas. This evening, we're pleased to host you at one of the most extravagant social events of the year."

Victor was half-listening as he fiddled with his MeshBit, trying to connect to Pearl. The device indicated that no signal was available.

Silk glanced down and noticed. "Ah, yes, Mesh devices won't work here. They're obsolete. The new Tangle network is ten times as fast but Mesh-incompatible. The changeover was exceedingly smooth for residents, but guests may be inconvenienced. You'll be issued private Tangle nodes."

Victor wondered whether Tangle would be a less intrusive communications platform than the Mesh devices that kept AU citizenry under the eye of anonymous surveyors working for European guardians of politics and culture. He looked up at the skyport's metal canopy. *How many cameras, and who's watching?*

A set of fogged glass panels parted as they approached, revealing a cavernous space and a silver vehicle with all the heft and sleekness of a whale. The air changed, becoming slightly warmer, though they weren't outside yet. Glowstrips illuminated rows of cars.

Victor gestured for Ozie to come over. "Before we go, I want to call Pearl," he said.

Ozie held out his cyberarm, showing his wrist where a red *X* lit the "skin" from underneath. "No signal," he said. "And there won't be for a while. We're in a blackout. All of us." Seeing Victor's puzzled expression, Ozie explained, "We're not contacting anyone until the King wants us to. We're on his timetable now."

With those ominous words, Victor expected fanfare and the Diamond King's playing-card face, as it had been described to him, to pop up on every surface. Nothing happened. But he wouldn't let his guard down; he kept his eyes roving, soaking up this new context, learning everything he could.

They climbed into the vehicle, sat in seats that were hard yet comfortable, and waited. Silk rode in the front, separated by an opaque partition. Any conversation would undoubtedly be over-heard, but they had the back of the vehicle to themselves. Austere classical music soothed Victor's nerves.

The drive was as smooth as an undersea journey and unevent-ful, since they couldn't see outside. No one seemed in the mood to talk. Maybe they'd said all they'd intended to for now. Yet it seemed like the quiet wasn't only surrounding him; his own thoughts were muted. He wasn't used to being quiet in his head; ideas usually careened in his brain and made him anxious. Curious. *Must be the soundtrack*, Victor mused.

They arrived in another subterranean and nondescript parking area to disembark. What percentage of the built environment in Las Vegas looked like this: bare, functional, soulless? Then he remembered the skyport and realized this was a land of dichotomies, extremes, and incongruity.

Silk led them into an elevator that could have fit five groups their size. Victor noticed the aesthetic change right away. There were panels on each wall with abstract paintings of rich and luscious crimsons, azuls, and verdigris. The highly polished, cream-colored floor was flecked like cookie batter. The tactile splendor of the elevator appeared to Victor far richer than anything he'd encountered in Oakland or New Venice.

The elevator chimed gently, and light flooded his vision as the doors retracted. With all the tricks the Diamond King had at his disposal, he could have arranged for the windows to be dimmed, yet he didn't. He wanted this bedazzlement, planned for it. Small tricks everywhere that Victor hoped meant nothing to worry about later, like a law of perverse expectations.

The flare of light subsided, and Victor and the rest exited to a gently sloping floor that ended in a tall and wide glass curve. Beyond this curve lay Grand Park far below them. Silvery sage-green plants lined shaded gravel walkways, where people ambled in the late afternoon heat through the cooling mists sprayed from the colorful kiosks. In the center, a monument depicted the city in miniature.

In the winter quadrant of the park, Victor noticed a group of individuals, all wearing gray coveralls, who carried a large, irregular parcel between them. After a moment, they left the parcel on the ground within the park's boundary.

"Is that a body?" Wonda said and pointed.

Onlookers in the park paused and then walked on, whispering to one another. They seemed unfazed. Silk barely glanced in that direction, but Victor was sure they'd seen a body. Burial and other alternatives for honoring the dead were widespread social norms. But not here? He wondered if this spectacle was orchestrated for his benefit. He'd been repeatedly warned of the strangeness he would encounter in Las Vegas. Was the body one of the Diamond King's many victims? Would there be more? This could be a message about the perils of disobedience. Or maybe it was a universal message, saying watch out, everyone, there's danger everywhere, and we're nothing more than organic machines whose time on this earth is finite, fragile, and at the mercy of forces beyond our control.

Cody Sisco

Duly noted, he thought grimly.

"Well," he said, turning toward Silk, who watched him with hands clasped in front, a slight smile curling up, seemingly oblivious to the horror below, "there's a lot to see here." He'd meant it to sound ironically portentous, but it came out sounding meek and overwhelmed.

"Sing it," Wonda muttered, but not critically. She offered a wan smile.

"Please, make yourselves comfortable," Silk said, gesturing to a large, curved couch that looked like a strawberry patch with its pale green fabric indented with red buttons. "What would you like to eat or drink? It's about three hours until dinner, so a snack is perfectly reasonable. Or if you don't want to decide, we can have a parade."

Victor thought maybe he'd heard wrong. "Excuse me? A parade?"

"It's a thing that's done here," Ozie explained. "Enjoy the show."

They found seats and stared out at the view, and soon, a robot rolled in, earning a groan and an eye roll from Ozie. Victor recognized the machine, which was a close copy of the top-hatted waiter robot that Ozie had built for the Springboard Café. Now savvy enough to be on the watch for subtle signals and signs, Victor wondered if this was meant for him or Ozie. Regardless, it motored close, waited until Victor hesitantly plucked a puck-shaped pastry from the tray, and then rolled next to Wonda and then around the room until all of them had taken one. Biting the treat revealed flavors of goat cheese, mushrooms, and herbs. A crispy crust may have had honey mixed in with the dough. Delicious, elaborate, and the first of many delicacies on offer.

The next few robots that tootled by were various shapes, some squat like piglets, some lean and lanky teetering on legs like giraffes; all of them carried delectable treats that subtly shifted from the savory to the sweet. Along the way, Silk quizzed each of them quietly about what they wanted to drink, each choosing various flavors and enhancements. Shortly thereafter, the beverage would appear. A brief interaction with Silk revealed that, indeed, a large supply of fumewort could be delivered to Victor's room, and he would find it there after the gala, which he supposed would represent the ratcheting up of the Diamond King's attempts to match Eastmore levels of wealth.

Too bad I'm not so easily swayed, Victor thought, although he was preemptively grateful for the fumewort.

Once they had all eaten and moved into their second round of drinks, Silk moved to one of the windowpanes, which darkened and became a vidscreen showing a banquet in a large room with a stage.

"The Citizens Ball," Silk said, "is one of our most treasured occasions. Felicitous that it comes early this year. We celebrate those among us making important contributions to the sciences and the arts. Poets, philosophers, researchers, theorists. I'm sure you're aware of awards programs elsewhere obsessed with categorization, one prize for this or that per year. We eschew that type of quota system. Individuals are nominated and evaluated by their peers; their accomplishments are measured by their impact on whichever field of activity, and the result is not a rubber stamp of approval but rather a celebration of the individual, their work, and the collaborative society that makes their achievement possible. Each receives a generous allocation of resources to help propel their promising careers forward."

"And everyone gets a big pat on the back," Tosh said sourly.

Silk took the comment in stride and continued, "Of course, we also celebrate our culture. I don't know what you've heard about the OWS, but I assure you that all your misconceptions will be cleared up during your stay with us." Smiling, Silk waved a hand, and the window cleared, revealing buildings that glinted with reflections of the setting sun, a dark-bellied thunderstorm in the distance, and streams of rain evaporating far above the hot desert floor.

"If you'd like to go to your rooms, we can help you prepare for the ball," Silk said.

Silk's compatriots, waiting at the edges of the room, made themselves known. They each wore multicolored, form-fitting robes that reminded Victor of ones he'd seen in Little Asia on the San Francisco Peninsula. They came forward and introduced themselves to the other guests. At the same time, Silk, who had remained by Victor's side, gently took his elbow and led him to an elevator. They rode ten or so floors up to the eighty-eighth, the top floor, Silk told him, and he exited into a tastefully decorated suite. It felt cozier than the previous room, with overstuffed couches, dark nooks, and bright outlooks on the city below, all balanced and harmonious. *Slick*, he thought, *the seduction continues.*

Playing along, he said, "It's really impressively designed."

Silk blushed. "Thank you."

Victor paused, hearing more gratitude and pride in Silk's voice than he expected. "You designed it?"

Silk nodded. "This is my craft. I happen to be one of the citizens being honored tonight. It's why I had the opportunity to meet you."

"Why would you want to meet me?" Victor asked.

Silk looked surprised. "It is simply an honor to meet guests who don't know what OWS society is like." Silk looked down, and Victor noted their lashes curved ninety degrees, giving Silk an air of elegance. "I've always wanted to distinguish myself somehow. Now I've found a way to please the King." Silk looked up and a sun-bright flare of ambition flickered in eyes that held Victor's gaze with the force of gravity. "I *am* honored."

There was no denying the earnest voice; Silk believed something that Victor wanted to think was nonsense or, worse, corruption. Adulation for the Diamond King couldn't be deserved, could it? The more Victor learned, the less he felt he knew, yet the moment when he'd be put to the test grew closer. He closed his eyes and remembered the safety and confidence in his granfa's warm embrace. He could use some of that now.

Silk watched him with curiosity and lingered a little too long. "Thank you again," Victor said, making it clear their chat was at an end. He wasn't so desperate as to need the touch of a stranger to make him feel better. Not yet, anyway.

28

The fatal flaws in the American Union pre-dated its birth. Without imperialism to bind disparate peoples, there was no common ground. Repartition opened a door that could not be shut, leading to parochial feuds and geopolitical myopia. Destiny became hyperlocal. Vitality withered. The soul of America vanished and could not be recalled.

—Robbie Eastmore, *The American Union: A Failed Experiment* (transmission date unknown)

14 April 1992
Amarillo, The Republic of Texas

Elena lost count of how many times she boarded a new bus or autocab with her bag of contraband gizmos. Four? Eight? The transit situation throughout the ROT was in chaos thanks to glitching systems that caused buses to idle in parking lots or trains to stop in their tracks, leaving the populace with makeshift and spotty options. She finally reached Amarillo around noon by riding in the back of a private van that jostled and bumped on poorly maintained roads. It didn't help that she couldn't see outside, and with each lurch, the seatbelt dug deep into her midsection.

The driver dropped her off, along with a few other passengers, at the center of town. Not an ideal place for her to turn up. She would be spotted quickly, which meant she had to find her Puros faster than the Corps could pounce. There were more tents than she remembered, each one like a new growth sprouting from the plaza's cracked stonework. Children played while parents kept an eye out. The blue, cloud-gauzed sky, decaying taupe buildings, and a few bright emerald trees were familiar, but Amarillo appeared dry and parched compared to the open water of the Passage and all its adjacent foliage.

Hoisting the bag onto her back, she hustled along one edge of the main plaza, past Café Magyar's green-and-white striped awning and into an alley. Three doors down, she buzzed the door to a hostel the Puros used as a cover to pass messages. She was admitted and entered a vestibule with a locked door at the end and a glassed-in reception desk on one side.

The older gentleman clerk looked her up and down. "Want a room?"

"Elena Morales," she announced softly.

This earned an eye roll. "I told Xavi I don't want to be in this game anymore. You're lucky he paid me so well."

"Just give me the message."

"Your parents are safe. They're on their way to San Antonio."

"Is that it?"

"Yes. Now, please, I want no more part of this."

"Where can I find Xavi?"

The clerk sighed. "Pizza parlor. Where the butcher's shop used to be. Take my advice—"

"No thanks." She started to breeze back outside, then stopped. She took ten gizmos from her bag and put them on the counter. The clerk scrunched up his brow skeptically. "These are for your guests," she said. "Real news." Hearing that, the clerk's expression changed, softening.

Hope.

It had been so long since Elena had seen the emotion that it took her a second to recognize it.

She stepped outside, feeling an unfamiliar buoyancy. Mama and Papa were safe. Good. That was a weight off her shoulders. Now to find Xavi and figure out how deep the troubles ran for the Puros.

Xavi wasn't at the pizzeria, though the teenage girl saucing a pie told Elena she had seen him the previous day. "Check at the cake shop a few blocks toward Center Avenue," she told Elena.

Tired of lugging her bag, Elena sat, ordered a pizza slice, and asked for the gossip.

"Things have quieted down," the girl said as she placed thin cheese disks on the next pie to go into the oven. "Xavi is the last one. Not much he can do on his own, right? The Corps like to act like they're in charge, but they don't do a damn thing. Except they don't pocket our profits, so a lot of people are happy about that."

The girl put a square slice of pizza on a slate. Grease slid off the cheese, glowing iridescent under the lightstrips. Elena's stomach gurgled and flipped.

The girl had a point. The Corps made their money selling stims and could rely on cash from Las Vegas. The Puros resisted that creeping corruption, and yet had mouths to feed, so yes, maybe they leaned too hard on local businesses and residents, but never with serious threats of violence—just a little intimidation—but only to build support. "Independence isn't free" was their catchphrase.

Elena finished her slice and left ten gizmos on the tables, telling the girl behind the counter they were freebies. The girl shrugged and slid a rectangle of pizza into the oven.

A few doors down from the cake shop, Elena caught up with Xavi in the courtyard of an apartment complex. The courtyard was filled with big leafy plants, which shielded them from any eyes that might have spied.

Bald, scartooed, man-smelling Xavi wrapped her in a surprising hug, which she returned, slightly puzzled. He'd never been one to emote, and their rivalry over control of the Amarillo Puros had been a source of tension for years. He seemed to sense her question.

"We're the last ones," he said. "Unless Chico ...?"

She shook her head, gazing at a small papaya tree's slender, scaly trunk. "He's still asleep or whatever. There's not much hope." She looked up into Xavi's ice-blue eyes. "Terry? Selas? All of them?" She didn't mention Davinth. She was still sore about his role in handing over Victor to the Corps.

Xavi's lips turned down. "No one."

"Well, shit," Elena said and sat on a short bench perfectly sized for a couple with nothing better to do than sit and stare at the plants. Gone. The family she'd found and come to, if not love, exactly, but care for deeply and depend on, all gone. It was unreal.

"Things are going better down South. I was thinking about moving on. Now that you're back."

"Tell it to me straight," Elena said. "Is staying suicide?"

Xavi dropped his head. "I'm surprised I haven't been taken out yet. Maybe they like me here as a symbol of failure. Or they're waiting for me to try something. Part of me wants to give them that satisfaction. With you here, though ... we would both be too sweet a target to pass up."

"I'll move on. No sweat, no fuss." She patted the bag with her. "I'll leave some of these with you."

"You're carrying around a bag of shocksticks?" he said with eyebrows raised.

"Nothing so buzzy. Some gizmos I picked up. Real news. Not fake Mesh bullshit."

"Picked up from where?" Xavi looked concerned. "You know the OWS likes to drop things like this before an attack."

"I got these at the LT border. They're legit. What's weird, though, is I think they're from Europe."

Xavi mimed his head exploding.

"I know," she said, "but things have changed. I think the Mesh is compromised. These things are more secure."

"Mesh operators are replacing their own equipment? For free? That's not like them." He pulled a leaf off a plant, shredded it in four quick movements, and let the pieces fall between his boots.

Elena said, "I think they're desperate. Think about it. If the OWS threatens the status quo, it's mainly Europe that stands to lose."

"They never helped us before."

Elena shrugged. "Like I said, things have changed."

"So, what are you now? A European agent?"

Elena blinked. She hadn't thought of it like that. She was only doing what little she could, based on a fluke encounter at the border. And she cared nothing for what was good for Europe. She only wanted to preserve a way of life in the ROT that was under threat. She'd been distracted by Victor, then Chico, and hadn't cared for her people. In a way, that's what Victor was doing: focusing on the people who needed his help the most, the Broken Mirrors. She needed to re-focus now on hers.

Xavi was still looking at her.

"I'm a European agent if I have to be," she said. "But I'm a Puro first. You know that won't change." He wrapped an arm around her and kissed the top of her head, which was far more affection than he'd ever shown her. She hugged him back, and they sat there for a moment, remembering the friends they didn't save. "Help me get out of town?" she asked.

"I'm going with you. Someone needs to watch your back. You're getting in deep, you know that."

"I've been under water for years," she said. "So, next up, Dallas?"

He nodded. "Puros are strong there still. Lots of international folks. Maybe you can contact whoever gave you these"—he grabbed her bag and lifted it, testing its weight—"and get more. Maybe they're willing to throw in some cash, too."

She said, smiling, "Let's go get our payday."

29

The social rating system was not meant to confer class status, privileges, or any official weight. It was an organizational scheme meant for internal use only. People asked for it; they wanted clearer communications and more structure. They got more than they bargained for.

—*A History of Las Vegas* (author unknown)

17 May 1992
Las Vegas, Organized Western States

When Victor saw his traveling partners again, it was after being coaxed into a form-fitting jumpsuit made of subtly glistening black material. Their transformation was no less stunning. He'd spent weeks with Tosh and Wonda in loose-fitting Human Life Movement robes, hitched into various arrangements that showed bits of legs, arms, and shoulders in a kind of shabby-sexy look. What they wore now was zero percent shabby and a thousand percent sexier—sleek, sultry, iridescent—turning them into a bunch of clowns to amuse the court of the Diamond King, Victor supposed.

This isn't my first gala. They're not going to win me over with nice clothes. I won't be distracted.

In a shrink-wrapped three-piece suit, Tosh looked like a bipedal slimmed-down sea lion. Wonda wore a gown of black material, fitted at the waist, and flowing down around her like an oil slick. The material was encrusted with a thousand different colors, glowing, pulsing, moving. Ozie was the least transformed. He wore trousers and a vest, which showed off his cyberarm, glowing and blinking with fewer, larger lights than Wonda's dress.

All four had refused any face paint. Would that mark them as outsiders, Victor wondered, and what exactly was this gala for? *To throw me off balance, probably. Well, they're going to be disappointed because I feel great.*

The effect of all this glitz should have been distracting and off-putting. Instead, he noticed that a curious type of calm infused the group. Even his own mind, as it moved from detail to detail, had a more neutral, perceptive quality than was typical.

Before he could open his mouth to remark on this, Silk beamed at them and said, "You all look splendid. Shall we go up?"

"The gala is here?" Wonda glanced up at the ceiling. "I was hoping it would be outdoors in the park." She made a grand, sweeping gesture with her arm, which caused a shimmer to move and rebound along the length of her dress. She twirled, squealing delightedly and gasping in awe.

A klaxon sounded in Victor's ears.

"I think you'll appreciate the venue," Silk said with a wink toward Wonda.

Victor finally broke through. "Have we been drugged?" he asked, trying to employ an angry voice. Instead, he sounded giddy.

"Do you not feel well?" Silk asked, looking concerned, but Victor caught a pink flash of amusement in Silk's eyes. Outrage, which should have overwhelmed Victor, failed to materialize. He could only muster a shallow sigh before his own smile returned.

"I feel great actually," he said. "That's what tipped me off. What did you give me?"

Silk said, "The avatars sometimes take it upon themselves to do what's best. I enjoy mood stabilizers to even things out. It's never harmful."

Victor said, "I need to know if and when you plan to drug me again against my will. It's kind of a thing for me."

"Me too," Ozie muttered.

"Me too," Wonda echoed, her voice raised. She wore a crazed, happy-angry smile that he found vaguely disconcerting. "You don't have to be mentally ill to want to stay pure."

Ozie glared at Wonda, though with less rancor than he might. "Mentally ill," he echoed. The words had always triggered bitter fury in him. He had every right to be angry. Mirror resonance syndrome was a difference, not an illness, a lesson they'd learned at great cost and only after more than a decade of being told implicitly, and sometimes explicitly, that they were wrong, bad, deficient, defective, and destined to become vegetative—lies upon

Cody Sisco

lies upon lies. Mirror resonance syndrome did affect the way they experienced the world, but so did addiction, greed, aggression, and all the other emotions and afflictions that made people do what they did—emotions that for him and Ozie were no less strong or legitimate for sometimes originating in others' minds. In SeCa, "ill" implied they weren't capable and that their fates should be placed in the hands of medical professionals. And look how that had worked out.

"Earth to Victor," Tosh said as he cupped the back of Victor's head and massaged his scalp. "I think we're all on board with the notion of consent"—this was a particularly twisted thing for Tosh to say, given what he and Wonda had done to Victor while he was blank, yet somehow it only provoked mild annoyance—"but I agree with Victor. I feel great. Let's get to the party and let the night unfold." He pulled Victor close and leaned into his neck in what appeared from the outside like a cozy snuggle, but his whispered warning was full of danger. "Don't let your guard down."

"That tickles," Victor said in a fake, high-pitched, boyish voice as he pushed Tosh away. They shared one brief glance of acknowledgment and then the group followed Silk to the elevators.

On the roof they could see the full-circle vista of Las Vegas below. Three other buildings reached similar heights, each one at the innermost edge of a different seasonal wedge of the city. Hanging off their building, like a giant balcony, was a flat expanse of concrete, painted in a grid of bright red squares. Two sky fliers stood about ten meters from each other with turbines cantilevered off their torsos.

"Do we split up?" Wonda asked in a small voice. She sounded like she was holding down a meal that wanted to jump from her throat. Her dress mirrored the stars above.

"It will be more comfortable," Silk said. "Unless you want to try to all pile in together. It's probably okay. The sensors will tell us if we're too heavy."

"Ozie, let's you and me go together," Victor said. Ozie nodded agreement.

Silk smiled. "We'll see you there."

Victor walked to the farthest sky flier. A bright yellow semi-circle protrusion, flat as a candy wafer, created a step for him to use as he climbed inside. Ozie followed and they both sat on the seat bench that faced forward. The top hinged down, enclosing them while affording wide views. Wonda sat in the other vehicle, facing them, looking as pale as he'd ever seen her, sandwiched between Tosh and Silk.

"Can you seriously not make a connection to Pearl?" he asked Ozie. "You, the great hacker, can't do that?"

"I am great. Problem is, she's not taking calls," Ozie said glumly. "Why?"

Ozie looked uncertain. He shrugged. "Aren't there times when you don't want to talk to anyone?"

Sure, he had moments of hiding from the world. And Pearl wasn't a people person either.

The engines thrummed to life, introducing a vibration into the cabin. When Victor looked at one of the floodlights illuminating the launch area, it jostled, or rather, his eyeball was jostling as he looked at the stationary light. He looked away, disturbed.

"Why all of this?" Victor asked with a wave. "Why the big show?"

Ozie said, "Everyone gets welcomed. It's a basic bit of psychology. There's a place for you here. Someone cares. Someone is looking out for you. We've got Silk. Everyone gets someone. It's a civic duty. No one is alone. No one is unsupervised."

"No one?"

"Thousands of people arrive every year. They're welcomed, they get housing and jobs, they're integrated."

"But we're only here temporarily, to make a deal," Victor said.

Ozie remained silent.

What deal had Ozie made?

What would a welcoming country be like? Boatloads of people fled conflict and destruction in Asia and arrived on the shores of Semiautonomous California. They were shunned and excluded, forced to fend for themselves in a dry and empty landscape where the best plots of land and the most productive urban areas were off limits to them. Here, they were welcomed, slotted in like pieces of an expanding mosaic. This seemed like a better solution. Yet it came with a cost that Victor didn't yet have the full measure of. There were dark, unexplored areas at the edges of his understanding.

"I need you to be honest with me, Ozie. How did you end up here? I never got the real story from you, did I?"

"Didn't you?" he asked. One of his braincaps lay on his lap.

His fingers idly danced over it, almost like they were repeating a pattern.

Victor thought about all the times in the last few months when he'd asked Ozie to level with him. This time was no different. Ozie evaded. He obfuscated. At the root of the problem was his distrust of Victor, and the feeling was reciprocated. They should have been confidants. They should still be best friends. But time and lies had come between them, and it seemed those were insurmountable barriers.

When Ozie spoke, it was in a distant voice, soft, as if his mind were a world away. "I told you I was already here when Jefferson found me. I escaped to the OWS years earlier." Tap, tap, tap went his fingers.

"You went missing in the middle of the semester. I didn't know if you were still alive."

"I had to leave. Once you're across the border, there's a whole society that's ready to take you in. Surviving here is easy. At first, they put me to work on a homestead halfway up the Cold Nile. I didn't tell them about MRS or what I could do with computers. They assumed I was just a silly college kid with dreams of a better life. That changed when I got bored. I started helping modify their Mesh feeds, getting deeper into gadgets. At some point, I became useful to the local Corps, and that must have figured into their scouting algorithms. But it happened slowly. They don't come at you all at once, usually." Tap, tap, tap. "You know the rating system?"

Victor had heard vaguely that OWS citizens had some sort of system to acknowledge and reward their contributions to society. It was a nation where largesse flowed from the government to the people, thanks to a centrally planned economy and vast automation that powered the most economically productive sectors. Taxes on labor were negligible and stipends were plentiful, doled out and scaled to a person's rating. Beyond that, Victor had no clue how it worked, though a rectangular image came to mind.

"Something to do with playing cards?"

Ozie nodded. His fingers tapped on the braincap as he spoke. "Yeah, it's the stupidest thing I've ever heard of, except it actually works. Privilege comes from your ranking. There's a floor on wages, so everyone makes enough to survive. Housing costs are capped, so you always have a place to live. All the basics of the economy are stable and guaranteed. Above that, though, is where everyone plays. There are incentives for cultivating and demonstrating ambition, creativity, and innovation. Everyone starts at one, and you reach five by twenty years old if you work at it. It's similar for immigrants. The scheme rewards service, altruism, and all the good things in life. The tough thing is that there's no tolerance for complacency. You can move down too, so there's no getting lazy. There's no time for selfish goals. Interdependence is hard-wired into society."

The lights of the city receded as they headed over a dark landscape. The vehicle was oriented toward a string of lights on the horizon. Off to the side, Victor glimpsed the other vehicle, a twin set of beacons and a reflected glow from the windshield and fuselage. He wondered briefly what Silk was telling Wonda and Tosh, or vice versa.

"I happened to be able to help people use and adapt technology in a place that prizes that kind of service. By the time I started Springboard Café, I was an eight, which for a guy in the wilderness is a lot. Usually, you've got to be a district council member or a cutting-edge researcher to get that far. I was a hacker who happened to be ahead of the game. I beat it."

"What do you mean?"

"I hacked the rating system."

"Isn't that dangerous?"

Ozie laughed loud and long. He wiped his eyes, his chuckling fading slowly. "Do I look like someone who can't handle a little danger? Do I look that helpless? Victor, remember who tricked out your car in the desert. I put missiles on there—illegal, globally controlled missiles." Ozie laughed again, this time more quietly, like he was savoring a private memory. Victor noticed that Ozie's obsessive tapping on the braincap had stopped, which put him at ease, although why, he couldn't say.

"The Diamond King doesn't usually interview people until they make ten. Or at least he doesn't personally contact you. He's got an army of intermediaries. The Corps showed up at my door with an ultimatum: 'Give us all your data about hacking the rating system and we won't break your neck.' I was a bit less self-preserving back then and probably would've gotten myself killed, but the thought of them burning down the Café and everything I'd built there got me cooperating. I moved up a rank. More importantly, I'd been noticed. They knew who I was and what I could do, not just with the rating system. They looked at everything. The braincaps, the Mesh hacking, mirror resonance syndrome, all of it."

The bright line was drawing closer, revealing a more extensive, more geometric patterning than had been visible before. A line of hills some twenty kilometers from the city was ringed with lights, like contour lines of a topographical map. At the top, on a plateau, was an array of buildings. The sky fliers began to descend.

In SeCa, I was part of the lowest class and the highest. Caught between worlds. What would my rating be here?

Victor realized he'd missed what Ozie was saying. "Repeat that."

"Nothing like Jefferson's name to capture your attention," Ozie muttered. "I said that's how Jefferson found me. Via the Diamond King."

"Wait," Victor said. The vehicle was descending in a straight line toward a landing area. So why did it feel like he was tilting sideways? Memories he'd pushed away jostled back into place maybe. Ozie put an arm on Victor's shoulder, bracing him. He *had* been tilting sideways. "That means ..."

"Jefferson had already made contact with the King. They were working together on research into mirror resonance syndrome."

"You found this out—"

"From Jefferson, yes. Victor, by the time Jefferson came to me, he'd already started working with the King, he'd already been poisoned, he'd already decided to make the data egg—that's why he needed my help, and he came to me saying the King had said I could help. This was maybe six months before he died."

"I don't know why I assumed ... I thought he turned to the King for help after—after Circe poisoned him."

"No. They were in business already." Ozie looked like he was on the verge of saying something painful. Then he stiffened and looked away. He started tapping again on the arm, apparently lost in his thoughts.

Victor closed his eyes and rubbed them with his palms. This was going to be a long night.

A change in momentum caught his attention. He opened his eyes and saw lights on the mountaintop drawing closer. Their shape was distinct now, concentric squares and smaller shapes, marking out different areas. At the center a bulbous, curvilinear building dominated the scene. The sky fliers took them past the building and then lower, to a landing area nearby.

After disembarking and reuniting, the group of five entered a large banquet hall through an opening in glass walls encasing the structure. Large pillars rose and blossomed into many-fingered support beams for the undulating roof. The impression it gave was like having been shrunk down and wandering beneath an enormous metallic mushroom forest.

Clusters of people filled the building, moved, and coalesced around semicircular tables. "Is the Diamond King here?" Victor asked Silk. Anticipation sent tiny shivers through his chest.

"It's not a polite discussion topic at a formal event like this," Silk said, for the first time betraying annoyance. They took his elbow, sending a wave of pleasure up his arm, and led the group from the entrance doors toward the tables at the front of the room. "This is for the esteemed citizenry, in acknowledgment of their accomplishments, and for special guests."

Victor stopped, shrugged away, and held up a hand to indicate to the rest of the party they would go no further. He wasn't there to be esteemed and gawked at. He was there to make a deal and get home. The Diamond King had insisted that he come. So where was he? "What is the point of all this? We're here to do business with the Diamond King, not ... not whatever this is."

Silk's eyes widened. "Please, don't make a scene."

Sensing he had the upper hand, Victor rooted his feet and looked around. They had been noticed. Curious glances and sly gestures showed them to be the center of attention.

Victor faced Silk. "Why are we here?"

"To celebrate!"

"Why, really?"

"I don't know. I only know I'm to be your escort for the evening. When you get an order here, you don't question it! Please!"

The din of the crowd faded, growing quieter, curiosity giving way to dread. The event was clearly meant to be an enjoyable spectacle, not anything objectionable or controversial. Victor and his entourage, by interrupting the flow, created a problem, and in Las Vegas problems could be serious indeed.

He was on the verge of walking out the door, climbing into the sky flier, and whirring back to the city when Wonda sidled up to him and whispered, "We're here. We might as well chat up everyone so we can get more information. If this is the dumbest thing we've ever done, let's at least do it smartly, right?"

Was she wise or was she naive? Victor knew she'd grown up in poverty, scrambled to find her place in society. Was all this opulence intoxicating? Or was she savvy enough to find her way to the heart of power? With Wonda, it was somehow all those things at the same time.

Victor let the drugs in his system return him to calm lucidity and indicated for Silk to resume showing them to their tables, saying, "We'll go with you if you answer our questions. All of them."

Silk nodded gratefully and led the party to an empty table at the center of the room.

Battalions of robot servers began conveying plates of food. Their table was served first. Each robot deftly maneuvered dishes on pneumatic arms that looked like tentacles.

Victor sliced into a pasta square filled with mushrooms and cheese and covered with sage-butter, though it had a slightly strange texture, and he wondered if it was non-dairy. The least of his concerns.

"Silk, have you met the King before?"

"Met? You mean in person? Of course not. My rating ..."

Wonda growled, a frustrated sound like an engine that wouldn't start. "Could someone explain this rating thing to me? Like you literally have a score that runs your life?"

Silk stiffened. "In a way. But it's not controlling you. It reflects your contribution to society. It's earned."

Tosh added, speaking with his mouth full of pasta, "Ten is the highest number. After that, you're elite. Then it gets complicated. But there are other factors. Suits are your professions. Clubs are mercs; bureaucrats too, anything government related. Diamonds are for business. Hearts are for the arts, sports, communications. And spades are the technologists, the scientists, right, Silk?"

"Yes. All that's an oversimplification of course. And the suits aren't official."

"Show me your rating," Tosh demanded.

Silk looked surprised for a moment, then acquiesced, pulling out a small vidscreen and showing it to everyone: an eight of hearts. "I chose the heart insignia. It wasn't assigned to me. It's not a nickname or a title. It's like ... like a tribe, one that I chose to be part of. Nothing is off limits to anyone based on suits. It's just a shorthand way of saying, 'I'm into these types of things.' And it's a topic that provokes endless discussion."

"What about teachers? Which suit are they?" Wonda asked.

Silk gave Wonda a blank look.

"I was an art teacher in the LTs before—" Wonda glanced at Victor with a soft glaze of sadness. Turning back to Silk, she repeated, "So, teachers?"

"I'm not sure what you mean."

Ozie looked up from the delicate job of eating with one human hand and one cyberhand. "There's no public education system. No official teachers, and yet everyone is potentially a teacher. It's all assisted learning. Standard course materials. Interactive modules. Mentors. That type of thing. When someone masters the coursework for a given subject, they enter into an apprenticeship. Learning by doing. There are learning groups for sports, arts, and science projects."

"And that works?" Wonda asked, clearly skeptical.

"Of course," Silk said. "Knowledge is there for the taking. Experience has to be—"

"Has to be earned," Tosh spoke over them. "That's pretty much how everything works here. There are no free riders. Everything is possible, but you have to work for it."

"Exactly," Silk said.

Victor thought back to all the seconds, minutes, and hours he counted down, waiting for the end bell to release him from school's social hell. The Las Vegas system sounded too good to be true.

Doesn't matter. Stay focused.

Jefferson had dealings with the Diamond King, and look what happened. Death by radioactivity. However attractive this society's portrait was, it wasn't the whole story. Victor's survival wasn't guaranteed. And back in New Venice, a host of bodies waited for resurrection.

30

Lights beaming down from the canopy sizzled in their sharp brightness, making Victor queasy until they dimmed, leaving only the
stage illuminated. A woman with long bright green hair, wearing
a sleek red dress, came on stage while the crowd applauded. She
announced a rank increase and a special award of a kiosk in Grand
Park to a man who sidled up to her meekly, clearly awed by the
gathering. He accepted the award, then stood alone on the stage,
clearing his throat. He wore a cream-colored suit, a gold and blue
cravat, and bright yellow shoes. People in Las Vegas liked a bit of
pizzaz. The presenter announced his name and title: Dr. Killean
Brücktwyn, Chief Civil Engineer for Las Vegas. Now, that was a
profession of importance, Victor thought, building real things in
the real world that affected what people could do and what the
world looked like. All his brain science, computer coding, and social
dynamics permutations seemed suddenly ethereal in contrast.
Human ideas could be dismissed or changed on a whim, whereas
concrete, steel, glass, and all the new materials technologists could
manufacture were the bones that held up this society.

Behind Brücktwyn, a video screen the size of a large bus showed
a map of the Organized Western States. Brücktwyn began speaking, at first stiffly but then loosening up after a minute. He'd
given this talk before, apparently. Victor listened eagerly, bliss-
fully transported beyond his self-centered concerns. It felt like
escaping gravity.

The presentation focused on water resource management in
the OWS, with a particular focus on Las Vegas and its reuse of
wastewater and how that had changed over the years, bringing
the city ever closer to being self-sustaining. Historical figures for

rainfall and river diversions, groundwater usage, and recycling swam onto the screen and accumulated as the man continued speaking. The audience, seemingly in tune with Victor, was rapt. He could almost sense the weight of water moving across the land, through its tunnel and tubes, funneled into the infrastructure making this part of the desert, if not green and wasteful, then at least satisfied and wet-whistled. The presentation concluded with a summary of the specific actions that Killean had spearheaded during his career. A standing ovation followed. The engineer left the stage, replaced by the presenter, who indicated the next award would be announced in twenty minutes.

Victor looked around, expecting an excited conversation about aqueducts and water recycling technologies. What followed instead was a deluge of offers for mind-altering substances. There were candies, pipes, tinctures, canisters, powders, gels, and various pills in different shapes. Vidscreens on the table detailed their effects and recommended dosages when held close to the vidcapper. Several people at Victor's table remarked on their favorites and what they liked and didn't like on occasions like this one. A few said they already felt spectacular and would likely not "augment."

In various ways, Victor's crew conveyed that the evening was a delight but a little overwhelming, so they would abstain. Looking across the room at the other tables, it was apparent most citizens indulged their inclinations.

Brücktwyn was added to their table's complement. He knew a few of the other people sitting with them, and when introduced to Victor and the rest, he seemed already familiar with their status as respected guests.

"I would be curious to hear," Brücktwyn began, "what you think about how we're managing our resources, especially compared to other nations in the AU."

"None of us are engineers," Victor said. "I don't know what we could say about it."

Brücktwyn appeared to be disappointed and looked around anxiously.

"I'll admit," Wonda added, "I don't know much about all this stuff. But it seems—I don't know—I mean, sure, you've made progress and all, but I don't see why it's so important. I know rain is scarce here, but you have the Cold Nile. Literally, all the water you could want comes by canal."

Brücktwyn smiled and seemed to be heading toward more comfortable territory as he responded. Maybe he was feeling pressured to keep them engaged. Or distracted. "That is true. It is a marvel. And yet, there are limits to how much can be shipped. The canal has a maximum flow capacity that is currently sufficient for deliveries. However, settlements are expanding up and down the length of the project. We're planning to ensure we can meet demand for years to come, even if we never receive a centimeter of rain in the basin for an entire year."

Tosh smiled his wolfish grin and leaned forward, which was a sure sign that he was on the attack. "There's also the fact that the Cold Nile represents the single most vulnerable piece of critical infrastructure in the OWS."

Ozie shook his head in warning, but Tosh didn't see it or didn't care. Tosh continued, "What does this city need? Power. The solar towers have that covered. The city exports power beyond the OWS. Semiautonomous California and the Louisiana Territories pay loads of AUD for it. But what do you think would happen if the Cold Nile was bombed or sabotaged?"

"Tosh!" Ozie gestured to the shocked faces of Silk, Dr. Brücktwyn, and the other citizens. "You're freaking them out, and I doubt you-know-who likes the sound of this."

"You-know-who is way ahead of everyone in gaming this out. Why do you think we're hearing from a middling water engineer? No offense, Mr. Brücktwyn, but you're not that impressive a speaker, and what you've done is essentially a hack plumbing job, albeit on a gigantic scale."

"None taken," Brücktwyn said, though his face turned red. "I moved up one rank tonight, which is nothing to sniff at but not so extraordinary at the end of the day." He sounded sincere. Whatever pride he took in the night's acknowledgments was probably more to do with the fact that he really liked civil engineering. As he put it, the status bump and public praise were unavoidable and inevitable parts of the job. Victor couldn't help but think about people with MRS in SeCa, those Class Threes like himself, who, no matter what their contributions to society, would be shunned, their accomplishments minimalized, sidelined from public praise and recognition. How would they be treated here? Just like anyone else?

"So," Tosh continued, "you-know-who wants Las Vegas to be self-sufficient, and not because he's got a warm place in his heart for the people here, but because it patches up a vulnerability well before the battle."

Victor frowned at Tosh. He should drop it unless there was a point to his badgering.

"What battle are you referring to?" Brücktwyn asked. "The nations of the American Union are at peace, among each other and with the great powers."

"For now," Tosh admitted, "But when war comes—"

"War is always a last resort," Brücktwyn said.

"Yes, exactly," Silk added.

"When war comes," Tosh continued implacably, "there's another unaddressed vulnerability in the amount of goods transiting by rail along the Cold Nile to and from the port in Columbia Sound. What would happen if the rail portion of the Cold Nile were to find itself inoperable? My guess, since you're wondering—"

"We aren't," Victor said caustically. The bleak looks on their Las Vegas hosts' faces made his stomach churn. This seemed like socially taboo terrain, yet he was curious about where Tosh was going with his questions. They were here to get help with the Broken Mirrors in the LTs. Did Tosh not care about that or was this an oblique tactic to influence their bargaining stance with the Diamond King?

"Is that vulnerability going to be patched, too? I bet tonight or another night not so far into the future, we're going to have ourselves another award winner who presents on the progress in expanding the road and rail links between the southern OWS and its neighbors, particularly to the south where Imperial Mexico is busy developing its own port infrastructure on both the Pacific and Gulf sides of its territory."

Silk and Brücktwyn gave each other surprised glances.

"Am I wrong?" Tosh asked them.

"Indeed," Brücktwyn said, "you're not. There's been much talk of it. The Southern Network it's being called."

Tosh sat back and crossed his arms, seemingly satisfied to have made his point.

"That was a mistake," Ozie said.

"Again," Tosh answered, "you, my friend, mistake honesty for criticism and obvious facts for secrets. I don't know what you've been fussing around with here on behalf of our lord, the Diamond King, but you may not want to keep your head so tightly wedged up your ass."

Silk winced at this, and Brücktwyn frowned to an exaggerated degree. Ozie stared coldly, remaining still as a stone.

Tosh seemed to revel in the anxiety he was causing. He explained, "I've been trying to figure out what the other nations are going to do in response to all these moves. How much do they see the OWS as a threat? And what are they prepared to do to counter it?"

"And?" Wonda asked. "You want to let us in on your 'honesty' and 'facts'?"

"There will be a war. And only one side will be prepared for it. Because no one wants to see what's plain as day: the OWS is prepared to win."

Victor looked at Ozie. "You basically said the same thing at dinner with my parents. You agree with him, don't you?" Ozie tapped on the table, ignoring Victor.

Brücktwyn looked down his nose at Tosh. "I will say it again because perhaps you didn't understand the first time. War is only a last resort."

"Keep telling yourselves that," Tosh said.

"But don't you see?" Silk said. "A war is counter-productive. It would be unnecessary. We're an ongoing economic miracle that the rest of the world is lucky to trade with. We provide a model for the other nations. Our technology and social innovations can lift up the AU."

"I'm sure you'll be willing to share all of this," Wonda said.

Silk answered quickly, unreservedly, "Of course."

Wonda slammed her palms on the table, rattling the flatware. "Whether we want it or not! The way you shared your little helping doses with us whether we wanted them or not. And the way that stims are being pushed whether the other nations want them or not. And probably whatever things he's cooking up." She jabbed a finger toward Ozie, who looked away, finger tapping agitatedly.

Victor had tired of the bickering and speculation and was about to say that a simplistic debate about something as complicated as trade, technology, and society wasn't particularly relevant or useful in the current moment when smoke began to rise from the stage. Alarmed, he was about to jump to his feet but paused as the lighting above them dimmed, and a green and blue glow infused the smoke. He caught a whiff of salt spray and kelp. He turned to Wonda to ask if it was just his mind playing tricks, when he saw, rising from the stage, ten or so tentacles.

Thick as tree trunks yet more flexible, they rose and swayed, forming a circular screen. Drums and low-resounding oboes and didgeridoos thrummed a languid rhythm. The tentacles parted, radiating out in sinuous arcs, revealing a woman, apparently naked, standing center stage. Her skin was sea-green and iridescent, and a cap covered her hair.

Victor expected her to break into song, maybe a low wailing number to match the music. Instead, she extended her arms to the side and then pulled them in. The tentacles responded, moving outward then retracting, so clearly reversing their previous expansion that it looked for a moment like time had reversed. She intertwined her fingers and palms, lifted them to the ceiling, and beneath her feet, the tentacles wove together into a platform that began to rise. Ten meters in the air, it halted.

She moved to the edge of the platform, lifted one leg, and a tentacle split from the others, its raised end flattening, broad like a leaf, and she stepped onto its rock-steady firmness. She raised another leg, and a tentacle created the next platform, a little lower this time. And again, she stepped down. She was accelerating her decent, green leaves forming at the precise moment she needed them, a staircase solidifying beneath her feet. She ran down, spiraling toward the ground one platform at a time.

When she looked poised to sprint onto the stage, she lifted her arms straight up and a slim tentacle extruded swiftly into her gripping hands. As she swung forward, another slick pole shot out, catching her behind the knees, and she revolved on it; again, one met her hands, and around she went, revolving, forward and back so fast that Victor could hardly follow her movements. Her body and the tentacle structures no longer seemed separate, and when she twisted, the tentacles twisted to meet her. With one leg hooked around a tentacle, her body splayed out, her arms moving with the music, appearing to draw the air and the spectators closer.

Short of breath and feeling out of body, Victor let his gaze drift. The light show pulsed on every surface, false colors reflecting dim outlines. He considered going blank briefly to get some relief from the frenzied lights and cacophony.

The crowd, initially laughing at the act's novelty, now stood cheering, screaming, and gasping with delight. The dancing-flying woman was flirting with a tentacle, drawing closer then away, looking bashful then brazen. While a crowd-pleaser, it left Victor cold. Everyone here was laughing and cheering, and in New Venice the comatose patients were waiting for him to wake them up. If he could get the Diamond King's help. If there really was a deal to be made. He was starting to doubt it.

Victor sensed movement and saw that Ozie was standing over him, looking flushed and panicked. Bending down, Ozie hissed in his ear. "We need to talk. I have a suspicion and it's melting my brain."

Victor noticed a weight on his head that hadn't been there before. Ozie had slipped a braincap on while he was distracted.

The crowd was still screaming at the comedy act, while the other tentacles behaved like interested, jealous suitors of the woman on the stage.

"You want to talk now? Really?" Victor asked.

"I didn't see it before. It's the Diamond King. I thought we could play a trick hand, outmaneuver him." He laughed bitterly. "How could I not see it?" He watched the performance, his fingers tapping on his collarbones, self-soothing. Something was really freaking him out.

"What happened? You seemed to be doing fine before."

Ozie's eyes widened. He grabbed Victor's suit by the lapels, bunching the fabric in his fists to the point that Victor felt the breath squeezed out of him. Ozie roared in his face, "You're not paying fucking attention!" before letting him go.

A few nearby citizens looked concerned. He smiled meekly and waved, pretending he and Ozie were having a joke. He play-punched Ozie for good measure but forgot which arm was his human one and landed the cyber one instead. Pain flashed in his knuckles. He yelped and nestled his hand in his armpit. Ozie didn't laugh as Victor thought he might have. He only shook his head and stalked away.

What was bothering him? Why couldn't he come out and say it?

Victor watched the rest of the woman's act, which now seemed to be showing off all the ways she might try to kill herself by falling. The tentacles deftly saved her every time. But he was too busy thinking of Ozie. He probably didn't like that the action was on his turf now, that's all. He'd preferred to send his drones to New Venice and mess things up there. Well, Victor wasn't arguing with his advice. He'd get whatever the Diamond King had to offer to fix the Broken Mirrors and then return home. He didn't see why Ozie had to get so bent out of shape.

What would he tell Alia, though? She and Torsten were desperate to find out what had happened to Anders. Instead of trying to find a lead, he was laughing it up with Las Vegas society. Maybe there was something to Ozie's warning after all. Victor wasn't in control; his hosts were leading him around like a dog on a leash, and he still hadn't been able to call or talk to anyone back in New Venice. Pearl could help him figure out what to do, but she'd been impossible to reach. What were they doing here, watching all this stage business? They should be negotiating.

The audience was applauding as the woman bowed, and Victor sensed this had been going on for a while. He got up, thinking he could sneak away and find Ozie. But as the crowd's noise reached a crescendo, the tentacles rose again and extended into the crowd, carrying the woman at the crest of their undulating waves, right toward Victor.

She was deposited in front of him, smiling broadly. She bowed and said, "I dedicated that performance to you in the hopes of good cooperation and collaboration in the future."

Victor froze under the gazes of everyone in the entire performance hall—he felt a gush of saliva in his mouth. *Don't let me throw up right now. Or go blank.* He noticed now that she wasn't naked per se but wore full body paint and a piece of fabric or plastic to cover her privates. "You were amazing."

She smiled again and inclined her head in gratitude. Pride in orange hues feathered her expression, yet a purpose lurked behind her eyes as she held his gaze.

Seduction. Again?

I've had enough.

What Victor said next, turning in a circle to maximize his audience, he said as loud as possible without screaming. "I want to talk to the Diamond King right fucking now, or I'm leaving Las Vegas tonight."

31

I always thought my dreams were meant to teach me something useful, like they were warnings or premonitions. If only I'd known the truth.

—Victor Eastmore, *Apology to Resonant Earth* (transmission date unknown)

17 May 1992
Las Vegas, Organized Western States

Pearlescent moonlit mountains surrounded the gala hall. Pale glowing slopes rose toward the stars while black shadows clustered in the ravines. Ozie avoided looking down for fear of seeing shapes there: ghosts of his imagination, sneering at his utter stupidity. Instead, he looked up at the Moon, its brightness a reminder that earthly problems could be surmounted and escaped if only he could outsmart gravity.

Tonight was a triumph. He'd done his job, dragging Victor to Las Vegas to bargain with the Diamond King. But he couldn't think about it.

Fuck, oh fuck, oh fuck; we are so fucked ...

Ozie cranked up his braincap. Victor had managed to forget days and weeks, entire arcs of his life, so maybe Ozie could forget this completely. Erase, delete, fucking burn it to zeros.

The brain pluggers surpassed all reasonable expectations. Grette had smiled the other day and congratulated him. The implants worked. The tentacle show had proved at least one non-military application of the technology—and it had broken Ozie out of his stupor. *Fuck!* He was in too deep. He should abort the mission, but the mission was more important now that he knew the truth. If he stopped now, if he complied, if he set aside his plans and allowed the future to emerge, history might never absolve him.

Why try to fight the inevitable? No one can hold back the tide.

We can at least build some seawalls and manage to retreat.

Ozie had tried to raise the alarm with Victor, but he wasn't deciphering the signals that Ozie practically screamed in his face. To be watched closely and to go unheard at the same time was a special kind of torture. It hadn't made a difference. Victor was falling under the Diamond King's influence, and Ozie couldn't speak plainly enough to warn him. Victor had always had a knack for not seeing what was right in front of him.

The patch of the artificial wrist where the Diamond King often made an unwelcome appearance to Ozie thankfully remained dark. Otherwise, he might have screamed. *I'm working for a monster, and nobody knows the truth but me.*

Over the sounds of partying within the great pavilion, he heard sand rasping across the plateau's concrete apron, the low hooting of an owl from somewhere within the trees in the deep valley, and coyotes' excited yapping for a kill. Yet everything was spinning into chaos. All was not as it seemed. Alarms rang in his head. Centuries ago, they called what he was planning "regicide." But he saw it more like an amputation to prevent an infection from spreading. Or a hard code reset.

He glanced back at the gala. The formal festivities had given way to unprogrammed merriment. Beyond tall transparent windows, people in gowns and suits danced and chatted. Ambitious social climbers sought out connections. Romances kindled; a few combusted. He should be in there, making a name for himself and riding the surging crest of his service to Las Vegas toward fame and fortune.

Get real. You're falling apart.

His body, a brittle, malnourished patchwork of goop and silicon chips, shook, torn between tension and exhaustion. He'd be lucky to survive the next few weeks with his mind intact. He looked at his cyberarm in disgust. It had been a wellspring of joy and wonder, but now it was a nightmare.

A figure approached, sinuous, shimmering. It was Silk, perhaps the most beautiful person Ozie had ever met, and all the more attractive for their intelligence and calm, assured confidence, which, at the moment, they were uncharacteristically lacking.

Silk stood half a meter away, every part of them fluttering. Ozie was sympathetic, up to a point. Silk was probably worried about saving face, whereas Ozie was concerned about the future of humanity.

"Why aren't you doing anything?" Silk asked.

Ozie stayed silent and waited. As a double-agent, he was getting very good at waiting. The risk was always in saying too much, putting too many cards on the table.

"I don't know what to do. How can I fix this?" Silk asked.

Ozie removed his glasses and pinched his brow, pressing hard as he stretched the skin outward along the lines of his eyebrows. It didn't help relieve the tension.

"Please. What do I do?"

"I don't know," Ozie admitted. Silk was deeply embedded in the system he intended to subvert. Something rumbled in his guts that wasn't guilt or shame. He was too good at rationalizing and self-preservation to be stuck in that socially conditioned filth. Maybe it was sadness and, perhaps, a bit of regret for a life spent using people, manipulating them, bringing them close if they were useful, or, if they weren't, leaving them to the figurative wolves. If he didn't play this right, he would lose his only friend. Compared to that, Silk was merely driftwood floundering in his wake.

Silk took a breath and looked ready to shriek.

Ozie said, "You've done everything you can. Let me figure something out."

Silk put a gloved hand to their mouth. Ozie should have faked a bravado he didn't feel, been more reassuring. But in this game, the high-value cards swept up the low ones. Silk was feeling an invisible hand's merciless disregard.

"What if he's angry?" Silk whispered.

Ozie didn't respond except to crank up his braincap. When he spotted Tosh exiting the gala and rushing toward them, he resisted calling out. He didn't trust his voice not to sound panicked.

Tosh glanced at Silk and then pinned a stare on Ozie that was as uncomfortable as if he'd been lanced in his stomach. He resisted the urge to defend himself and say, "I haven't told anyone we're planning treason." Tosh should think more highly of him by now. Or maybe Tosh was scared, too.

"We're going," Tosh said, gripping Ozie's bicep. Ozie began to protest, but a warning flared in Tosh's eyes, and an instinct for self-preservation sealed his lips. Better to appear cooperative. Tosh told Silk, "I think your part in this is done."

"No," Silk gasped. "Please, I can help. If you let me come with you …"

Ozie shrank within himself. This was how power worked in Las Vegas, by proximity, by access. Silk was being frozen out of the negotiations. A minor loss of status. Nothing world-ending. But status here was everything, and fear of the Diamond King made even a minor slip treacherous. Fearmongering was the most hideous of all tyrannies. This was why he'd committed to this path. The madness had to stop.

Tosh's face was a mask of cold sternness. "Go."

Silk shouted in a parting defense, "I didn't do anything wrong," before departing in swift steps toward the gala and into the pen of sheep. Time to meet with the shepherd.

Tosh slipped his arm around Ozie's waist. There was no warmth in the gesture, no intimacy, simply a dominant physicality with an arousing effect that surprised Ozie.

He gets away with too much. But in times of trouble, we need strongmen as much as we need eggheads.

Tosh guided him in an arc away from the ravine until, side by side, they faced a set of hills. City lights glittered in the dusk beyond. Tosh was staring. Ozie opened his mouth to ask but caught the subtle shake of Tosh's head. The man continued to stare out into the desert.

Toward the city, red lights cast their glow on the solar towers dotting the blackness. To his right, the foothills were unbroken stretches of shadow, faintly glowing in the moonlight, with one exception: a few lights clustered at the foot of the mountains where a two-story building sprawled and curled like a sidewinder on gravel. That's where Tosh was staring.

When Tosh spoke, his voice was soft and deep, though toneless. "Between times when I was running jobs for Jefferson in the Democratic Republic of Mexico, I met up with him a few times here. He kept me busy, mostly, but he also made sure I found time to relax and enjoy the company of locals."

Their arms were inches apart. How would Tosh feel if Ozie leaned against him? Could they share strength, connection, or lustful, desperate embraces? If only there were more camaraderie among the tools Jefferson Eastmore had assembled to carry out his will beyond the grave. Ozie sensed a hidden weight within Tosh's words but couldn't quite grasp why he was talking about what he assumed were brothels.

Let it be. Listen.

"Is that so?" Ozie asked, hoping Tosh would interpret the message as, "What the Laws do you mean?" or "Come a little closer and tell me." He cycled the program on his braincap. If Tosh was radiating sexual hunger, it was a distraction Ozie couldn't afford.

"There's more to find there than companionship. There's a kind of freedom."

Freedom.

Tosh had put no special emphasis on the word spoken in an unexcited monotone. Yet Ozie knew that was the key. It was the one word he'd desperately needed to hear to give him hope.

Did Tosh know the truth?

Ozie looked at the far-off building; mostly, it was a blur of light. He squinted and thought maybe it was an older structure that lacked certain modern conveniences like vidcaps, mics, and surveillance equipment that Ozie knew without a doubt were threaded through every building within the Grand Orbit circling the city. A place to speak freely? A place to learn how freedom might be attained? If the building was none of that, if it was only a brothel, that might be enough freedom to enjoy for a while.

"You're right," Ozie said. "We all need some ... relaxation."

Tosh nodded, removed his arm, and walked not toward the gala but on the path leading them directly to the skyfliers. Ozie followed. A wad of hope burned in his chest, but he feared it wasn't enough. What if, with each step, he wasn't moving closer to freedom and was only running down the clock of his indefinite servitude? Lacking any beneficent gods in a realm of covetous, greedy demons, he prayed for nothing more than an opportunity to escape.

32

The smart executive doesn't manage the business of today. Instead, she plans for the future, which she'll create with vision, insight, and dedicated effort.

—Circe Eastmore, *Race to the Top* (1991)

19 May 1992
New Venice, The Louisiana Territories

Circe declined Karine's offer to tour the tower's unfinished floors and review the progress with her own eyes. Instead, the BioScan chief welcomed Karine into her office and looked down with stoic reserve at the stone buildings of New Venice. Karine couldn't begin to understand how Circe felt about the place. The Eastmore family's deep connection must live in her bones. But Karine guessed that the wanderlust that had led Circe to Europe at an early age wouldn't ever be tamed.

Despite planning to do so, Karine wouldn't criticize Circe for blowing the roof off the travel budget, not to her face. She'd learned diplomacy over the years. She knew when to bring up a topic and when to let things lie. This was one of those let-it-lie moments. They had decades of history to help smooth any bumps in the road ahead.

Circe's attitude toward the BioScan operations had notably changed. Of that, Karine had no doubts. Before, Circe's efforts were energizing, and she had thrust herself in the middle of every decision, every deliberation, and nothing was too minor a matter to contend with—what a thrill it had been to watch her take the reins of the company and to see the fervor with which she whipped the operation into shape.

Now, that verve had gone into hiding. Circe looked out with sunken, tired eyes. Karine didn't think it was the hostage crisis that exacted this toll. Her gut said it was something else, something still unfolding. But how do you ask your boss why she looks so haunted? Would the answer give any reassurance, or would it make matters worse? Karine was well-versed in Eastmore psychology and would prefer not to dive deep again.

Karine broached the topic softly but directly. "You asked me to look at the MRS patient numbers. There are some jagged edges to this puzzle. I'm going to need to do some traveling around, interview some people, review their files. Are you comfortable with Victor in charge while I'm gone?"

This was a trap, of course. Victor had gone missing a few days ago. Karine had decided that it was still plausible that she remained unaware, so she'd framed the question thus. Victor was the source of many problems, and Karine wanted to keep her hands clean. He was the poison tainting what should have been close and trusting relations between her and her Chief, the way it had been for them back in Madrid. Now Circe was distant, so Karine needed to play games to protect herself. It was an entirely reasonable approach.

Circe waved a hand dismissively. "Of course. He'll have to get used to it if he's ever going to succeed me."

Karine felt her eyes nearly pop out of their sockets. "I'm sorry," she said. "Did you say—"

"Don't make this a big deal, Karine." Circe looked her square in the eye. Any fondness, any warmth that had ever been there, was gone, replaced by a cold, disappointed glare. "You can't be surprised that I'm grooming Victor. This is a family company, after all."

No, of course, I'm not surprised. That's what she should say. That was the diplomatic response. Submission. Capitulation. That's what Circe expected to hear.

Karine's mouth sealed shut. She always knew the smart course of action. She knew how to manipulate. She knew how to play a long game. But in the last few seconds, something had snapped suddenly, irrevocably, and unexpectedly. She couldn't bring herself to say the words. She couldn't pretend this wasn't the last fucking straw and that she wasn't fucking so completely done with Circe, Victor, the Eastmores, and their stupid company.

"Was that too flip? I apologize." Circe wore a sympathetic expression. Karine no longer cared to conjecture if it was genuine.

"Of course. I'll let you know what I find out," Karine said, keeping her voice smooth. She stood and saw spots and darkness.

"You can take a couple of days, you know, if you need them. We can't be burning ourselves out now, can we?"

"That sounds nice," Karine said flatly. "Safe travels."

Karine left the room, shut the door behind her. Around the corner, she stopped against a wall and closed her eyes.

She should have known.

You can't be surprised, she told herself.

But she was.

How? How! How could Circe possibly think Victor was stable enough, qualified enough to lead the company? It was absurd.

Yet she should have known.

Despite a strong urge to leave the building, board a train, travel far away, and never return, Karine didn't allow herself the luxury of nonsense fantasies. She'd dedicated years of her life to supporting Circe. Halcyon days of mostly independent operations at Gene-Us aside, the better part of a decade had seen her taking orders from a woman, who, it turns out, showed all the good judgment and upstanding character of a toad.

A toad in shit, Karine thought. *So, what now?*

Karine let the gears in her mind—so accustomed to business strategizing—start turning to analyze her situation. Circe's plans for Victor weren't urgent or imminent. She'd spoken offhandedly about a far-off day when Victor would take over. Chances were, Victor wasn't aware that this route had been plotted for him—he would probably be more shocked than Karine. For all his faults, he had few illusions about how other people saw him, and Karine knew he wouldn't deem himself reliable, capable, or qualified enough for the job of Chief, family business or not. It was iffy whether he could spearhead treatment for stim addicts and Broken Mirrors, a fiendishly complicated charge. In truth, he had been displaying more confidence, initiative, and dependability—his present unexplained disappearance notwithstanding. Still, he had a long, *long* way to go.

It was true that he and Karine also had a rapprochement, an extraordinary one considering what he'd done to her in that disgustingly dirty motel with his skeezy friends. Sweat materialized on her brow. Gooseflesh rose on her arms. The chair she'd been tied to pressed against her back. The ropes cinched tight. Her breath labored. A bright flash of pain echoed where Elena struck her cheek. Victor's spittle flew; his eyes were wild, rage-filled, murderous. She tried to shake off the memory. The paranoia in that room had been intoxicating. Not for the first time, she wondered about MRS's emotional contagion being a two-way circuit. Would alternative treatments fix *that*?

At the very least, she and Victor shared a goal of helping their patients. Along the way, surprisingly, without much bother and certainly without reciprocation, she'd gained his trust.

There's the solution.

A distracted Circe and an unwitting, trusting Victor created a situation Karine could exploit. Karine called her assistant, telling him to track down Victor, who wasn't in New Venice; she was sure of that. For a brief, hilarious moment, she almost thought of hiring Lucky and Bandit again to track him down, but that had ended so spectacularly badly last time she couldn't countenance doing it a second time around. She wasn't someone who made the same mistake twice. Perhaps Alia would know where he had gone. She placed a call, but the connection didn't go through.

She knew what she needed to do: start planning trips. On the surface, she would investigate patient transfers, recordkeeping, and supporting growth as MRS and anti-stim laws were enacted. The substance of her trips, however, would be known only to herself: she would interrogate BioScan facilities, operations, and finances and make a plan that would allow her to outsmart the Eastmores, siphon their riches, and leave them holding an empty container.

33

Psychoactive substances, in the right quantities and at the right moments, can make miracles apparent. That's one lesson the Catholic Church can take credit for.

—*A History of Las Vegas* (author unknown)

17 May 1992
Las Vegas, Organized Western States

Victor was waiting by the skyfliers when Tosh and Ozie walked up.

"Where did you two go?" he asked.

They exchanged a look like guilty dogs who'd stolen treats. A flash of jealousy came and went. No time for *that* silliness. It was time for the fish to go into the fryer. "I'll do the talking," Victor said. "Follow my lead." He was proud of the steel in his voice that indicated he was done following, fretting, and burdening everyone else. They would talk to the Diamond King, and he was in command.

Wonda walked up to them. "I'm ready. That party was a bunch of drugged-out narcissists."

Victor opened his mouth to point out multiple ironies in her statement when the interior screen of the skyflier glowed brightly. A vortex of pixels resolved into a playing card with the Diamond King at the center. It was a pale, cartoonish avatar drawn in slim black lines and sweeping curves. The face remained motionless as a robotic voice said, "The coordinates have been programmed."

Victor grabbed the handle, climbed in, and turned to help Wonda.

"About time," she said. Ozie and Tosh climbed aboard after her.

The cabin was lit only by the console blinking and reading out their telemetry and city lights in the distance, drawing swiftly closer. They descended vertically, sliding down among tall buildings. The skyflier landed on a ground-level pad in the Summer quarter. The pavement glittered, marking a path toward a building curved to fit the arc of a ring road that stretched a few blocks before vanishing around the bend. An empty atrium, ablaze with lights, opened its doors, and, as they walked in, Victor in the lead, followed by Wonda, then Tosh, and finally Ozie, he realized where they were. The Institute for Applied Biological Science. He'd been there before with Elena, pretending to be on a date, using Ozie's gadgets to steal the data encoding the MRS gene. If not a coincidence, then the Diamond King leading them here was … what? A message, perhaps? A reminder? Before he could puzzle too much over it, they were walking down a hall that wasn't part of the tourist route.

Their journey ended in a waiting room, not unlike a doctor's office. The majestic vistas they'd become accustomed to were gone. Nothing adorned the walls—no art, no sconces. Lightstrips were nestled in the joins between the walls and ceiling. Low chairs lined the walls, each with a small side table devoid of ornamentation.

They hadn't been offered anything to eat or drink. The ease and comfort forced on them throughout the day had vanished. So did their highs. The comedown was gentle, but a warm bed and darkness would be welcome. Did the Diamond King expect the change to influence their discussions? Seeking such a minor advantage seemed cheap and disappointing. Victor liked to think they wouldn't be so easily rattled.

Wonda plucked at her sleeves and looked around anxiously. Tosh sat down, his back straight, and closed his eyes. Ozie fiddled with his cyberarm, avoiding Victor's gaze. Whatever he'd been plotting with Tosh, now wasn't the time to ask.

He sat and mused and waited, his eyes closed. No means to mark time in the dull room, aside from Tosh's breathing. He knew nothing more about the Diamond King than he did a day ago, except he knew more about the society here. It was impressive, sure, but did that matter? Many people would swear it was a shining example for the rest of humanity. But it was a backwater, a landlocked curiosity, remote and unimportant. Part of Victor wished there was a dark corruption at its heart that negated everything good he'd heard about it. Despite himself, however, he was persuaded. The OWS would make a great refuge, a place to start over. He would entertain the thought of staying and contributing to such a grand project—if it didn't mean a complete abandonment of his past and principles. The other MRS patients deserved more from him.

It wasn't that he owed anything to the patients counting on him for help. Their lot was already vastly improved by being moved to the BioScan campus, where research could proceed and treatments beyond mind-numbing Personil could be explored. He did truly want to help them. That wouldn't be the deciding factor, though. He had to be totally, brutally honest with himself if he was going to emerge from this crucible as anything more than melted-down raw material for the Diamond King to mold. He wanted the cure for himself.

The door whisked aside. He opened his eyes. Wonda met his gaze and tried on a smile that died as soon as she saw the figure in the doorway. Swirling black fear and uncertainty hazed her expression. As he turned to look, his breath caught in his throat.

Victor had expected one of the Diamond King's many eager lackeys to walk through the door and escort them to a grand conference room or an office with another stunning view of the Las Vegas skyline. What he saw instead mystified him.

It was as if a mannequin had gained the ability of auto-locomotion. Into the room walked a gray creature, human-shaped, limbed with vague joints, wrought of a smooth material, synthsilk in appearance yet solid.

And more disturbingly, faceless.

It strode into the room and sat in one of the empty chairs next to Wonda, who stared with wide eyes, mouth open. Tosh remained motionless and watchful. Ozie wore a creased brow, his eyes crackling with intense curiosity as he stared at the thing in their presence.

The blank face glowed with light, and suddenly, the Diamond King's playing-card face was visible, more photo-realistic, like a vidcap image superimposed on a curved surface.

Ozie moved closer, peering intensely. "Glass? Is it flexible?"

"You've never seen this before?" Victor asked.

Ozie turned to him, shook his head, and then laughed darkly. "I guess I wasn't special enough. He's showing off his toys for you." His face clouded with some negative emotion Victor couldn't name.

"Toys?" Wonda echoed in a whisper. Then, with bitterness and disgust, she said, "This isn't a game."

"Let's begin." The Diamond King's voice came from the avatar's face, crystal clear, sounding as a human voice should, a man's voice, rich and deep. The thing remained motionless, though the face was animated, eyes blinking, lips curving in a slight smile. The image was high-resolution, not pixelated, appearing almost human, if not for the exaggerated red, gold, and black coloration. Victor was reminded of Orb Weavers, those bulbous, intricately patterned spiders the size of his thumb that spun webs of geometric precision. Granma Cynthia's garden was meticulous in every way, but she had a soft spot for the Orb Weavers and delighted in their constructions, leading the family to view them on dewy, humid mornings as the fog burned off and the plants steamed. Victor felt the same wonder now mixed with a desire to keep his distance.

"It's not simply a projection," Ozie said, scrutinizing the face. "It's got contouring! Look! The nose bulges. The processing power alone must—"

"Ozie!" Victor's hiss was loud in the small room. Tosh stood, crossed slowly toward him, and put a hand gently on Victor's shoulder, murmuring for him to relax. More quietly, Victor continued, "Let it go." Victor looked at the Diamond King's real-life avatar, wondering how to address him. "Since this is our first meeting, what should we call you? You must have a name."

"A title conveys importance symbolically. You may address me as your excellence."

Victor almost laughed, but Wonda caught his eye and shook her head gravely.

"Fine. Your excellence," he said, "we've come to bargain."

"Trade we shall. I will take possession of the data repository originally formatted by Jefferson Eastmore, which contains his research in addition to Samuel Miller and Victor Eastmore's neurograms. In exchange, I'll provide BioScan with equipment, software, and protocols for the neurological rehabilitation of mirror resonance syndrome patients. Agreed?"

Ozie breathed heavily in the silence. His hands were clenching a braincap so hard he might rip it apart. Tosh and Wonda looked to Victor. The avatar did too.

"Are the terms acceptable?" it asked.

Wonda elbowed her way in front of Victor to stand facing the avatar. "Hang on a minute. I'm the only one who knows where the data egg is hidden. As the custodian of Samuel Miller's legacy, it's just as much mine as anyone else's, and I have some demands, regardless of what you give him."

The avatar shifted to face Wonda directly. "Go ahead."

"First, information. What's your interest in Broken Mirrors?"

Although Victor was wary of Wonda inserting her demands into the process, he agreed and said, "I want to know that, too, actually."

The avatar was motionless as it said, "Mirror resonance syndrome is a puzzle that needs solving."

Wonda asked, "What does that mean? 'Solving'?"

The Diamond King's avatar replied, "We will conduct research and administer treatment."

A chill crept over Victor's body. He didn't mind talking with an avatar; in some ways, that made it easier. But something deeply troublesome lay behind the Diamond King's words that he couldn't put his finger on. The royal we maybe. Was he talking to a person or a group of people?

"No deal," Wonda said stonily.

All eyes turned to her.

"No deal. Treatment results in spiritual disfiguration. It's already a huge concession for the Human Life Movement to allow the research to go forward."

Spiritual disfiguration? It was absurd. The nerve to inject her nonsense beliefs and into what should have been a rational process. "*Allow* the research?" Victor repeated. "You don't get to decide."

Wonda huffed. "Maybe not. But I won't agree to anything that forces treatment either. And I'm surprised you'd want me to. Unless it's agreed to rely on prior and informed consent, I guess we came all the way here for nothing."

The Diamond King's avatar extended an arm in her direction. The smooth gray material shifted shape, becoming slender, and a finger extended, pointing. "You agreed to negotiate in good faith. We have not made all the relevant information available to you yet."

Wonda crossed her arms, shying away from the thing's reach. "Say what you have to say then."

"We are offering a significant investment in treatment for mirror resonance syndrome. That should be enough. If you need more convincing, we can show you the prototype treatment and—"

"Stop," she interrupted. "You're not listening." She got up, looming over the Diamond King's seated body-avatar. Victor read the tension in her hiked shoulders, how her palms were squeezed into fists, and most of all, the red-black squiggles wriggling like worms across her face. His synesthesia was in a particularly illustrative mode this evening. He wondered if the Diamond King had drugged them again, this time with hallucinogens. Or maybe the fumewort was wearing off. Ozie had closed his eyes. His lips were moving, and he shook his head, as if he were having some private argument with his demons.

Wonda poked the avatar, finger-nudging pixelated brow, but it didn't react. "You are responsible for the stims," Wonda said. "They're coming from the OWS. That's what he told us." She pointed at Victor.

"That's correct," the Diamond King said.

"Why? Why create so many addicts?"

"The addictive effects are unfortunate, but they're transient. Jefferson and I agreed on the need for additional research. At the time, MRS patients in Semiautonomous California were unavailable to us in the necessary numbers. And, of course, lab conditions never properly simulate the real world. Stims mimic MRS neural states. They're a convenient proxy." During this, the avatar remained upright, posture perfect, its voice replicating the sanctimonious and erudite cadence of a man who knows best. No wonder he and Jefferson Eastmore worked together; their styles meshed exquisitely.

Victor could hear Wonda's breath in the silence, ragged and on the verge of exploding. When she spoke, it was in a tightly controlled growl. "You let stims loose on the people, knowing the problem would grow, and you could study them like animals in the wild. Despicable."

Ozie pulled himself out of a fugue and glowered at the avatar. "I don't think anyone expected addiction to spread so far. Especially Jefferson. Stims were meant to give researchers here a window into the workings of mirror resonance syndrome. But the way they spread, it was like a forest fire. They couldn't control it."

Victor filed that bit of information away and one more: Ozie still hadn't told him everything he knew. The rift of mistrust between them ran deeper than anything could bridge.

The Diamond King's avatar said, "Remember that mirror resonance syndrome, as a formal diagnosis and a cultural phenomenon,

Cody Sisco

was confined to Semiautonomous California. People see the need for assistance only after they are aware of the trouble they're in. Here, the use of stims motivates the corrective. People need to see a thing to fear it, in other words. The same treatment, which we've developed and would like to make broadly available, will be effective for both MRS and stim addiction. We can inoculate against the threat. The flaw in the Classification Commission's approach was that it stigmatized the population. With sufficient resources and political will, with social acceptance, treatment can be made available to everyone."

Wonda resumed pacing. The avatar's gaze didn't shift to follow her. The Diamond King probably had vidcaps from multiple angles, the better to watch them all. "'Social acceptance,' he says." Wonda walked toward Victor, then U-turned, shaking her head. "Like here, where everyone is on drugs and couldn't care less about purity. He's providing drugs *and* treatment. It's giving me mental whiplash."

"Would you like a sedative?" the King asked. Victor wasn't sure whether it was meant to be a joke.

Ozie circled the avatar, inspecting it, prodding it, until the avatar gently but forcefully pushed his hand aside.

The negotiation was going nowhere. Something slippery in the Diamond King's logic put Victor on edge. It combined misdirection, conflating issues, and dismissing concerns—how the powerful played with perception, cognition, and concepts—tools of propaganda and indoctrination so invisible, it was near impossible to see them operating. Wonda hadn't said what she really wanted. Prior and informed consent was a sidetrack, not the main obstacle. They still didn't know why the Diamond King cared about the data egg.

"What about you?" Victor asked. "The way you hide. The way you evade. We don't know who we're dealing with. And your reputation is not spotless. Why would we agree to deal with you when you treat your people this way?"

"Victor," Ozie said, his voice low in warning.

Victor shot Ozie a look to stay out of it. He'd come all this way, waited, and gone through the silly motions of learning about Las Vegas society. He'd been more than patient. Now that the Diamond King was in front of him, sort of, what the shocks was this avatar business about anyway? He needed answers.

Victor continued, "I don't see why you couldn't meet with us in person. Are you so afraid?"

"Victor!" Ozie said. His eyes were wide, fear coiling around them like black wisps of smoke. Victor's heart thumped in his chest. *Thanks, Ozie, for that bit of emotional contagion.*

He looked again at the avatar. Its curves suggested a body, but it wasn't really. Whatever the material, it wasn't skin and bones and nerves like the rest of them. And the face was an illusion, too, the freakishly persuasive suggestion of personality without being one. And behind it all, what was there? A man in a room somewhere nearby—or maybe not. Could he be from far away? Another continent, perhaps?

"Are you a European agent?" Victor asked.

The Diamond King's laughter filled the room, ten times louder than the previous volume, a sharp, grating laugh that carried more than a hint of hysteria.

Victor exchanged glances with his allies and saw they were as disturbed as he was.

"Do you know how much European agents fear me? They have a war room dedicated to countering me. They're right to be afraid. I have no political allegiance," the Diamond King said. "The OWS is a convenient testing ground, it's true, but, mostly, a historical accident accounts for my presence here. My ambitions, however, are expanding."

The weight of his words settled over them uncomfortably. Wonda glanced at Victor, worried. Tosh stared grimly at the avatar. Ozie held his head in his hands, bent over as if grieving or about to vomit.

"Are you okay?" Victor asked.

"We have to go," Ozie said. "We have to stop this." His fingers danced on the rim of the braincap he held.

"What? Why?"

"I'm trying to tell you! The Diamond King is—"

The avatar silenced Ozie with a hand on his shoulder. "Victor and I will now speak privately."

"Why?" Wonda asked loudly. Then, more quietly, "What will happen to him?"

"I will persuade him."

Victor wanted to reassure Wonda and say, "It's okay. I'll see you soon," but his mouth clamped shut. Ozie's fear had made a home in his brain and rearranged the furniture into a fortress of panic. A constricting pressure circled his neck. Swallowing took great effort. Words were impossible.

Ozie came over and put his hands on Victor's shoulders. "You'll be fine. As long as there's a deal to be made, you'll be safe."

The avatar walked to the door, opened it, and gestured for Victor to proceed. After a moment's hesitation, he walked through it and left behind Tosh, Ozie, and Wonda.

Alone in a hallway, lit by lightstrips in the ceiling, Victor asked the avatar, "Will I see your true face now?"

"In time. Come see how I help people with MRS."

The Diamond King's avatar, still wearing the playing-card face, moved forward in almost-human steps. Victor followed, watching it closely. There was something slippery about the way it moved. A door at the end of the hall opened, and they passed through, heading further into the building.

It no longer felt like seduction. It felt like a trap.

34

The avatar led Victor down a maze of hallways with so many twists and turns that he knew he wouldn't be able to find his way out again on his own. A tactic to get him isolated and powerless? Maybe. Yet he was also being treated like an honored guest. Via the avatar, the Diamond King spoke about galas, sights, delicacies, and delights that Victor could avail himself of. It had become clear that Victor was expected to stay for at least a week. He hadn't yet told anyone at BioScan of his absence. Worse, he was still without Mesh access. They would be wondering about him by now.

He also couldn't place a call to Pearl, whom he wanted to hear from. She'd have some good advice or at least some perspective that would help him keep his wits.

After riding an elevator for what felt like many floors downward, they continued walking. The avatar now spoke of brain scan data, algorithms, and translation protocols, which sounded far beyond what he thought was feasible. Significant portions of information passed him by at a rapid pace. The Diamond King reassured him that this was only a brief overview; the full data would be made available for his review.

They entered a room full of staff in lab coats who glanced up and then resumed their activities as if working and receiving visitors through the middle of the night was normal. Some patients, wearing forest-green jumpsuits and odd-looking, semispherical hats, lay in beds, and others stood or sat in chairs with their gazes fixed on wall-mounted video screens.

"I am Grette," a woman said, coming over. She had close-cropped blond hair and carried a type-pad clutched to her chest. She gestured to the beds along one wall. "These are mirror resonance syndrome patients receiving treatment. They, too," she said, pointing to the ten or so individuals watching the vidscreens, which mostly showed vistas of nature. A few were lying down, with their eyes open, Victor noted, staring into space and still wearing their hats, which was odd.

Grette, in an accent Victor recognized as European but vaguely so, said, "There are not many cases in the OWS. We treat them as our precious subjects. Every one of them has shown signs of improvement. Our treatment works."

Subjects as in research, or the kind you rule over?

"Some sort of brain stimulus?" Victor asked, looking at the avatar, which he realized was a bit absurd given that he could ask the flesh-and-blood person in front of him instead. He turned back to Grette. "The King was telling me about it."

She looked at the avatar, bowed her head, and closed her eyes in a discomfortingly sincere movement. "Yes," she said, gesturing for Victor to approach one of the patients, a young man of East Asian descent, standing nearby. A refugee from SeCa, maybe? "Of course," Grette went on, "we have not so many patients initially comatose as in Semiautonomous California, but many experience frequent debilitating episodes. We have eliminated these episodes."

Eliminated? That was impressive enough to get him interested. He watched her carefully. "With braincaps?" he asked.

Grette didn't nod or answer affirmatively, Victor noticed. Instead, she said, "With electromagnetic stimulation of inhibitory neural responses, we restore normal function. It is intermediate step to cure."

Victor turned to the avatar. "And this is the treatment that could be deployed at BioScan?"

It answered: "You will see improvements in all your patients. There's something more."

The avatar gestured to a door.

"We're done here?" Victor asked, puzzled.

"It was important to show you patients," Grette said. "For trust."

Victor looked at the young man in the green jumpsuit and moved to intercept his gaze. "Hello, I'm Victor. How are you feeling?"

The man frowned and cast a brief questioning glance at Grette. She nodded encouragement without smiling.

Victor took a breath. He'd been too aggressive. It was more than rude to probe someone's emotional state so directly; it was an assault. Still, he had to get a handle on what was happening, and he would use every skill he had.

Victor asked, "What's your name?"

The patient hesitated.

"It's okay," Grette prompted.

"My name is Huang Xi," he said, smiling but staring at the floor.

"It's good to meet you," Victor said.

There was no response. Was it faulty cognition, contextually appropriate gaze avoidance, shyness, or something else?

"This way," the avatar said.

Reluctantly, Victor followed the avatar through the doorway. As it shut behind him, Victor felt suddenly alone, a sensation that didn't change when the avatar spoke again.

"You may not be aware that one of the variant proteins associated with mirror resonance syndrome occurs more predictably than can be explained by randomness or inheritance. There is an environmental factor."

"What? I've never heard anything about that."

They stood on a metal gangway overlooking a large workroom. Below were six large capsules that looked like ceramic cabbages. Each capsule had one door big enough for a person to walk inside without ducking, though some workers did anyway. Victor tried to understand what he saw, but the Diamond King's words distracted him.

"Environmental factor?" Victor said, dragging his mind back to the conversation.

"Every cell in the human body, though it shares a genealogy with every other human cell, leaving aside the matter of the symbiotic and adversarial microbiota that make up most of the cells in the human body, has a history of division that may include mutation. This is true of neurons as it is true of other types of cells, and the neural environment is a factor in what happens to the DNA molecule as it replicates."

Victor took a moment to extract the point of the King's statement, then said, "The neural environment influences mutations? You don't mean epigenetic changes, do you? That I would believe."

"No. Mutations. Changes in base pair sequences. The natural world is full of analogs for the environment's influence on evolution. Geologists have long focused on plate tectonics and other earth-based physical and climate systems models. But their models were missing a key environmental factor: the extraterrestrial environment. Space, though sparse, is anything but empty. Dust, rocks, planetoids, and various cosmic energies originating both within our galaxy and beyond impact the Earth and influence it, adding mass, energy, and chemical compounds to the terrestrial system. Similarly, the external world impacts neurons that form the substrate of human consciousness."

"Hang on. What exactly do you mean by 'external world'? That's potentially, like, everything. And the blood-brain barrier, well, it's not impermeable but nearly so."

"Human brains have plasticity of varying degrees throughout their lifecycles. With your help, with the data you can provide, the nature of external stimuli on brain development will become clear."

That's a non-answer. What's he driving at?

"Okay," Victor said. He would return to this question of an environmental factor, but for now, he'd insist the Diamond King shed some light on his aims. "That's why you want to help treat the MRS patients, for the data. I get that. But why do you want the data egg? My and Samuel's neurograms aren't much data compared to all you'll get from MRS patients here and in New Venice."

"The most important segment of a time-based data set is the beginning. We are collecting data from our current patients. But yes, we need historic data, which happens to be very rare."

"And that's what's so special about Samuel? Because he was the first person known to have MRS—"

"He was not the first."

Victor's head swam. For as long as he could remember, everyone had referred to Samuel as the first Broken Mirror. It was part of how Semiautonomous California had told and re-told the history of the Carmichael Massacre: Samuel was the first, and thus, extreme caution and extraordinary care were needed to prevent more. "If Samuel wasn't the first, then who?"

The avatar ignored the question and walked with uncanny ease downstairs to the workshop floor below. Victor watched it go, and a queasy dread pulsed in his stomach. After breathing and recalling the owl mantra, he followed it down the stairs and came to one of the capsules with an oval door hinged down to create a ramp to its entrance.

The Diamond King's eyes twinkled on the avatar's face as he said, "Climb inside."

"What is it?"

"The means to an answer." His image faded from the avatar. It was a gray, blank stick figure again.

Victor hesitated at the entrance. Matte silver walls curved to the apex, like the inside of an egg. His throat was full of panicked squirrels, a racing and chittering vortex of agitated fur. He swallowed. It felt like drinking a cup of ash. Inside was a chair, not unlike the scanning chair he'd been in many times for his Classification appointments.

Victor said, "Tell me what happens if I sit in that chair."

"Only what you consent to." Victor took a step inside the threshold. A vidscreen facing the chair lit up with the Diamond King's playing card face. "This pod contains an advanced magnetic resonance imaging system, a rough and insufficient technology. But when paired with more detailed neural imaging and feedback solutions, it will create a neural environment suitable for treating mirror resonance syndrome. It's also portable. BioScan will be provided with a more expansive modular installation under the terms of our agreement. I need your help to answer a research question."

Victor took in the pod's interior. It looked like an expensive brain scanner. One little brain scan? Was that the price? "Are you going to share what that question is?"

"You know what the question is. What is mirror resonance syndrome? The genetic mutation answer has always been a misleading and insufficient explanation. What is MRS really? What causes it? I aim for a sufficiency of explanations. Do you want to understand? Then sit."

Victor gulped.

A few steps, a short descent, a synthleather chair. *Relax and let the cards fall where they may.* He imagined a fist around his heart unclenching, the tension in his brain releasing. How much better could he think, if he could think about what he wanted when he wanted, instead of what the world demanded.

It was too good to be true. He'd been shown so much, the beginnings of answers he'd searched for—years of his life spent hunting for scraps, and now the table was laid for a feast.

But who was really being fed?

Could Grette and the Diamond King be trusted? They said their treatment helped comatose patients recover. To what degree? Were there side effects? The patients he'd seen hadn't been chatty and high-functioning. Victor knew he didn't have the gift of gab, but he had some common sense, a healthy dollop of paranoia, and alarm bells rang in his head.

"No," he said.

"No?"

"No. Not until we have a deal. Not until I know more."

"I can show you."

Victor exited the pod, paying closer attention to the exterior. Nozzles, maybe for refueling. Odd protrusions around the base. The outlines of hatches or panels toward the top. He made a few orbits, trying to picture the pod standing outdoors somewhere. It would fit snugly at the apex of Triton's Deep Crossing.

Clanging steps on the catwalk broke his reverie. Grette and an aide used a lift to lower a gurney to the workshop floor. They wheeled the gurney up the ramp and into the pod. Panels in the floor of the pod opened to reveal slithering tentacles that snaked forward, slid between the gurney and the patient, and lifted him into the reclined seat. The aide wheeled the gurney aside, and the door closed.

"We shall observe here," Grette said, leading Victor to a vidscreen on the wall. It showed the pod's interior from a vidcap in the ceiling. The patient's scalp was being shaved skin-close by blades at the end of a tentacle, dropping curls and wisps to the floor. Another tentacle with a hollow tip vacuumed up the hairs. Victor felt pressure behind his eyes. He couldn't look away. The razor continued to move precisely and efficiently across the patient's scalp. Victor's head tingled with each stroke. He leaned forward, trying to spot any blood or nicks, but didn't see any.

Grette glanced at him, and in his peripheral vision, he guessed a smirk was forming on her lips. "It is a very precise operation. Brain surgery must be."

Victor looked at her to see if she was joking. She met his gaze briefly, no hint of a joke on her face, and then returned her attention to the video screen.

More instruments mounted on the ends of tentacles started to descend. One sprayed something on the scalp. Another traced a semicircle around the patient's skull. A moment later, Victor realized it had actually been slicing, not just tracing. A forceps contraption pulled the skin back, revealing the skull. Vacuum suckers prevented blood from spilling down the patient's head, and an IV was inserted in one arm almost quicker than the eye could follow.

"You will see now the implants."

Tentacles gripping a curved object no bigger than a large hat descended from the ceiling to within millimeters of the patient's skull. The vidscreen shifted, no longer a vid, it showed a schematic of a skull.

"This is real time. This color indicates elevation; this pattern is the pressure. The skull is abraded and replaced with the implant, which immediately penetrates and bonds with the meninges. My doctoral research focused on interactions between the pia mater and filament coatings. We've not yet experienced a single intracranial infection with this method."

Victor thought about how would he explain this to BioScan staff. "Like replacing the cork in a wine bottle without spilling a drop or letting microbes slip inside?"

She gave him a puzzled look.

He cleared his throat. "I mean that it's extraordinarily difficult. And once the, er, plugs are in?"

"They extrude filaments throughout the brain's neural tissue. Both to map and influence neural activity. Inhibitory circuits strengthen, counteracting the MRS pathology. The plugs transmit and receive data externally via spectrum relays."

The vidscreen returned to the overhead camera view. The machines were already retreating.

"Quick, you see. That is how we expect every surgery to proceed."

"In less time than it takes to eat a sandwich," Victor muttered. He was impressed—how could he not be?—but he also felt sick.

The Diamond King's avatar, which had stood motionless during the surgery, approached again, wearing the pixel face. "Once our deal is concluded, you will return to New Venice with this patient. Are you satisfied with the demonstration?"

Victor's stomach lurched, and he couldn't tell if it was bile rising or the effects of inertia as his torso spun him around, and his legs sprinted for the door. He ran back up the stairs and down the hall. He must have turned in an unexpected direction. He didn't come upon the lab with the MRS patients, so he couldn't ask them what it felt like to have tiny wires looping through their gray matter, if the plugs itched, and if sometimes fluid leaked from the seams. He puked yellowish-red chunks, spraying them across the wall in an arc like a palm frond. Turning away from the gore, he shuffled down the hall to a clean spot away from the smell and sunk down, ass hitting the floor with a thud and knocked his jaw shut.

I have to get out of here.

The avatar appeared at the end of the hall.

His stomach flipped again. "Stop!" Victor yelled and gasped. "Give me a minute."

The avatar's pace slowed, then stopped. It waited silently, far enough away that Victor could look straight ahead at the blank wall and not scream from its proximity. It was a spider. It wanted to wrap his brain in a web of conductive nanofibers and suck out his consciousness. Absurd perhaps. Maybe it wasn't a rational thought. But that's what his mind was screaming, and it was time to listen to his intuition.

No. Never. Not me. Not now. Nope.

An edifice of hope came crashing down. It wasn't relief, anger, self-pity, or any emotion on the hot-cold spectrum from self-immolation to self-preservation. It was the gravity of an epiphany bending toward a certainty in his core; an explosion, a multispectral nova that radiated light, revealing the truth: he didn't want a cure, he didn't want to change *like that*, he didn't want to be transformed, he didn't want to be reborn.

He was by no means perfect. Maybe his flaws got him into trouble. Okay, yes, he'd gotten into *a lot of scary trouble*, but it wasn't only his brain at fault.

The world was a steaming pile of interconnected foolishness and brutality. In the grand scheme of things, his eccentricity was as harmless as one of those weird, little moons that orbited backward and sideways. The universe operated according to rules, both known and mysterious, but the universe didn't *seek* to change. It emerged.

He did not want or need this kind of cure. He could walk away right now.

35

"I'm done," Victor said. The hallway was vibrating, the lightstrips were humming; a music of resonance that only he could perceive.

"You are not yet convinced," the avatar said.

Victor started to answer, then shut his mouth. The contents of his stomach swirled and gurgled, threatening to escape. The image stuck in his head was the thin membrane under the skull punctured by nanoscale tendrils. What forces stopped brain juice from leaking out?

He got to his feet, bent over with his hands on his knees, pausing to breathe and let his gut settle. He straightened. "I'm leaving. Show me the way out."

The avatar showed no sign of disappointment as it led him through monotonous, indistinguishable hallways. Maybe the Diamond King was cursing in his rooms, off mic. Mute, grim, and heavy with dread, Victor followed the avatar into an elevator, up twenty floors, and onto a balcony. He gulped fresh air as if he'd been holding his breath for minutes.

"Can you schedule our flight home? Please." He would have to break the news to Ozie, Wonda, and Tosh and face their disappointment. He didn't have it in him to worry about logistics.

"Shall we recommence negotiations tomorrow? You seem tired." The King's voice was gentle, calming, exactly what Victor needed at that moment.

"No." He pictured skulls sliced open. Brain implants. A direct mind-machine interface. He'd wanted a cure, but this was far too much.

The avatar didn't move. The face stared, passive.

"I said, 'no.' You're not going to convince me. Brain implants! You don't have data on long-term efficacy. Sure, the patients can stand, blink and say their names—that's not enough. I don't know who you are. I don't understand what all this is about."

"All this?"

"Yes, everything. You, Las Vegas, and the OWS. Your interest in mirror resonance syndrome. I don't even know who you are."

"You don't trust me," the avatar said. Victor imagined gears turning, new strategies clicking into place. The Diamond King wasn't going to let him go easily. "Let's try to change that."

"No deal."

"Give me one day to convince you. I promise to answer your questions. You'll have a good rest tonight, well, this morning, really, and by sunset, if you still want to leave, we'll part ways."

Victor stood shakily with one hand against the wall. His palm pulsed against it. His arteries vibrated in sync with his staccato heartbeat. What was mirror resonance syndrome, really? No one knew. The Diamond King shared his curiosity—okay, no, his *obsession*. Why?

He would leave without a literal brainhacking cure, but maybe some new crumbs of truth would make the trip worthwhile.

"Okay, fine." He wiped a hand down his cheek. "I want this day to end."

Victor had nodded off in the skyflier. Now, half-awake, he rode the elevator from the roof to his apartment. He fell fully clothed onto his bed and into deep unconsciousness, dead to the world.

Sometime later, he was awakened by a small robot on wheels singing "Let's Go to the Cemetery" by the Boob-Head Dickies, a song he loathed for having both dumb lyrics and an unforgettable melody. He quieted the robot with a simple command, then noticed the vials of fumewort tincture it was carrying. He downed them and sighed, feeling the familiar sting in the back of his throat.

Victor tried to slip back into sleep, but his heart was thumping. He'd promised the Diamond King a day to make his case. Might as well get on with it. As long as he didn't have to witness another surgery, he would soldier through whatever gimmicks and tricks the Diamond King had in store and be home in his own bed by midnight.

After showering, he scrubbed his foul-smelling, slimy mouth and teeth and dressed in a fresh pair of pants and a tunic. He followed the robot to a taxi and climbed in, wondering what the rest

Cody Sisco

of his group was up to. As he reached to close the door behind him, he heard the robot whining like a puppy in distress. He picked it up—it was lighter than he expected—and put it on the seat next to him and shut the door.

"Can't you act like a person?" Victor said.

The robot meowed and said, "You'll like be better as an animal." Victor wondered if this, too, was an avatar of the Diamond King.

The driverless autocab navigated the streets and tunnels, moving toward the city's southern fringe. Buildings were shorter here; the tallest had maybe five or six floors, with plenty of two- and three-story townhouses interspersed. Occasional green space, playgrounds, and sports fields were tucked into intersections of major roads that dipped toward underground roundabouts.

The autocab stopped at a three-story sandstone-colored building with terraced balconies fronted by glass and covered by solar-collecting sunshades. Victor got out and put the little robot on the ground. It moved to the side and said it would wait for him there.

The home's front door opened as he approached it. A middle-aged woman with short salt-and-pepper hair stood on the threshold, bearing a curious expression. "So, you're the young man throwing all our breakfast plans into disarray."

"I'm sorry," he said, taking a step back.

"Nonsense, I'm only teasing. Come inside. We're all interested to meet you."

She smiled and led him down a hall. The walls were covered in framed photographs showing a family of five: two adult women, two teenage boys, and a girl of maybe six or seven. Every picture showed one or more of them in sports gear and team uniforms.

They arrived at a shaded patio. The air was thick with moisture from walls of plants on either side. They overlooked a yard that sloped downward to a paved trail, where joggers and bicyclists wove around each other. Watching the people, Victor marveled at their resilience to the heat and was reminded that he was thirsty.

"I'm Monica," the woman said. "This is my wife, Kendrel; our boys, Ethan and Parker; and that's little Priscilla."

"Pris," the girl corrected.

"Hello," Victor said.

Kendrel was dazzlingly beautiful. She had a willowy figure, high cheekbones, and skin the color of creamed coffee. She moved effortlessly, like some kind of goddess, and Victor felt his throat tighten in awe. Her confidence and warmth were palpable.

"I'm not sure exactly why I'm here," he managed after a moment.

"It's a bit of a surprise to us as well. Come, sit. We can compare notes." Kendrel pulled a chair back from the table and nodded for him to sit.

When they were all sitting, Monica poured water from a pitcher into their glasses. The two boys were watching Victor with big smiles on their faces. He smiled back weakly, thinking how few moments he'd had at that age to feel such unburdened joy and enthusiasm. His first instinct was to fault them for their good humor, and he felt bad for it.

Kendrel said, "We were told you're visiting from the Louisiana Territories. Welcome."

"Thank you. What else were you told about me?"

The women exchanged a mysterious look. Monica said, "I'll bring out some lemonade," and excused herself.

"That's all we were told," Kendrel said. "Our situation is a bit unusual. We're tech-averse."

One of the boys, Parker, Victor thought, noticed his puzzled expression and explained. "She means we don't use computers. We heard you were coming from a neighbor who does."

"We're six-fixed," Ethan added.

"Huh?" Victor blinked. It was stunning how quickly language could evolve in different directions.

Pris laughed at Victor's confusion. "*Six is the fix*," she sang. "You don't know?" She laughed again when he shook his head.

"You've heard of our rating system here, right?" Monica returned with a pitcher of lemonade and glasses.

"I've heard a little."

"Most people are motivated by ranking up. They're always looking for more: more opportunities, more privileges, more bragging rights. Well, we're part of a community that says, you know what, a six rating is all we want, and we're happy with that."

"Being a seven wouldn't be *so* bad," Parker said with an exaggerated wink.

"Oh, but think about what it's like for the tens!" Ethan said in a mocking stuffy tone. "Penthouse apartment. All the fancy clothes and mixing with high society."

"I'll get the sandwiches," Kindrel said.

"She deserves a seven!" Ethan shouted.

"Ethan." Monica gave him a serious look, and the boy calmed down.

What I wouldn't give to be so easily calmed, Victor thought.

Monica took a sip of lemonade, then said, "We don't have computers in the house. I use them in my work as a manager for a social work agency, and the kids use them for their schooling, but that's about it. We're mostly analog. If you compare our community to the rest of Las Vegas, we seem like misfits. No ratings. No totems. But it works for us. What matters in life are people and relationships, and being safe and satisfied. We've got everything we need. What more could we want?"

"An eight," Ethan said.

"Oh, or a nine," Parker chimed in.

Monica laughed and sighed. "Teenagers, right?"

The boys put on such overly shocked expressions that Victor laughed, too.

"And you don't get harassed or anything? For doing something different?" Victor asked.

Monica smiled yet seemed sad. "If someone were harassing us, they'd lose standing. So, while we try to remove ourselves as much as possible and not let it affect our daily lives, the rating system does benefit us. We're protected because other people are so motivated by it. Pretty ironic."

"There was a fight at school once," Pris said in a serious tone, "and one of the boys dropped an entire level. He was so sweet after that."

The sandwiches were passed around. Victor tasted roasted vegetables and salty cheese. Simple and delicious. His next thought made him laugh out loud. When they looked at him funny, he figured he better explain.

"I'm used to looking for the dark side of things. The drawbacks. The opposite of the silver lining: all the shadow-maybes. I'm sitting here trying to talk myself out of feeling good and taking at face value everything you're telling me, and it's surprisingly hard. I'm unsure if that's what the Diamond King meant to show me."

Monica looked frightened, and the kids looked shocked. "Please go finish your lunches inside."

They swiftly stood and took their plates inside as guilt settled in Victor's stomach alongside the sandwich. "I'm sorry. I didn't—"

"It's all right," Monica said, cutting him off. "Of course, there would be more to your visit than appeared at first glance."

Kendrel changed seats to be next to Monica and rested a hand briefly on her shoulder. Their support for one another was touching. She said, "We know we're being watched like everyone else. We try not to mind. To stay sixes, we avoid taking political stands, but that can be difficult when ..."

Monica picked up where Kendrel had left off. "There are many rumors about what the Diamond King does to his political opponents. We stay out of it. We try not to frighten the kids, but their friends and teammates talk." She met his gaze for a long moment. "Why are you here, Victor?"

How long would it take to explain mirror resonance syndrome? Could there be any connection to this family living on the fringes of a seeming utopia with a dark secret? He thought probably not. "I don't know. I think I'm here to get a local view of Las Vegas ... and maybe him." With a laugh—how odd it was to be the one holding the reins—he said, "I'm being pitched a deal."

Monica nodded, seemingly to reassure herself. "The Diamond King never breaks a promise. He honors every contract. That's all I'll say."

"Should I be worried?" Victor asked.

Monica's lips pressed together.

"I don't put a lot of stock in rumors," Kendrel said. "Most times, a rumor is started by someone scheming to get what they want and can't get by honest means. I think about what I have, how grateful I am for it, and what I would do to keep it. What do you have to lose, Victor?"

His chest tightened. Could she tell just by looking at him? Was it written on his face in neon letters? Seeing this happy family had underscored the truth, and the realization opened an empty pit in his soul: He had so very little left to lose, and the Diamond King knew it.

36

Victor saw himself out. The heat was already rising, and sweat immediately broke out on his brow. The small robot rolled up to him and suggested a walk. "I know a cool place nearby," it said. When Victor agreed, a motorized rollerboard that had been waiting on the sidewalk moved toward him. Reluctant at first, he stepped on the plank, prepared to fall, but it adjusted as it moved to make the ride so smooth that soon he was lost in his thoughts as it whisked him through a neighborhood then into a commercial district dominated by a dome the size of a city block. Victor left the rollerboard outside, and the small robot rolled alongside him as he entered the dome.

Inside, it was cool, dark, and damp to the point of being foggy. Grateful for the opportunity to stretch his legs without breaking into a sweat, he followed circuitous paths, stopping to savor a pocket of cool air rising from damp ground. From ground to ceiling, verdant bushes and trees created the illusion of being deep in the green rather than surrounded by the city. The glass above must be calibrated to block the sun's radiation, a layer of protection against the hostile environment. *Not unlike a skull.*

The Diamond King was offering to drill, insert, and patch MRS patients with skullplugs. The surgery would enable them to effectively become people with less-reactive minds. *You might as well call it a personality transplant. Would I wake up unburdened, or would I wake up as a different person, a dim reflection of who I am now? Is that what I want?*

He walked slowly, paying attention to his gait, the weight of each step, and the solidity of the earth. Each footfall landed softly without kicking up dust. This was a sanctuary from the desert, a glimpse of a distant, wetter epoch. Below, in trapped pools of sludge, the buried carbon remains of limitless fern forests were shrouded in the darkness of geologic time.

Cloying, moist air swirled over his skin. Fern fronds glistened with dew. One unfurled spike like a curved finger waved at him, beckoning. He moved deeper into the domed garden. *Stop being so selfish.* Didn't he owe it to the MRS patients in New Venice to come to an agreement? Was the offer an improvement on the alternatives?

The temptation to leave the path was overwhelming. He pushed into a dense clot of vegetation and stood, breathing quietly, letting indifferent, vibrant nature soothe his nerves. The robot didn't try to follow. Stretching out his arms, soft vegetation caressed the pads of his fingers. He didn't care if anybody saw him behaving strangely; they were all plugged into a system that controlled their careers, their lives, and probably their relationships too.

He sighed heavily. He was stalling. *I can't hide here all day.*

A bird landed on a fern frond, looked around, head tilting, listening, and took to the air again, darting into the canopy. His brain was sluggish in comparison.

Could he leave Las Vegas empty handed? He would be returning to patients with slim hope of recovery, no new treatments, cared for by a company on the verge of bankruptcy. A difficult situation to turn around, but weighed against the trauma of brain surgery, it seemed the best course of action.

He moved to a bench overlooking a small pond, expecting to be found and guided to the next revelation intended to win him over. Unsurprisingly, the small robot companion rolled toward him a few minutes later and offered to take him to Silk, who was reportedly enjoying cocktails with a friend.

Victor nodded and stood up. *What was a utopia without the things that make life worth living? I am thirsty. And it will be good to say goodbye to them.*

The robot chirped sharp and loud like a towhee announcing sunrise, and Victor was ushered away again, passing through harsh desert light and desiccated air, into a climate-controlled solar-powered autonomous vehicle that drove him to a familiar building. He got out and brought the little robot with him to an elevator, up to a high aerie, which turned out to be Silk's balcony salon.

A large painting of stars and galaxies caught his eye. He saw a face, faintly, staring back. It looked too alive. He turned away with a shudder and moved on, hearing voices. Silk and their friend were in a frenzied discussion, sitting around a table with a mosaic of a blue fish. What they were debating was unclear. Victor approached and stood behind an empty chair.

Silk said, "The image exists. Its meaning is a mirage."

"You can't ignore the artist's intent." Silk's companion paused and introduced herself as Davita. She was a skinny wisp of a woman with pink hair and acne-pocked skin, a fast talker whose fluttering hands frequently reached toward the sky as if grasping the wind.

"I don't want to interrupt," Victor said.

"Nonsense. Sit. Cucumber margarita?" Without waiting for his reply, Silk poured a glass for Victor from a pitcher and refilled their own and Davita's glasses. Victor sat down.

"Are you hungry?" Davita asked.

"No, I ate."

"Well, then, a snack." She ordered a few types of sushi from a robot waiting by the door.

"Surprising to have fish in the desert," he said.

"Not really," Silk replied. "It's not only water that travels along the Cold Nile."

"Mmm, that's good," Davita said, sipping the margarita. "As I was saying, the meaning is an amalgamation of the artist's intention and the audience's understanding."

Victor tasted his margarita, trying to suppress the feeling that Davita was reading his mind. But then she veered into philosophy and pop culture, referencing articles he hadn't read, plays he hadn't seen, and people he'd never heard of. Silk would chime in occasionally, edging out Davita to make a point. Victor let their words pass by as he visualized the hours and minutes counting down until he could return to New Venice. He was starting to wear his failure more comfortably. It helped to believe that he was taking a principled stand against an unproven, invasive treatment. Ethics demanded his refusal.

His wandering mind snapped back into place when he heard Davita talking about her rating.

"You look like you have a question, Victor," Silk said.

"I do, yes. How much do you let the rating run your lives?"

"Well, I wouldn't put it that way," Davita said. "It is part of the Cold Nile Miracle. The totems, too." She waved her glass at Silk in a loose, careless way, suggesting she was more than a little tipsy. "Where would we be without them?"

Silk looked at Victor calmly. "When you arrived, you had a MeshBit?"

Victor nodded.

"Back home, you always keep it with you, right? What does it do for you?"

"Do? Well, it's the key to all my financial accounts, accessing computer interfaces, messaging my family."

"It's a key, yes," Silk said, "only the door it opens swings both ways. You are monitored. You are controlled. The difference between that and what happens here is that we are not being monitored for control. The purpose is fundamentally different. We are being ... uplifted. We are challenged to live up to our potential. Ask yourself: why are they watching you? To what end? If you don't know the purpose, how could it possibly be to your benefit?"

Victor was dumbstruck. As a Class Three Broken Mirror, he'd lived under the watch of the Classification Commission for years. He'd bristled under the surveillance even as he accepted the reality of it. He'd never considered American Union citizens subject to a slightly different flavor of surveillance through Mesh devices. That was Ozie-level conspiracy talk.

A sushi platter arrived with chopsticks, tiny plates and bowls, napkins, a tray with pickled ginger and generous dollops of real wasabi among carefully arranged slabs of fish and cut rolls.

For a moment, they were silent, serving themselves, before Davita began describing an art installation involving robots dancing like bees when she mentioned totems.

That word again. Monica and her family had a thing about totems, too, Victor recalled.

He swallowed a portion of eel and rice, then said, "What do you mean by 'totems'?"

"Here," Davita said. She put down her chopsticks and picked up a type-pad, tapped a few times, and then turned it so Victor could see the image of a fox that was an uncanny blend of a photo-real image and a cartoon. The fox's face took up most of the screen. Its eyes were half-closed, reminding Victor of the lazy feeling after a big, satisfying meal. Its tongue lolled almost doglike, but then it began to lick the back of a paw, and the resemblance to a cat became stronger. The fox stopped licking and roved its gaze across the three viewers. It appeared to be smiling.

"This is my totem," Davita said. "I named him Copper. Some people change their totems every year or whenever suits them. I've had mine with a few modifications since I was ten, the day after the Miracle Breakthrough."

The fox image bounced and retreated, becoming smaller on the type-pad. It curled up and appeared to sleep. "Copper," Davita said, "you lazy devil, come back; Victor wants to talk with you."

Copper's ears swiveled.

"You talk to them like they're alive?" Victor asked. He glanced at Silk, trying to gauge whether he was the butt of some sort of joke.

Silk smiled and said, "Of course. They wouldn't be much fun otherwise."

"But what's the point?" he asked.

"Copper, what's my rating?" Davita asked.

The fox lowered its snout as if sniffing the ground, then snapped its jaws, capturing something it brought closer. The prize, held in its teeth, became clear: a playing card showing an eight of hearts. The card slipped from the fox's bite and floated down to sit in the corner of the screen, shrinking as it went.

"How do I become a nine?"

The fox barked in laughter and then spoke in a breathy, high-pitched voice. "If only it were that simple, dear!"

"Please, I want to know what I have to do."

"Achieve your goals," Copper said. "Would you like to see them?"

"Sure."

The fox barked repeatedly, accompanied by a gust of smoke that swirled upward. The letters assembled into a numbered list that Victor skimmed, noting an overuse of the terms "expressive creativity," "community-centric," and "self-actualization" along with a few more tangible criteria.

Silk gestured at Davita's goals on the type-pad. "You told me the art center idea wouldn't work out."

Davita blushed. "I was stubborn and didn't listen when Copper said it was already being done by other people three ways. I need something more *me* and more challenging. What do you think, Copper?"

"Oh, now you're listening to me?" the fox said. "All those new arts centers are going to need exhibitions. You're already working on funding and production. Why not complement your efforts with curation?"

Davita chomped the last cut roll and smiled broadly while she chewed. "That's so perfect. I wonder if I would have thought of it without you." She turned toward Victor. "See? I'm never stumped, lost, or confused. There's always a good answer waiting in a totem."

Victor blinked. People had prescribed him many good answers over the years, and they usually missed the mark. He hadn't always come up with the right answers, but they were his to search for. "It sounds like the next few years of your life were decided in a few seconds by a—whatever the totems really are."

"I suppose you could look at it that way. But what's the harm? He knows me and my place in society. If it's the right answer, who cares how it arrives?"

"Don't you want to decide for yourself?" Victor asked.

"I did." Davita looked ruefully at the type-pad. "I don't have to accept Copper's suggestions. But look what happened when I didn't. If the goals are a good fit for me, if working toward them brings me fulfillment, why wouldn't I say yes?"

Silk chimed in, "The rating is merely an assistive illusion."

"Right. It's a wonderful recognition of the work I've already done. Copper reminds me all the time that it's my life to live."

"Don't paint it all one color," Silk said to Victor. "I think any economic system that rewards advancement needs a social coun-ter-corrective so we don't all become too obsessed. We have to be happy wherever we are. The economic motor can't run at full speed without burning us out."

Victor remembered the happy family at breakfast, determined to stay sixes and eschew totems. Society here had already devel-oped a counter-corrective. It all seemed so ... *balanced*. That was the only word that came to Victor's mind. A utopian oasis on the surface—aside from the rumors about the Diamond King's cruelty, the provocative and destabilizing actions of the Corps, and the feeling that something below was rotten.

There had to be limits to the totems' usefulness. *Hey, Copper,* Victor wanted to ask, *what should I do about my aunt murdering my grandfather and this big bad MRS thing going on in my head?*

Victor said, "How can you live inside 'an assistive illusion'? Don't you want to know the truth?"

Cody Sisco

Davita shook her head. "This illusion or that one. It doesn't matter in the end. I've accepted Copper into my life. He is always there for me, knowing me better than I know myself."

Silk raised a glass to that, Victor mimicked them, and the three clinked and drank to being true to oneself while also accepting self-delusion. His head swam. Noises from the street below filtered up, sounding gentle and muted. Even as Victor noticed heat coming through the canopy, another sunshade shifted into place, darkening the patio further.

"So, as far as I can tell," Victor said, "the rating system runs the city, the economy. And you have the Corps carrying out the will of 'the people.' And right there at the center, you have the Diamond King, pulling all the strings. Am I getting this right? Is that how it works?"

"It works, that's enough," Davita said, a bit sharply.

Silk looked unhappy, their brow dipping, lips pressed into extinction. They were happy to chat about philosophy and art, but politics and current events scared them. What kind of political system makes people scared to discuss it?

"The Cold Nile Miracle was not just about uplifting the people, you know," Silk said quietly. "It put a lid on bad behaviors. You can't eliminate ambition or greed, but you can keep them in check. In other places, I don't think such a top-down system would work, but here, everything moves in service to both the greater good and individual wellbeing."

"As I like to say, power works differently here." Davita's tongue seemed to be slackening, her words slightly slurring.

Victor refilled the glasses until the pitcher was empty. A robot rolled up the table and took it gently from his grasp before rolling away.

Davita took a long gulp, swayed in her seat, and said, "I'll tell you how power works here. Officially, the local council rules Las Vegas. Same in other places. Every polity sends a delegate to the OWS national council. But unofficially, and here I'm diverging from the truth-on-paper to talk about the truth-in-execution, everyone knows that national policy and enforcement are determined by the Vegas local. The Cold Nile Miracle succeeded in fundamentally tying together local jurisdictions. It concentrated power in the hands of the financiers. The officials in charge here only rule if they don't defy the wishes of the Diamond King; may he rule peacefully, forgive us our trespasses, and bless us with long life, pleasant dreams, and good sex." She winked at Victor.

Silk frowned and said, "I hope our writer friend here is nearing the end of her soliloquy."

"It's okay. We have a good system. The Diamond King isn't a miracle worker, you know," Davita said, "but—"

Victor cut in, saying, "Who do you think he is?"

Davita smiled, big teeth, eyes closed, maybe close to passing out. "The King is a totem, like all the others."

It sounded like a dodge. "Come on. For real, what do you think? Who are the totems?"

Davita and Silk exchanged wary glances. Davita broke the silence with a smirk. "I don't like to indulge in conspiracy theories."

"Then don't," Silk admonished with an eye roll.

"Shush, you," Davita said ponderously, drawing out her vowels. "There's a different kind of power in him. Possibilities. Transformation." Her gaze sought to pin him and wavered instead. "'When lightning strikes the desert sand, the sound, oh, Lord, is thunderous and the way is paved with glass; the Cold Nile Miracle, our righteous path.'" Davita grinned. "Not my best. Path's a tough one to rhyme. Math. Bath. Bottom line: he's part of a different pantheon. You don't fuck with the Diamond King."

He wasn't getting anywhere with her. He stretched out a hand to Silk, palm up, beseeching. "Who is he? He'll show up on a screen, a cartoon, but doesn't want to be seen in person. What is that about?"

"You find the idea of a cartoon leader insufferable?" Silk asked with a lilt Victor couldn't interpret. They were sitting straight-backed, meeting his gaze with a cool, guarded expression. His MRS symptoms were well in check; they were no help in decrypting Silk's emotions. If his younger self could see how far he'd come in managing his condition—to hope for an episode and the clarity it might bestow—it would have stunned him and maybe given him hope he'd desperately needed.

"I think it's brilliant. 'The King'"—Silk made air quotes with slender, hooked fingers—"is unaccountable, inscrutable, elusive. That's purposeful. How do you oppose a mirage? It would be like fighting the wind."

"I agree. It's genius," Davita said with her eyebrows climbing high. "You can't coup a cartoon."

Both Davita and Silk's Tangle devices chimed. On Davita's,

Copper vanished and was replaced by an image of the King. Silk made her message play on the vidscreen on the wall.

The Diamond King's avatar appeared and said, "Your presence is requested at dawn tomorrow in Grand Park for a Breakthrough announcement." The image vanished.

The expressions on both Davita's and Silk's faces were strangely reverent.

"What is it?" Victor asked. "What does he mean?"

"A breakthrough," Davita said, musingly.

"After the one last month." Silk noticed Victor staring and seemed to remember that he didn't know their ways, not all of them. "Breakthroughs are rare. Some years, there aren't any. When one is announced, everyone participates."

"The entire population is going to Grand Park?" Victor asked, incredulous.

"No," Silk said. "Everyone gets a slightly different invitation. The lower ranks will go elsewhere. Grand Park is usually only nines and up."

Davita looked thoughtfully at her MeshBit, then laughed. "For a second, I entertained the ludicrous notion that I might jump a level. I'm thoroughly confused as to why I might be invited."

Silk said, "Perhaps you're expected to keep Victor company. You've done a good job thus far."

Davita blushed. "I'd be honored, of course."

Silk looked again at Victor. "The last Breakthrough was when we switched to the Tangle network and stopped using the Mesh. Everyone got new devices. The old ones were collected. It was a logistical triumph. My totem's resolution more than doubled."

"Mine too," Davita said. She showed Victor the fox-totem's image again. Its tail swished fitfully.

He stood, unsteady, more drunk than he'd intended. If this was the Diamond King's way of getting a deal signed, it wasn't going to work. Deep down in his gut, Victor knew people with MRS weren't defective; they were connected to the world in ways that were challenging but reflected a deep sensitivity to their surroundings. They were full of untapped potential. Yet the Diamond King was the first person to corroborate that viewpoint. Could he turn his back and leave the puzzle unfinished when all the pieces were sitting there waiting to be assembled, returning to New Venice without the Diamond King's technology?

For years, Granfa Jeff and Dr. Tammet had guided Victor, much like Davita seemed to be guided by Copper. But he couldn't put his trust in either an image or absent guardians. He would have to guide himself.

He'd arrived a skeptic, not believing the Diamond King had much to trade. Now there was something valuable on the table, but it carried immense risk. He knew that the worst way to enter a negotiation, according to the late great Jefferson Eastmore, was to be vague or conflicted about what you wanted. Victor wasn't worried about his granfa's approval; he was worried about being blown wherever the winds of change might take him. He was torn.

The robot signaled that it was time to join his friends. Sunset was approaching. It was time to make his decision.

Cody Sisco

37

Victor stumbled to his apartment, ushered gently by a robot on wheels with soft, velvety arms. A waking hangover seemed to take hold. He drank two glasses of water and was contemplating a third when someone came in, obscured by the bright reflections of the setting sun. When the person came close enough, he was shocked and delighted.

"Pearl!"

"Hello, Victor."

No one in the world had shaped Victor more than his granfa's herbalist friend, and she'd done it only once the man was dead. No one else could reach into his brain and reshape it into something new as she could, with her strange theories and surprising observations. She was unorthodoxy personified, a take-no-bullshit, speak-no-lies spiritual juggernaut.

He stumbled as he went to greet her and sat down hard on the settee instead. *I'm too drunk for this right now.*

She approached, squeezed his arm with a fierce grip that belied her seventy years, and smiled, revealing glistening, perfectly aligned fake white teeth. Her face was less wizened than he remembered, less lined and wrinkled than when he'd last seen her a couple of months ago. She left New Venice before Wonda stormed BioScan with her cultists. Now, she wore a blue business suit patterned with loud, colorful flowers; she was an orchid in a glittering desert oasis. It didn't seem at all like her scene.

He'd been hoping to talk to her since he arrived, but one thing or another prevented him. And now, on the cusp of momentous decision, she was here—was this part of the Diamond King's plan? "Where have you been?"

She cleared her throat. "They keep me busy here."

Victor blinked, realizing. "You work here ... with the King?"

Her smile had faded into a calm expression that was slightly sad and proud, definitely weary. Pieces of the puzzle began assembling in his mind. Was she a spy or a traitor or something more strange?

"We share a commitment to helping MRS patients recover. How could I say no?"

Jefferson. Ozie. Tosh. Wonda. Now, Pearl. They'd all thrown in their lot with the Diamond King. Why was he making such a big deal of it?

The wise owl listens, that's why.

"Do you know about the skullplugs?"

Pearl spoke slowly and carefully, choosing her words with delicate precision. "We know that some patients will never regain consciousness without intervention. The implants work: there's no question in my mind. I could recite all the reasons to worry or fear, but the future is emerging here, and I wanted to be part of it."

Something shifted inside him. Pearl had always been cryptic and cagey. Is this what she'd been hiding? She and Tosh always portrayed their interest in Victor as loyalty to Jefferson. Was it more complicated than that? Was it the Diamond King influencing her actions?

So much uncertainty. So many unknowns.

But he couldn't stay paralyzed. He had a choice in front of him.

Pearl looked at him with fondness. "In strange times, emergence happens everywhere. A warm, strong heart can weaken. Even the dead can dream." She sounded tired, not at all her usual sprite-like, enigmatic self. It felt like their brief time together was already nearing its end.

Victor was concerned and said, "I can make some tea. Or a tincture. We can sit and talk about—"

"No. No. You've got some decisions to make. I wanted to see you. But I don't want to hold you back." Pearl patted his shoulder and said, "We are alike, Victor, because we believe in possibilities. There's more to life than the things we can see. Until next time."

Victor barely had a moment to regret her departure. Minutes after she left, Wonda, Ozie, and Tosh came onto the balcony with the Diamond King's automaton avatar. Ozie looked hungover, like swampy roadkill. Tosh was in bright spirits, as if he'd fucked his way through an entire brothel—probably had.

Wonda asked Victor quietly, "Are you okay? Are we doing this?"

She stood next to him as they faced the sunset, a comforting presence. Despite the bad blood between them, they both hungered for a kind of peace that remained out of reach: autonomy and the simple, uncomplicated joy of being in good company.

Sparse, wispy clouds above the mountains glowed with gold and pink highlights. Closer, the Summer quadrant was rust-colored, glorious, divided from Autumn by a broad avenue bright with the sun's fading light.

The stars would appear soon. He was eager to be dazzled by their fierce, hot light in the great cold expanse of the universe, eons away, shining all the way from the distant past, from a time long before this wondering, worrying, and weary moment of indecision.

"Are we?" Wonda asked.

Victor responded carefully, noncommittally. "There is a treatment. It's ... intense. I would need to see proof that it improves outcomes. I need to understand the risks. I want to see the data."

Wonda searched his face then shook her head. "No," she said.

Victor sighed. Just ... *no*? Leave it to Wonda to have a strong opinion based only on her gut.

"No, that's not enough," she said. "He still hasn't told us the truth."

Over by the door, the avatar made a loud sound like a distressed bird. It held out its hands, palms up, not in surrender but exasperation. Victor was certain the Diamond King was making the same gesture wherever he was hiding while controlling that thing. "The truth about what?" the avatar asked plaintively.

Wonda responded coolly, "Why you are so interested in mirror resonance syndrome."

She was right. All the things Victor had been shown today were shades of dark shadows against that black mystery.

"It's an itch I need to scratch." The avatar raked one spindly finger down its pixelated cheek. "Satisfying one's curiosity is a thing even money and power have trouble delivering. Don't you like solving puzzles?"

"Money and power, hmm?" Wonda began to pace, shooting looks at Victor or Tosh and the avatar. Then, turning to face it, she said, "Victor makes the final decision. But I'll sign if you agree to two demands. First, I want refuge and autonomy for the Human Life Movement. Property. Arable land. A tract with income from trade. Somewhere along the Cold Nile would do. And we want no part of the rating system you've got here. We want to be left alone."

The Diamond King responded warily, "There is no precedent for an autonomous region within the Organized Western States."

"Call it semiautonomous if that makes you feel better. You have counties, don't you?" Wonda insisted. "They must have some powers."

The avatar folded its spindly arms in an uncanny mockery of a human gesture. "There are ninety-six counties within the OWS that have local councils, but—"

"Give us one of those *and* effective autonomy."

Ozie barked a harsh laugh. In response to his friends' disapproving looks, he said, "What? She's impressive."

Wonda pressed her lips together in a mixed expression of displeasure and pride.

Tosh was nodding. "It would work. Everyone is used to taking orders here. Whichever county she gets, all the residents would get a bump in their statuses and agree to comply or move out, leaving her with the land. Or with new subjects. Precedent doesn't stand for much out here." He gestured toward the avatar.

Wonda responded, "The residents can stay if they agree to a purity pledge."

"You'll make a terrifying queen," Tosh said with a cutting smile. "No qualms about taking charge. Not a care for who suffers."

Wonda bristled, but Victor thought Tosh had her entirely figured out. She said, "I don't want to be a queen. I just want a place where we can be free. If they stay, they live by our rules. We will have the ultimate authority to regulate medicine and other substances. No drugs."

The avatar said, "The OWS will retain the right to impose quarantines and mandatory testing and treatment for infectious diseases. This is nonnegotiable."

"Fine, as long as it's understood that MRS is a special case, no matter what," Wonda said. "Treatment is not obligatory."

"What is your second demand?" the avatar asked.

"That was it. No treatment for those with MRS that refuse it."

Tosh smiled again. This time it was genuine. "Checkmate."

"No treatment?" Victor muttered, his palm against his forehead.

Wonda approached and took his hands. He disliked the touch, cool and clammy.

"Remember when you chose not to take Personil? The price for that was exile."

She didn't need to remind him that he couldn't step foot in SeCa without risking arrest. He didn't want to return, but it galled him not to have the option. "Isn't it fair that people with MRS get to decide whether to accept treatment without coercion?"

He opened his mouth, unsure what to say. He didn't like her tone, but that was a petty response, and the stakes were too high to be bothered by it. What about comatose Broken Mirrors? What about stim addicts on the verge of suicide? Nothing came out of his mouth. The treatment he would bring to the Broken Mirrors was far more invasive than a little pill. He should tell her about it now. But that might jeopardize the deal. And she didn't care about the patients; she cared about her own power and dominion.

The ethical dilemma he never wanted to face—why should he have to decide?—was now staring him down. Should MRS patients be given the option to *not* be treated? Personil was a false cure; he'd rejected it on the hunch that he'd been lied to and forcibly stupefied. He should have been given a choice, but the Classification Commission denied MRS patients that basic right. This was different, though—this was a real cure, wasn't it? This was liberation, not oppression, wasn't it? This would help Broken Mirrors recover their minds from the horror of blankness. *But what was blankspace, hmm? I still haven't solved that mystery. Not yet, anyway. Maybe the Diamond King could help with that, too?*

"Give them a choice," Wonda pleaded. "You would have a choice, too." She squeezed his hands hard, and their chill became a burning heat.

A choice now and a choice later. That was the crux of it. Now that he'd seen the MRS treatment, did he even want it? No. But what if one day he did? Didn't all patients deserve that option? The saliva in Victor's mouth had dried, leaving behind a combination of gooey and parched indecision. "Some patients won't be able to say whether they want the treatment, but—"

"But once they're lucid," Ozie chimed in, shifting his eyes left then right in a parody of alertness, "and communicative, we'll confirm if they want to continue treatment. Or we'll reverse it, if that's possible." He glanced at the avatar, flinched, and looked away, mumbling. He sat down, rocking in his seat, and closed his eyes. It was more than a hangover. He was decompensating.

Victor wondered if Ozie would opt for the treatment at some point. If he didn't stop with the surgeries, he would be more machine than man. The leap from braincap to skullplug wasn't far.

Victor said in a rush, "The treatment is an implant. They'll have computer chips in their skulls. Brain plugs." He needed them to understand. He needed them to tell him it wasn't monstrous. Or that it was.

Wonda seemed surprisingly nonplussed as she asked, "Can they be removed?"

The avatar shook its head.

"Can they be shut off? Powered down or whatever?"

"Over time, yes," it responded. Victor looked to Ozie for confirmation but got none.

"Okay then," Wonda said, "from a purity standpoint, there's not much distinction between an implant or a pill—they're both forbidden. I can't stop a flood, but I can find high ground and defend it."

Victor looked to Tosh, who shrugged and, with a wink, said, "What's the harm?"

Everything!

Ozie roused from blankness, stood up, eyes wild, and shouted, "We can't do this. It's going to take over the world. Everyone will be caught in its net. It's the end of everything!"

Victor turned away to minimize Ozie's paranoid contagion from seeping into his brain. Tosh manhandled Ozie back to the chair and held him there with a forearm against his chest, whispering quietly, tenderly.

Breathe. The wise owl needs some peace and quiet. Look at this rationally.

Victor didn't want to say yes. He could leave right now and forget all this—forgetting was easy, after all. He could resume his not-at-all-normal life to stew eternally like a vegetable in the consequences of his failure, softening, disintegrating into the murky broth of his sad surroundings.

Or he could return to New Venice with a revolutionary treatment for mirror resonance syndrome. Hopeless patients would be on the road to recovery. He would have more resources to call upon than even an Eastmore could dream of: technology, money, a powerful ally, the future pulling him toward his most golden visions. BioScan would be saved, his status within the company would be assured, and he could usurp Circe's position as chief. He could decide later, perhaps much later, when long-term data was available, whether the treatment was for him. And then there was the not-insignificant promise from the Diamond King to explain the true nature of mirror resonance syndrome.

All it would cost was committing to an uncertain future.

There was one more domino to fall to reach a deal. Alia had begged for help to find Torsten's brother, and he was finally in a position to try. The Diamond King seemed to be able to work miracles. Why not ask for another?

"There's something else," he ventured. "Not saying I agree yet, at all, but it needs to be discussed."

The avatar asked, "What are your additional terms?"

"I want your help in finding Anders Lund. He's gone missing, and Alia—Alia Effendi—his sister-in-law-to-be through Torsten Lund, her fiancé ..." He paused, shook his head, and started again. "Alia thinks Anders is in Las Vegas, and she wants him back. It needs to be done quietly. Torsten is running for office. He's Ander's brother. You can look him up." He was glad Alia couldn't hear him stumble through that clumsy plea.

The Diamond King's avatar blinked and smiled slyly. "No need. The patient whose treatment you witnessed yesterday will return with you to New Venice."

Victor froze. He looked blankly across town, dusk was thickening, and a planet, maybe Jupiter, twinkled above the horizon. Somewhere in that direction, in one of those inscrutable buildings, deep in the bowels, a surgery had been conducted, one he'd witnessed. The scalp peeled back, the skull sliced. Bile rose again, and Victor gulped it down.

The Diamond King knew. He knew what I was going to ask for, and he dipped into the well and gave me a drink before I said I was thirsty. Am I doing or saying anything surprising to him? Do I have any freedom at all?

Victor stared at Ozie, still pinned by Tosh's forearm, realizing. "You told him. About Anders."

"I couldn't keep a secret if I wanted to." Ozie's fingers were tapping urgently on the braincap again, and it felt like rough fingers pawing at Victor's flesh. On Ozie's face, black and blue waves churned, a tempest of terror and sadness. Victor had to look away.

Far below, people were strolling in the evening shade, some tasting one another's ice cream scoops, others jogging and sweating in the cooling air.

Why was Victor always surprised by Ozie going behind his back? Watching Anders undergo surgery had left a sour taste in his mouth. What would Alia say when she saw the scars on Anders' scalp and learned what had been done? No. He couldn't worry about how she would react. The surgery would help Anders kick his stim addiction. If a brain implant was the price, well, it had already been paid, hadn't it?

Victor trembled. He was so ready to be done and far away. He would leave empty-handed if he had to. He faced the avatar. "I'm going to ask one last time. Why do you care? Tell us the full truth this time, or we all walk away."

"Perhaps I can show you," the avatar said.

A video screen on the wall suddenly lit up, showing a map of the American Union and a timestamp at the bottom: 1971, the year of the Carmichael massacre. The cool, dusky breeze that had caressed Victor became an ice vest, squeezing his chest. A red dot flashed in Semiautonomous California's Long Valley, followed by another, then another.

"What are we looking at?" Victor asked in a small voice.

The Diamond King's voice came from sonobulbs near the screen, not the avatar. "The number of people with mirror resonance syndrome has seen an unsteady rise. The data was difficult to assemble. The Classification Commission's approach countermanded good epidemiological practice. The first cases appeared in a cluster near Carmichael and then spread to Oakland & Bayshore."

Wonda said, "MRS is genetic, though, right? It's not communicable, so this could just be showing how the tests were rolled out?"

Victor didn't comment. He was too busy trying to make sense of what the vidscreen showed. In an eerie way, the map illustrated a spreading caseload that mirrored his life's path. The timestamp, advancing slowly, showed the early eighties when his parents moved back to the Eastmore Oakland Hills mansion with Jefferson and Cynthia. He'd roamed the gardens in a gauzy post-traumatic fog not yet intensified by Personil. The glow in Carmichael remained at the same level, while throughout Oakland & Bayshore, it deepened, the sign of an intensifying number of cases. Throughout Semiautonomous California, additional hotspots appeared and grew.

In a voice filled with queasy resignation, Ozie explained, "Those would be the Classification Commission facilities."

The display advanced by years at a time. A new glow appeared to the east in the Louisiana Territories. In New Venice. A cluster of people with MRS.

"That's the transfer of patients," Victor said.

"No," the King responded.

Victor looked at the timestamp again. April 1991. Months ago. Right after he arrived in New Venice.

"No," Victor whispered. He repeated, "No."

"Victor, what is it?" Wonda asked.

"Shocks," Ozie said in a low whisper. His hangdog gaze roved over the display. He motioned at the timestamp. "That's before the patients were moved to New Venice. Before Samuel Miller was transferred. But after Victor arrived."

Wonda studied the vidscreen. Then, she stood ramrod straight, still as a statue. A single whispered word left her lips: "Emergence."

Tosh looked at her and shrugged. Then he turned to Ozie and asked, "Is it the stims, do you think?"

Ozie wiped a hand down his stubbly cheek. "I'm speculating, but stims alter brain chemistry, and epigenetic changes can occur with prolonged use. So, maybe?"

"Partly, it is the stims," the Diamond King said, his voice lilting softly. "Partly, I suspect, it is something to do with you, Victor. Don't you want to find out?"

"It is emergence. This changes everything," Wonda said, seemingly to herself.

No. No. No, no, no, no.

Victor walked to the railing and steadied himself with a hand on it, gripping to keep from sliding into blankspace.

The wise owl listens before asking who. The dark forest hides the loudest cuckoo. The wise owl listens. The wise owl flaps away!

No. Fuck! I need to understand what he means.

Victor turned to the vidscreen and asked for the display to be run backward. It showed a few dots representing cases in New Venice before 1991, which gave him some relief but not much. The Diamond King was doing a really good job of freaking him out. Was that the point?

MRS as an epidemic that originated in his own brain?

The others were looking at him expectantly. The Diamond King was promising to explain the mystery that haunted his entire life.

Can any dark fate truly be avoided?

Victor let out a long breath. It felt good to let go. He would go along with the deal, despite his doubts, despite the risks, because he believed in possibilities emerging. He would enter the dark forest. He would find the cuckoo.

Having decided, for himself, the world shifted around him. No more hesitation. No more feeling stuck. Gravity shifted. Wind was at his back. He was ready to believe in the path forward. He was committed.

Saying no was never an option. He'd had no choice. Was he a fool to pretend he'd ever had one? There was nothing to be gained from resisting the future.

"I'm in. Let's get this over with."

The avatar stood, its body motionless. The superimposed face, which previously had been animated during silences, eyes blinking, looking at each negotiator and observing, now seemed stuck on pause. A long moment extended. Victor wondered if the Diamond King, wherever he was physically located, was speaking with his team of scientists or policymakers to understand the ramifications or if he was swearing up and down to be faced with their demands.

Then animation returned to the avatar's face, its arms spread wide, and it said, "We agree."

Wonda let out a long sigh and sat down, hugging her arms around her middle. Ozie was hiding his face, clutching at Tosh, possibly crying. It was too much.

Victor looked toward the sky in the east, where the rim of the world was darkening to a lush, inky purple. He'd had no choice, really.

38

Amarillo was nestled in the ass crack of nowhere and Elena was glad to leave. The Republic of Texas capital of Waterloo, where Elena and Xavi were headed, was hundreds of kilometers to the southeast. In their path lay dry arroyos, broken plains, oily marshes, and stretches of hardscrabble farms, some abandoned, others drilling deep for scant pockets of depleted aquifers. Their train route involved several transfers and long waiting periods, sometimes overnight. They suffered one particularly difficult stint in a cramped transfer barracks with flimsy partitions that didn't mask the sounds of other visitors' fighting, snoring, and fucking. During long, noisy hours past midnight, Elena lay awake with one hand gripping the shockstick under her pillow.

During the day, stalking the platform with hundreds of shifty-eyed travelers, she experienced a twinge of sorrow. The ROT had changed. The destitution couldn't be ignored: people with flimsy travel bags, haunted looks, stringy hair, and rags for clothes. She'd always made it a point to curate a wardrobe that blended in, even after Eastmore money gave her a big income boost. But in a place like this, isolated, dangerously close to the OWS border, and full of transients, she looked hopelessly conspicuous in clothes that weren't threadbare.

As they approached the capital, the train ride smoothed out, meaning they proceeded on tracks that hadn't been hastily repaired after bombing by what the OWS called "home-grown ROT rebels" and what Texan authorities called "foreign agents." Call them whatever; the saboteurs were bad news for travelers. Elena and Xavi were grateful when they finally arrived at their destination.

Elena glanced back at the train car as they collected their bags on the platform and wondered how long until this route was cut off for good. She hefted her bags, shook off her doubts, and focused on getting through this day. One step at a time. She assumed it would be a grinding audition process to meet with Puro leaders in Waterloo, figure out how to fit herself into their plans, and let slip, *Oh, by the way, I met this spy from Europe who says he wants to help. Anyone want some tech or weapons?*

Too big a goal. Start small. Find a place to stay that night.

Xavi wasn't much help.

"I'm more of a small-town guy," he said when she asked for advice. He'd been to the capital only once or twice. He preferred wide-open spaces. She should call the shots. His newfound subservience surprised her. Maybe he was too exhausted to act as the alpha male. Or something had broken him. Maybe this was the new normal, and she should simply appreciate they were no longer butting heads at every crossroads. Hopefully, this was a sign he would defer to her leadership when push came to shove. Honestly, Elena preferred it when he bothered to display more machismo and confidence. She didn't like the new Xavi and wanted the old one back, but it wasn't her job to pep him up. He'd have to regain his mojo on his own.

The device from the farmer-spy guy at the border, which she'd taken to calling her "Bitter Pill" because of its lozenge shape, among other reasons, was a big help in tracking down accommodations. It identified a hotel within walking distance from Central Station marked "ROT Loyal" with reasonable rates. Xavi insisted on carrying more than his share of their bags, which she admitted was a rare example of machismo being a positive societal adaptation, at least as far as minimizing her exertions was concerned. His face was wet with sweat by the time they arrived at the hotel.

She approached the reception desk. The area was dim, lit by thick amber lightstrips hanging in meter-long coils from the ceiling like glowworms about to drop onto the guests below. They rang the buzzer for a clerk.

But before anyone appeared, ten plain-clothed paragons of physicality swept into the lobby and cut off every avenue of retreat. Elena had been in ambushes before. Usually, there was a loud noise, maybe some distracting theatrical smoke or explosions, and then the troops rolled in to knock down anyone standing.

However, this time, it was smooth, slick, and silent—she didn't realize it was an ambush until she and Xavi were surrounded. And it was nice that they didn't use force—a sweet touch.

Their leader was a tall, big-boned blond woman, who was pretty in a you-ain't-seen-me-be-ugly-yet way. She walked up and faced them.

"Elena Morales," Blondie said, sizing her up.

"Probably," Elena responded. She was outnumbered and ill-prepared for a confrontation. Denying what was easily confirmed would only appear weak and evasive, which seemed like a short path ending in pain.

"I'm here to escort you to a meeting with Senator Alberto Montero. Come with me, please."

"What if I don't want to?"

Blondie smiled thinly for the first time. "That doesn't factor into it."

"I'm coming with her," Xavi said.

Elena had to admit that he looked cool, like he could throw down with these muscle types and do some damage. Still, she put a hand on his elbow, leaned in, and whispered, "In case I'm going to meet the Grim Reaper instead of the Senator, I need you to stay here and carry on and find some friends who can light a candle in my memory."

Xavi, whose consent clearly didn't matter to the big blond and her beefy friends, nodded, and Elena was ushered out.

After a quick trip in an armored van's rear compartment—no windows meant Elena didn't need to be blindfolded, so that was nice—she was unloaded and escorted through an underground parking garage and into a transparent plastic cage containing only a chair and holes where gas could be pumped in. They made her give up her shockstick and endure a pat down by Blondie. Then she was led into a building that looked cozy for probably being an underground bunker: the lightstrips were a tastefully muted blue-green, and the wall decorations were pleasingly simple polychrome curves. Blondie strode quickly on her giantess legs. Elena hurried to keep up, helped by two guys behind her who would step on her heels if she slowed down.

They entered a carpeted office with a desk, bookshelves, some cozy chairs, and no view whatsoever. The best of bunker style. Behind the desk sat a man with salt-and-pepper hair with a cute curl. He had a kind and handsome face that reminded Elena of an uncle who'd always given her good birthday presents before he died in a brutal fight when she was six. His hands looked as weathered as country fence posts.

"Elena, please sit down. I'm Senator Montero. Please call me Alberto. Thank you for visiting."

"It was an irresistible opportunity," she said sweetly. "Blondie wouldn't have taken 'no' for an answer."

"It was important that we speak. You can go," he said, glancing past her. Blondie and her guys left the room and shut the door. Elena had the impression they wouldn't go far.

The Senator smiled sadly at her before picking up a device resembling Elena's Bitter Pill. He said, "I was given information about you. Alliances that seemed unthinkable in the past are now a necessity. For too long, the Puros have been on the outs with the administration of the Republic of Texas. That changes now."

Elena narrowed her eyes. "Well, thanks so much for finally taking your collective heads out of your collective asses. I guess you'll just ignore the body count."

He cocked his head. "If the situation weren't so urgent, we could discuss reparations. That will have to wait."

A just cause snuffed out by expediency was nothing new. Her temper blazed, but she kept her voice cool. "I take it back. You're still a bunch of head-stuffed assholes."

Senator Montero threw his head back and laughed at the ceiling. Then he said with a slight smile yet serious eyes, "Don't paint us all with the same brush. It's been a deadlock here for a decade. That's about to change. Even the pacifists and isolationists are coming around to realize something must be done about the OWS. However, there's only so much we can do without a big shift in public opinion."

"That must be where I come in, having exactly zero percent experience in that area." If he wanted to use the Puros for a political stunt, the conversation was a waste of her time.

Montero frowned, and Elena could feel, peeling away, the thin varnish of pretense that this would be a voluntary cooperation. It just made her want to wallow in sarcasm that much more.

"Tell me more about the pacifists we're going to arm," she said.

"Please. We're aware of your history with the Puros. We also know you have a connection to the Eastmores. Both of which may be useful."

Elena shifted in her seat. "I don't see what the Eastmores have to do with this."

It was Senator Montero's turn to look a bit surprised. "You don't know?"

He stood, walked around the edge of the desk, and beckoned her to sit in a pair of more cozy-looking chairs next to a tall shelf displaying spines of leatherbound books. She began to wonder how much a man of the people he was. What was his background? Native or colonizer?

The first wave from Europe had mixed with locals, creating a subsistence society with strong trade links to the Mexican Empire. The second wave held themselves apart, bringing their old-world fortunes, their penchant for exploitation, and the blessings and moral convictions of the Catholic Church. Elena looked around the room for a crucifix but didn't see one. If Montero was devout, he was a smart enough politician to hide it. As the home and origin of the Communion Crisis—that domino fuck train of disasters that mortally wounded the Catholic Church—the ROT would always be fanatically secular. Texans could never abide being known as suckers.

Montero offered her sweets from brightly colored ceramic bowls, dulce de leche taffy on the right and caramel pops on the left. She chewed on the taffy and waited for his explanation of what-the-Laws the Eastmores had to do with her being summoned.

"The OWS may not have declared war yet, but they are waging one. We won't let diplomatic formalities stop us from fighting back. Thanks to Circe Eastmore, we may be able to do so effectively. She is singularly responsible for convincing Europe to intervene in a way that doesn't prey on the AU's divisions. I'm referring to revised trade terms and amendments to the War of the Atlantic concessions. She pushed for those. She may be single-handedly responsible for saving the American Union from the most significant crisis of our generation."

"So, she gets a medal. Great. What does this have to do with me?" Elena had a sneaking suspicion that she wouldn't like the answer.

"It's come to our attention that Victor Eastmore is currently in Las Vegas. We want to know why."

Elena rose to her feet and spit the candy on the ground. "You brought me here to talk about Victor?"

The Senator looked at her with an expression of genuine surprise that she would have found funny if she wasn't using every part of her will to not shake his stupid body until his head popped off.

"We're done here," she said, moving toward the door.

"Wait! Elena! He's only one of several reasons. Please, we do need your help. We have resources. We can help your family."

She paused at the door and breathed. The safety of her family was worth everything. Mama and Papa had been on edge for years, tight with money, jumpy from all the violence. She could give them a tidy, safe, and pastoral home away from the unrest. Abuela Julia could keep her warmthless house. This was an opportunity to give her parents the retirement and space they deserved. Shocks. Why did she have such a hot head and a soft heart?

She turned and faced the senator, who looked at her expectantly. She gave him a quick nod. "You take care of my family, make them comfortable, make them safe, and I'm all yours. What do you want me to do?"

"We need an inside source."

Fuck.

"Well, this won't be my first time spying on Victor. Let's talk plans."

39

Narcissism, selfishness, and selective hearing are terrible personality traits. That's a self-evident truth. In my experience, they're also the traits that successful executives use to secure an advantage.

—Circe Eastmore, *Race to the Top* (1991)

20 May 1992
Las Vegas, Organized Western States

Victor looked down through obscuring mist at the people below, sitting at cafés and shaded by looming buildings and photosynthesizing awnings that dripped biofuel into collection pots. Victor, Tosh, Ozie, Wonda, Silk, and the Diamond King's avatar were gathered on the patio of the apartment Silk had designed, looking out over the city. After a full day of working through the finer points of the agreement, they were there to review and sign the contract. But unreality veiled his senses. Sounds were muffled. People and objects had liquid, blurry outlines. Victor had a looming sense of history in the making that lurked at the edge of his vision, an invisible giant farmer sowing seeds to be reaped in years and decades to come. A good crop or a bad crop? A future he wanted to meet or the biggest regret of his life?

I'm losing it.

Victor asked Ozie for one of his braincaps. They seemed like toys compared to the skullplugs, and he indulged without hesitation, cranking the program to maximum. A calming thrum flowed like water down his back, quieting his nerves.

Victor had arrived prepared to get the deal over with. The contract had already been reviewed by Karine, who'd been shocked when Victor looped her in via vidfeed. "I want to proceed without Circe," Victor said, insisting.

293

"That's not a problem from my perspective. I'm in Billings, of all places, looking at invoices and purchase orders. Based on what I've seen throughout my travels, we're a month or two from insolvency. You came up with a solution at the end of our rope. The funny thing is, I've had trouble with most of my communications, and from what I'm hearing, it's a problem throughout the Louisiana Territories. Something is happening in the Mesh, and it's disrupting everything. Your vidfeed is coming through clearly, but I couldn't contact Circe if I wanted to." Victor wondered about that. Circe had been an absent chief, preoccupied by BioScan's European operations. But Karine usually managed to reach her. "It's not a problem," Karine said, "I'll run the contract by one of the lawyers here." She told him the firm's name, which reassured him; they were legit.

After an hour of waiting, most of it spent with the braincap on, their vidfeed resumed with Karine smiling. "Marvelous trick. I'm in a total Mesh blackout, but I can get you within a few seconds." The document raised no red flags during her review, she reported. "I didn't think you could do it," she told him. "When you went missing again, I assumed we wouldn't hear from you for weeks. It seems that you've single-handedly rescued the company from bankruptcy. Quite an achievement."

"You don't see anything in the agreement that looks like a trap?" he asked.

"No. If anything, the terms are too generous. The rider for your review of treatment efficacy data is rock solid. I agree it seems too good to be true. But BioScan could walk away in a year with tens of millions of AUD in investment, and the Institute would have nothing to show for it."

She logged off with a shrug and a half smile, looking more than a little pleased.

Victor shared the summary and judgment of Karine's lawyer with his companions. Under the contract terms, the Institute for Advanced Biomedical and Neurophysical Research would provide technology and resources for installing surgery and treatment pods at BioScan in New Venice. Anders Lund would be transported there in the morning. Wonda and her Human Lifers would be given a county along the Cold Nile to run as they saw fit. Class Two or Three Broken Mirrors could elect treatment or refuse it. Class Ones would receive the treatment, and they could elect to discontinue once they regained verbal function. In exchange, Wonda would turn over the data egg to be copied. It all looked exactly like what they'd discussed. The trickle of hope he'd been nurturing became a whispering stream.

The avatar picked up a type-pad from a whirring robot that zoomed up. Mist coalesced into drops that ran down its arm, falling on the tiles beneath their feet. The agreement had been signed not by the Diamond King but by the Executive Director of the Institute. The Diamond King said the contract would be honored. Everything Victor had heard suggested that this was true. He signed first, and then the others followed.

A joyous monks' chant rose in his ears. No one else heard it.

With the signing done, all eyes turned to Wonda.

"Okay," Tosh said, "tell them where it is."

She spoke quietly. "It's in New Venice, well, not really. It's on the Qaddo land where I was staying."

"You will bring it here," the avatar said.

"You want me to go and come back with it?" she asked.

"Yes," it said.

"Can Victor come with me?"

"No."

Wonda frowned. "Why?"

"I have more to show him."

Victor bit his lip. *Will I finally get to meet him in person?* Or can I look forward to more MRS revelations?

Wonda looked to Tosh and Ozie.

"I'm busy," Ozie said. "There's so much to do here."

"Tosh? Please," said Wonda.

"I'll go," Tosh said with a sigh. "Unless you object?" His question was directed at the Diamond King's avatar.

"You may."

Victor sighed quietly to himself. It would all work out. There was a clear path ahead. He would deliver a cure for MRS. For the moment, he could put aside the question whether he would ultimately submit himself to the treatment.

Silk sidled up to the avatar. "Before Tosh and Wonda go, we'll attend the Breakthrough, the best Las Vegas offers. We're celebrating a new commitment to improve humanity."

Wonda smirked and said, "That commitment would ring more true if you didn't drug your guests and hold them hostage."

"Don't," Ozie warned.

"What?" she replied. "We made our deal. He can't back out just because I'm critical of this great society he thinks he's building."

Silk's gaze slid away from Wonda toward Victor, and they said, "Hopefully, you'll have a better opinion after a few days of getting to know us."

"I've seen a lot already," he said, thinking of how Silk and Davita got nervous or defensive when talking about the Diamond King.

In the awkward pause that followed, a new voice sounded. It didn't belong to any of the four guests or Silk; it wasn't the Diamond King's, yet it wasn't unfamiliar. The haunting voice came from the avatar. "Since when are you so skeptical, Wonda. You believed in me, didn't you?"

With his heart hammering, Victor turned toward the avatar and saw an image superimposed on its gray head: the face of Samuel Miller.

"No." Both Victor and Wonda said it at the same time. Victor's utterance continued a low-voiced, rapid repetition, "No, no, no, no, no, no, no, no."

"Wonda," the voice of Samuel coming from the avatar continued, "we agreed you would have land and resources and a social easement allowing you to organize your group as you see fit. You'll worship me. Isn't that what you wanted?"

"You're not Samuel," Wonda whispered.

"Am I not?" The avatar's head turned left and then right. The image of Samuel's face looked as it did before he died: wide, dark, hollow eyes on a long, pale face, thin lips turned down severely because he never smiled. It looked real, lifelike, and convincing. "If I act as he did and think as he did, how am I different?"

"You're not him," she repeated, putting more force behind her words. Grief and rage were red and black shadows like bruises on her cheeks and neck. She missed the man, how powerful he made her. His death had unmoored her, set her adrift toward an uncertain fate.

"But don't you want me to be?" he asked.

"Stop this," Victor said. "Stop tormenting her. We don't need to see this."

The Samuel-avatar's gaze locked on him, and for a moment, Victor felt a gut-wrenching urge to knock the thing down when Samuel's face was suddenly replaced by another: Jefferson Eastmore's.

Victor couldn't speak. Couldn't breathe. It wasn't Jefferson. It was just an image.

Yet when the voice came out, it sounded just like him. "I know it pains you, Victor, but you must learn to accept things you can't change. The wise owl listens before he asks who."

The fires of a volcanic eruption would be quenched and liquid lava frozen where it flowed and rocks the size of houses would crack open in the unworldly chill that Victor reached for. He had to stay cool, or his body would vaporize in the heat of his rage. The Diamond King was wearing Jefferson's skin like a cloak, mimicking his voice like the mythical crow monster that uses deceit to draw out its prey. "Stop," he whispered. He smashed a fist against the vidscreen. He pounded three more times until it cracked. "Stop!"

He felt arms take his shoulders and cried out, relieved, when Ozie said, "It's okay, it's me."

Tosh added, "We're right here, Victor."

He opened his eyes. Wonda was crying, sitting on the ground with her face in her hands. Silk was gaping at them all, bewildered.

Victor breathed and tried to regain his calm. Why? Why was the Diamond King showing them this freakish illusion? He must be recreating speech patterns and images from recordings of the two men. But why?

Wonda looked shaken. She glanced at Victor, and a change came over her. She squared her shoulders and lifted her chin. "I'm going. Now. I'll be back," she said. Victor thought she might leave then, quickly and quietly, but she began to cry as tears slipped down her cheeks. She came over to him, wrapped him in a hug with her face pressed against his chest, tiny sobs echoing within her torso, wetting the front of his shirt with her tears.

He wrapped his arms around her and murmured, "We'll be here."

"I didn't know," she said with a low moan. "I didn't know how badly this would go. Be careful."

He held her shoulders and looked into her eyes. "You'll be back. You're doing this. We're doing good."

She nodded, looked beyond his shoulder at the avatar, then met his gaze. "I'm doing this for you, yes."

She went to Ozie and squeezed his human arm. "Goodbye."

Ozie shrugged away, never missing an opportunity to show how much he scorned her.

Silk swept Wonda into a hug and cooed affection.

To Ozie, Tosh said, "Relaxation will have to wait," and winked without looking amused. Tosh nodded at Victor and then left.

Victor watched him go. A sort of grim caution settled in his belly. He wouldn't be dragged into whatever Tosh and Ozie were planning, and he wouldn't let them spoil his plans. He turned to the avatar. The Diamond King was a deep well of poisoned secrets. Victor needed to learn them all.

"Show me the pod again."

Victor entered the pod and sat down in the chair, expecting at any moment that tentacles would burst from panels in the floor, wrap him snugly in the chair, and hold him down while scalpels sliced into his skull. The contract guaranteed the skullplug operation could not be performed without his consent, and still, his gooseflesh rose in terrified anticipation. Was he stupid to trust in the power of an agreement with a maniac who toyed with dead people's images just to spook people? Or was there some deeper manipulation going on?

The door closed behind him. A faint humming in the walls began. Light, which had glowed diffusely, dimmed until complete darkness. A tentacle descended from the ceiling. He didn't see any sharp edges or needles, only a helmet, which slowly came to rest on his head.

His breath was loud in the silence.

Then, stars.

Stars in countless numbers lit up the vidscreen and the pod filled with ethereal glimmers. Pinpricks of light, bright yellow, red, and blue hues pulsed and sent out streaks in every direction. Layers and depths of connections between them, a vast latticework of communication.

It dawned on him. "This is my brain, isn't it?"

"Yes." The Diamond King's voice had returned to the deep, raked-gravel baritone that was now so familiar. "Your neurograms in the data egg will be compared to these we're taking now to look for changes in your neural pathways."

"What do you expect has changed?" Patterns of light raced across the screen, unintelligible terabytes, perhaps petabytes of data. "Why are you showing me this?" Victor asked.

"You're the key to solving a puzzle. How does MRS spread, Victor? Are you aware of what you're doing?"

Cody Sisco

"No," Victor whispered. "No," he repeated more forcefully. "That's ridiculous."

"And yet the evidence points to you. We spoke of an environmental factor. We've ruled out pathogens and environmental contaminants. You are the catalyst that makes people susceptible."

"Susceptible? Susceptible to what?" His heartbeat galloped. The display showing his brain's inner workings changed. The patterns shifted, and roughness smoothed. Jagged spikes became sparser. At the same instant, Victor felt a calm wash over him like a windstorm ebbing to a gentle breeze or thundering rain fading into a softly descending mist. His vision sharpened; sounds became distinct.

When he took a breath, he felt a rush like pure oxygen. "What did you do?"

The image on the screen showed bright tendrils pulsing at his brain's perimeter. Some force was extending into his mind. His skull felt emptied, enclosing only a vacuum, its contents obliterated. Real silence.

Which made him question the absence. What was now missing? What was it that had been so ever-present in his perceptions that its lack felt so novel, so pure?

With wonderment, Victor realized that his connection to blankspace, that hovering doorway into nothingness, was gone.

"What is this?" Victor asked.

The Diamond King's voice was soft and distant. "People with mirror resonance syndrome experience an uncommon sensitivity. Most perceive that sensitivity in relation to other people's emotional states. In addition, they have sensitivity to a signal, which is now blocked."

What signal? A cold icefall formed in Victor's belly. What insanity was this? What delusions had he opened himself up to?

"What signal?" he asked.

"How do you feel?" the Diamond King asked.

"Something changed, but it's hard to put into words. What's happening?"

"We'll find that out together. You've experienced episodes of blankness. What changed after you stopped taking Personil?"

"The episodes became more … intense."

"Try now."

Silence.

"MRS results from a deficiency in neurotransmitter receptors that preferentially affect inhibitory neural circuits. The magnetic fields generated inside this pod are stimulating those circuits, crudely. With time and a better map of your neuroconnectome, the effect can be more finely targeted. Or you could opt for the plugs."

"No," Victor said quickly. "I don't need to be fixed. Setting aside the classification system, which would put me at a high-functioning Class Three if the tests were fair, and they're not, I'm good with how my brain works, volatile as it is."

"Even without the implants, these pods can be a sanctuary for you. How do you feel?"

"It's ... I feel ..." A lump caught in his throat. He couldn't bring himself to say: I don't feel broken anymore. "I'm not sure."

"Would you like to stay in Las Vegas?"

"I—I'm not sure yet."

"How about a trip to blankspace?"

"What?" Victor began to say, but before he could, his world inverted.

It was like being turned inside out. Bile rose in his throat. A pressure sensation filled his brain. Blankspace returned, a nearby negative pressure pulling at his thoughts. He slipped into its embrace.

Whiteness that wasn't light, shadows that weren't dark, textures that appeared inside vast transparency, and the feeling of movement. There were figures in the mist. He was unbodied, adrift, seemingly at the whim of winds that blew him like a leaf in a storm. A voice burst into his ears, thrumming loudly, incomprehensible, too close, too loud. A period of intense pain followed, and then, at last, as the blankspace faded, the words became clear, and they resounded in his ears, as familiar as his own voice, "Yours is not the only universe."

Victor fell out of the chair, banging his knees, nearly knocking his head on the lip of the control panel. He sprained a middle finger, arresting his fall, and he cried out.

"Tell me what you experienced," the King demanded.

Victor was on all fours, gasping for breath. He dry heaved. The transition to and from blankspace had never been so rough, had never torn at his brain that way. His ears were ringing as if the sounds from that place had been real. *Yours is not the only universe.* Words spoken in his own voice. He dry heaved again.

Cody Sisco

"What did you hear?" the King asked again.

Victor shifted to sit against the pod's hull. The data would have showed activation of the parts of his brain that process sounds and language. But without the plugs' super-precision, the Diamond King couldn't translate the data into words. Fuck him. Let the monster behind the screen try to guess. "Nothing. There's nothing there. I want to go."

The pod door unfastened and swung out like a petal opening to the sun. Victor emerged on shaky legs. That brief minute of respite. He wanted it again already. But the way it had been ripped away, turned inside out, and perverted—he never wanted *that* again. He mistrusted the urge to return to the pod and forced his feet to take him down the ramp. That minute of bliss illuminated the taxing stamina required every second just to be himself. The shift in and out of blankspace had drained the last of his flagging energy. He collapsed on the floor, a darkness weighing him down toward unconsciousness, but not before he felt the avatar's arms under him. The arms stiffened, akin to water firming up a length of hose, and he was lifted and carried away.

"What did you do?" Victor asked once he'd regained consciousness and found himself lying on the bed, back in the apartments Silk had furnished.

The avatar stood by the window, blank faced. Beyond its figure, sunlight glinted off rooftops and windows of the tall buildings.

Without moving or displaying anything on its face, the avatar said, "There is a signal. You should be familiar with it. It's been with you for most of your life."

"What signal?"

The Diamond King's playing-card face appeared on the avatar, its fuzziness becoming crystalline and finely pattered, yet still not looking fully human. "The answer to that question is supremely important to me. It eludes. It frustrates. It hides in plain sight. We can see the signal's effects but can't detect its source. Everywhere and nowhere. I've not come across a challenge this exquisitely amorphous." The avatar reached out a hand to help Victor off the bed, and he took it, rising and testing his legs. They were steady beneath him, thankfully. He realized almost immediately that he was desperately hungry.

"Food," he said, "and you can explain while I eat."

A real-life waiter served Victor a steak with a pink center and charred exterior, announcing with an air of mischievousness that it was vat-grown meat. Victor shrugged and chewed a forkful, far more interested in the Diamond King's explanations about the signal.

"We learned of it by examining the neurograms of the first MRS patients."

"We?" Victor asked, taking another bite of steak. He chewed until it dissolved. No gristle. This was a good cut, an expensive, over-the-top luxury. No, it was fake but maybe even better than the real thing.

"A figure of speech," the King answered almost too quickly. "The same patterns kept cropping up in different patients. We checked whether comatose patients were conscious but unresponsive—they weren't aware of their surroundings, but they were doing *something*. Whatever is going on in their brains is not a result of their perceptions, as far as we can tell. The patterns are similar to dream states. However, when we started to compare the neurograms of patients, a startling fact emerged."

Victor's throat tightened, and he put down his fork. He understood now why the mystery got the Diamond King so worked up; it was the same one Alia had come across a few weeks ago. "Their states were coordinated. Synched up."

"Precisely."

Heat penetrated his skull like hot skewers. MRS patients were connected to each other somehow. How was that even possible? Then, a sudden rush of cold grief doused the fire in his head, grief for all those years of believing there was something wrong with him, when, in fact, nature couldn't be wrong.

"If the research in SeCa hadn't been halted," he said quietly, "we would have learned of this years ago. A decade or more, wasted." His shoulders had hiked up, and his jaw ached. If only he could be a child again and free of the terrible burdens he carried. He willed his muscles to relax.

Thinking back to what he knew of those first days after Samuel Miller's massacre in Carmichael, when the SeCa research staff had the mandate to find out what was wrong, Victor recalled hearing about a nurse who killed himself.

"Is there any evidence this signal affects people without the MRS gene?"

"Inconclusive. We call it a signal, but we don't know what it is, how it works, or even where it comes from. We need more information."

"You said I'm a catalyst."

"It's a hypothesis we need to explore."

Victor pushed his plate away and took a drink of water. How should a person react when they learn that the world is not what it seems? With the bloody-charcoal taste of steak in his mouth, a lump formed in his throat. Tears emerged and tracked down Victor's cheeks. Something about the world wasn't right, a fact he'd known all along; confirmation didn't help. He sobbed quietly, thinking that nothing had been solved and something undefinable had been lost. He would have given anything to feel his granfa's comforting arms around him. Instead, he had only the cool gaze of the Diamond King's avatar, inscrutable, unyielding, and patently inhuman.

40

What the Mesh accomplished was extraordinary. It taught humanity that virtual communications were a privilege, that authoritarian control of information was the norm, and that the slice of any individual's knowledge or concerns should be limited to what was in front of them. When it came apart, there was no common-sense philosophy to orient the public to a new state of affairs. Chaos was the only possible outcome. And some thrive better in chaos than others.

—Robbie Eastmore, *Another World* (transmission date unknown)

21 May 1992
Oklahoma City, The Louisiana Territories

Wonda had barely shut her eyes when she was shaken awake. The jet touched down, slowed to a bumpy roll, and parked on the tarmac in Oklahoma City. She rubbed her face—oily, grimy, unclean. Tosh was in a similar state. He'd been handsome and commanding at the gala; now he was looking worn out. She needed a good night's sleep and a shower. They both did. Who knew when that opportunity would come? Things were moving fast, and she needed to keep up and keep control, or she'd be swept along like debris in a flash flood. No time to nap, despite how much she wanted that sweet release. Exhaustion was simply the price to be paid for her commitment to purity. Purity was virtuous. Purity gave her a voice. Purity meant giving up the seductions most people used to mask the truth of their lives. No caffeine to jolt tired nerves. No stims to fill wasted, empty hearts. Only the pure, white-hot satisfaction of the moral high ground.

Tosh walked ahead of her toward a car waiting on the curb near the terminal building. The warmth he sometimes showed her when Victor was watching had vanished. They weren't going to be intimate, he'd made that clear, but she couldn't tell where that left their relationship. Tosh had always kept to the periphery of the HLM, involved himself when it suited his purposes, and otherwise acted aloof and seemingly unconcerned, which had worked perfectly, to be honest, much better than if he'd been interfering and second-guessing her all the time. Their alliance during the hostage-taking had been useful but not easy.

Giving him some credit, he'd been a hard, sharp instrument of her will at vital moments. It had nothing to do with her preaching, she was sure, and it was not because he *believed*—his thoughts, goals, and values remained a mystery to her—but he'd cooperated, whatever his reasons. And now, again, he was there when she needed him. Her luck hadn't run out yet.

Her followers would welcome the move. They had to. The Human Life Movement's roots on Qaddo lands would never reach nourishing depths; they snaked across the hard, waterlogged, and infertile clay rimming the lake. She had no illusions that their new home in the OWS would be permanent. She had no delusions about the risk she was taking—addicts shipped to the OWS to clean up while the rest stayed in New Venice on a mission to gain converts—this could be the end of it all.

Or, as with everything, it could simply be a new beginning. They believed in Wonda. She'd gambled on Samuel and won. His martyrdom solidified their faith in her. They trusted her to deliver miracles. Assuming she'd interpreted the Diamond King's demonstration correctly, with Victor's help to deliver a miracle, she would. The remaining disciples were the hardcore, truth-seeking followers she would usher through this crucible.

Tosh waved at the private autocab waiting for them, and its doors opened. She raised an eyebrow at him. A private vehicle was an extravagance, even in the tourist haven of New Venice.

Tosh responded to the unstated criticism. "You bargained your way into controlling an entire county, and you think I'm splurging with a nice ride?"

This wasn't a time to sweat the small stuff. She grunted and got into the cab with a bag full of small Tangle-connected devices that a Corp with a ponytail and full beard had pressed into her hands at the skyport. She said, "I guess I'm not surprised. But it makes me wonder what else you've been up to these last few months."

Storage containers in the rear compartment of the car gave off whiffs of plastic and metal, factory-fresh and toxic. Probably more weapons. Tosh climbed in and sat facing her. *Everything looks like a nail when all you've got is a hammer, and everything looks like something to be blown up when you're Tosh.*

"Slipping across the border doesn't happen without a lot of work. A lot of palms greased and a lot of persuasion of the gentle and not-so-gentle kind," Tosh said.

"I appreciate everything you do," she said with over-the-top sweetness.

Tosh snorted, although his lips quirked in a smile so rare on him that she smiled back immediately, genuinely. "It amazes me how little thought you put into the future, yet somehow, it seems to work out."

She watched trees pass by in a blur as the autocab picked up speed on the highway. "Does it look that way to you?"

From her perspective, life required banging on all the doors until one opened. This was the true way of things: they worked or they didn't. The trick was finding a way to push through. Tosh had a point, though. It helped to think ahead to remove roadblocks before they impeded the journey. Emergence happened no matter what, of course. But it didn't spring forth from nothing; it was shaped by what came before. It was an active process that could be directed, something to keep in mind over the next few hours.

Tosh stared glumly out the window, keeping his thoughts to himself.

"If this works, it'll be a miracle," she mused.

He frowned. "Don't count on me to cheer you up."

"I don't need you to," she bit back. Anxiety had gripped her out of nowhere. However, it was no good alienating Tosh when she needed him. She took a breath and added, "You've been helpful. I'm grateful for that."

He made a smoothing away gesture like sweeping crumbs off a table. "Earlier, what I meant was that you successfully negotiated with the King. You walked through flames and didn't get burned. That's a rare feat. And it rarely lasts."

"I created a path. The hard part will be getting my people to walk it with me."

"You have a plan?"

This was her opening. He wouldn't ask unless he was prepared to help. He didn't know what it might cost, though, so she had to pull him in.

She grimaced and lowered her gaze. "You might not like it."

Out of her peripheral vision, she saw him bristle. Nothing like a little challenge to stoke his ego.

"Try me," he said.

Here goes.

"I need your help with the Qaddo leadership."

His expression hardened, eyes squinting, lips thinning. If he were a dog, he would be baring his teeth and giving off a low growl.

She leaned forward and spread her hands. "They're our hosts but only reluctantly. I need them to move from reluctant to unwilling to worse. We're getting comfortable here licking our wounds. Complacent. Soft. I need them to expel us so that the OWS becomes our only option. Do you have any idea what could make the Qaddo do that?"

He looked at her stonily, betraying almost nothing, but she'd spent enough time with him to know when his mental gears were whirling away. Quiet, thoughtful, calculating, icy in outward appearance but a raging white-hot fire beneath.

When she spoke, it was in a soft voice. "If you think it would be better for me to go to the Chief alone ..."

After a moment, he muttered, "I don't think that matters." More loudly, he continued, "You need a reason for him to change his mind. An incident. Or a line crossed."

He was right, of course, and she'd known that, but hearing it helped her shape what she would do. She would create an incident. Importantly, perhaps more so, Tosh was now on board.

She looked out the window. The high stone walls of the cemetery flashed by, overarched by tree limbs waving in the wind. The car's windows were up, and the chiller gurgled in the side panels, exhaling small gusts of cool air. "About the incident ..." she began.

He looked at her and waited.

"It'll be a one-two punch. Punch one, stims. I've tolerated them for too long. After Samuel was gone, they suffered. They would sneak back into town and trade with some of the addicts at Pond Park. Stims gave them mysticism. A bond. If I take a hard line out of the blue, it'll cause a rupture. However, if an incident requires a response—"

"A violent incident?" he asked.

"Possibly," she said. "Punch two is our deal with the Diamond

King. If the Qaddo know we have somewhere else we can go, they won't feel obligated to shelter us."

"That's more of a gentle push than a punch. You need more oomph."

The autocab turned off the highway and navigated through the tightly packed streets of New Venice and then over Bozart's Bridge. Wonda stepped out of the auto cab. Cemetery Hill loomed close above. The BioScan tower seemed a pale imitation of wealth and power compared to what she'd left behind. To the north, Pond Park was dotted with tents and makeshift shelters. Westward, the stone buildings lining the canals were squat, clunky, and medieval compared to the soaring towers of Las Vegas. She wrinkled her nose, smelling sulfur and rot. The fetid water that sluiced over the pavements and roadways was only slightly less disgusting than what flowed through sewers. Steam from geothermal vents in the hills smelled fresh and clean by comparison. In the distance, Qaddo Lake and its depths of despair. She wanted to be gone from there and return to the desert as soon as possible.

"What are we doing here?" she asked.

Tosh pulled a large crate from the storage compartment and set it on the curb. "Special delivery," he told her, then said something inaudible. The box unfolded and disintegrated into hundreds of little blobs with tendril-thin protrusions. They looked like the unholy spawn of rats, spiders, and centipedes. The freaky hybrid babies streaked up the steps, following shadows, and moved swiftly toward the administration building and the hillside tower.

BioScan's newest vermin residents.

Which gave her an idea.

"We need to do some shopping while we're here."

Tosh looked at her warily. "For what?"

She gave him her biggest, sweetest smile. "A present for your tribe. Punch number two involves dolls."

41

Wonda enjoyed the shopping spree. Buying out every Qaddo-style doll in New Venice took some time, but the haggling was fun, and her plan put wind in their sails. It was helpful having Tosh follow her awkwardly around with bags and bags of dolls in the Qaddo-style—simple stitching to create the impression of a face and colorful, tailored clothing. Watching him squirm was a nice cherry on top. And the shopkeepers' quizzical looks were priceless.

Back in the car, their body odor was rank and heavy, so Wonda lowered the window and stared at a line of hills and rocky outcroppings that shaded Qaddo canyons. It was a more interesting view than the expanse of muddy water on the other side. They left the highway and began to climb the switchback over the ridge. On the other side, a roughening road and a decades-old, pitted sign announced they'd crossed a border into the sovereign Qaddo nation.

"It's not just the dolls," she explained when Tosh told her, with enough venom to down an elephant, to just spit it out already. "The second punch is totems." She gestured to a bag of devices buried under bags of dolls. "We put these in some dolls and spread them around town and among my people. Qaddo dolls ... with the Diamond King's avatars speaking through them. That's got to be taboo, unholy, or whatever. The Chief won't tolerate that kind of humiliation, right?"

Tosh frowned in a way that said he was impressed but didn't want to show it.

"Stims and totems. That's the one-two punch," she said.

"I'll arrange for the Chief to visit the camp. Make sure you get the data egg first. That's the whole point of this stupid trip."

"Hey," she said, smiling. "You want to know where I hid it?"

He looked down at her lap. "If you say, 'on my person,' I might throw up right now."

"Pervert," she said laughingly. "It's in the hot spring. The big one in our camp. I took Victor there when he visited. He looked right at it without seeing."

When Tosh laughed, it sounded like a drum beating in his chest. "That wouldn't be the first time he didn't see the truth staring back at him."

"Yeah," she said wanly, wishing she knew what Victor was up to. He was erratic at the best of times, but when in a new place amid a messed-up situation, even more so. "Let's take care of this quickly and get back to Las Vegas."

After another quick ride, they arrived at the Human Life Movement's compound but didn't rest. Her people got to work undoing stitches on the Qaddo-replica dolls they'd been making, inserting the avatar sonobulbs, and sewing them back up.

Using a long set of metal tongs, she retrieved the data egg from the steaming pool at the edge of the compound and put it in a zippered pocket.

Wonda didn't tell the Lifers why they were removing price tags from the dolls, ripping their seams, stuffing gadgets inside, then sewing them back up. She took one doll into a room and spoke to it, outlining her plans, and verifying the dolls would function as a new digital pet, life coach, and instrument of the Diamond King's surveillance operation.

Finding the Chief was the next step. A brief stop at the tribal center sent them following a string of clues, and eventually, they came to a park with grass and a few tall trees at the mouth of a canyon. At one end of the park, a group of men and women from the tribe, most of them elderly, sat on small logs arranged in a hexagon around a small steaming pool. Water flowed into the pool via a stone sluice no wider than a child's shoulders. A similar outflow directed the stream toward the lake. The pool was a meter deep and clear, showing a stippling of red and yellow mineral deposits on the smooth stones at the bottom. She wondered how many of these pools existed under their feet, buried deep, unnoticed. Surfaces always deceive.

Tosh motioned for Wonda to stop while they were about a hundred meters from the group. Bird calls and cicadas' humming filled the air. The group glanced over during their approach but continued talking, though Wonda got the feeling that whatever they had been discussing had shifted to include her and Tosh.

"You never told me much about your childhood here," Wonda said. It came out sounding like she was baiting him. A slip. She hadn't meant to. She needed to be more careful.

He looked at her a moment, then sneered, "You are fucking intolerable, you know that?"

Wonda smiled, a big fake grin to prove his words had no power, though she wondered about his reaction. She hadn't intended to poke at old wounds, yet he'd bit back as if attacked. Maybe that was his default mode. No, she'd seen him exercise control and hold an icy mask in place even when he was boiling inside. Perhaps he was comfortable enough with her now that masks weren't called for. Or maybe there was no space in their relationship for tenderness, honesty, and true connection.

After letting him cool off, she said, "I thought it might be something to talk about. If we have to wait here for seemingly no reason."

His response was flat and final. "Now isn't the time."

"Is it ever?" she asked.

A breeze pulled at her sleeves, and she wished to shed her clothes and run naked across the ground, to feel freedom as a breath of wind on her skin, and to leave all this struggle behind. To give up was a tantalizing fantasy. Nonetheless, she wouldn't abandon all that she'd fought for. She wouldn't stop fighting to survive. Her people needed to take the next step. Perhaps one day soon, she could sit still, enjoy the sun on her face, and just breathe. As Tosh said, though, now wasn't the time.

Chief Iwi waved at them, not a friendly wave, more like a come-here-and-let's-get-this-over-with command. Fine. Wonda was eager to be done with it, too.

They approached and took seats on an unoccupied log. Wonda noticed the long exchange of glances between Tosh and Chief Iwi. There was definitely some history there. Tosh would open up to her sooner or later.

Tosh eyed Iwi and noticed crow's feet, sagging cheeks, and bags under their eyes. The face was still handsome, despite the passage of time, yet the gorgeous young sibling that Tosh had obsessed over and clashed with had matured and now seemed on the verge of a decline. Memories of their time together, as venomous and sharp as a scorpion sting, came back in a rush. The silence after they'd sat down extended. No one seemed in a hurry to speak.

"We don't want to interrupt," Wonda said after a moment.

"You're here," Iwi said, though it wasn't clear if they were speaking to her, Tosh, or both.

Wonda cleared her throat. "We would like to thank you for providing refuge for the Human Life Movement. We'd be desperate without it."

Iwi glanced at her, then returned their gaze to Tosh. "And you, Tashah? Why have you returned after so many years? You live in the city now, we know. This isn't your first visit, but it's the first I've seen of you." Nodding heads around the circle. They'd noticed him keeping his distance. Not a surprise.

"Are you mad I didn't come sooner?" Tosh asked, trying to smile and feeling that he bared his teeth instead.

"This is your home," Iwi said slowly and carefully, obviously resisting Tosh's attempt to snag the conversation on personal grudges. Tosh admired them for it. "Though I heard you renounce your heritage, you cannot change where you came from."

"Or where you belong," said a woman Tosh didn't recognize at first. Then he looked more closely and saw it was Natti Niish, a woman he'd called Auntie growing up. She'd aged more than years alone could account for.

Memories threatened to overtake him again. A boat trip on the lake. A beating for a childish lie. The taste of frybread, and the scent of sulfur wafting on the breeze.

Tosh hadn't wanted this reunion. He'd resisted the Human Life Movement taking refuge here to prevent precisely this scenario from unfolding. He turned to Wonda. "Say it now, and let's be done."

She smiled, although anxiety showed on her face for all to see. The tribespeople didn't trust her—he could tell by the focused way they watched her.

Brightly, Wonda said, "We are planning a ceremony this evening to express our gratitude. It will include a discussion of our beliefs and yours. We hope to find common ground."

"You want us to join your cult," Natti barked with a laugh. She'd always had a quick and mean tongue.

"Not at all," Wonda said. "It's purely an opportunity for dialogue."

"We don't want you here," Natti said.

Iwi looked at Tosh and kept their gaze on him as they said, "I think they know that, Natti."

"We have gifts for you," Wonda said. "Dolls. Handcrafted in the Qaddo style."

The tribespeople looked at each other slyly. Dolls were for children. They sold them to tourists of all ages, sure. But did they look down on the buyers? Tosh thought so. They didn't have high opinions of the townspeople, who were generally out of touch with their heritage. Rootless. Shifty. Ambitious. Iwi had said Tosh would show himself to be all those things if he left, and he'd been right.

The joke was on them, though, because this was Wonda's genius move: an offer of gifts couldn't be lightly brushed aside. The Qaddo dolls appealed to the tribe's reverence for heritage and tradition, while at the same time invited down-the-nose looks. Why concern themselves with a childish gift?

Seeing Iwi and Netti sitting side by side afflicted Tosh with a sense of loss, like a hungry stomach aching on the third day of a fast. He could miss them, but that didn't change the fact that they were hypocrites. They claimed to respect all life, and that may be true. However, they looked down on society outside the tribe as a broken, mangled reflection of the good life they embodied. The world outside had technology and so-called cultural sophistication. Yet, Americans let successive waves of capitalism wreak destruction across the continent and embraced their destroyer more closely when faced with a crisis.

What the tribe didn't understand, as Tosh did, was that their disdain and separation didn't protect them. Their sovereignty was an illusion, only as durable as the nation that had sprung up around them. Their culture wouldn't survive being overrun by the Diamond King. They shouldn't expect to survive in the face of any overwhelming force if they wouldn't take precautions. That's why Tosh had left: to understand the threats and do his part to counter them.

He got no credit for the sacrifice.

But in the end, he deserved none.

Somewhere along the way, his own drives replaced his idealism. Now, the only goodness left depended on finishing what Jefferson had started and resisting the Diamond King. That included being there for Victor when threats he was too naive to see coming crashed against him.

Tosh examined the faces of his estranged friends and family. They were good people. They lived in harmony with the natural world, not out of principle, but because there was no other way—the gap between nature and civilization was a misconception, a Western delusion. But their philosophy didn't equip them to adapt when faced with an existential threat.

Some of them would come to Wonda's ceremony just to laugh. Let them laugh all they wanted, as long as they were properly outraged by the demonstration he was planning. Thanks to Wonda and the Human Life Movement, the Qaddo were now on the Diamond King's radar. If all went as planned, the tribe would expel the Human Life Movement, and this particular threat to his people would be deferred.

If only the true menace of the Diamond King were so easily ended.

42

"What happens in Las Vegas is simply the future."

—Intercepted message on Mesh 1.0 devices

21 May 1992
Las Vegas, Organized Western States

The night before the Breakthrough announcement, Ozie showed Victor the "micro-pods," as he called them, which would be shipped to BioScan's facilities and assembled into a surgery bay and imaging center.

"The standalone normal-sized pods, like the one you saw earlier, are too big," Ozie explained. "You couldn't get one of those into the building. So, what we've got is a larger installation made up of these smaller components. It needs too much power to run on solar cells and biobatteries, so it'll hook up to the grid. Each is priceless; the materials alone are worth millions of AUD, and the technology exists nowhere else. Are you feeling rich yet?"

Victor scratched behind his ear, noticing the length of his curls. He was due for a haircut. "That's a weird thing to ask an Eastmore."

These last few whirlwind days in Las Vegas had begun before dawn with tours of the King's research centers and treatment facilities and extended long into the night with programmed social gatherings. He looked forward to returning to his relatively anti-social life in New Venice and the calm it afforded. For how long, he didn't know. His idea of home was in flux.

"You're not wrong," Ozie said, "but the King makes you Eastmores look like paupers."

"Maybe." Victor looked around the room at so many carefully engineered components. The scientific and economic resources they represented were staggering. "This seems like more investment than BioScan needs." He trailed off, thinking seriously about a looming, too-long-unanswered question: What would he do about Circe?

Thanks to Victor, BioScan would now have a treatment for MRS and a way out of their financial predicament. He had a feeling Circe's reaction would not be praise. She had some history with the Diamond King that was wrapped up in Jefferson's death, though the truth of that story depended on who you asked and who you believed. In any case, he wasn't sure she'd appreciate the achievement this deal represented. She liked her own plans better.

As Victor looked at the tightly packed cubes, another thought occurred. He put a hand on Ozie's shoulder. "You'll be there to supervise the installation, right? Maybe you can stay and keep an eye on the surgeries and the recovery."

"I can't," Ozie said. "I'm needed here."

"For what? What are you working on that's more important than this?"

"It's not something we can discuss." Ozie glanced down at the robot waiting, then to a speaker above them.

Victor got the message. They were under surveillance. He suspected as much, but when would they have a chance to speak? Never? Ozie wore a no-expression mask—a long-practiced trick that walled him off from the world and its dangerous influences. Victor had been fooling himself into thinking they might reconcile. Ozie was incapable of acting on his feelings. He wasn't going to change.

"I'm leaving tomorrow night, so I suppose we never will," Victor said heatedly.

Ozie's face fell. "Don't," he said quietly. After a moment, he looked up. "Don't give up on me yet." He touched Victor's arm gently, but the pulse of adrenaline that shot through Victor was the opposite of gentle. "Come on." Ozie led Victor outside to the street, down the block, and into an alley used for deliveries to the high-rise loading bays.

A van pulled up and opened its door. As they got in, Victor noticed it was surprisingly empty—unlike Ozie's souped-up van, which was crammed with gadgets, cables, and numerous devices. This one had netting on the walls, ceiling, and the floor, and slabs of batteries stacked and daisy-chained together. Victor turned just in time to see Ozie jump in, seal the door, and tap something on the pad next to it.

"What are you doing?"

"Hang on." Ozie tapped on the cyberarm. Sweat trickled down his brow, which he shook and sent droplets flying. "It's active. We're in a Faraday cage."

While Ozie fussed with his arm, Victor blinked, vaguely remembering what he'd learned about an inventor who discovered how to shield machinery from electromagnetic interference. Of course. Ozie would want a shielded space, away from spectrum relays, Mesh signals, and any devices that could relay information to the Diamond King. They had stepped inside a black box so they could talk.

"You should come to New Venice," Victor suggested. "You can take a look at the patients."

Ozie shook his head, still focused on his cyberarm. "I don't dare leave. Besides, he's got eyes all over there."

The Diamond King was already spying on BioScan? How?

Victor steadied himself with a hand on the van's wall, his mouth filling with spit. Tosh. That's why he'd been so eager to instigate the HLM hostage-taking: it was a perfect opportunity to scatter his bugs everywhere. It was too much wishful thinking that the tower, built after the crisis, would be free from surveillance. It wouldn't take much to bribe a BioScan employee or a building contractor.

"There. It's powered down." Ozie looked up. "Okay. There's not a lot of time. This thing"—he glanced at his limply dangling cyberarm—"has been listening. It's in a low-power diagnostic reboot, so it can't record, but I've only got a minute or so more. The van's shielding means nothing can transmit or receive. We're clear."

"But—"

"You've got to listen, Victor. What the King is planning is worse than you can imagine. He won't stop until he controls everything. He's—"

The fingers on Ozie's cyber hand curled. He jerked like he'd been zapped and looked down in horror as the arm moved, bending at the elbow, bringing the fingers to his neck where they flexed and probed. They began to squeeze. Ozie looked panicked and tried to speak, but nothing came out of his compressed windpipe. He was suffocating. His lips mouthed the word "help."

Victor tried to pull the arm down, but it was locked so tightly that if he pulled it away, it might rip skin and tendons. Ozie's lips were blue. Victor lurched to the door and used the type-pad to unlock and open it.

The cyberarm relaxed. Ozie choked in a huge breath and coughed, bending over, trying to fill his lungs.

"That's it, then," Ozie said eventually. "I can't help you. I can't even help myself. It's up to you now."

Ozie slumped against the side of the van's cabin. His cyber hand rested on the rear step. Victor had a brief imaginative flash. What would happen if he slammed the door on the arm and ripped it away? Would Ozie be free then? Would he bleed out?

"It listens," Ozie said. "It listens and it plots and it schemes. There's no use resisting."

"I wish I could help," Victor said. It sounded weak. His friend was in trouble; all he had was a wish and no power to make it come true.

"It's no good. Leave, Victor. There's still time before your world comes crashing down. Go! Leave me alone."

"I don't understand. What's bothering you?"

Ozie closed his eyes. Victor saw the resignation. Ozie was serious: he was giving up. Victor didn't recognize the expression on his friend's face; it was entirely unfamiliar.

"Wait," Victor said, "I've been meaning to tell you something about my feelings. And you can *tell me*."

Victor reached over and took off Ozie's glasses and set them aside. He put his hands on his shoulders, bringing their faces close, their lips almost touching, their breath crossing the distance, Ozie still panting. Victor's breath hitched in his chest from excitement. Their lips pressed into a kiss.

Without drawing away, Victor whispered, "Remember how we used to talk?"

Ozie pulled Victor, crushing them together. Victor simultaneously became aware of several facts. One, Ozie's real hand clenched rhythmically, repeatedly in a familiar pattern, tapping out SOS in Morse code. Two, Ozie's lips moved, and he moaned, but not in an aroused way. He shaped the barest outlines of words with his lips, adding enough sound to fill in the details. The tapping! Of course, Victor had been an idiot the night of the gala and hadn't picked up on the code Ozie tried to use with him. Three, Victor knew they were about to covertly communicate, but the feelings inside him had nothing to do with communication. Lust, longing, sadness, and fear mixed into earth-spinning cocktails. He breathed hard. He wanted this moment to last for days, bodies pressed close, breathing each other's air, feeling the heat build.

It would look like they were cuddling. To the Diamond King or anyone undertaking surveillance, they would appear to be genuinely getting it on. What shocked Victor was that it was genuine. He had wanted this, hadn't dared acknowledge it, but now it was happening, however twisted it was, he saw a broken reflection of how it should be.

Victor pushed Ozie away, catching his breath from the shock. He read the look on Ozie's face: pure black fear and a tiny sliver of golden hope.

Does he feel the same way? He's fighting for his freedom, and I'm chasing a sexual high. It's not right.

Victor shook his head to clear it. "If you want a relationship, let's start again," he said, hoping the subtle emphasis on *start again* was clear enough. A look of relief passed across Ozie's face, and he nodded.

They were close again, lips together and "kissing." Victor was less distracted this time, although Ozie's sandalwood smell competed for his attention. They needed a simpler way with fewer distractions.

"Acrostic," Victor whispered into Ozie's mouth.

That short message took several repetitions for Victor to be certain Ozie understood. When he nodded, Victor was relieved. Not wanting to give up physical contact, he moved to sit beside him in the empty van. They now had a way to communicate without the Diamond King knowing, and it didn't require mouth-to-mouth. The message would be verbalized using a letter-by-letter approach they'd developed at university during delusional spells when they thought the Classification Commission was spying on them. The first letter of each sentence was the content of the message; the rest was simply a way to confuse potential codebreakers. Looking back, though, their paranoia in SeCa had been justified. Was it again? Or was Ozie slipping away?

After a minute, Ozie said, "Man, it's great to see you again."

M.

"It's been a while," Victor responded, indicating with a brief nod that he got the letter.

"Actually, it wasn't my idea to bring you here. It was the King's. He took an interest in you a while back."

A.

Victor kept track of the letters as unease began climbing out of his stomach. The Diamond King's interest in him and the link to MRS spreading could not be less reassuring.

"I know. He told me about the signal, too," Victor said. He knew this was dangerous; if the Diamond King or one of his spies listened, they would pay close attention whenever he was mentioned. Hopefully, their words would be taken at face value.

Ozie seemed to hesitate. He looked around, like he was searching for the right word. Or maybe a vidcapper. Any number of which could be hidden anywhere in the loading bay or the alley. A cold chill spilled down Victor's back. What data didn't the Diamond King have access to?

"Chances are, he's listening right now, but I don't think he'd mind us speaking like this. He's making amazing improvements in cyber human interfaces." Ozie nodded at his artificial arm, and Victor read disgust on his face.

Chances signified a *C*. Or could it mean *CH*?

"That's confidence for you," Victor said. "Not chicanery, chiral, or chancy luck. Right?"

"Oh," Ozie said with a sad grin. "Yes, correct." He emphasized *C*, not *CH*.

Okay, C.

Victor was relieved. "Well, I'm glad you could take a break and come here." Emphasis on the word break while he was looking at the cyberarm. If Ozie needed to break away from the arm, they needed another chance in a Faraday cage, a clamp to hold the arm in place, and some quick surgery. It would be bloody, painful, and horrific, but it had to happen. They would also need help. It was nothing Victor was qualified to do.

They continued this charade, moving the surface conversation away from the Diamond King to earnest statements about their friendship, overcoming past disagreements, and maybe even exploring new terrain together. But Victor took all this with a grain of salt. Although Ozie seemed sincere, Victor didn't dare get his hopes up. This wasn't the time to get distracted.

"Later," Victor said, not wanting to confuse things.

Ozie's code had thus far spelled *M-A-C-H-I-N-E*.

Machine? Or the beginning of machinery? Maybe the message was something about OWS industry and the Diamond King's plans. Or was this about building a better Faraday cage?

Ozie said nothing for a moment. Then, deliberately and slowly, he said, "That's it. That's what you-know-who is." He let the silence extend for two full beats and then continued, "And the world can't stop him."

The message was complete.

The Diamond King is a machine?

Victor thought of the Diamond King's digital and physical avatars and the totems. He'd always assumed people were speaking through them, animating them somewhere. In a hidden room, people with human intentions and psychology controlled them. Was it even possible? Machine learning on Bose Drives to feed chatbots through spectrum relays to every available sonobulb and vidfeed?

Ozie had been tinkering with computer programming for as long as Victor could remember. He could make little servant gadgets, create mind-calming braincap programs, and hack into the hardest-to-hack equipment.

But Ozie had always said synthetic consciousness was hundreds of years away, if it was even possible. Computer architecture couldn't recreate the brain's architecture. The information density required was out of reach. Humans emerged from the womb with no self-awareness and lacking intelligence. It took years to develop. Could it be emulated? Was a synthetic consciousness possible? Was such a thing animating the Diamond King?

"Now you understand what all this means," Ozie said. He waved toward Grand Park and the skyline glinting in the sun. "The implants ... we're all totally fucked."

Black stormy panic, struck through with lightning, swirled in his vision.

"Couldn't there be another explanation?"

Ozie looked at him coldly.

Victor said, "What I mean is that the Cold Nile Miracle is unbelievable."

"You think I'm crazy." The patronizing smile Ozie showed had zero humor in it. The warmth between them chilled; air condensing to frozen mush.

"I don't know," Victor said. "What can I do? There's no going back."

"That's what I'm saying." Ozie gave him a grave look. "What can any of us do?"

I could have said no to the deal!

A wave of anger toppled Victor, and he sat down hard on the ground, resting against the van's bumper. It was too late. He looked at the cyberarm again and wondered what he could say to make it start choking Ozie again for not warning him.

Long ago, as a new student at Ludlum Middle School, still reeling from the violence he'd witnessed in Carmichael, Victor sat alone and watched other students playing "rattling chains" in the yard. One of the games they played had them linking arms in a long line, facing in alternating directions. The player at one end would stand in place while twisting back and forth, causing the next person to stumble a few steps, first forward and then back. The next person in the chain was forced to keep up, to take more steps even faster, again forward and then back, and the next had to sprint to keep up, racing forward then stumbling back, all the while staying connected in the chain. Inevitably, players at the far end would lose their grip and fall, tumbling, squealing, until many splayed out on the grass, moaning.

Victor knew Ozie was yanking his chain back at the Springboard Café when they reunited; it was always the predominant pattern in their relationship. Ozie was forceful, knowledgeable, motivated; he made plans and pushed forward. Victor was pliant, confused, persuadable. He reacted, always felt two steps behind everyone else. It wasn't an ideal friendship, but it had worked for a time, and when Ozie came back into Victor's life, he'd hoped it could work again.

But Ozie wasn't the first player in this chain. Ozie was being jerked around by the Diamond King. And Victor was at the end, whipped back and forth, not seeing clearly until now who—no— *what* was yanking the chain.

Ozie looked at him miserably. Victor was glad. Ozie always had a good enough reason to lie. It was his turn to be flung to the ground. Victor hoped it would leave him with big purple bruises and the sharp sting of regret. The deal had been sealed. The Diamond King was a synthetic consciousness that had taken an obsessive interest in mirror resonance syndrome and why and how the condition seemed to trail after Victor.

"You should have told me," Victor said.

"I tried."

Could Victor back out now? Should he walk away?

No. He intended to see it through, get answers, help the other patients. But he probably should have asked a bit more about "who" first. The wise owl didn't listen hard enough.

43

People say the Repartition of the United States returned power to its roots. That's tarted-up ass puckery. Power evaporated after the War of the Atlantic. Repartition was the makeup you put on a corpse for its wake. That body's been rotting in the sun too long. At least people now see the truth.

— Republic of Texas Senator Alberto Montero (unpublished interview)

21 May 1992
New Venice, The Louisiana Territories

I love my fiancé, but sometimes I want to murder him.

The thought came to Alia fully voiced, dropping into her head like a stone in a pond, leaving a wake of concentric what-the-fuck-is-wrong-with-me waves as the limousine that carried her and the delegates from nations of the American Union cruised forward. If only she could feel so unbothered.

It's the stress of the conference. Too much on my plate. Why did I let Torsten lead me into this?

She ran her fingers through her hair. A glimpse in the window's reflection showed skillful makeup camouflaging the bags under her eyes. At least she *appeared* put together. The sad thing about being prepared was that you didn't get to enjoy it. Some new, fresh, unpredicted hell was always popping up. She was as ready as she could be.

Let it be enough. Powers above, give me grace. I just have to breathe and push through.

She sat up in her seat, mindful of her posture, as the caravan carried the AU emissaries and support staff toward the meeting place. Onlookers stopped and gawked at the unblemished vehicles passing through town, brown like the river. She watched Torsten where he sat opposite her, leaning toward his guests and embarking on a long-winded digression. He called it "marinating," introducing concepts and vocabulary and immersing listeners in his frame of reference to influence their thinking during the real discussions. He was going to have mixed results. The emissary from the Organized Western States wore a disdainful expression, looking down her nose at the idea that there was a stim epidemic. During the planning discussions, she'd claimed there was no stim problem and, therefore, no need to discuss it. Alia wanted to drag her by the ear through Pond Park, asking, "Can you see *this*?" Thankfully, the consensus-minus-one rule meant that a single voice couldn't sway the proceedings, and the other emissaries had insisted on placing the topic on the agenda.

I'd better breathe easily with the little wins, or I'll be choking on the losses.

After the vote, the OWS delegate complained loudly. "Everyone should be free to explore every facet of their personal development."

Her facet is probably dry, tight, and full of venom, Alia thought, noticing that the Semiautonomous California delegate, Mía Barrias, had frowned at that statement.

Mía was a steely woman. Alia admired her strength and compassion as well as her storied biography: survivor of the Carmichael Massacre, a key player in the BioScan hostage crisis, and most recently, she had successfully negotiated her release from another hostage situation back in SeCa. Mía looked like she had something to say but remained silent. Her grit was inspiring, and Alia had a feeling that whatever she was holding back would be fascinating.

The motorcade passed through the Buffledyn Tunnel, left the highway behind, and entered the camp formerly belonging to the Human Lifers near the outflow of Ouachita Dam. The trailers and modest buildings assembled by the displaced group now comprised a BioScan-run stim addiction treatment center. Patients were cordoned from the gravel road as the motorcade passed by, watching with agitated faces, some of whom Alia recognized. Not even the New Venetian gentry were immune to the siren call of stims.

She suggested beginning the deliberations here because it would underscore the severity of the situation and impress upon them the need to address the crisis before it spread further. Already, every nation bore a portion of the burden, but none more so than the Republic of Texas, Semiautonomous California, and now, with growing urgency, The Louisiana Territories. Alia didn't believe the OWS claim there was no problem there at all, fearing they had

Cody Sisco

perhaps eliminated the problem in an unpalatable way. Rumors of capital punishment, outlawed throughout the AU, had spread. She didn't believe they were true, but rumors grew in fertile soil.

Seeing the patients' miserable faces beyond the glass made her doubt the wisdom of choosing this location. They looked like how she felt inside: exhausted and discouraged. The crowd's noise was more jeer than cheer. They might be making too strong an impression.

The motorcade stopped to avoid a patient who'd ducked the barricade and flailed in the street for attention. His words slurred together in a frantic stream of nonsense. Looking closer, Alia realized now that the expressions on the patients' faces—desperation, agitation, and frustration—were not likely to inspire empathy; if anything, it was the opposite. By pressing the case so blatantly, she might have overplayed her hand.

Torsten looked at her and gave her a tight smile—his standard poker face—though there was calm approval in his eyes. On another occasion, he would have squeezed her hand or offered some other small physical reassurance. Not today. Everything today would be played by the book, restrained and focused, with no leeway for small things like comfort. She forced a smile and nodded back at him. They would get through this.

The motorcade stopped again.

"What now?" the OWS representative complained. Alia looked at her more closely, not bothering to hide the strength of her disapproving gaze. Some people would never be won over by politeness or kind eyes. The woman was middle-aged with skin the color of dark-stained oak and gray hair wildly fringing her face, which played host to many bright hues of makeup: sapphire glitter, rose-red sheen, and silvery luster.

The sonobulb in Alia's ear piped in an update from the driver: "Group of stimheads linked arms in our path. They'll be cleared, and we'll be moving soon."

Alia had to weigh the benefits of pointing out the severity of the stim problem against drawing attention to security concerns that would distract the delegates. She didn't want to admit that their security was lax.

"A brief delay. The venue is nearby," she said with a fake and bright smile, hoping she'd scrubbed all the irritation and anxiety from her voice.

The OWS woman raised an eyebrow. From the way she'd loudly contrasted her transportation via private airship within the OWS to her trip from Oklahoma City to New Venice—via train in a private cabin the size of a blue whale, complete with dining room, sleeping accommodations, petite gym, and lounge area—Alia had the impression the woman was never satisfied outside her superior OWS company town. The OWS woman glanced at Alia dismissively, snorted her disapproval, and then returned her gaze to the window to scoff at the surroundings.

The bald Black delegate from the Southeastern Confederacy, Clive Marlow, smiled at Alia. He'd already distinguished himself as the group's most positive, engaging, and peacemaking personality. Though Torsten, she knew, was holding some charm in reserve for when it would be needed to sway the group to his viewpoint. Clive made a sound like someone might make after sipping a fine wine. "Would you look at that?" he said. "Those garden plots are bursting with bounteous pleasing produce."

Alia and Torsten exchanged a glance, smiling more fully now, knowing the other was thinking the same thing: *Who on earth says, "bursting with bounteous pleasing produce"?*

Clive continued without missing a beat. "As someone who tends his garden by hand and with an ancient connection to the soil, I do approve."

Margie, the New England Commonwealth representative, was a young pretty woman with a pale, freckled face. She asked, "When you say your family has an ancient connection, what do you mean? Are you of native descent?"

Clive's expression lit up, and he favored Margie with a smile. "Can you tell by looking at me? It's true my lineage draws connections both with the native peoples from a coastal community that was forced to march west, as well as freedmen who'd labored in slavery for more than a hundred years following their horrific journey from their soul home in Africa. The providence of the Civil War, Reconstruction, and the Permanent Enlightenment means that our oppression has been rectified, leaving me free to play in the dirt for leisure and produce. Such a beautiful thing brings me great joy."

Alia had traveled to the Southeastern Confederacy once she was old enough to acknowledge her prejudices and gauge their accuracy. She knew it was indeed true that enlightened personages of the South crafted their words with airs as befit the heirs of the Permanent Enlightenment's originators. She found herself grinning in appreciation of Clive's efforts to improve the mood.

She spoke to him in a register that echoed his. "Joy can be a solid, weighty contentment derived from the righting of grievous wrongs. The legacy of slavery can never be erased, but justice prevailed at long last."

The mention of the atrocities perpetrated by the United States of America—something people from the Southeastern Confederacy were always happy to bring up, in Alia's experience—twisted the mood toward somber remembrance.

"Prevailing into the future, I hope," Clive responded. "We sustain the Permanent Enlightenment by naming injustice and, beyond that, rectifying wrongs." He swept a hand slowly by the van's window next to him. Did he mean to remind them all that it was their duty to look for ways to help people suffering from the affliction of stims? His approach might be too subtle for this audience, Alia thought, looking at Margie, who seemed not to know how to respond, and at the delegates from the Greater Ohio Constitutional League and the Dominion of Florida and Cuba, who seemed to prefer silence to dialogue. She hoped they'd open up later.

The motorcade stopped again about the same time Alia's sonobulb buzzed with the message that they'd arrived. Louisiana Territories security personnel opened the doors and directed the emissaries to a large transparent half-dome over a paved depression. This had been the Human Life Movement's assemblage. No longer. The white synthsilk tent fabric had been replaced by transparent soundproof material that interfered with all non-visible wavelengths of electromagnetic radiation. The emissaries had agreed wholeheartedly with Alia's suggestion that extreme counter-surveillance measures be taken. Any communications among officials from the nations of the American Union would be an attractive target for Mesh operators and, by extension, European intelligence agencies, as well as the other AU nations, who guarded their sovereignty jealously, all the more so now they had been too diminished to meet their ambitions.

The most they could ask for was privacy. Not that they would get it. Torsten and Lisabella had convinced her of the necessity of Europe's constructive involvement. Though Alia wished that didn't require her to spy for them. It was a perversion of loyalties, though she believed it was for a good cause.

As the dignitaries were being served water, tea, and real coffee, the security chief quietly approached Alia and requested a private chat. They made their way to an unoccupied couch along the far arc of the tent, though they didn't sit.

The security man was tall, his pale skin flushed red by alertness, and he had the physique of someone who could wrestle a cheetah. "There's nothing to worry about now, Ms. Effendi," he told Alia. "I just wanted you to know that we stopped a few Human Lifers outside the facility."

Alia kept her composure, allowing herself only a raised eyebrow while her stomach coiled. "Were they armed? How close did we come to an incident?"

"We removed them well in advance of the motorcade. They're in custody. They weren't armed, per se." The man hesitated, running a hand over his bald head. She noticed the faint tic of amusement at the corner of his mouth.

"Do you mind sharing the punchline?"

"Yes, of course. It's just that each one of them was as high as I've ever seen a person. We all had a laugh about the purer-than-pure Human Lifers using stims."

"Indeed," she said. The tension in the pit of her stomach eased, replaced by curiosity. What was Wonda up to now? She'd do anything to grab an audience.

"That's not the thing, though. They had these dogs."

Perhaps she'd misheard him. "Dogs, did you say?"

"No, ma'am. *Dolls*. This big." He brought his hands together as if cradling something the size of a large grapefruit. He then took out a MeshBit with a screen the size of his palm and showed her an image. A dark-colored doll with wild white hair and a purple dress in a conservative cut filled the screen, an obvious homage to the OWS delegate. He went on, "They had one for each of them. The stuff they were saying was gibberish. Something about freedom to cross over and throwing off the shackles of oppression. They called you the mistress of literal thinking."

Alia wondered, *Did they make a doll of me too?*

"It was a lot of garbage," he said. "You don't need to be worried. The bigger problem is what's inside. We found devices. We think they're for surveillance. We haven't been able to hack them yet, but we will. Question is ..."

She picked up his trail: "Why?"

"Exactly. Why do they care about this summit? I mean, they're all for purity, right? You'd think they would want to stop stims from coming over the border."

"That would make you guilty of literal thinking, I think," she joked. The smile on his face was a welcome break from the tension that had been building all day. Thanks for letting me know."

"We'll keep an eye out for any more unexpected attention. I've got guys watching everything that comes and goes from the Qaddo Lands." He gestured to the dignitaries. "This venue is clear of any bugs. No worries about that." He'd returned to his all-business manner quickly.

She nodded and thanked him and made her way to the refreshments table. She was parched, and some emissaries had yet to take their seats. They huddled in twos and threes, strategic groupings, looking for common ground with allies before the formal deliberations began. She didn't envy their positions; how does one speak for an entire nation?

Her mind turned to the dolls. That was new and odd. The Human Lifers perhaps had too much time on their hands, stuck within the bounds of the Qaddo sovereign lands. Now that she thought of it, the dolls suggested more interplay between the Human Lifers and the Qaddo than expected. The Qaddo had been reluctant to host the HL refugees. Was that changing? She didn't want to think they could influence her Qaddo friends, some of whom were as close as family, closer really, since her parents had been removed from the equation.

If they were spying, who were they spying for?

She stopped herself. This wasn't the time to speculate. She had a mission, and she needed to focus. With a polite smile, she sat on the chair that had been reserved for her, one slightly apart from the others, outside the circumference drawn by the mind's eye when taking in the position of the other seats. She set her water on a transparent acrylic side table, leaned forward, and started listening as Torsten kicked off the meeting, putting aside all thoughts of little dolls made by people who believed in fanciful, magical alternate worlds.

The running list of agenda items that Alia kept grew quickly. Each topic required long discussions, with every emissary having their say. The meeting proceeded more or less smoothly, until the Greater Ohio Constitutional League emissary said something that silenced the gathering.

The middle-aged man of Germanic descent, round-faced and white-haired, repeated, "I move that we add a discussion of the refugee situation to the agenda."

The other emissaries scowled at him, except for the emissary from the ROT, who looked pleased.

"There's no need," the LT delegate said.

With a sigh, the Southern Confederacy emissary said, "I suppose a discussion could be helpful." After a moment, he added, "I second the motion."

"Would you like to call for a vote or debate?" Alia asked.

The GOCL man looked at his fellow emissaries and, reading their body language, said, "A debate would be insightful."

A debate about a motion to add an agenda item. *Give me strength*, she thought.

44

21 May 1992

Qaddo Allotment, The Louisiana Territories

Wonda stalked through the camp, calling for a meeting and telling everyone to assemble under the large oak tree marking the edge of their allotment. There was some grumbling and many curious questions. "We've got a big decision to make," she told them.

When everyone had assembled in a rough circle, she recounted her trip to Las Vegas and the land she'd bargained for. The way the Human Life Movement members stoically took in the news impressed Wonda. A less disciplined group would have shouted and demanded clarifications, but her flock seemed willing to wait until she finished, for which she was thankful. She was sure, however, the uproar was merely delayed.

"And that's where we find ourselves," she said. "We now have a new home, with land, with infrastructure, with a framework for running our lives free from interference, not dependent on reluctant kindnesses. There's more, though. I promise you, when we arrive, there will be a new, profound, ground-shaking revelation. Now, I'd like to hear what each of you thinks. Sally, why don't we start with you?"

And she heard them, one by one, as each expressed surprise, hope, skepticism, worry, and anger to different degrees. Of course, they recognized their current situation was untenable, but the challenges of moving to a different country—the risks and uncertainties had to be reckoned with. She heard them, keeping back what she truly thought, encouraging them to each have their say. This was all prelude, not that any of them knew it. She was stalling for time for the Qaddo to assemble and for Tosh to arrive to start the show.

They had four more initiates waiting to comment when noise from the parking area nearby stopped all conversation. Engines gurgling, gravel hissing, doors opening and slamming, voices calling to one another. The Lifer discussion ground to a halt. Iwi led a dozen or so Qaddo from their cars to join the Lifers in the shade. Wonda asked a few initiates to bring folding chairs from the camp, which they did, and the sharing paused until the Qaddo were seated. Wonda saw Tosh walking across the dry grass with an opaque plastic crate in his arms.

It's go time.

Wonda raised her voice so all could hear. "We've said time and again that we're grateful to the Qaddo for their hospitality. And this is how we've repaid their generosity."

Tosh walked to the rough center of the gathering. At Wonda's nodded command, he took the top off the container and tipped it over. Hundreds of vials poured out. A tinkling chatter erupted from where they landed, piling up a rough glass pyramid of stim addiction discards desecrating the Qaddo Lands. The Human Lifers and the tribe shared a disdain for drugs. However, the Qaddo were less hardline about it, leaving room for their traditional ceremonies of plant-based intoxicants and hallucinogens. But this demonstration, this defilement, it had the effect she predicted. The Qaddo swapped angry glances and traded shouts of dismay: "What is this? What have you done?"

A string of curses erupted.

Just when it seemed they were all about to lose their shit and start yelling, Wonda shouted, "Wait, please! We want to apologize with these gifts!"

She signaled for the dolls to be brought forward. Two of her flock carried a wicker basket filled with dolls and placed it on the ground. When they heard the dolls speak, she hoped the effect would be like a bomb going off. She wanted their outrage and fury.

"Wait," Tosh said. "Wonda, I can't let you go through with this."

"What are you doing?" she asked, layering panic and outrage onto her voice. She moved to block him, but he warned her away with a glare. It was his turn to perform.

Tosh glared at Wonda. Of course, she would think this prank was all about her and her plans. To her, anything shiny and bright looked like a mirror. She only saw herself and the limits of her power. And she knew fuck all about history, though she was good at creating a scene.

She couldn't understand the size of Tosh's debt to Jefferson Eastmore, how much he feared what the Diamond King was unleashing on the world, how much he hoped Victor would find a path of his own to follow. For a long time, plotting revenge for Jefferson's murder was the panacea for the guilt he felt at failing to protect him. But now? Now, alliances were shifting, and plans were in motion again. And the Qaddo needed to wake up and understand the threat. This wasn't the return home he'd hoped for. But reconciliation wasn't ever in the cards.

He remembered all the times he argued with his sibling about the tribe's relationship with the rest of the world. Iwi wouldn't listen. When a Qaddo delegate was offered a seat on the Louisiana Territories council, the lone tribe to be offered such a seat, Tosh objected. The Qaddo should not be the only tribe to be recognized. He'd been working with dozens more to bring their suits to court. When the LTs cut other tribes out of the process, it splintered the Alliance. Iwi had not seen the value of solidarity, arguing instead that the tribe should focus on its own problems, saying it wasn't a betrayal; they would still write letters of support, but their time and effort were better spent using their newfound political power. Iwi had become Chief. Humiliated in front of his allies and family, Tosh left.

Tosh wasn't breaking any bonds; they'd all withered long ago. But green shoots could grow in well-tended soil.

He picked up one of the Qaddo dolls and ripped it open. He then plucked out the thumb-sized device and held it up for all to see. "This is the future we're fighting against, and she brought it here!"

He said, "This is what they think of your traditions. A means to a deceitful end."

Iwi smoldered. "What are you saying?"

Natti shouted and gestured angrily, first at the stim vials littering the ground, then at the dolls. "This is too much!"

Tosh took several steps back, leaving the Wonda and the Human Lifers to stand awkwardly and bear the full brunt of the Qaddo's revulsion. In the commotion and outrage, Iwi had forgotten Tosh. The reverse was not true. Tosh watched Iwi carefully; flames gathered in their eyes. Wonda's plan was working.

The sound of wheels on gravel interrupted them. A black gendarmerie van pulled off the road, and two women emerged, heading directly for them.

Tosh saw Wonda's surprised and concerned expression, as if she hadn't written this script. She was also a skilled actress, mostly because her sense of reality was extremely malleable to her will. Everything was going as planned.

The gendarmerie agents approached. One of them noticed the bin full of dolls and nudged her partner. "What a funny coincidence," the taller one said.

The other agent, who had a short black crop of hair on top, shaved sides, and skin a pleasing deep brown color, echoed her partner's tone. "Well, that is a coincidence. We were on our way here to chat with you about some dolls we found at the security summit. We have some questions."

The taller partner nodded and said, "Chief Iwi, nice to see you again."

"We have some questions as well, Agent Quinn," Iwi answered. "We can both ask why the Human Life Movement corrupted our craftwork."

Agent Quinn surveyed the Lifers. "Where did you get the devices?"

Wonda stepped in front of her flock and answered, "I found them in the park. There were bins full of them. The signs said, 'Free.'"

"I saw them too," one of the Lifers said.

"Do you know what they are?" the shorter agent asked.

"Some new kind of MeshBit, I think," Wonda said tentatively. "When I picked one up, it said it was looking for a home, and it was very tired and needed a place to sleep. It sounded cute."

"The device *said* that? It spoke?" Agent Quinn asked.

"Yes. I took them home, but they've been silent since."

"And the dolls?" Quinn prompted.

Wonda blushed and Tosh could have kissed her for how beautifully she played her part. "We're not exactly flush with cash here, Agent Quinn. I thought they would make a good toy for the market. Is there a problem?"

"That's what we're looking into." The shorter partner whispered something and glanced at Iwi. Quinn nodded and then turned to the crowd. "Thank you for your time. If we have questions, we know where to find you."

As quickly as they'd arrived, the two agents were back in their van and driving north out of Qaddo lands.

Two Human Lifers had started picking up shattered glass and putting the pieces in plastic bags. The basket with the dolls was removed from view. The rest muttered quietly to one another.

Wonda said, "I'm sorry if we've caused any trouble, Chief Iwi."

Her naivete at that moment was threadbare, and her cunning showed through. Tosh found it annoying and was sure the tribe would as well. They'd all just been humiliated to have the agents come onto their land, asking questions and interrupting. None of them looked pleased.

Iwi waited until the ground was clean and then he spoke.

Here it comes, Tosh thought. *Iwi loves an audience.*

"When colonizers came and took our lands and forced us west, we struggled and wept. We did not give up. When the Civil War ruptured the unholy trinity of slavery, capitalism, and elitism, there was fertile ground to plant the seeds of a new society. They call it the Permanent Enlightenment. We call it the Listening Season. The Qaddo tribe supported the three R's ..."

Iwi paused as if waiting for Tosh to respond like he was in a grammar school lesson. Tosh bit his tongue. The tribe would listen until Iwi was done. The Lifers were looking around in confusion. *You can't teach a hungry dog to dance.* "Reparations for Indigenous communities, formerly enslaved people, and women ensured that participation in the political system could take place on equal ground with equal opportunities for self-determination and socioeconomic advancement. Repartition returned control to communities and laid the groundwork for a community of nations opposed to imperialism and injustice in all its forms. And Rebalancing investment prioritized human development. Many tribes refused to support the three-R reforms because they saw it as giving up the principle of sovereignty. We saw it as an opportunity to regain what we'd lost. We pledged to take in any tribe member from that point forward. We wouldn't divide. We wouldn't exclude. We wouldn't abandon our family—our human family."

Iwi paused. They weren't done speaking, and no one chimed in even as the silence extended uncomfortably. Wonda watched Iwi and stared. It was a look that would have provoked anyone else. Iwi noticed but was not flustered. Tosh almost felt sorry for Iwi; they were being played so easily, but the Lifers had to leave, and this was the way. Tosh didn't want the Qaddo to shoulder any blame for what was to come.

When Iwi went on, they spoke directly to Wonda. "You have violated our trust. We say all are welcome, and we mean it. You test our patience and forbearance. We will not ask you to leave, though, by your actions, it seems you are pushing us to do so. Until the cloud over our relationship is lifted, our goodwill is suspended. You no longer have our permission to stay. You are not welcome at our ceremonies. We will provide no more aid. We will not partake in any dialogue with you for thirteen moons. You may go."

Wonda hung her head, a sign of defeat. Tosh had noticed that while listening to Iwi's decree, a smile ticked onto her face and vanished repeatedly as she struggled to contain her glee. The plan had worked. Perhaps not perfectly or definitively. But it would be enough for Wonda and the Lifers to claim their slice of the Cold Nile Miracle and walk unknowingly into the lion's den, clearing the way for Tosh and his allies to topple the Diamond King and Circe Eastmore.

45

When the United States committed to anti-imperialist principles, the rest of the world laughed at the upstart, isolated nation that thought it was doing the world such a favor. Little did they know.

—Robbie Eastmore, *Another World* (transmission date unknown)

21 May 1992
New Venice, The Louisiana Territories

Alia needed a win. The delegates were bickering again, bogged down in recriminations and suspicion. Torsten leaned in, looking interested as he listened, but Alia could tell he was frustrated. Meanwhile, New Venice was sinking into the muck, and strange rumors relayed by twitchy European agents implied a vague threat from the West, looming, making the work of the conference that much more urgent. She reminded the delegates they were only halfway through their agenda.

"Yes, I can read, sweetie," Margie snapped as if she were a bitter has-been rather than a fresh-faced thirty-something. She then softened to say to Alia gently, "You must have been the prize pick for study group at school."

Alia didn't have many fond memories that far back. During a particularly low moment post-graduation, after she disavowed her parents and their rigid, constricting religious beliefs while she was bouncing between low-rent studios, friends' couches, and Qaddo-run social service shelters, she joined a kung fu school. Learning and practicing flying kicks, dragon stances, and lightning-fast attacks might have saved her life or maybe her soul. The teacher was a slim, quick, beautiful woman, a daughter of refugees from the Great Asian War who had been forced from their land in Henan. During lunch hour, the teacher ran Alia through exercises and drills five days a week. It became her most reliable routine during a chaotic period. She often stayed after class, hoping the teacher would drop her fierce instructor mask and ask Alia on a date. It wasn't until later that Alia realized she had traded one form of punishment, her parents, for another: her teacher's cold, antiseptic, and disappointingly non-sapphic authority.

Maybe it's time to stop choosing hurt.

The delegates lounged on padded sofas arranged in a circle with adjustable tables on swing arms to bring their papers closer when needed. Alia suffered on a rigid bench that made her ass ache, one more pain in a long list of psychic woes this conference had inflicted. She chose her punishment when she agreed to this debacle and made herself a punching bag for the warring delegates, letting their political barbs and jabs land on her instead of each other. She absorbed the injuries, and her blood soured. It had become a running joke how unqualified she was. However, someone was always willing to chime in that she was doing a fine job and that anyone would struggle to facilitate a convening of such big personalities and weighty problems. She was starting to think they might find some common ground by the end of it, as long as she could soak up their distress.

A motion Clive made grabbed her attention. Torsten was smiling. A proposal was on the table. The delegates, aside from the one from the OWS who refused to do anything except try to slow down and derail the discussions, were aligning around an agreement to share intelligence. The scope was shaping up to include the spread of the stim epidemic, the manifestation of propaganda and illicit media sources, and the movement of refugees. Sharing information wouldn't solve any root causes of the troubles. Still, it would help people who were hurting and give authorities the information they needed to understand the magnitude of the challenges.

It was a win. A rare, unexpected, honest-to-goodness win. The implications—for her, for Torsten, for people who need help— made her giddy.

Alia made a ritual of the victory, asking each delegate to share how the agreement would be received back home and what it might mean for the future.

A shouted explicative interrupted them. Everyone's gazes snapped to Mía at the tent's aperture. She said she had unsettling news. An OWS citizen had escaped overland, made an arduous trek through the craggy heights of the Sierra Nevada, across

Cody Sisco

fire-burned foothills, down into the flats, and arrived at a remote SeCan town in the Long Valley. Crucially, the place he found refuge was one with a government representative stationed there so the news could travel onward quickly.

"He delivered evidence of chemical propellant manufacture throughout the OWS," Mía said grimly when asked to repeat herself.

There goes our agenda. This could ruin everything.

Torsten had no chill; he looked ready to explode.

I have to address it head on.

Alia said, "We have some wiggle room in the schedule if we'd like to discuss this situation briefly before moving on to the next topic." Alia sensed agreement. The Treaty of the Atlantic concessions had strictly regulated projectiles and weapons systems, including chemical propellants, to reduce the proliferation of arms. No AU nation had dared violate the agreements before. "That is if the delegate from the OWS agrees."

The delegates' gazes shifted to the woman from the OWS, who had remained stone still during Mía's explanation, her face a mask of unsurprised, glacial calm.

Two seconds passed before she erupted. "This is outrageous! I will not sit here and listen to these fabrications." She stood up. "You can consider our participation in this summit terminated. I will be communicating my fervent dissatisfaction at your conduct"—she paused for a breath while glaring at Mía, then turned to Alia, who couldn't help feeling that she had indeed failed to keep the peace—"and you can be sure the repercussions of this slander—"

"Let me ask you to take a moment," Torsten said calmly as he stood. He seemed to have regained his ease, or he was faking well. "I'll admit these statements come as a surprise to all of us. We should hear more." Torsten beckoned the OWS woman to return to her seat, but she stood her ground. "If this is a problem with malicious third parties spreading false information, we'll want to get to the bottom of it. Agreed?"

The woman opened her mouth. Nothing came out. Then she surprised everyone by nodding and taking her seat, smiling thinly.

Alia saw the trap Torsten had laid and was impressed. By raising the possibility that the information was false, he invited the OWS delegate to stay to argue that case. Alia, however, had noticed the delegate's expression when the news broke; she'd been completely unfazed until she chose to make a stink. A calculated response. She hadn't been caught off guard; she had known the truth all along.

As the delegate sat primly, her hand twitched, rising and then returning to her lap as if fighting an urge to check her watch.

Lisabella had briefed Alia on the political situation in the OWS. On a jog along one of the dirt paths overlooking the Passage, Lisabella parceled out the facts she'd gathered from interviews with Mesh editors and European operatives. Alia focused on keeping her footing and setting a slow pace. She noticed Lisabella's breathiness—as a taller woman with more to her figure, Lisabella worked harder to keep up.

"Do you want to stop?" Alia asked.

"No," Lisabella wheezed. "This is great. I needed … to get out … too many men in the Mesh house, if you know what I mean." She summarized the OWS's recent political history. As bizarre as it sounded, the evidence was persuasive. An entire nation of the AU had slowly, inexorably come under the control of an individual so shadowy and elusive, so masterful in the arts of propaganda and social engineering that no one, not even the citizens enduring such an autocracy, knew him only as the Diamond King.

"How do you anticipate the actions of a leader when you don't even know who he is?" Alia wondered aloud.

"We collect clues, and we don't stop until we figure him out."

Recovering her presence of mind, Alia looked around the room at the delegates and asked them to share their thoughts on Mía's news.

"We have no reason to believe the information isn't true," said Margie, speaking on behalf of the New England Commonwealth, sounding again much older, like there was metal in her voice. Alia cringed. If the OWS woman took it as an accusation, she might decide to leave—she seemed to be on a hair trigger. Margie went on more delicately, though, facing the OWS delegate and smiling as she said, "We want to believe you. Give us a reason to doubt its veracity."

Ah, that's her method. Cold, then warm. Now I know what to watch for. Alia observed the OWS delegate smooth the sleeves of her jacket. *Too bad warmth is lost on that bitch.*

After a moment, the OWS delegate regained her composure and said quietly, "This is an unsettling development. I move that

Cody Sisco

we adjourn to review whatever information our colleague can share with us, confer with our offices, and return in two hours to discuss it."

Torsten smiled one of his polite, functional, charmless smiles that said we both know you're screwed. He said, "If that's as much time as you think you'll—as we'll all need, then I second the motion."

"A vote?" Alia asked brightly.

She polled them, and unanimously they agreed to a two-hour break. Enough time for the OWS delegate to report back to the Diamond King and receive her orders? Alia didn't envy the woman's predicament. But were any of their situations much better?

Faced with this new information, they must decide how to play their part. Juggling national interest, internal politics, and foreign relations wasn't a game Alia had ever wanted to play. She shuddered. Why was she realizing so belatedly that Torsten's direction might not match her desires?

The gathering was slowly dispersing. She closed her eyes for a moment to fight a feeling of vertigo. A sweet waft of calm followed that made her smile with gratitude. One moment a crowd of people surrounded her; the next, silence and absence. She opened her eyes and saw that only she remained in the room.

"What the hell just happened?" she asked herself. A chill brushed Alia's skin from her neck to her toes.

Looking around, she realized Torsten had disappeared too. Probably to confer secretly with the LT delegate to see if there was more information. Propellant manufacture in the OWS? Did that mean they were making rockets or, maybe, missiles?

She left the sealed dome for fresh air. Beyond the security cordon, patients watched with curiosity in small groups. They weren't allowed to gather more than six at a time. She took out her MeshBit and checked her messages. Most were from BioScan, the usual signoffs and requests for information or changes to work orders. One message stood out. Bill, her godfather, Peace Chief of the Qaddo Lands. It was marked urgent. She placed the call, and he picked up after a single tone.

"Alia! Laws, I miss your face." His face filled the small vidscreen on her device. She held it up and smiled at him.

"Hey, Bill. You okay? I've been in an information blackout and just saw your message."

He frowned and furrowed his brow. "I could complain, but that would take me all day. Something funny going on with the Lifers."

Alia grimaced. "What's funny about them?"

"They're busy. Usually, they laze around like dogs on a hot day. We keep telling them that if they want a safe place, they must do the work to make it safe. Now they're busy. All of them. Moving stuff around, talking, something's going on, Laws if I know what. Chief Iwi talked with them, but I haven't got a download yet."

Most people in New Venice assumed that the Human Lifers, now that they'd sought refuge with the Qaddo, were neutered and harmless, which was a kind of out-of-sight, out-of-mind magical thinking as far as she was concerned. She'd seen firsthand their relentless obsession and ability to shed and morph morality, transforming completely from rapacious caterpillars to venomous butterflies. She worried about what they might get up to, that they might mess with the Qaddo somehow. And that thing with the dolls ...

"Anyway, I thought you should know. Pass my regard to Torsten while you're at it."

"Of course. I appreciate it. Let me know what you see, please."

"Will do. And Alia?"

"What is it?"

"I don't want to raise alarm bells or invite ghosts to supper."

"You've never been that excitable, Bill. What aren't you saying?"

"Probably nonsense. But I heard it a couple of times this week. Same story. Not from people I've yet had cause to doubt."

"Okay?"

"You seen any lights that aren't stars blazing down at us?"

She wanted to say, *What the Laws are you talking about, Bill?* Instead, she took a breath. "Lights? No, I haven't."

"Keep 'em peeled, would you?"

"I'll let you know what I see and hear."

"Appreciate it. Come on by when you can."

"I will."

Alia closed the connection and returned the MeshBit to her pocket.

Lights in the sky? Did this have something to do with chemical propellant? Everyone knew what a rocket launch looked like. Every time a Moonbase resupply mission went up, the news was distributed throughout the Mesh, one of the few bits of content

shared globally. Europe had a monopoly on rocket fuel manufacture, which was strictly for scientific exploration, officially.
People suspected Europe had transcontinental missiles, but no
one believed they would be used without provocation.

The OWS, on the other hand. Who knew what type of weapons
the OWS might put on top of a rocket and aim at their neighbors?
What did a falling rocket look like? She didn't know, hadn't seen it
herself, but she could picture Oklahoma City towers blasted flat,
poison gas drifting through the streets. Avenues of imagination
that she didn't want to travel.

She was startled when Torsten put a hand on her arm. He
looked at her with concern.

"I'm fine," she said preemptively.

"You sure? You went away for a while."

She tapped her pocket. "That was Bill. Something's going on
with the Lifers. He doesn't know what, but he thought we should
know."

"If it's not raining, it's a flood. We don't have time to worry
about the Lifers too."

"He said something else about blazing lights in the sky. I think
he meant rockets."

Torsten looked at her, clearly spooked.

Her skin crawled, and weakness threatened to buckle her knees.
She put a hand on his chest. "Tell me. If I'm going to worry, I might
as well have cause to."

He gave her a pained smile, kissed her brow, and brought his
arm around her shoulders. She nestled as they walked back into
the secured space. "Is it time to talk about why the OWS is making
propellant?" she asked.

"Are they now?" He had grim disappointment in his voice. "The
official word is that such things must be confirmed to be believed."

"You're saying ... Oh, Torsten, I'm sorry."

"Yes, it seems I was a bit too clever, and the trap I sprung has
snared us all. The OWS can now deny the accusations as lies and
propaganda. The situation is a test of our ability to work together.
And I'm afraid we're going to fail."

Mía approached Alia, and they hugged. She shook Torsten's
hand.

"Before we get started again, I need to tell you something. The
news is worse than what I shared," Mía said.

Alia's stomach seized. How could things possibly get worse?

"The OWS has a new capability for digital forgeries. Text, audio, video. They've been able to infiltrate the Mesh, and we should assume all digital communications are compromised. Did you know already?"

Alia was only able to shake her head mutely. Victor wasn't responding to her messages. Was he receiving them? Could the news she read this morning be trusted? Were the delegates' messages to their counterparts back home being messed with?

"We're fucked," Torsten said.

Mía frowned. "It's going to slow us down right at the moment we need to be sprinting. Lisabella is still around, right? I'll make sure she's aware." She jogged away.

"What the hell?" Alia said, looking after her. "It's like nothing can go right all of a sudden."

Torsten wrapped her in his arms and pressed his lips down on her hair. "We're right. That's not changing," he said. It helped, but it didn't stop the feeling like everything good was draining out the world and leaving them all to navigate a colorless, joyless existence.

Cody Sisco

46

There's nothing I mistrust more than people with unshakeable convictions.

—Victor Eastmore, *Apology to Resonant Earth* (transmission date unknown)

22 May 1992
Las Vegas, Organized Western States

On the morning of the Breakthrough Ceremony, hours before Victor was due to fly back to New Venice, he stood on the balcony and stared at city lights growing dim below. The sun would soon crest the horizon, and subtle pink, blue, and violet hues would be erased by harsh glare and deep shadows.

His thoughts turned around and around. Ozie's declaration that the Diamond King was a synthetic consciousness defied belief. The Diamond King's fibers reached into every aspect of OWS society and economy. How could that have happened? How could people let that happen?

The Diamond King had taken a special interest in Victor. Or so it seemed. Maybe that's how every citizen felt about their totems. Cared for by a higher power. It wasn't simply the metaphysical comfort of believing oneself part of an ethereal plan. There were tangible, copious benefits: a roof over one's head, food, society, belonging, purpose. The list went on. Material wealth going hand in hand with spiritual submission made for a potent combination.

In Victor's case, a great wish would be fulfilled at a seemingly trivial cost. Did his knowledge about the nature of this specific genie change anything about what he had agreed to do? Too late. He'd already rubbed the lamp.

After a breakfast of eggs, toast, and juice, Victor was summoned to Ozie's office, but when he got there, Ozie was sitting sullenly in the corner and refusing to speak.

A vidscreen on the wall blinked with the message: *Micro-pods arrive at BioScan today. The staff will receive your instructions. Would you like to record them?*

"Can I speak to them in real time?" he asked.

The Diamond King's voice came from a sonobulb. "No."

"Why not?"

The vidscreen blinked, and Victor was now looking at a map. Superimposed on a field of black were glowing green outlines tracing the edges of every continent. The land was shaded in a range of pastels to reflect national borders. Thin blue arcs and clusters of red lights indicated the networks and nodes that made up the compusphere knitting together the Mesh. Other smaller regional systems were shaded in different colors, including the Tangle network glowing yellow throughout the OWS.

Victor slowly grasped what the vidscreen was telling him. Everywhere around the OWS territory, yellow fireworks severed blue arcs. Messages from the Mesh, which had previously passed through the Tangle's links unhindered, were being rejected. They doubled back on themselves and searched for new paths via circuitous detours. The swath of territory being affected was vast. Messages on the Mesh network from Semiautonomous California would have to detour thousands of kilometers through the First Nations of Canada or the Holy Empire of Mexico to reach other nations in the American Union. A digital blockade of sorts. The non-Mesh hole in the Mesh was growing. Yellow arcs penetrated Mesh territory, with a dense knot around New Venice, and extended across the Atlantic, moving both East and West, a sign that back-and-forth cyberattacks between the OWS and Europe and its overseas holdings were accelerating.

After examining the schematic for a moment, Victor understood. It showed a world at war—not a real conflict of troops and equipment, but a cyberwar of communications blackouts, sabotage, and subterfuge.

Ozie was staring at him angrily. Victor switched off the vidscreen and turned away. What could he do about cyber incursions? He couldn't even help his friend. Granted, Ozie bore all the responsibility for his situation. He'd wormed himself into the heart of the fruit, enticed by the secrets at its center, eager to access the world's most advanced cyber research center. The passage he'd made had sealed up behind him. Now that he had what he wanted, there was nowhere he could turn. No escape.

Why was Ozie's glare so accusatory? Victor couldn't undo the past. He couldn't wipe the slate clean. They were all living with the fallout from choices made and paths taken. There was nothing Victor could do but walk his path. The distance between him and Ozie grew as their trajectories diverged.

A chime caught Victor's attention, and Wonda's face swam to the front of the vidscreen.

"Mission success," she said.

"You have the data egg?"

"Of course. Not without some drama. The Human Lifers were kicked off the Qaddo Lands today. Tosh is on his way back to you with some of them and the data egg. I'm sticking around to work on recruiting some followers now that I've got a sweet pitch of promised land to offer them. Not only that, I can promise them Samuel's ghost."

For a moment, Victor was back in Carmichael, flames ripping through homes, smoking climbing into the sky. In a quavering whisper, he said, "Please say you're not serious."

Wonda stared at him, or, more accurately, her image stared. He'd seen the deepfakes the Diamond King was capable of making. How did Victor know this was truly Wonda?

"Come on, Victor," her image said. "I'd be a fool not to take advantage. You saw Samuel talking to us. That was part of the deal, formal or not."

"It wasn't real."

"It looked like him to me. It sounded like him. Think how much more persuasive it might be with the data egg's neurograms. Samuel is still with us. That's what I'm telling people. He can be our guide and mentor."

"Your totem," Victor said.

"Join us. We won't need Samuel if we have you."

He refused to respond. The only thing worse than being a cult member was becoming a cult leader. And he was tired of her taking advantage of him.

Wonda sighed. "I'll see you when you're back in New Venice. Then we'll talk about the future."

Her tone set off alarm bells in his head. "What do you mean?"

"Are you going to get the plugs?" she asked. The question caught him off guard. Her voice was soft and light. It sounded innocuous, innocent. His stomach churned, remembering the speed and precision of the surgery. What happened to the pieces of skull they cut out? What would it feel like for nano-tendrils to push into brain tissue to light up his neural pathways? Wonda's lightness was a lie. She didn't want him to get the plugs—more than anything, she wanted his brain pristine. He was part of the purity mythology she was trying to grow around MRS, to make it some holy Emergent phenomenon. A truly bonkers idea. So, why ask the question so lightly? Was this even Wonda?

"We'll talk when I'm back." He cut the connection.

Was the Diamond King sending messages to Wonda, using simulations of Victor's face and voice, to convince her to use Samuel as a selling point in her proselytizing? It wouldn't take much convincing.

Ozie was staring at him. Then, he abruptly got up and started toward the door, signaling Victor to follow. Another escape attempt, probably. He was going to get himself in trouble.

As if all this wasn't trouble enough.

They climbed into an autocab, which circled Grand Park before heading out the avenues dividing Autumn from Winter. They passed the last boulevard and entered a vast construction zone. Towers in various stages of completion arced left and right. Trucks trundled with their steel, concrete, glass, and fiberboard cargo. Cranes lifted. Robots climbed vertical surfaces, installing panels and gear as they rose.

The autocab pulled up to a set of trailers at the edges of the construction zone. Ozie hadn't said a word about where they were going or why. Victor replayed Wonda's voice and image, asking himself if that really had been her and finding it impossible to decide. A chill crept up his spine. He could never trust any vidscreen again.

Ozie led him up a set of steps to the trailer door and opened it, beckoning Victor to step through. He did, but only after peeking inside and checking it was not full of scalpel-wielding tentacles. Seeing a dimly lit room with beds and people asleep, he decided it was safe, though his skin prickled. What the Laws were they doing here?

Ozie raised the lightstrips' output by tapping on his cyberarm. He looked around. "Everyone asleep?" he called out.

None of the people stirred.

"What are you doing?" Victor asked.

"These are pluggers. None of them have the MRS gene. They volunteered. The Diamond King is determined to bring skullplugs to anyone who wants one. Sorry, anyone who earns one."

Victor scoffed, "Why would people without MRS want implants? I mean, I guess if we're going to use them to treat stim addictions, they could help other addictions, too. Or neurodegenerative diseases, maybe. Epilepsy." He hadn't thought through all the potential applications.

Ozie flashed him a look of dismay. "Addiction isn't half of it. Haven't you noticed how strange it is here? Like how obsessed people are with ratings? They'll do anything to climb the ranks. They're already invested. Why not plug into a mainline to pipe reward and punishment directly into your brain? To not do so would seem suspect. I guarantee if you come back here next year, there won't be a non-plugged human left."

Ozie's voice had climbed in volume throughout, and now he was shouting. None of the sleepers had awakened. Victor looked around, double-checked that the nearest person was breathing, and was reassured to see their blanket's steady rise and fall. Still, in the close confines, such loud speech should have roused them.

"Are they damaged?" Victor asked.

"No," Ozie said with a sigh. "They're assisted-sleeping. I'll wake them up."

He tapped on his arm.

A woman levered up, yawned loudly, and stretched, looking mildly surprised when she spotted them. A few other people rose quickly, tossed off their blankets, and started dressing and putting on shoes. Others awoke more slowly, some pulled type-pads from under their pillows and began browsing and chatting. Within a minute, they were all awake, bustling, and generally seemed happy.

Victor, on the other hand, got the message. Something as fundamental as the sleep-wake cycle was no longer a matter of biology for them. It was no longer an intrinsic function. It had been outsourced. Ozie used his control over these people, but it wasn't his hands that ultimately held the reins, was it?

Victor walked out into the harsh sunlight of mid-morning, his mind whirling, unsettled. They'd given up control over not just their lives. Their consciousness, their entire subjectivity, was now open to influence. They would go about their days smiling only if they cooperated. It was nightmarish. It was ghastly. It was horrifying.

And yet, this wasn't his problem to solve. It wasn't something he could stop.

Again, Ozie was trying to make him feel guilty for something outside his control.

An autocab pulled up. His Tangle gadget told him that it would take him to Grand Park for the Breakthrough announcement. Ozie watched Victor from the doorway of the trailer. Skullplugged people passed him chatting, talking about how they were surprised to be up so early and refreshed when they'd only had three hours of sleep.

"Goodbye, Ozie," Victor said as he entered the autocab. He made sure to speak loudly enough that Ozie could hear him. "Good luck."

47

22 May 1992
Las Vegas, Organized Western States

On Victor's orders, the autocab dropped him off a few blocks from Circle Way. He would walk and try to collect himself. The blazing heat discouraged long rambles. Even at ten in the morning, with shade provided everywhere by trees, artificial canopies, and misters at every corner, it was oppressive. But he needed to think. The leash the Diamond King had him on had grown longer now that the deal was done. Silk no longer escorted him everywhere. He wasn't whisked every free moment to some new appointment. He could summon an autocab, walk through the city, or take a monorail, and no one would stop him.

Should he leave?

Did he want to?

Las Vegas was foreign and exciting, with more layers to explore than he could count. The vibe was good, too. People smiled as they passed him. The Breakthrough announcement had spread a giddy joy. People were rushing to wherever they'd been invited, brushing past him. Every close encounter added some of their velocity to his. Small groups headed to Grand Park, passing him quickly, chatting and speculating about what the announcement could be. Victor told himself it had nothing to do with him. It was just a coincidence. One final bizarre custom to witness before he boarded the jet this evening that would take him back to New Venice.

Giant sunshades like circus tents created large shadows that protected the ground from direct sun. A vast stage, overshadowed by its support structure, had been erected at the park's center. The crowd was tens of thousands deep. Large vidscreens provided a close-up view.

Victor triple-dosed on fumewort, more out of habit than necessity. He aimed for glacial calm, rejecting the revelations that battered his mind: The Diamond King was a synthetic consciousness, and he, Victor, was responsible for spreading MRS. He wanted to believe none of it. But his mind had accepted those assertions as truth and somehow not been upended by it. His few brief trips inside the Diamond King's scanning machine seemed to provide a halo of mental stability that gradually faded. He was surprised and pleased. Somewhere deep down, he was probably in shock. Nonetheless, after a few days, he continued to enjoy some of the therapy's protection. This, more than anything else, convinced him to accept the current state of affairs and move forward with his plans. As long as he didn't get the implants.

As he navigated through the crowd, their enthusiasm was an electric buzz filling his battery. Giddy with excitement at being so close to a cure, he took out his Tangle device and tried connecting to Pearl again. She would want to know that he was on the cusp of something great. Miraculously, his call went through this time, and she accepted though audio-only.

"Pearl! Are you going to the Breakthrough?" he asked.

"I got out. I'm in Oakland," she said, quick and clipped, unlike her mysterious, sometimes accented lilt. "Can't get through to Carmichael. The transit hub is closed. The National Council building is occupied. City service workers are striking. It's a mess. I get the feeling it will get worse before it gets better. The protesters have the upper hand for the moment. Like the seventies."

He'd sat through commemoration ceremonies, vid screenings, and lectures throughout his school days, all of them celebrating the heroic police force that tamped down the flaring protests. The tone of the narrative had always galled him. It was so one-sided, so absolutist. It never voiced the concerns and grievances of the protesters. Semiautonomous California was a land of stark contrasts, black-and-white precepts, and determinative moral consequences. You were either good people who benefited from every largess society could bestow, or you were one of the bad ones, deserving nothing less than perdition. In the retelling, protesters were unequivocally bad. He knew from personal experience how SeCa treated its bad ones.

"Are you okay?" he asked.

Pearl sighed, a whoosh of air that sounded to Victor like surf at the beach. "I don't know anymore. This whole thing started because of the rumors about MRS patients, but now … it's taken a turn. There are new announcements every day. The Mesh isn't behaving normally. People are getting all sorts of wild stories and rushing into the streets. Authorities are distributing new devices they say are safe to use, but the protesters accuse them of failing to protect the people and spreading lies. Which is nothing new, to be honest, but there's something different this time."

His heart thumped. He didn't worry about his family. By now, they would have all arrived in New Venice for the reunion. But Pearl was still in SeCa, as was Mía.

"You sound scared," Victor said.

"I am."

"What about Mía?" he asked.

"She's in New Venice now. They got her back unharmed."

"What do you mean got her back?"

In the silence that followed, Victor imagined Pearl taking the device away from her ear and looking at it scornfully.

"When was the last time you spoke with her?" Pearl asked.

"I've been—oh, shocks, it's a long story. I haven't heard from her in a while."

"She was kidnapped."

"What?"

"She's unhurt. The thugs who took her revered her. But being locked up for that long …" Pearl sighed heavily.

"I didn't know."

The crowd around Victor began to cheer and hoot. The sound rose, blocking out everything. The crowd's scent was like campfires and savory, roasting meat.

He couldn't hear Pearl. "I'll call you again soon," he yelled, then cut the connection.

A few burly men approached Victor, nodded, and cleared a path. People moved aside and looked at him with curiosity. Some seemed to recognize him and smiled. His anxiety was on holiday; he found himself smiling back and didn't fight it. Emotional contagion could be helpful as often as hurtful, if the people around him were friendly and feeling good.

Toward the stage, colorful rugs helped mark out different spaces. Large umbrellas provided shade to those who needed it. Mist rose in wafting clouds, decorating his vision with rainbowed, cottony wisps. An area was cordoned off with waist-high barriers that looked too flimsy to stop even a child. However, the crowd gave them space, and he could see stations with playing-card images and people consulting their devices to know where they should stand.

He was led to the frontmost area reserved for VIPs and raised a meter above the rest of the crowd with a better view of the stage. In their clothing and mannerisms, the people around him exuded the smooth, polished, and effervescent aura of wealth, power, and wisdom. They were nines, tens, and face cards. The Las Vegas elite had gathered together in the sunshine to witness the latest transformation of their society. They would embrace and lead the change. That Victor was among them was not a huge surprise, but it wasn't where he wanted to be. The flight to New Venice seemed far into the future, yet it couldn't come quickly enough.

A line of green-blue tentacles obscured the stage, rising like sea-grass and rippling rhythmically. Looking into the wings, he caught glimpses of machinery, vast and complicated scaffolding, and what looked like a giant metal nautilus above the stage. Glancing backward, Victor saw that Silk, Davita, and Dr. Brücktwyn, the engineer, had gathered and were standing on the other side of the VIP barricade. They smiled and waved at him, and he returned the gesture in a daze. It felt like his life was running at triple speed; all he wanted was for things to return to normal.

This is normal. This is your life now. The wise owl is flying high.

The tentacles onstage retracted, revealing one of the pods that Victor had seen in the King's workshop, only transformed. As opposed to the sleek egg-like surfaces he'd seen previously, this one had open panels and exposed cables, and it stood on five landing struts similar in texture to the tentacles. The more he looked at the pod, the more he realized it resembled one of the early Moon landers.

Victor's eyes widened. Was this the Breakthrough? Would the Organized Western States go to the Moon and end Europe's long-standing monopoly on space habitation?

There was a change in the light as if clouds had moved across the sun. The ceiling above the stage dilated, retracting open at the center, and now he could see a giant balloon dozens of meters across, hovering above the stage. It lowered tentacles, hooked into the top of the pod somehow, and lifted it. The landing struts retracted, panels closed, and the pod looked like a white and chrome teardrop. As the crowd roared, the balloon rose, lifting the pod dozens of meters and then hundreds. They ascended together until the naked eye could barely make out anything but a speck of darkness in an otherwise blue and cloudless sky, and then it was gone. Hoots, hollers, and cheers quieted, but the electric mood only increased as everyone watched the vidscreen showing close-up views of the balloon and pod from different angles. The images must have been beamed from ground-based telescopes or others high in the atmosphere or perhaps low Earth orbit or drones rising in tandem. The balloon and pod seemed to reach the edge of night. Maybe it was a trick of perspective, but no one was sweating the details. They were waiting with one held breath.

The tentacle dangling from the balloon disengaged. The pod dropped. It descended, reaching terminal velocity, falling straight down. The images zoomed out, showing the rapidly growing distance between the balloon and the pod. Gravity pulled Victor, wanted to slam him to the ground. He steadied himself as the vidscreen focused on the pod and drew closer. A panel opened at the top. Out blossomed a parachute. The pod's descent slowed. He and the crowd were floating, feeling the tug of parachute lines, wafting in the atmosphere at the whim of immense, invisible forces. The vidscreen view shifted to a schematic of the atmosphere, a three-dimensional representation of wind-speed vectors, with a single red line threaded from top to bottom. The line changed color going down, blue overtaking red, and Victor realized it was tracking the pod along its projected path.

A slight breeze rattled sand around his feet, and the scents of the crowd in perfumes, musk, and sweet, fried food washed over him. In a way, he was a fraction of the organism of humanity, a cell in a tightly packed organ, like they were all neurons in a giant brain seeing the world through digital lenses instead of eyes.

Several minutes passed as they watched the vidscreen. The blue portion of the pod's path was growing, the red portion diminishing. The line traced a wavering lightning bolt downward. Victor hadn't thought there was that much dynamism in the atmosphere, yet now it was clear there were more invisible forces acting on the world than was apparent from surface-level weather. The things that he or any human could know would never again surmount the streams, lakes, and oceans of data available to computer minds. He couldn't say why he found this a sad thought, but he did.

Looking up, only the parachute was visible at first, and then the pod was discernible as it descended, closer, nearly on top of them. Jets sprang from the pod to the sides, and below, the parachute morphed shape, becoming smaller and streamlined, reducing the effect of wind and drag, until it was all gathered into the top of the pod, which resealed smoothly. Jets maneuvered during the last seconds of the pods' descent, and it landed in the exact spot where it had been before, with Victor and the crowd looking on. The cheers, which had started when the pod became visible again, rose to a crushing roar when it touched down.

A door slid open. Steps extended, growing like exotic flat-leafed fungi from the side of a tree, and the Diamond King's avatar stepped onto the stage.

The crowd hushed. An eerie silence extended across thousands of people.

Victor listened as the avatar, with the Diamond King's playing-card face, began to speak in a voice that was evidently a fraudulent version of human. It announced the next phase of social evolution, which would extend beyond the OWS to encompass the American Union. This evolution would include the knitting together of humanity under one social protocol, aided by the technologies that Grette, Ozie, and countless other technicians had made possible.

The Diamond King announced that, eventually, his gifts would extend to the entire world, and the crowd roared its approval.

48

Victor wanted to escape from the Breakthrough Ceremony, but it was impossible. The crowd penned him in, not to mention Silk, Davita, and Dr. Brücktwyn all had him in their sights. And surveillance in Las Vegas was ubiquitous. He was stuck.

On stage, Grette presented the research on skullplugs via carefully selected footage from the first pluggers, including the woman who had danced with tentacles a few nights ago.

A budding MRS episode grew stronger as Victor's questions and doubts about the Diamond King became impossible to ignore. Where else could he escape to except his own private mental hiding spot? He'd partnered with a thing capable of wholesale murder and mass manipulation. The fate of MRS patients hinged on his cooperation. Alarm in his mind grew like a siren's wail, loud, insistent, unavoidable, while blankspace tendrils promised soft, mercilessly quiet oblivion. Although he stood still as possible, he could feel his body vibrating subtly. His hands wanted to flap at the ends of his arms while his feet stamped the dirt. A growl, inaudible over the crowd's murmuring, grew in his throat.

The escape hatch of blankspace unlatched. He dipped into it as easily as taking a deep breath. Unpleasant bodily sensations transformed into palliative vacuity, a kind of negative pressure. He was without form, a phantom in ecstasy, forceful as the wind and as free.

Then he heard his own voice, saying, with grave sadness, "This is my apology to a universe destroyed." Overwhelmed, he fled blankspace, arriving back in reality with a stumble.

Tosh was at his side. Solid, loyal, grim, and provocative Tosh. Grette's presentation seemed to be over. The applause cascading

361

into the skies was dwindling, and people were turning to chat excitedly with their neighbors.

Tosh looked at Victor appraisingly.

"You're back," Victor said.

"You noticed? I thought you were blank."

"I was."

Tosh gave a brief nod. "Did you see any of this?" He cocked his head toward the stage. "Or were you off in nowhere land for the whole thing?"

"I saw enough," Victor said grimly.

"Then let's go celebrate!" Tosh said at a screaming pitch packed with giddy hysteria. The crowd nearby cheered. The mood was exuberant—Tosh had mimicked and added fuel to it. Yet his smile was toothy and sharp, and the glint in his eye looked dangerous and wild. He was the only person in the world that Victor trusted at that moment.

They hurtled through the crowd together, taking turns going around or busting through groups that were talking excitedly, whatever route would let them escape the quickest. Shouts of effusive nonsense buffeted their passage. They were clapped on the back, hugged, cheered, and wailed at for precious seconds, but they kept moving and eventually reached a monorail station.

As they boarded the slick pod, Tosh wrapped an arm around Victor's shoulders and said, "This is the quickest way to your apartment. We have time before your flight."

Victor responded by looping his arms around Tosh, pulling them into an embrace, and resting his head against the taller man's chest. It was exhaustion. There was nothing sexual in the gesture, he told himself, despite the very urgent message his groin was sending. The gesture was childish, a reflex that communicated: help me, take care of me, protect me. Oh, well. Any pride he'd had was gone. He needed help and would take as much of it as he could.

"You gave it the data egg?" Victor asked.

Tosh said, "That was the deal. Nobody breaks a contract with the King."

If not break then what? Victor wondered. *Bend? Braid it with other priorities and deceptions? What would Jefferson do?*

Victor whispered into Tosh's ear, "We have some urgent unfinished business. The dogs."

Tosh disentangled himself to look Victor in the eyes.

"You-know-who will knows now," Victor said. "It's only a matter of time. Can we get there first?"

The monorail car slowed and stopped at the Vernal Equinox station. Tosh seemed uncertain. The doors opened and a few folks got off. Right when passengers waiting on the platform began to board, Tosh grabbed Victor by the arm and hauled him out, nearly knocking them over. "Sorry," Victor yelled behind as Tosh pulled him along with one hand and spoke into a Tangle device with the other. When they reached the street, Tosh kept them walking until a van pulled up and they both hopped in.

Tosh managed the controls while Victor sunk into a black synthleather seat. He was a tumbleweed in a blustery, chaotic storm. The easy thing would be to let go and ride it out in ROT luxury. Instead, they were fleeing.

As the road transitioned from city arterial to desert highway, Victor leaned forward. "Can we talk without being heard?" he asked.

"You bet," Tosh said as he tapped the dash-pad.

"Can the King track us?"

"I'm sure his Corps will try. If we make it out of the city, then we'll be okay. I'm confident we'll, ahem, *reach orgasm tonight.*"

"What? Oh." It was the acrostic code. Ozie must have explained it to Tosh. "But this van has to be off grid somehow anyway. Since the King isn't listening, you don't *need* to be gross."

Tosh winked. "Don't I?"

Victor punched Tosh's meaty shoulder. "Asshole. So, I think I know what you hid at the Lone Star Kennel, but you never actually admitted it, did you?"

Victor had known there was something suspicious about the kennel. He pictured choking Tosh for keeping the secret so long but suppressed the desire. Answers were more important than brutal satisfaction.

"No. You're right. I guess it's time." Tosh's smile was wide and delirious. "Victor, how about we get you Jefferson's real cure for mirror resonance syndrome?"

The vehicle took a hard turn off the highway, and they hurtled deeper into the sun-scorched desert.

TO BE CONTINUED

Afterword

Thank you for reading *Altered Bodies*, the third volume in the Resonant Earth series.

Indie authors depend on word of mouth. Tell your sci-fi friends about my books, and please consider leaving a review at the retailer where you purchased *Altered Bodies* or on Goodreads or other platforms. You can find links on my website at www.codysisco.com/books.

You can read more about the events that set Victor Eastmore's journey in motion in "Believe and Live," a short story set during the Carmichael massacre. Newsletter subscribers can read the story for free by signing up at www.codysisco.com/contact.

About the Author

Cody Sisco is an author, editor, publisher, and literary community organizer. His LGBT psychological science fiction Resonant Earth series looks at the stigma of mental illness and the hellish distrust and alienation that goes with it. As a freelance editor, he specializes in genre-bending fiction. In 2017, he co-founded Made in L.A. Writers, an indie author co-op dedicated to the support and appreciation of independent authors. His startup, BookSwell, is a literary events and media production company dedicated to lifting up marginalized voices and connecting readers and writers in Southern California and beyond.

For more information, visit: www.codysisco.com.

www.ingramcontent.com/pod-product-compliance
Lightning Source LLC
Chambersburg PA
CBHW021235190726
48289CB00005B/1340

* 9 7 8 1 9 5 3 9 5 4 2 5 1 *